Amir Muhammad publishes books (under Buku Fixi as well as its imprints such as Fixi Novo and Matahari Books) and produces movies (under Kuman Pictures).

When not drawing, **Chin Yew** directs TV shows and commercials for a living. He also likes to brew rice wine and screen films at a screening club. @ashingtray

FIXI NOVO MANIFESTO

1. We believe that omputih/gwailoh-speak is a Malaysian language.

2. We use American spelling. This is because we are more influenced by Hollywood than the House of Windsor.

3. We publish stories about the urban reality of Malaysia. If you want to share your grandmother's World War 2 stories, send 'em elsewhere and you might even win the Booker Prize.

4. We specialize in pulp fiction, because crime, horror, sci-fi and so on turn us on.

5. We will not use italics for non-American/non-English terms. This is because those words are not foreign to a Malaysian audience. So we will not have "They had *nasi lemak* and went back to *kongkek*" but rather "They had nasi lemak and went back to kongkek". Nasi lemak and kongkek are some of the pleasures of Malaysian life that should be celebrated without apology; italics are a form of apology.

6. We publish novels and short-story anthologies. We don't publish poetry; we like making money.

7. The existing Malaysian books that come closest to what we wanna do: *Devil's Place* by Brian Gomez; and the Inspector Mislan crime novels by Rozlan Mohd Noor. Look for them!

8. We publish books with the same print run and the same price as those of our parent company, Buku Fixi. So a book of about 300 pages will sell at RM20. This is because we wanna reach out to the young, the sengkek and the kiam siap.

CALL FOR ENTRIES.

Interested? For novels, send your synopsis and first 2 chapters. For anthologies, send a short story of between 2,000-5,000 words on the theme "KL Noir." Send to info@fixi.com.my anytime.

The Big Book of Malaysian Horror Stories

Edited by Amir Muhammad
Illustrations by Chin Yew

Published by
Fixi Novo *which is an imprint of:*
Buku Fixi Sdn Bhd (1174441-X)
B-8-2A Opal Damansara, Jalan PJU 3/27
47810 Petaling Jaya, Malaysia
info@fixi.com.my
http://fixi.com.my

All rights reserved. Except for extracts for review purposes, you are not allowed to duplicate or republish this book, in whole or in part, without the written permission of the publisher. Although to be honest the idea of pirated books is kinda cool and we'd secretly take it as a compliment.

The Big Book of Malaysian Horror Stories
© Fixi Novo 2022
Copyright of each story © its author

First Print: December 2022

Edited by Amir Muhammad
Illustrations by Chin Yew
Cover and layout: Teck Hee
Consultants: Azmiera Aliah Syuhada Zairulhisham,
Alyssa Mohamad and Matthew Yap

ISBN 978-967-0042-36-7
Catalogue-in-Publication Data available from the
National Library of Malaysia.

Printed by:
Vinlin Press Sdn Bhd
2 Jalan Meranti Permai 1, Meranti Permai Industrial Park
Batu 15, Jalan Puchong, 47100 Puchong, Malaysia

Contents

✕

INTRODUCTION	8
CAMPFIRE STORIES Rizal Ramli	11
WHAT HAPPENS IN KLCC STAYS IN KLCC Raja Ummi Nadrah	23
KLANG CROW Joshua Lim	31
A SLICE OF HEAVEN Chua Kok Yee	45
MAN IN THE MIRROR Adrian Chase	57
SLAVE OF MINE Joshua Lim	71
DREAM HOME Yanna Hashri	87
GUNIK Collin Yeoh	95
JANICE Nurul Hafizah	107

FACELESS PORTRAITS
    Joni Chng   119

COVET
    Tina Ishak   129

DEATH IN THE POWER STATION
    Muthusamy Pon Ramiah   143

DEAD MEN DON'T CLOSE CALLS
    Ethan Matisa   159

DON'T GO FAR-FAR
    Hadi M Nor   173

SIO BAK
    Wong Jo-yen   183

SKINS
    Nadiah Zakaria   195

THE DESIRED ONE
    Malachi Edwin Vethamani   207

A KULIT FOR THE SHADOW KING
    Ismim Putera   221

THE GIFT
    Bissme S.   237

THE ORIGINAL MOTHER
    Atikah Wahid   247

THE TALISMAN
    Eileyn Chua   261

THEY CAME FROM THE SEA
    Nathaniel Sario   273

TURBULENCE
    Izaddin Syah Yusof   287

BAD SPIRIT OF GOOGLE TRANSLATE
    Saat Omar   297

THE BREAK-IN
    Terence Toh   307

THE RED KEBAYA
    Venoo Kuppusamy   321

I AM A TRIATHLETE
    Lai May Senn   333

BIPEDAL
    Paul Gnanaselvam   345

IN THE VINES OF PARANOIA
    Reuel Rawat   359

LINE(AGE)
    Nat Kang   367

BIOS   382

Introduction

✕

Hello, punters!

I started Buku Fixi in 2011 because from what I could see at the time, the market for commercial fiction in Malay was dominated by romance titles. At least nine out of the 10 books on the bestseller lists would have *Cinta*, *Kasih* or *Rindu* in them, and this made me want to hurl.

Nothing wrong with romance per se – it is escapist fun like any other popular genre – but I wanted more variety. So Buku Fixi started with 10 novels in 2011 and the 10th, *Kelabu*, was a certified bestseller; it has sold over 41,000 copies to date. (The fact that the genre for *Kelabu* is romance, but with a twist, need not detain us for now.)

Fixi Novo is our omputih-language imprint. We started with the novel *Son Complex* by Kris Williamson in January 2013 and went on to publish over 30 more titles so far. Some were single-author collections or novels while the rest were anthologies featuring various writers. From the first type, the bestselling title is *Horror Stories* (2014) by Tunku Halim (33, 500 copies). I am still not sure why this did so well; when we tried a cash-in sequel called (wait for it) *Horror Stories 2* a couple of years later, we only managed to shift 9,000 units – but that's still far higher than what our average Fixi Novo title would sell.

Among the anthologies, the four bestselling ones were the first four of the *KL Noir* series, named after the colors of the Malaysian flag: *Red* (2013; sales 18,000), *White* (2013; sales 13,500), *Blue* (2013; sales 7,800) and *Yellow* (2014; sales 7,500). In 2021 we came up with a belated coda *KL Noir: Magic* – which not many people seem to know about, so buy lah, it has some of the strongest stories in the whole series.

The main *KL Noir* quartet did well because it brought a brash, unfiltered energy – replete with serial killers, psychopaths, vigilantes – to a familiar place. Our local movies and TV shows are so heavily censored, so the brazenness of the books seemed like a liberating option for people (and who could these people possibly be?) in search of sex and violence.

Since we are patriotic af, we tried anthologies set in other Malaysian cities too. These met with varying levels of success: *Love in Penang* (sales 6,500) *Hungry in Ipoh* (3,000), *Lost in Putrajaya* (3,500), *PJ Confidential* (2,000) and *Chronicles of KK* (1,600).

We have published hundreds of writers by now. A few went on to bigger and better things – we published Hugo Award-winning writer Zen Cho's first book *Spirits Abroad* (2014), and short stories by Hanna Alkaf, Lee Eeleen and Karina Bahrin before their novels were published in First World countries. (#doneclaim) Would they have succeeded without us? Of course they would have, they're talented and determined. But we would like to think they got a slight nudge of encouragement from us.

Anthologies always take a lot more time and work than single-author books. All anthologies by their very nature are 'mixed bags' and it is the task of the editor to pick the stories that are not only interesting in their own right but will also fit into a reasonably coherent whole. This book went through several drafts and took over a year to get done. It was a draining process and please remind me to never do something on this scale again.

The theme of horror was chosen because I thought it would sell. No, just kidding: The theme was chosen because horror, most explicitly of the supernatural variety, is inextricably entwined with Malaysian life, and the forms that these ghosts take are subtexts for the actual anxieties, fears and prejudices that we have. No, just kidding: The theme of horror was chosen because I thought it would sell lah.

This book opens with a bunch of friends talking cock and sharing ghost stories, an experience that would be familiar to many Malaysians, then proceeds to an urban legend in a popular contemporary building and then a tale that crosses liminal boundaries of not only time but species. (I just used 'liminal', so you know this is a serious Introduction.)

Along the way there are horrors that manifest themselves in the form of ghouls and demons, but also in seemingly more mundane elements, like a tracking device on a car or an itch that refuses to go away. Some reimagine historical events or have audacious spins on themes that would otherwise have a solemn approach (such as environmentalism). We also have cannibals; they seem to pop up in most of our anthologies.

If I would suggest a common thread for this book, it would be: How we deal with tradition, and how tradition deals with us. What legacies do we inherit, and how do they enrich or damage us? Although prohibitions like 'don't piss in the jungle without seeking permission' are well-known, there are stories that show a more complicated relationship we have with forces beyond our control: these are the ties (historical, familial, cultural) that can not only bind but choke.

I write this just before Malaysia's 15th General Elections – when, once again, 'inherited' fears, traumas and bogeymen are amplified on the national stage by the usual dodgy suspects. Will we ever break free from politically engineered mistrust? Perhaps sharing stories are one small way to break free; we have the power to determine the tiny elements that make up the 'grand narrative' of our imagined community anyway. Which is why the final story here is probably the boldest when it comes to bringing together past/present, real/unreal, horrors we experience/horrors we impose, and asks where we can go from here.

We tried to be diverse in this selection, at least in terms of geography and social demographic, but we know there are blind spots. If you think there are stories that are not here but need to be written, perhaps it's because *you* are meant to write it. Who knows? Maybe this anthology can be the start of a series. Even without knowing the results of this election yet, I can sense that some of the outcomes might bring forth even more opportunities for horror.

Amir Muhammad
1 November 2022

Campfire Stories

✕

Rizal Ramli

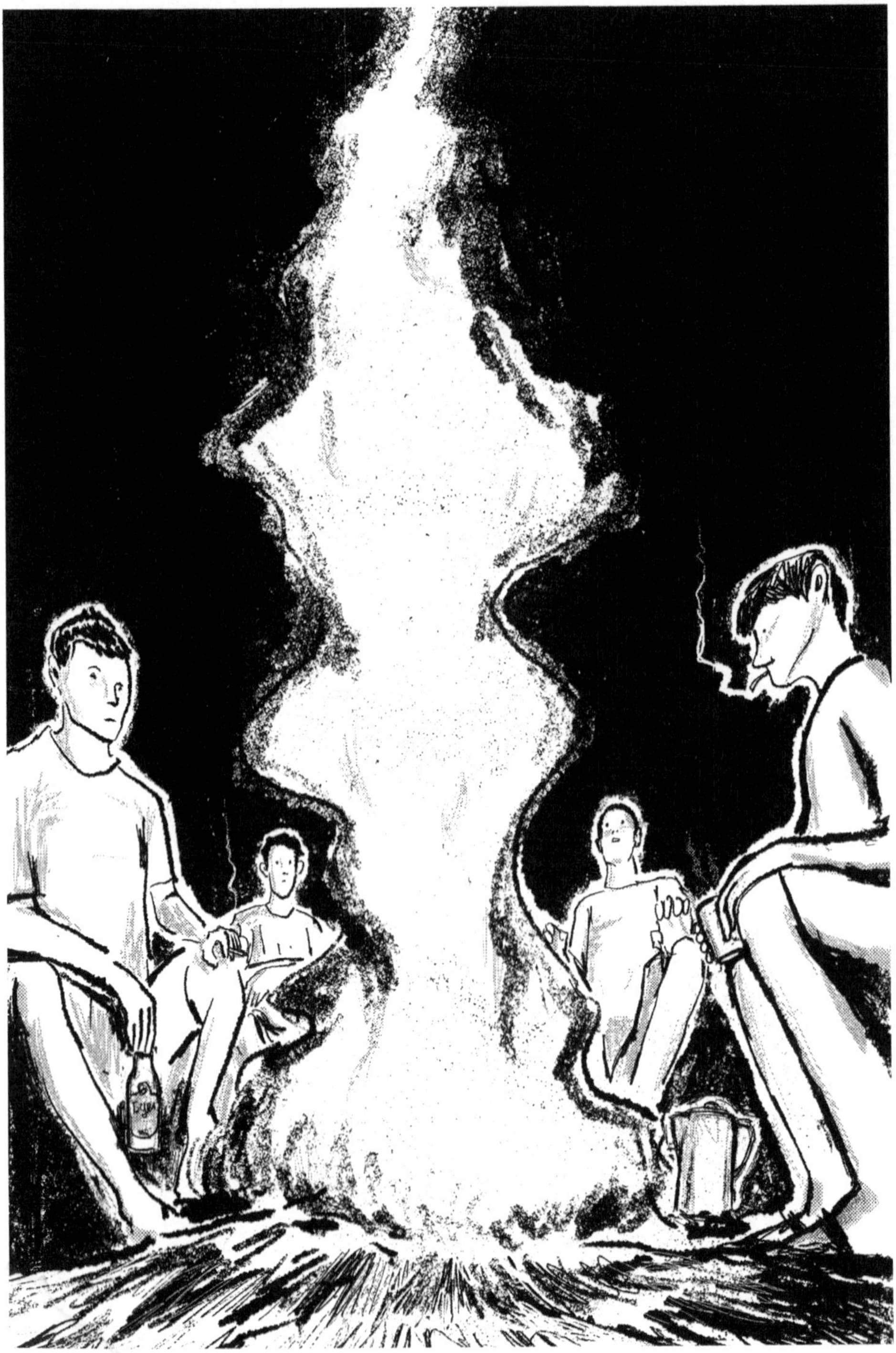

"...and when the guard poked his head outside the booth, he saw a lady in white with long hair standing by the factory's main gate. She was crying and cradling a baby in her arms," Ali recounted the story he'd heard over and over again.

The campfire lit up his stern face, making the mood spookier. Firewood crackled, sending embers floating upwards like fireflies. Everyone was immersed in his tale except Ah Chong. He was stifling a laugh, his whole body trembling.

"Haiya, always the same one. Lady in white. Long hair. Boringlah!" he chortled.

"Dey! Don't interrupt lah." Muthu held his palm out to Ah Chong. Then his fist bumped his friend's shoulder. "Spoiled the mood la you."

Ali and Jasvinder sighed and clicked their tongues. The mood was indeed gone, and Ali's story had lost its suspense.

"Okay, okay. Sorry. Wah, so serious la you guys." Ah Chong put up his hands.

"If you don't like the story, don't interrupt la brother. Potong steam la!" Jasvinder barked.

"I said I'm sorry!"

"Okay, okay. Guys, let's continue." Ali leaned forward. "The guard got out from the booth and looked around in case the woman was not alone. She turned her head and hid her face."

The woods got darker and colder. The shrill chirps of insects reached a crescendo. Monkeys howled in the distance, sounding like screaming children. Everyone was a bit disturbed by the howling, but this was the reason they camped out here: the adrenaline rush and thrill of telling scary stories in the woods. They wanted this.

"The woman was still crying. He got closer and asked the woman: 'Excuse me, Miss. Are you lost?' She didn't respond. So he asked again: 'Are you in trouble?' The guard walked around her so he can see her face, but she kept hiding her head, like she's very shy or something. So the guard finally tapped her shoulder."

A shrill scream from the trees startled them. It came not far from where they were huddled around the fire. Everyone's heart leapt into their throats.

"Aiyo, that one was very close la macha!" Muthu looked up.

He flashed his torch up into the trees. Hairs on the back of his neck bristled when his wild imagination expected to see a pontianak or hantu raya squatting on a branch.

"Relax la. It's just the monkeys. Let's continue." Ali cleared his throat. "After the guard touched her shoulder, the woman stopped crying. And she said slowly: 'My baby is hungry.' And then she held out her baby to the guard. She wanted him to take it. He was shocked at first, suddenly passing him her baby, but he took it anyway." Ali mimed the movement, cradling an invisible baby in his arms.

"The baby was very heavy. So the guard lifted up the blanket covering its face…"

He leaned forward, closer to the fire and lowered his voice for extra effect. "…and he was shocked to his core when he saw what the woman was holding all this time." Ali looked around at his friends' eager expressions. "It was a gravestone. Still have grave dirt on it."

Everyone rubbed their arms and the backs of their necks. Jasvinder let out a nervous laugh, acknowledging the creepiness of the story.

"The guard froze. Too scared to say anything. Then the woman turned her head slowly. The poor bugger wet himself right there on the spot. Because the woman HAD NO FACE!" Ali grabbed Ah Chong's shoulder.

They all laughed.

"Good one. Good one. Very creepy." Muthu put up a thumb. Jasvinder nodded.

"But still can be scarier if not for this fella's interruption." Ali tried grabbing Ah Chong's ear. His friend hid his head behind his shoulder.

"Stop it la wei! I said I'm sorry, kan?"

"But these monkeys also play-play with us. Like they know we're telling ghost stories. Maybe they want to join us?" Muthu chuckled. Everyone did.

As if on cue, the monkeys let out ear-piercing howls. This time they were very close and sounded like they came from above them. Everyone yelped in panic and almost fell from the logs they were sitting on. Muthu's torch caught a pair of red glowing eyes on the nearest branch. The animal hissed and flashed its sharp teeth before swaying from branch to branch, leaving the four terrified friends. More howls and screams in the distance and then things simmered down.

"Son of a bitch! Fucking monkeys!" Ah Chong stood up and yelled at the trees.

"Aiya the thing already gone now you berani huh?"

They all laughed, albeit still creeped out.

Ah Chong lit a cigarette. Ali poured the rest of the hot Nescafe from a small steel jug by the fire into his mug. Jasvinder stirred the embers in the fire pit, and then added fresh firewood.

Muthu looked up to the branches one last time before starting the next session. "Okay. It's my turn now. My story is scarier than yours, Ali." He nodded to his friend, confident in outdoing Ali's no-face woman story.

Ali and the rest grinned.

"This story happened in a haunted school hostel many years ago. I'm not sure which school but it's about…" Muthu turned to Ah Chong. "Oh, sorry bro. This is another lady-in-white ghost story," he chuckled.

Ah Chong rolled his eyes. "Haiya. Okay la, okay la. Continue."

"I heard this one from my cousin. Every night at this school, the girls always kena kacau. Some got possessed. Always start around Maghrib. There's one time the asrama students had extra night class because it's almost SPM. This school was surrounded by the jungle, you know, so their class was at the bottom and can clearly see straight into the thick trees. You know how people said, 'If you see, hear or smell anything suspicious at night, don't say anything'? Huh? Jangan tegur? Right?"

Everyone nodded.

"So during the class, there's one boy who sits at the windows. When he looked out he saw a woman in white with long hair waving at him by the fence near the jungle. This boy ar, very celupar one, he asked the teacher out loud: 'Cikgu, who's that at the fence?' Everyone including the teacher saw the woman.

"And then the woman moves very fast one! Like whoop! Whoop! Whoop!" Muthu held out his arm and pulled back his hand towards his face in three jerking moves.

"The woman like ninja suddenly moved to the windows and scared everyone. She looked inside, showing her ugly face. She had big bulging eyes. And her mouth was very wide, almost reached her ears. She just laughed and moved her eyeballs looking at everyone." Muthu's eyeballs moved wildly, staring at his friends.

"Walaowei!" Their eyes lit up.

"Everyone in the class screamed, and some hysteria. Or maybe possessed, I'm not sure. Boys and girls all screamed. The woman disappeared right away. The teachers had to call the ustaz and kasi settle."

"Asrama school always haunted la wei. Especially new schools. They cleared the jungles, and then build a school. Confirm haunted." Ali lit a smoke.

"Well, that's one story. There's another famous legend about that school. Scarier than the last one."

"Wah, pontianak jump scare you at the window still not scary ah?" Ah Chong said.

"This one happened in the girl's hostel toilet. It involves a pervert who likes to skodeng the girls. Very nasty one this fella. So one night he sneaked into the girls' hostel and climbed into the toilet's ceiling. This pundek just waited up there quietly, waiting for someone having a shower, or maybe buang air."

Everyone grimaced.

"Ugh, I don't understand why people can get turned on watching people shit," Jasvinder said.

"So around midnight someone got in. She just standing around, looking at the mirror and doing nothing. And then she turned over the sanitary napkin bin. The mat skodeng saw all the bloody towels scattered on the floor. The woman picked one towel and then slowly..." Muthu flicked his tongue out in the air. "She slowly licked the blood on the towel. And she sucked it like siput sedut some more!"

"Ugh, disgusting bodoh!" Ali cringed.

"The fella almost screamed but he covered his mouth quickly. The woman still heard him. Then her head snapped, not moving slowly, but snapped like she had no bones in her neck. It turned 180 degree. Just like the woman in my first story, her eyes very big, almost come out of socket. Her mouth wide and her bloody tongue very long one. Her eyes moving everywhere while looking at the ceiling, because she cannot see the mat skodeng hiding inside there. Then her head moved side to side and her neck got longer and longer, going up to the ceiling, like a snake.

"The pervert saw everything through the peephole. He's fucked anyway. Can't move, can't talk. Only can watch the snake head thing moved closer and closer to his hiding spot. He wet his pants. The head asked slowly: 'Where are you?'" Muthu sang the last part in an eerie melodic whisper.

"The fella closed his eyes and mouth and didn't move. He stayed like that for almost a minute. When he thought the coast was clear he opened his eyes. The bathroom was empty, only scattered bloody pads on the floor. So he was lega la. When he was about to climb down, a voice suddenly said: 'Found you!'

"The woman was right in front of him inside that tiny space. That fella screamed la wei. Like crazy. He fell down through the ceiling some more. And broke his legs. What a fucking loser. My cousin said he got expelled because he trespassed into the girls' hostel. People also said he went nuts after that. Something got loose inside." Muthu's finger tapped on his right temple.

"Of course la. Anyone sure gila if kena kacau like that. Scary wei," Ali said while stretching his legs. "Whose turn is it now? Is it yours, Singh?"

The screaming monkeys came back, but still sounded far away, somewhere in the trees. More firewood was added into the fire. Jasvinder sipped hot coffee from his steel mug and smacked his lips.

"Okay. My story doesn't have a pontianak. It's about my friend kena kacau while working late in office. He just started working. So he didn't know the pantang larang there. Never heard any ghost story. Maybe because he's new so nobody talked to him at first. So one day, his boss asked him to stay back for overtime. My friend said nothing. It's his first job you see, so he wanted to show rajin la in front of boss besides making extra money. Nobody else stayed back. Everyone went home after 5 p.m.

"Last minute only came one kakak told him to be careful in the printer room. My friend thought she was only joking. You know like trying to scare the new kid in the office. So later that night, he already forgot about it. He printed out all his work and went into the room to pick them up.

"While he was in there, he felt someone was watching him. You know the feeling you get when you think someone's in the corner, in the dark watching you, or when you sense another person in the same room with you. My friend felt that. Very strong one. His hair everywhere got goose bumps. When he was about to turn around, a white figure moved very fast behind him. He saw the damn thing like in the corner of his eyes." Jasvinder waved his hand near his ear.

"Suddenly he smelled something rotten, like dead animals and wet dirt. My friend dropped his stuff and quickly got out. Then he got even more scared when his boss surprised him at his desk. His boss told my friend he left something in the office. My friend told him about the white figure in the printing room. His boss told him to just ignore it. That's how people deal with it.

"So my friend went back into the room, not so kan cheong la because his boss was there with him. He resumed his work while the boss watched him from behind. Then his phone rang. It was his boss' number. My friend quickly turned around and no one was there, so he thought his boss went back into his office.

"He answered and his boss told him to compile all the documents and slip them under his office's door before going home. My friend asked if he's still in the office and his boss said no, he's at home. He left at five like everyone else. At that moment my friend felt like running.

"The white figure came back behind him while he was still on the phone. Then it floated from behind my friend and moved slowly past him towards the toilet. It was a pocong. Its face was all black and rotten. One eyeball hanging from the socket."

"What the fuck. What did your friend do?" asked Ali.

"He cabut la. Didn't even turn off the power or lock the door. Lucky they have guards in the building lobby. Tomorrow he resigned 24 hours. The company and his boss called him but he never pick up. He still can't work alone at night until today."

"Wah, not bad. Pocong in office building. Scary." Ali nodded.

Everyone stretched and yawned. Ah Chong stood up. His bladder felt heavy. He looked around, contemplating either to ask someone to come with him or not. Being called a scaredy-cat was more embarrassing and painful than holding in his pee. He sighed and made up his mind.

"Guys, don't start without me. I have to pee," he said.

"Of course, we can't start without you anyway. It's your turn."

"Go somewhere very far from camp. We all know how your pee smells after several bottles of beer."

"Only two bottles je la wei!" Ah Chong walked away from the camp leaving his laughing friends.

He sang *My Heart Will Go On* while tip-toeing over tree roots with the help of his torch. His friends' voices faded, drowned by insect chirps and screaming monkeys. Sometimes an owl hooted somewhere in that creepy orchestra. He stopped and turned around. The fire from his camp glimmered far in the distance, almost hidden in the dark, behind tree trunks and foliage. Like a fading lighthouse in a sea of darkness.

Ah Chong decided that he'd walked far enough from the tents. He unzipped and finished his business in a long relieving stream with a hint of a stinging sensation. His torch was tucked firmly under his armpit. His eyes darted wildly in the dark, hoping he wouldn't find anything.

After he finished, Ah Chong turned around and scampered back towards the camp. At first he couldn't find the fire. He panicked and called out for his friends.

"Over here!" someone's voice replied faintly.

Ah Chong followed the voice, and after a few clumsy steps, he saw the fire again and hastened his pace.

"...and when the guard poked his head outside the booth, he saw a lady in white with long hair standing by the factory's main gate. She was crying and cradling a baby in her arms," Ali said.

"I said wait for me la! And why you tell the same story?" Ah Chong came out from the bushes. "It's my turn now. I –"

His friends were all huddled around the fire. And there were four people instead of three. The fourth guy was sitting in Ah Chong's place.

"G-Guys. Wh-who's that?"

All four guys stood up with their heads bowed down.

"Guys?"

Then they all looked up to Ah Chong. Each person there had no face, except for a very wide mouth, with a long tongue lolling out.

His feet turned to jelly. One of the figures dashed forward and covered Ah Chong's mouth. The terrified guy's scream was muffled behind the icy hand. Then the rest of them surrounded their victim.

$$\times$$

"Where is he? Almost ten minutes already." Ali lit up another cancer stick.

"Maybe he's a taking a shit," Muthu responded.

"Shitting rock is it? Very big one."

"Aiyo! Need more than ten minutes la."

They both laughed.

"What if he gets lost? That feller is very careless one." Jasvinder craned his neck into the woods, expecting to see Ah Chong tottering his way back to the camp.

"Ah shit, I'm afraid you might be right. Useless la that fella. Let's go search for him. I also need to pee." Muthu stood up. "Ali, you stay here in case he came back. Let's go Jas."

Jasvinder Singh and Muthu left Ali by the fire and made their way through the path that Ah Chong took earlier. A dark brooding sensation enveloped the campsite. The temperature suddenly dropped. Ali noticed it got quiet all of a sudden. Insects stopped chirping, monkeys no longer screamed, only the rustling of tree branches brushed in the wind.

"Haiya, fuck you la Ah Chong. Always spoil the mood," Ali said under his breath while stoking the embers.

The cold bit through his skin. "Why suddenly so cold?" He hugged his arms.

A scream broke out in the distance. Ali stood up, startled. He spun around 360 degrees, head snapping in all directions. He subconsciously was sure the scream sounded more like a human's than a monkey's. Then more screams. This continued for a few seconds until he was sure again they were monkeys. Then the insects and owls joined in. The jungle came back to life.

Ali was still on edge when a twig snapped behind him. He screamed and turned around in panic.

"It's us." Ah Chong, Muthu and Jasvinder appeared from behind a bush.

"Son of a bitch. You guys almost gave me a heart attack," Ali tittered. "Wait, did you guys hear the screams?"

"Relax, Ali. It's just the monkeys," Ah Chong said.

"Forget about the monkeys. Let's continue. Whose turn is it?" Muthu grinned. He put his arm around Ali's shoulder.

"What are you doing?" Ali pulled his head back and stared into Muthu's face with one eyebrow raised.

"You look cold, Ali."

"Yeah. But not that cold."

Something was in Muthu's eyes: a light orange glimmer, probably a reflection from the fire.

"My turn now!" Ah Chong put up his hand, grinning as gleefully as Muthu.

Ali glanced at Jasvinder who was also smirking. *Something's off about these three*, he thought. Then it dawned on him. He began to understand the ruse. Ali chortled.

"Okay. I get it. HA-HA! Very funny guys." He clapped.

The other three kept on smirking and giggling.

"This story happened to my…close friends. They went camping in the jungle, having fun, eat BBQs and telling scary stories," Ah Chong began his tale.

"So at one point, one of them had to take a piss. He went out by himself, but never returns for a long time."

Ali stifled a laugh.

"Then two of his friends went out looking for him, leaving behind one friend at camp. Then after a while, the three of them finally came back. But they were acting suspiciously, like they're not themselves."

Ali finally burst out laughing.

"It's because the three friends probably died already and have been replaced with ghosts? Is that the story? Hahaha pundek la wei. Very scary one." He clapped again.

Muthu's arm never left Ali's shoulder. Then Ah Chong and Jasvinder closed in on Ali, and they all hugged him.

"Hey, what the fuck are you guys doing?"

The fire faded out, until there were only embers left. The jungle came to life, even louder and more chaotic than before. It was a crescendo of chirps, hoots, roars and screams. The screaming was the loudest of them all.

What Happens in KLCC Stays in KLCC

✕

Raja Ummi Nadrah

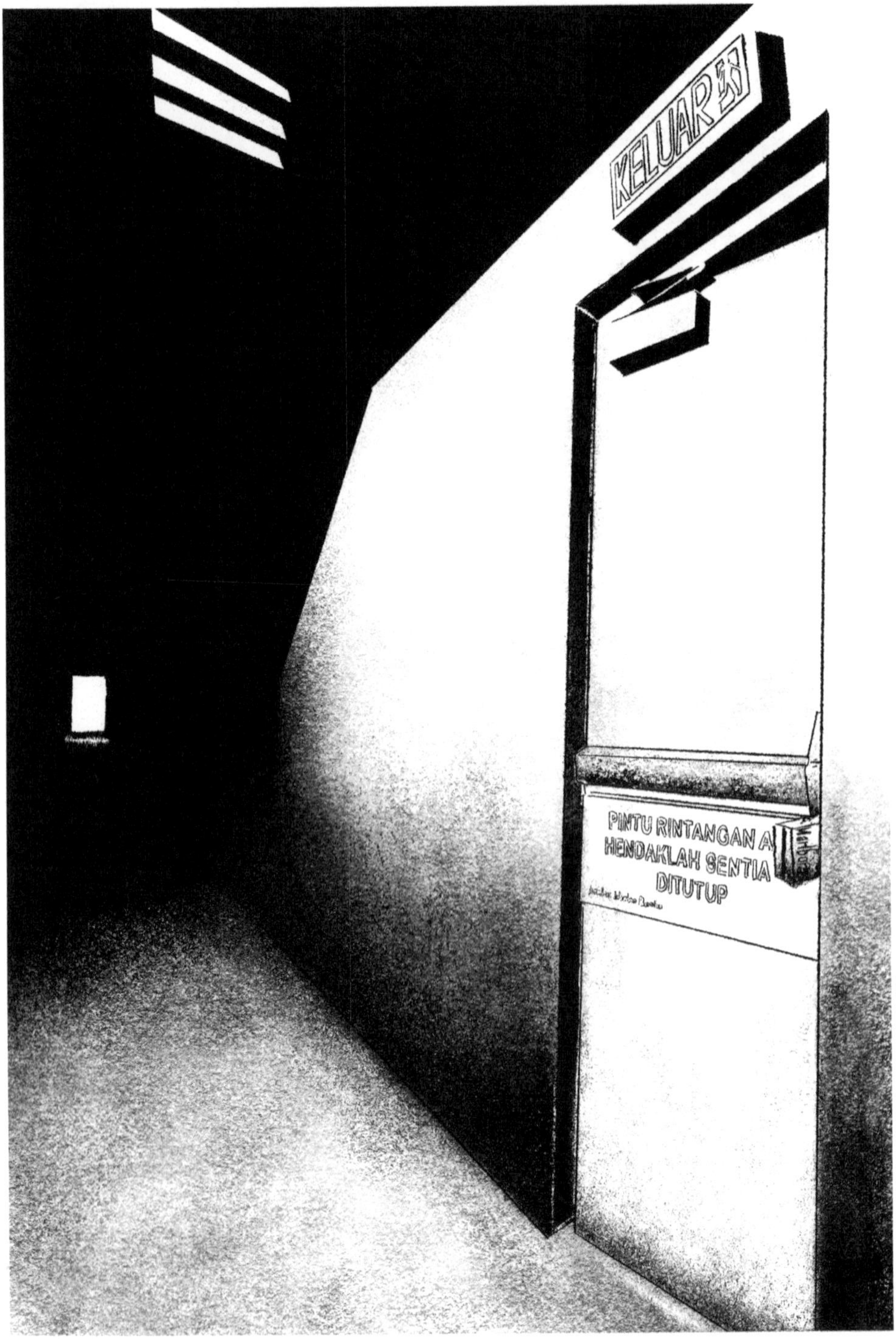
KELUAR
PINTU RINTANGAN A
HENDAKLAH SENTIA
DITUTUP

When you think of haunted places, the first images that come into your mind would probably be those of cemeteries, hospital morgues, abandoned houses or deserted paths in the woods. Dark, quiet places that rarely see humans. Or places that are often associated with illness and death.

But what about crowded places like the airport, LRT stations and shopping malls? Places with heavy footfall all day every day, all year long. What about the most iconic buildings in Malaysia, the Twin Towers? Would you have guessed that there were ghosts there too? Surely there can't be any, can there?

But ghosts, or spirits, or whatever you may call these paranormal entities, do exist all around us. In between the throngs of people waiting to board the train, at the corner of the elevator, or on the seat next to you at the pantry table where you usually have your lunch. Their presence can be felt, heard, smelled, and sometimes seen. If you take a moment in your busy day to stop in your tracks and pay attention to your surroundings, the sights, the smells, the sounds, or the general vibe of the place around you, if you paid *really* close attention, you might slowly begin to feel it. That strange coldness that tickles the hairs on your neck. That sensation of someone — or something — intently watching you.

In 2012, after graduating from college, for lack of a better job offer, I began my waitressing stint in a restaurant in the shopping mall at the foot of the Twin Towers. Back then, it was the only restaurant on the first floor. The others were mostly on the ground floor with alfresco seating facing the fountains, or on the fourth floor, near the food court.

As one of the most prominent tourist attractions in Kuala Lumpur, the shopping mall is busy day in and day out. Our restaurant opened at 10 a.m. Around 11, customers would already arrive by the dozens. By noon, it was a full house. Queues would form at the hostess stand, snaking all the way to the escalators. After the lunch crowd dissipated, we would close off the section at the back, but it was by no means a time for us to relax. We had to clean the section, wipe cutlery, refill the server stations and prepare for dinner while simultaneously attending to customers who had come in for afternoon tea.

The working hours were long. The minimum was 10 hours, from 9 a.m. to 7 p.m., but very rarely did we get to work minimum hours. On most days, it could easily stretch to 12 hours, or 14 if we were terribly short-staffed. The kitchen's last call was at 10 p.m., but customers would stay for dessert and tea and coffee and chit chat. We had to wait for the last customer to leave before we could start closing. The bottles of sauce and ketchup would then need to be wiped, the salt and pepper shakers refilled, the floor mopped and scrubbed, the tables sanitized. By the end of the night, the whole service and kitchen crew would be sprawled on the sofa seats, some even on the floor, waiting for the company transport to arrive and shuttle us home. On nights when the sales were good, or if the manager was in a festive mood, we could help ourselves to any drinks we wanted from the bar. Sometimes even our van driver would join in, getting drunk late into the night and early morning.

With so much time spent at the restaurant, workplace romances were common, even among the ones who had spouses waiting at home. Most of the foreign workers had been away from their wives and husbands for many months anyway, so it was not all that surprising to see how — amidst the chaos and exhaustion of this grueling job in this lonely foreign country — the yearning for some tender loving care slowly cropped up.

I remember well the tall, fair-skinned, almost Chinese-looking guy named Piolo. He had a secret lover: the new young waitress, Tina. They were polar opposites of each other. Piolo was a married man in his thirties, with two kids back home. Tina, as far as I knew, came to Malaysia right after completing high school. While Piolo towered at 5'11", Tina was petite, to put it mildly. While Piolo was loud and gregarious, Tina was demure and didn't talk much. In fact, I don't think I ever really talked to her except for the occasional times we were in the same section. The only memorable thing about her was that long, enviable shampoo-ad hair that she always wore in a bun during her shift but would let loose after work.

They were migrant workers from two different countries. We knew they were trying not to make their relationship too obvious, but a secret like that was difficult to hide for long, especially when they couldn't keep their eyes off each other. They often disappeared during lunch breaks and after closing time, only re-emerging from their hiding place just in time to get on the ride home.

×

The restaurant was designed in such a way that it was long rather than wide. From outside, it looked like a small outlet — just one shop lot — but once you entered past the waiting area, you'd see that it stretched all the way to the back. On the right-hand side were floor-to-ceiling windows overlooking the park. On the left were the bar, dessert display, payment counter, and lastly the kitchen. But before you reached the bar, you'd see a large louvered black door. This opened to a private room where the restaurant staff stored their belongings, held meetings, or took naps during their lunch breaks. Only for special occasions would this room be cleared to make way for customers, usually VVIPs who didn't like to be seen by the public.

At the corner of this room was another door that led to a passageway that was used primarily by suppliers to deliver stock. It also served as a shortcut for us to go to the washroom. Exiting the passageway at the other end, we would find ourselves flanked by two luxury watch boutiques. The toilets were just a few steps farther.

The passageway was a straight path with not many nooks or crannies to hide in. You could steal a hasty kiss, perhaps, but nothing more. However, on one side, there was an emergency exit leading to the stairs to be used in the event of a fire. This emergency exit, like most emergency exits, had push bar locks that could only be opened from one side. That means, if you accidentally closed it behind you, there was no way you could get back in unless you banged on the door until someone came to your rescue. So those who wanted to go and spend a few minutes at the staircase would put something between the doors, usually a wad of tissue paper or an empty cigarette box, to prevent it from locking them out.

I think all of us had gone to the staircase at one point or another. It was the perfect rendezvous spot for those workplace lovers who wanted to take their romance beyond a hasty kiss. Some people went there simply to steal a few puffs of smoke. Or just to get away from it all for a short while. So, if you saw the doors slightly ajar with something wedged between them, you'd know that someone was in there doing their secret business, whatever that may be. We were careful to cover our tracks so as not to be detected by the building management. Very occasionally, some clumsy fellow would leave behind a cigarette butt or a used condom, but thus far we never got in any trouble.

✕

Piolo and Tina carried on their heady affair for about half a year until it suddenly came to a halt. Tina was absent from work for a couple of days and when she came back, they were no longer talking to each other. The happy couple was no more. After what we assumed to be their breakup, Tina became a lot more withdrawn. We let her be. Eventually she stopped talking to all of us.

We watched in silence as her stomach grew rounder and she switched to bigger, baggier shirts. As the months progressed, the manager assigned her to do only cashiering work, further isolating her from the rest of the floor staff. She no longer joined us in our drinking sessions after work. She would go home on her own, not wanting to be squished with us in the van that was meant to seat seven but could fit up to 12 if we squeezed in tight.

That was why, on the night of the tragedy, we didn't realize anything was amiss. When we didn't see her after clocking out, we simply assumed she had gone home early as she had been doing for the past few months. Her body was only found the next morning by a security guard doing his rounds. She was lying in a pool of her own blood on the stair landing, with her stillborn baby by her side. The emergency exit door was tightly shut. The cause of death was severe hemorrhage.

It was a gloomy day for the rest of us. The restaurant was closed for the first time that year as we were reeling from shock and grief. After the police ruled out foul play, we spent hours trying to clean up the blood. But no matter how hard we scrubbed, the dark stain wouldn't go away. It seemed to have seeped into the cement, as if Tina herself had willed it to stay there to remind us all of its dark history. Obeying an unspoken agreement, we stopped visiting that secret hideout. Now the passageway is used only by unsuspecting suppliers and the newer waiters who don't know any better. For the rest of us who have worked there long enough, we would rather go out through the main entrance and take the long way to get to the washroom.

Tina's death destroyed whatever camaraderie we had. It changed the atmosphere in the restaurant. We were plagued by this uncomfortable feeling that continued throughout the day, but especially during closing time. It was as though there was some kind of negative energy reverberating from behind the fire exit door. The hairs on my neck would stand every time I walk past. I might have been imagining it, but sometimes I swear I could still detect the sickly metallic smell of blood wafting in.

It has been 10 years since the incident. The restaurant has been renovated almost beyond recognition. I have found a better job somewhere else. Piolo, on the other hand, went back to his home country a couple of months after Tina's death. Rumor had it that he contracted a mysterious illness during his last few weeks in Malaysia. He was seeing things that were not there and had to be restrained when he tried to gouge his eyes out. I have no idea what became of him after that.

But the story spread throughout the shopping mall. Some people claimed to have sighted a long-haired woman trying to breastfeed a baby, whose lifeless, bloated body was evidently decomposing, the skin almost black and blue. Some reported seeing a placenta, or chunks of it — with the umbilical cord still attached — soaked with blood that trickled down the stairs. And sometimes there was the faint humming of a lullaby. Then again these were all just stories, told from one person to another, with every possibility of being exaggerated or even fabricated. No one could ever verify them.

But maybe you could. So, the next time you pay a visit to the Twin Towers, look for those two luxury watch shops on the first floor, and the gray double doors between them. If you're feeling brave, go in and see the passageway for yourself. Find the fire exit and the big dark stain on the cement floor that I'm sure is still there. Does it still have that smell? Then look around you. See if the stories have any truth in them. Strain your ears. Can you hear the lullaby? I should tell you that the lights at the staircase are operated by motion sensor. That means only the light above you should be on. If another light at another part of the stairs suddenly flickers to life without you going there, maybe you've got company. Remember not to shut the door behind you.

Klang Crow

✕

Joshua Lim

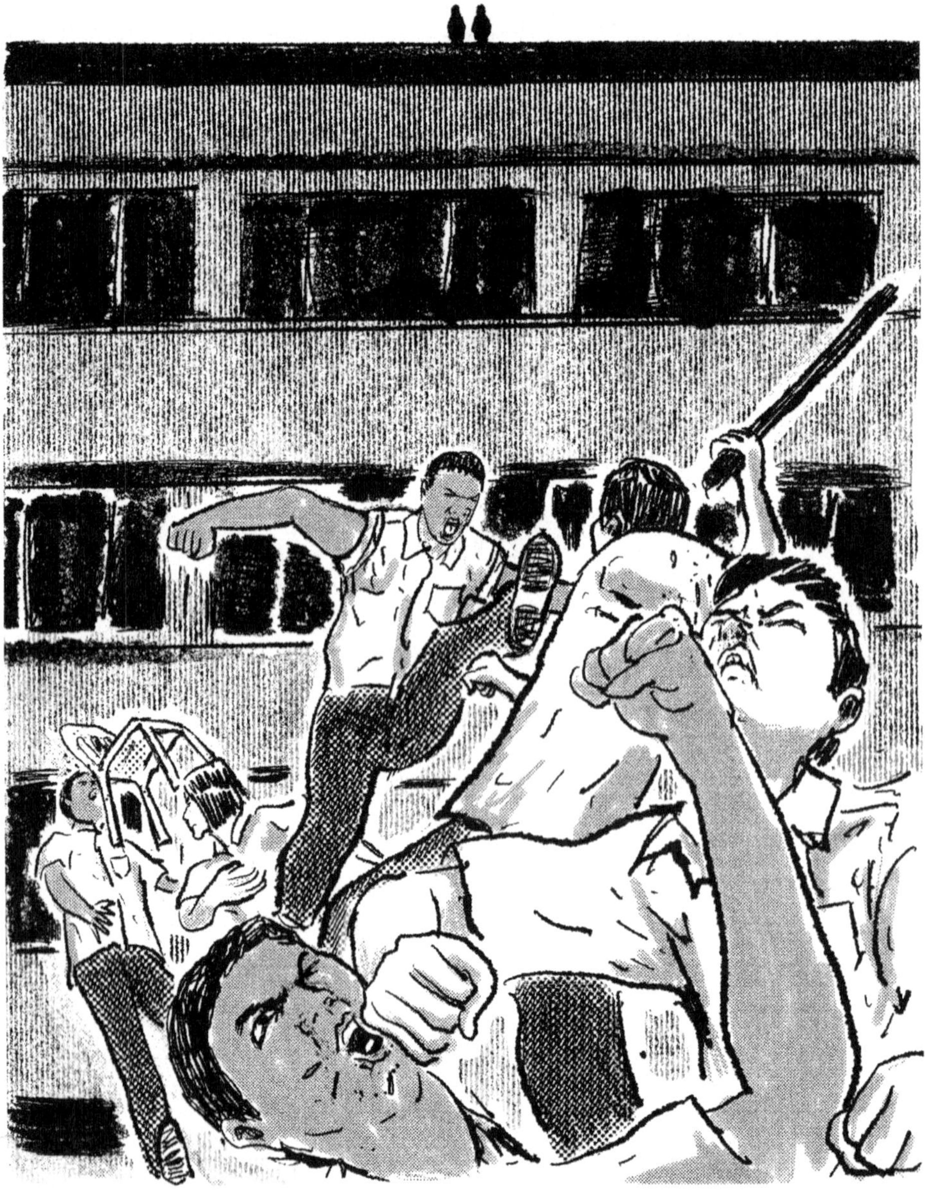

You are a crow in Klang, and you wake up trembling again.

The sun is rising, but the sky is still gray. You stir in your nest of twigs, looking out at the Ng house just across the road. You flap your wings, and your brothers and sisters and friends and neighbors start waking up all over your tree. The residential area you live in is still quiet and sleepy, but something in the air does not feel right.

Mr. Ng comes out from his house, dressed for work. He is about to enter his car when he notices a small white mark on the windshield of his Proton Wira — a drop of bird poop.

"Fucking crows!" he roars. He disappears into the house and bursts back out, clutching a long broom, going off in a Hokkien tirade. "These fucking birds — go away!" He slams the broom repeatedly on his metal gates, raising an awful ruckus. "Si oh ah! Go die!"

All the crows in the nearby trees scatter into the sky in a cloud of feathers, squawking and cawing, causing a terrible din of their own. You hear the cursing of Mr. Ng's neighbors and the slamming of windows. You hang around to watch, a sinking feeling in your heart. *Is the curse manifesting itself today as well?*

Mr. Ng's wife appears in the doorway. "So early, why bang bang bang?" she shouts at her husband. "What's your problem?"

"You're the one who made us move to Klang!" retorts Mr. Ng. "What the hell, not just the crime rate so high, crows everywhere also. I'm going to complain to the town council, shoot them all! What kind of town is this?"

"Oh, now you blame me? I am the problem?"

You have heard enough. You spread your big black wings, feel the wind currents and leap into the sky, climbing higher and higher until you are soaring above the tiny rooftops and looking down over the town.

From above, Klang is a labyrinth of houses and shops and streets and schools and offices stretching for miles and miles around. You let the wind carry you as you drink in the scenery with equal parts wonder and sorrow. The morning sun touches the tips of the buildings, reflecting off a million windows with a sparkling glimmer — but you feel no joy, only a creeping apprehension.

Gwa!

You veer off course, hearing someone call your name.

It is Rokk, your third-in-command, flapping his way up to join you. Behind him are the rest of your team. You, Gwa, are the leader of fifty crows, and you silently vow to keep them all alive today.

Did you feel it too? cries Rokk. *The curse?*

You clench your talons and nod.

Give us orders, Gwa!

Where is Ungu? you almost ask, before you remember. *Rokk, you are the new second-in-command. Take half the team, spread wide and search! We need to calculate how much food we need!*

Shall I call Hanuk? asks Rokk.

Yes, call him!

Rokk acknowledges and cups his wings, going off towards North Klang, taking half the team with him. Klang is split in half by the meandering brown river that crawls across the plains, and the south side is your jurisdiction. Hanuk is in charge of the reserve unit — juveniles, old decrepit birds and such — based in the north. On bad days, they drop in to provide support.

You glance at the sun. Twilight is at 7 pm, so you have around twelve hours. You have been doing this for years, but the curse has been manifesting itself more frequently, and the fear grips you harder every time.

Let there be no blood today, you pray.

✕

At noon, you run into Traak's team at the southern end of Klang, in Taman Sentosa. You can hear their loud and raucous cawing from far away. You hone in on their voices and dive into the back alleys among rows of workshops and restaurants.

Traak is perched on a rooftop gutter, watching his crew rummage through the humongous pile of black rubbish bags that have overflowed out of the dumpster. He cries a greeting as you alight on the gutter beside him. Many of the bags have ruptured, and the crows are plucking edible scraps from the spilled contents. The smell that wafts out of the mountain of rubbish stings your eyes.

The curse feels bad today, Gwa, says Traak. He is a senior and experienced bird, grizzled and deft of beak and claw.

You nod. *Yes.*

A woman comes out of a shop's back door, cursing at the crows in Tamil, and tosses a squishy plastic bag into the heap. The crows hop away but return once she has gone back into the shop. They peck and tear open the plastic — there is some rotten meat inside, and some rejected parts of food.

That won't do, observes Traak. *We'll need more than that. A body, at least.*

Was blood spilled? you ask. You have scanned the wealthier neighborhoods all morning. People have been arguing everywhere, fights started and punches thrown, but so far no terrible news.

There was an armed robbery at dawn, says Traak. *Some small gang altercations among the Indians. A few people were wounded.*

Your heart sinks further. So it has begun.

You'd better check Pandamaran, says Traak. *I'll handle the search around this area. Call Hanuk from the North — you'll need more help today.*

I've sent Rokk, you say. You salute Traak with a flap of your wings and fly west — towards Pandamaran.

Traak's Taman Sentosa might have one of the highest crime rates in all of Klang, but Pandamaran is the most violent and dangerous area in town. Since olden days, the power of the Chinese gangs or 'secret societies' has never fully left the area, and it is still the hub of everything unlawful. As you soar and ride the wind, you pray that the curse has not reached them.

Not today, please not today.

There are many high-rise apartments in that area: cheap and affordable housing for undesirable characters. You arrive to find that the flat apartment roofs and the nearby roads are swarming with crows. Kaww Kaww's troop, no doubt.

You see a particularly large huddle of crows on a sidewalk, so you dive in among them. *Please be a body, please be a body.*

It is a dead dog. Perfect.

Kaww Kaww and his core group of lieutenants appear around the bend of the road, hopping along with total disregard, picking at the scattered rubbish that had been thrown out of cars. Pedestrians and drivers even steer out of the way of the crows. You silently resent them for their boldness, for they may contribute to the curse.

Kaww Kaww hops up to the dog. It is a pariah dog, dead since last night, eyes already pecked away by some overeager crow. It seems to have been beaten to death by a stick.

Is the curse bad? We need this dog today? cries Kaww Kaww to you. He is a youngster with shiny black wings and strong claws, one of the newly-appointed leaders, still learning the ropes.

His crows are flapping around, excited by the corpse but unsure what to do. Typical of the roadside crew. They get lazy and stop thinking for themselves after too many easy roadside rubbish pickings, and they wait for a leader like you to give the order.

Yes, we need it, you say. *Get to work. Use the nearby drains for shortcuts.*

Kaww Kaww flinches at the mention of drains. You see the nervous ripple that spreads throughout the troop. You ignore it and continue speaking. *Use the drains. Did you see any crime today? Was any blood spilled? How is the gang war?*

No blood spilled, but there was a snatch-theft, says Kaww Kaww. *But I think the gangs went over to the North today. Didn't see them around here.*

You breathe a little easier, but you remind yourself to check the North.

Some car starts blasting its horn at a few idiotic crows who are blocking the road. "Oi, gagak, pi mampus!" you hear the driver yell. The crows scatter, and you propel yourself into the sky again, heading north. You see Kaww Kaww and the others hopping back to start butchering the dog.

Cars and their drivers are the biggest problem.

Second to the cawing of crows, if there is a sound that defines Klang, it is the car horn. The effect of the curse waxes and wanes, but it seems to have a permanent effect on the drivers on the road. There is not a day that thousands of people do not devolve into road-raging maniacs while stuck in phenomenal traffic — and the moment it starts loosening up, they drive like maniacs too.

Rokk meets you in the sky above the Road of Schools. You can see he has a lot to tell you, so you lead him down into one of the nine high schools lining the Port Klang highway. It provides a chance for you to check on the school gangs as well. You settle on a red-tiled roof over a school courtyard, and Rokk lands beside you.

Six car accidents today, Gwa, reports Rokk.

You groan. *Any deaths? Any fights?*

One death, two fistfights. The traffic in the Old Town is horrible.

You bury your head in your wings.

Do we have enough food yet? asks Rokk nervously.

One dog.

Is that enough?

A boy shouts.

You and Rokk look down into the courtyard. Two school gangs are advancing on each other, some armed with sticks and plastic chairs and one boy swishing a thick rotan. Many just roll back their sleeves and bare their fists.

"Come on!" shouts one Malay boy. "Your father is a —"

A chair flies across the yard and slams into his face, ending his insult. The boys yell and break into a charge. For a moment they are running, shouting wordless cries of fury, waving their weapons, and then everything becomes chaos.

You turn to Rokk. *No, one dog is not enough.*

Does that mean — we have to hunt and kill again?

I hope not. But if we must, we must. We cannot afford to run short again.

Rokk shakes his head. *I wish Ungu was here.*

You bite back the urge to snap at Rokk. He is young, but you have seen many crows live and die under the curse. Ungu was your stalwart second-in-command before he died, but now Rokk has taken his place, and Rokk must learn to be strong. You are going to say something, but the flapping of wings distracts you.

A female crow swoops down towards you.

Gwa! Gwa! Hanuk has news of a murder!

Where?

In Kapar! Hanuk says to meet beside the river!

You and Rokk exchange a glance.

Gather the crew and join Hanuk, you say. *I'll drop by the Sultan's palace and rendezvous with you at the river.*

✕

You pass over another traffic jam near the Sultan's palace. You can hear the honking from far away, and the intense red glow from the car lights makes your eyes hurt. *Maybe the red color contributes to the curse, making people more angry,* you think.

Klang is the royal town of Selangor. You find the palace peaceful as ever. That gives you a momentary spring of relief, but the palace is at the top of a hill, and at the bottom of the hill is the famous Little India street. Clouds of pigeons and gray feathers fill the air as you try to pass through. You dive and weave through swarms of stupid squawking birds, knocking them aside with your wings and claws.

There are a few young crows behind a Bombay Jewelry shop trying to drag a dead rat into a drain, so you help them shoo away the curious pigeons that crowd around. You try your best to stay away from the drain, but you find yourself near the edge, and you look inside.

It is almost like a small creek, flowing under the surface of the town. The drain is more than a meter wide, clogged with rubbish and filth, but the black and oily water is still drifting downstream. You know it will inevitably lead to the river. You shudder and look at the sun to gauge the time.

Five o'clock. Time to meet Hanuk.

Hanuk and a hundred crows are waiting for you on the north bank of the river. They are lined in black rows along the telephone wires and roadside railings, raising a deafening clamor with their cawing and arguing and jostling. Even the crows are not immune to the curse. You have previously seen two crows battle each other to the death on a particularly bad day.

Rokk is among them. You dive and land beside him and Hanuk in a tree.

Tell me about it, you say.

The murderers are bringing the body to the river, says Hanuk, ruffling his old graying feathers. *I have two youngsters trailing their truck.*

This man, killed in the gang wars?

Most likely.

Any last vestige of your relief dissolves into ash.

There they are! cries Rokk.

A nondescript lorry rolls off the road and into the cover of the thick trees and bushes along the river, with two crows sitting on the canvas roof. At your command, all your crows hop off their perches and creep closer to the truck.

A lean Chinese man jumps out of the truck. He squints at you and your comrades. "These crows look like they know what we're carrying," he says in Hokkien. "I swear, they seem too smart for their own good. Shoo! Go away!" He waves his arms.

"Don't care about them," grunts his stocky partner. "Quick, drop it in."

You watch as the men toss a few trash bags and an abnormally long sack into the brown water. No human is there to witness, only the crows.

Good thing they decided to throw it in the river, Hanuk says. *If they burnt it like the last time, we might have to kill a random dog or cat again, and she doesn't like substitutes.*

The men leave in their truck.

Get the body, you command.

The sack has sunk into the river, clearly weighed down with rocks. Fortunately, many of your crows are good divers. They dive in and slash the sack apart with their beaks and claws. It takes almost an hour to get the sack open.

The corpse finally breaks free, drifting just below the surface, barely noticeable from above. It is a man, and his throat has been slashed open.

Normally they don't float so fast, you say.

He was killed in the morning, kept in a hot truck all day, answers Hanuk.

You direct your crows to search for pieces of discarded wood and floating styrofoam or plastic objects — all of which are abundant in the murky Klang river. They collect the materials quickly, and you try to insert them under the body to float it.

With a beating of wings, Traak arrives to join the party, followed by his team. He is carrying shreds of unknown meat in his beak. *I was almost about to start the pigeon hunt*, he says. *I was afraid we could not appease the curse.*

She'll want this body, not forty dead pigeons, you answer.

Fifteen minutes later, you have the corpse lying on a raft of styrofoam. You get thirty crows to straddle the body, semi-concealing it from any inquisitive passerby, and then you and Rokk shove off the bank, heading downstream. Traak and Hanuk take wing to watch from above.

Sailing on the corpse-raft, you watch the sunset.

The setting sun is a ball of orange fire, suspended above the horizon among splashes of pink and purple that color the evening sky. The clouds hang low, glowing with twilight. The brown water of the river reflects the dying light in shimmering shades of gold. For a moment, Klang makes you smile.

Crowds of crows are circling overhead. Rokk is shouting beside you, urging the rowers as they beat at the water with their wings, propelling the raft forward. Steadily you move down the river, passing underneath the Klang bridge, hearing the din of thousands of car horns honking at each other. You watch for debris and call directions to the rowers, steering the raft, always watching for the cave opening.

Steer left! you shout when you see it. *Left! Left!*

On the southern bank, there is a gigantic drain that flows out into the river. You can see the cavernous circular opening where black water and rubbish slowly ooze out into the weak current. With lots of flapping and diligent wetting of wings, your crew guides the corpse-raft toward the drain. Piles of garbage and trash are heaped like sediment around the opening, so your raft is beached easily.

Dimly, you hear a crow's call echo from deep inside.

Hordes of birds drop out of the sky and dive into the tunnel. You see Kaww Kaww and his troop fly in with the dog's parts, and you focus on your task. It takes sixty birds to grab the corpse's clothes and lift it with the power of their beating wings. Slowly, inch by inch, you and your crew flap your way into the drain system.

Inside is pitch black, but the cawing of countless crows echo along the sides. The drains of Klang are a maze under the surface of the town, and you head deeper and deeper, followed by your faithful troops and your gruesome burden. Your eyes adapt easily to the dark, and your good hearing guides your way. You slip and skid on the slimy, dank inner surface. All the way you are praying, *Let the food be enough.*

It feels like hours before you reach the cavern with the open drainhole.

Every few hundred meters, there is a wide space where numerous drains combine into a single tunnel. A drainhole in some neighborhood was left open and never covered, so there is a shaft of light shining into the dark halls of the underground. Now, at twilight, the light is dimmer but still shines like a sun for the lightless depths. It illuminates a flat rock in the center of a pool of filth.

You manage to get the corpse onto this rock, then you back away, putting a good distance between you and the rock. The crows scatter and settle in perches all over the walls. Rokk stays close to you.

The cawing dies down. All grow quiet.

You wait.

Deep in the darkness, the Great Crow moves.

She drags her feathers along the sides of the sewers as she inches her way forward. Her claws slosh through the cold, dirty water — they are like curved spears attached to her gnarled feet, and they send clicking sounds echoing through the tunnels. You tremble and lower your head.

She comes into the spotlight — her misshapen crooked head with milky white eyes and a razor-sharp beak, with feathers like oily leaves tacked to a rotting tree. She opens her wings, extending her gargantuan wingspan to fill the cavern. The Great Crow has awoken, and she is hungry.

She raises her head and screams.

The fury and anger in all of Klang, channeled through half a million souls, pours out of her harsh voice. You and your comrades cower under her ghastliness. She has been here for centuries, since the days when wars were waged between power-hungry princes and blood watered the ground. In those times, the Great Crow fed on the corpses of men slain in battle.

Klang was placed under an eternal hex by a foreign prince who was betrayed by a Klangite; the town would be constantly plagued by anger and hostility, doomed to spill blood on the ground forever. Sometimes the curse grows weak. But it always comes back stronger, and when it does, the Great Crow awakes. She is the spawn of the prince's vengeance, born to ensure that death and slaughter will always torment this town.

And you — the crows of Klang — are the only ones who have kept this memory since the old days, and you are all that stands between her and a destructive rampage.

Kaww Kaww is the first to come forward. He lays the innards of the dog before her on the rock. His crew presents the rest of the dog in bits and pieces. Traak and his crew bring shreds of meat and rotten slices of pork. The young crows lay their dead rat beside the dog.

The Great Crow sniffs at the food, but she looks expectantly at you.

You clear your throat. *Tuanku, here is the proof of blood, spilled on account of the curse. Eat your meal, and be satisfied.*

For a second, you remember Ungu. *Please Tuanku, be satisfied*, you wish silently.

The Great Crow lowers her head to the human corpse. She pokes at the body with a large talon, scrutinizing it. She takes the man's head in her beak, pulls it off and crunches it, swallowing it in the next gulp. She grunts with delight, opens her wings and lets out a great *caw*.

You shudder. Today she will not eat any of your comrades.

You are a crow in Klang. When the humans see you, they curse and throw objects and telephone the town council to shoot you down. You dread the day when they finally drive you away, and the Great Crow is left hungry under their feet.

A Slice of Heaven

✕

Chua Kok Yee

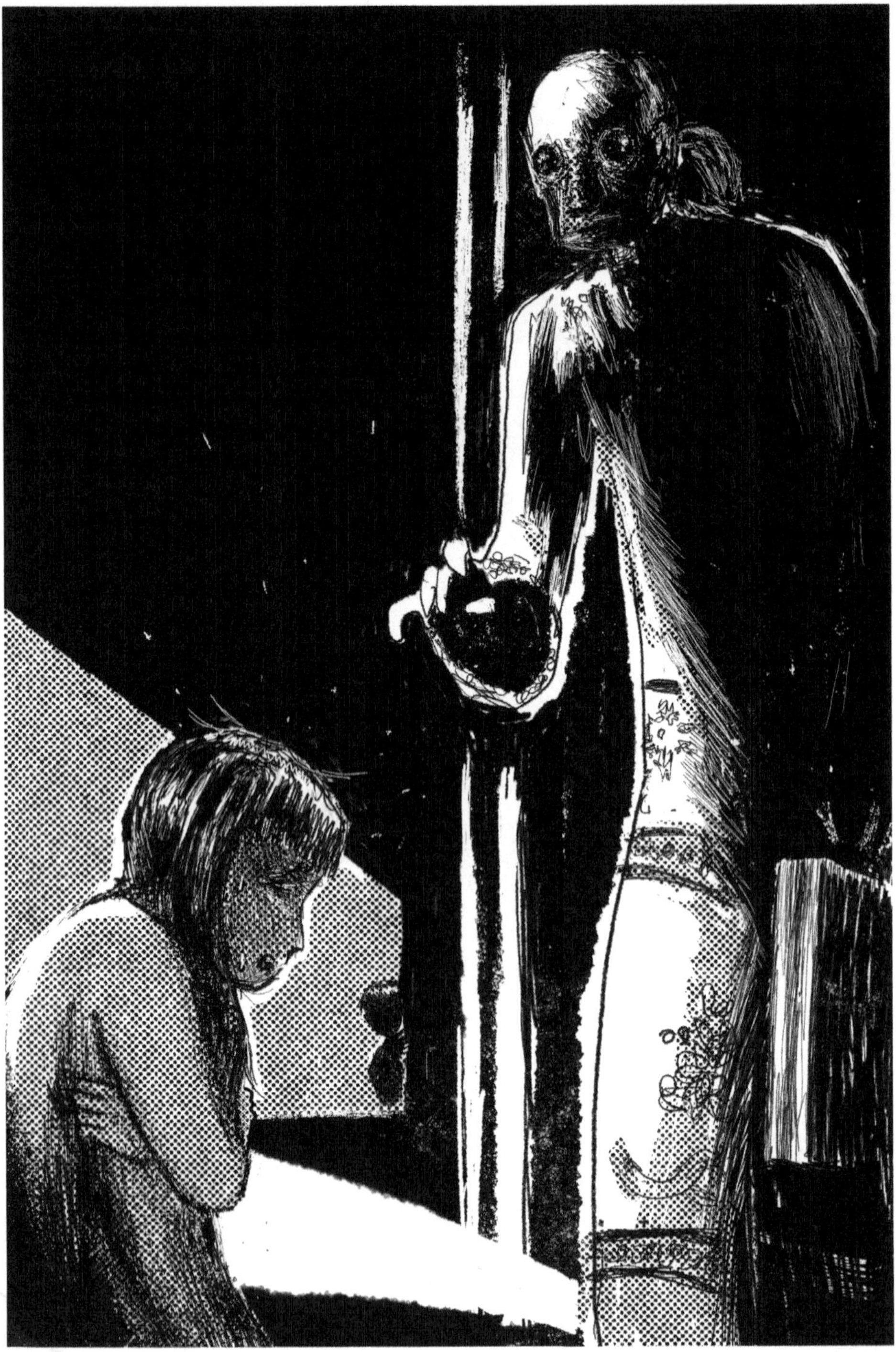

"Can I go see her?"

"She's very sick. We can't disturb her."

"I'll be quiet and won't disturb her, Papa. I promise."

"No."

"I've not seen her for a long time."

Papa shakes his head. I refuse to give up and keep asking him, until Papa gives me that look. His eyebrows come together and drop towards his nose, while his lower lip extends out in a pout. That is his angry face, so I stop asking. Disappointed, I trudge back to my room.

Papa has been telling me a lot of things. I am not supposed to run around in the kitchen because I might hurt myself by knocking into something hot or falling onto sharp knives. Birds can fly because they have wings and feathers. Plants can make their own food using sunlight and water, which is the reason he waters the garden every morning. I know all these because Papa told me. But when it comes to Lili, Papa refuses to tell me anything. I do not know why she is sick, or the reason Papa does not allow me to see her.

Worse, I know Papa is lying to me about her.

I love Lili, even though she is not my real sister. She came to live with us after Papa went to Indonesia about two years before. Papa told me Lili is the daughter of an old friend who passed away from an illness. I was happy because I always wanted a little sister. Most of my friends have siblings, and they do not have to play or do homework alone at home.

At first, she was very quiet. Mama said that was normal, as Lili was missing her old home and getting to know us. Mama was right, as usual. After a few months, she started talking and playing with me. She is very good at drawing and coloring. There is a huge poster of Spider-Man that she drew for me hanging on the door of my wardrobe, and a few smaller pieces I've kept inside my drawer.

Lili had a lot of time to draw because she did not have to go to school. Papa once tried to explain why she could not join my school, but I honestly did not understand. That was okay; I was happy for Lili as she could skip school every day. The only sad part is I am still doing my homework alone.

✕

I last saw Lili about three months ago.

That evening, I was in my room playing games on my iPad instead of studying and doing my homework. I knew Mama or Papa would not be checking on my homework, like they used to do in the past. Nowadays, they are too busy arguing with each other to pay much attention to Lili and me. In a way, that was fine for me as they were not so strict anymore, and I got less scolding from them. Yet, at the same time I felt sad whenever they started arguing.

I heard some conversation downstairs when I went to the toilet. My curiosity was piqued when I heard a voice I did not recognize, so I tiptoed to the top of the stairs. Crouching in the darkness, I spied on my parents from above.

In the living room, Mama was sitting on the long sofa next to Papa. On the opposite side was an elderly man I had never seen before. This stranger was wiry and tall, with a long ponytail of white hair. I did not like his eyes; they were widely spaced and bulging, like the eyes of a lizard.

Lizardman, I decided to call him.

"No, it has to be a member of the family. And it must be done in your home," Lizardman said.

"Why?" Papa asked.

"Think of it as our insurance policy. We got into trouble a few times in the past when the clients changed their minds and placed the blame on us."

The living room went silent. Lizardman was looking at Papa, who was staring down at his feet. Mama's eyes were darting back and forth between them with anxiety etched on her face. After a minute or so, Papa nodded. Mama let out an anguished cry.

"There must be another way, please don't do this," she pleaded.

"What other way, you tell me?" Papa retorted.

"But she's a young child, not some…"

"You're the one that brought this on us! How many times did I tell you to stop gambling? Do you think I am printing money? We have no other options now!"

Papa's voice was harsh and scary. But he was not always like that. Before, Papa was polite and seldom raised his voice at anyone. He started becoming moody and rude after the previous Chinese New Year. Since then, he scolded Mama often. It was always about Genting, Ah Long and debt. I know where Genting is, because Papa brought us there for holidays before. But I've never met this Ah Long person, and I did not understand the debt part.

Once, I asked Mama why Papa scolded her, and she said it was 'adult problems'. She told me 'adult problems' were for grown-ups to handle, and a good little boy like me should not think about them. She refused to tell me more, even after I explained that I wanted to learn so I can help them.

The following morning, I asked Papa to explain the 'adult problems' to me while he was washing his car. Papa raised his eyebrows before giving me a bemused half-smile. He told me the restaurant was not doing well, and he was facing money problems.

As I said earlier, Papa always told me things. I nodded and told Papa I understood, even though I did not. Until now I do not truly understand why the restaurant and money were called 'adult problems', and how they were linked to Genting, Ah Long and the debt.

The only part I understood was the restaurant. Papa was the owner and chef of a restaurant in Kuala Lumpur. His signature dish was Fatt Tiu Cheong or Buddha Jumping Over the Wall, and it was featured in newspapers and magazines before. I know the restaurant is very important to him, and to us, because it brings us money. Without the restaurant, Papa explained, we would not be living in our big house, wearing nice clothes or going on overseas holidays. He looked dejected when he said the restaurant was losing a lot of customers and might be closing down soon.

"But your food is very tasty, Papa. Why are we losing customers?"

"That's the nature of business," he shrugged. "Customers always want something new, and they will go away if we cannot give it to them."

I scratched my head, and that was the last time I asked them about the 'adult problem'. Mama was right; it was too complicated for me. The sound of her sobbing brought my attention back to the living room.

"We'll have to do it tonight," Lizardman said. Papa stood up and began to walk towards the staircase. The creepy Lizardman, carrying a black briefcase, followed him. I dashed back into my room, but left the door slightly ajar, just enough for me to peep through the tiny gap. When Papa reached the top of the staircase, he threw a glance in my direction. Luckily, I had switched off the light in my room so he could not see me. Papa must have thought I was sleeping.

He led the old man towards Lili's room, which was at the other end of the corridor. Papa knocked on her door softly. The door swung open, and I could see Lili standing at the doorway in her white and blue striped pajamas. She must have been reading on her bed again, because her hair was tousled. Her lips curved upwards when she saw Papa, but the smile faded when she noticed Lizardman. She raised her eyebrows at the elderly man for a second, before dropping her gaze to the floor. Lili was quite shy around strangers.

Papa said something to her, which I could not hear from my room, and stepped inside. My heart skipped a beat when I saw the Lizardman following Papa into the room. As the door was closing behind them, I caught a glimpse of Lili's face. She was biting her lower lip and staring at the old man with narrowed eyes. She was as suspicious of the Lizardman as I was.

✕

The next morning, Papa told me Lili was very sick, and they had to send her to a special hospital. He told me she left in the middle of the night because her health was getting worse. I did not even have the chance to say good-bye to her. *That was strange,* I thought, *because Lili did not look sick when I last saw her.* But I believed what Papa said because I trusted him.

Unfortunately, I found out a week later that Papa was lying. To be frank, I felt sad and disappointed. Papa always told me to tell the truth, but he himself was being dishonest with me. I know Lili is not at some hospital as Papa claimed. She is still inside her room. I discovered this one night when I tried to sneak into her room in the middle of the night. My intention was to return a coloring book I had stolen from her desk a few days prior. The door of her room was locked, but I could hear soft sobbing coming from inside.

"What are you doing?" a voice whispered from behind.

I turned around, and saw Mama standing there.

"Mama! Someone is inside…"

She knelt and placed a finger on my lips.

"Sshhhh…" Mama pulled me back into my room. She closed the door and leaned against it.

"I heard some noise from inside Lili's room. Someone is inside there," I told her.

"That's Lili, son. She is very ill and staying inside her room."

"But…but Papa said she…Lili is in…a hospital." My tongue was twisted by confusion. "Is Papa lying to me?"

Mama did not answer. Her lips were moving without making a sound, as if she were struggling to find the words. I had not seen such misery on her face before. After a long stretch of silence, I realized Mama would not be answering me.

"Is this another adult problem?"

"Yes," she nodded. "Don't tell Papa about what happened tonight. Just pretend you don't know Lili is inside the room."

She planted a kiss on my forehead before leaving the room. That night, I could not sleep as I tried to figure out the situation. In the end, I failed to come up with any answer. I did not know if Lili was truly ill, or the reason she was confined inside her room. But I learned one thing for sure: I could no longer trust my Papa.

Since that night, I have been outside her room five times. Each time, I gave the door three fast knocks, followed by two slow ones. That is our secret door-knock. We use the secret knock whenever we want to go downstairs to watch TV without waking Papa and Mama up. On each occasion, I waited and counted to ten. I knew she was inside as I could hear soft sobbing. But Lili never opened the door for me, not even once. There was not even a 'go-away' whisper that she used to give me when she did not want to go downstairs.

"Fine! I don't want to see your sick face anyway!" I whispered every time as I trudged away. I was lying. I missed her so much that I cried after I went back to my bed. Sometimes Lili was cruel towards me, like calling me Shorty, pulling my ears or hiding my *Spider-Man* comics. But I love her, and it made me so sad to think that she was sick, miserable and alone inside her room.

Mama, too, has been heartbroken since Lili became ill. She looks thinner because nowadays she seldom joins us for dinner. Mama spends most of her time inside her bedroom. Every evening Papa brings food home from the restaurant and sends it up to her. The last time I had dinner with Mama was about a month after Lili became ill.

During that dinner, Papa cooked us a huge bowl of Fatt Tiu Cheong. I tasted a spoonful of the warm broth and let out a gasp. While Papa's soup has always been excellent, this was by far the best I had ever tasted.

"It's very good, right?" Papa said with a smile on his face. He turned his head and looked at Mama. She seemed to enjoy the soup but did not say a word. She seldom talked much anymore. Whenever Papa said something to her, she would just stare at the floor, nodding or shaking her head. We sat there enjoying the soup in silence.

Papa stirred his bowl and scooped up a mushroom with his spoon. It was white with dark red dots, unlike any mushroom I had seen before. Papa said the mushroom was a new ingredient he added to the soup.

"My customers are coming back in droves because of these mushrooms. They say eating them is like biting into a slice of heaven."

Mama stared at the mushroom before she abruptly stood up. She pushed her chair back so hard it toppled to the floor. As she rushed into the kitchen, her eyes were bulging out of their sockets, and her face was pale like a ghost.

"Mama, mama! What's wrong?" I chased after her.

She was bending over the kitchen sink, retching. My heart sank; I was worried Mama had caught Lili's illness. I did not want Papa to disallow me from seeing Mama too. Papa stepped into the kitchen and told me to go finish my dinner. He had that look on his face, that angry look, so I dragged myself out. I heard Mama yelling about those mushrooms, but soon her voice was drowned out by Papa's scolding. I pressed my hands to my ears, not wanting to hear their horrible argument. A couple of minutes later, Mama stormed out from the kitchen and went upstairs. She looked a bit pale but seemed okay enough to walk upstairs by herself. I was just glad the argument was over.

Somehow, Papa is the only person in our house that does not seem sad since Lili fell ill. In fact, Papa seems to be in a better mood lately. Maybe it is because his restaurant business is getting better. Earlier this evening, he promised to bring Mama and me to visit Hong Kong soon. He said Mama was not very happy, so he wanted to cheer her up. The thought of a holiday brought me joy, but only for a second. I asked if Lili would be coming with us, but Papa said she could not.

"Maybe one day when she's out of the hospital," he said.

I felt angry and disappointed. I almost wanted to tell Papa I knew he was lying; that I knew Lili was inside her room and not in a hospital. Without saying a word, I turned around and ran up to my room. Papa kept calling after me, asking me what was wrong, but I refused to answer him.

It is two hours past midnight.

I want to go knocking on Lili's door again. *Maybe now she is feeling well enough to open the door for me*, I hope. As I quietly turn the knob on my room door, I hear footsteps outside. Cautiously, I open a small gap at the door and peep out.

I see Papa standing outside Lili's room. The door is ajar, and the escaping light allows me to see the kitchen knife in his right hand. There is a plastic container under his other arm.

After Papa steps into Lili's room, I sneak out from mine. I am excited to see Lili again, even just a glimpse, and remind myself not to make any noises. I know Papa does not want me to see her, even though I cannot understand the reason.

A few steps from the room, the sound of her sobbing reaches my ears. It is very soft, as if she has lost energy. My heart is pounding as I press my body against the wall next to the door. I crane my neck to peek into the room.

Lili is lying on the bed, looking very pale and thin like a skeleton. There are plastic tubes coming out from her nostrils and the hole in her throat. Her shoulders and neck are like a pin cushion with tens of needles sticking out from her flesh. Every time her chest heaves, soft wheezing and sobbing escape from her trembling lips. Her eyes are open, but they are so cloudy I cannot find the irises. The most horrifying parts are her naked chest and stomach: they are covered with some weird growths. The smaller ones are brown and short like Papa's cigarette stubs, while the bigger ones are the size of a twenty-sen coin, and white.

Papa, sitting next to her, is pinching a big one between his fingers. With a slice of the knife, he cuts it off from Lili's left rib. Thick dark fluid oozes out from the hole on her skin, and her body shudders. Papa puts it into the container at his side, before cutting another piece off Lili. This time, he lifts it in front of his face, giving me a clearer view of the growth. It is white with dark red dots, looking exactly like the new mushrooms Papa uses for his soup.

I scream.

Papa turns around with a startled expression on his face. "Wh…why…aren't you in bed?"

He puts the knife and container down before making his way towards me. I turn around and run to the staircase. Papa yells after me to stop. I continue running as I want to get out of the house, away from him. What has he done to Lili? How can he hurt her like that? My Papa is a monster!

As I descend the staircase in darkness, a tear begins to roll down my cheek. In my haste to get away, I miss a step and lose my balance. My body tumbles down the flight of stairs. As every part of my body knocks and bounces against the hard wood, I close my eyes and scream.

"Oh GOD!"

I hear Mama's voice as I lie at the bottom of the staircase. I try to turn my head towards her, to ask for help, but my head will not move. My voice has disappeared too. This is strange; I thought falling from so high up would hurt but I feel nothing, as if my head, body and limbs have disappeared.

I am dead! I think.

Well, this might be better than seeing Papa's face again.

Man in the Mirror

✕

Adrian Chase

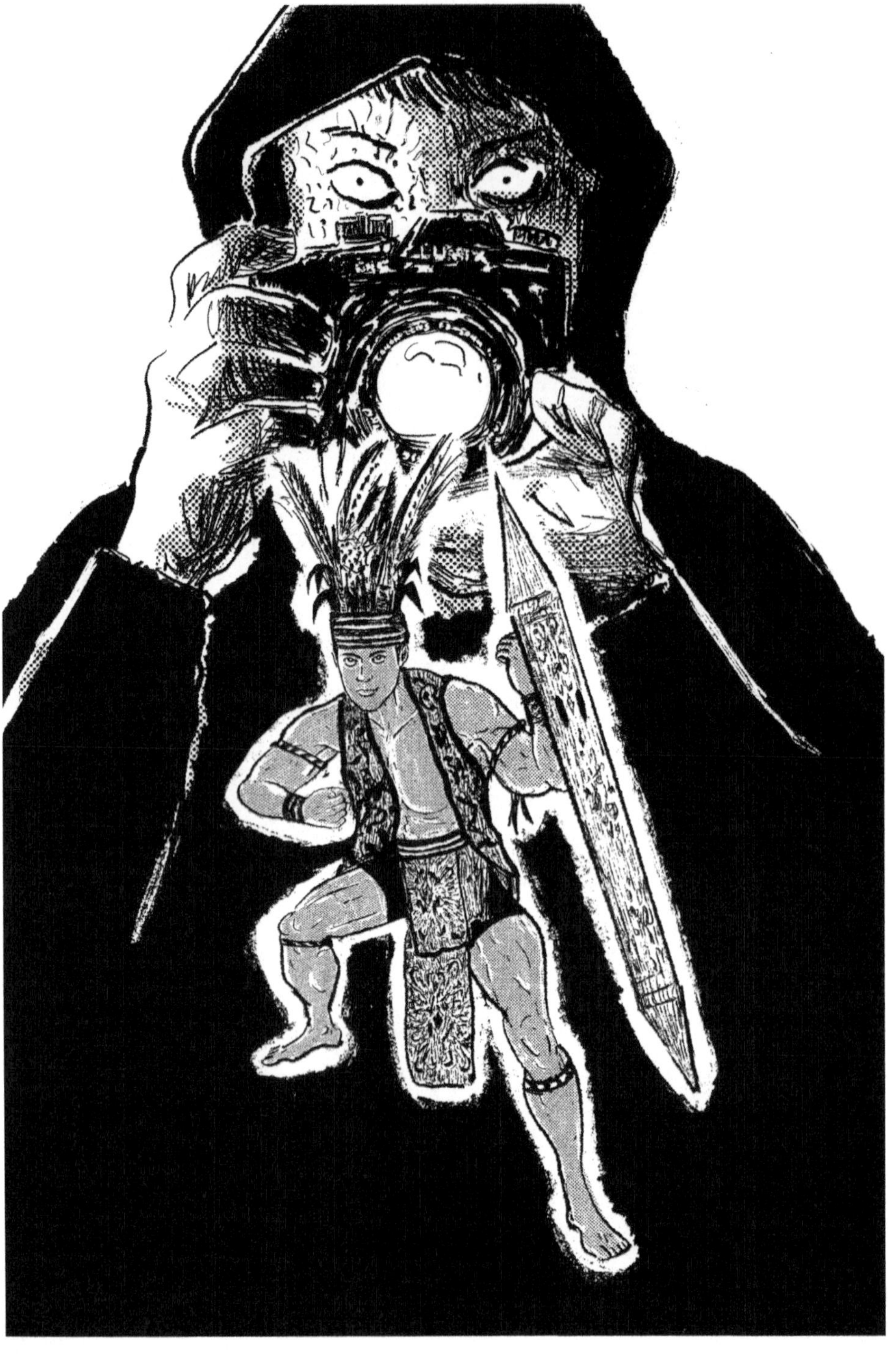
LUMIX

Tadau Kaamatan. The harvest festival sacred to the Kadazandusun of Sabah. Legend has it that Bambaazon, the spirit of the paddy, is ushered home by shamans during this festival, so that she may return to the field during the next planting season.

I guess I should give thanks to the bobohizans of my bloodline for the gift they have passed down to me, though I am quite sure Grandfather would squirm in his grave if he knew I would twist his legacy to harvest something else altogether.

I don't particularly like visiting the Kadazandusun Cultural Association center during this time. For one, I have to park my rickety Wira on the uneven field almost a kilometer away, and the burly man who guides me to my parking spot is barely helpful but charges me RM10 for the 'service'. I'm quite certain what he and his gang of other burly middle-aged men are doing is illegal. There must be over a hundred cars parked on this bald and dusty field alone.

I lug my gear as I make my way to the squat white-and-brown building surrounded by grassless fields in the scorching sun. I'm sweating under my hoodie, and people are looking at me funny, but I'm used to it. I ignore them, and they ignore me, eventually. In one vintage leather bag I have my standard camera getup: the body, two prime lenses and one telephoto lens, the flash, and spare batteries. I'll use the camera to capture the photos of the festival, and of the Unduk Ngadau beauty pageant. In the other bag is where I store my most precious possession: the camera I built myself. I guess the extended years of learning engineering as an undergraduate didn't go to waste. This one I'll save for the one shot that matters the most.

I jostle against the throng at the entrance. I hug both my bags close; people cannot be trusted. Thieves, all of them. I take a copy of the event pamphlet and check my wristwatch. The Unduk Ngadau main event won't start for another hour, so I have time to kill. I head for the open tents erected at the actual parking lot of the compound. Some of the people, especially those with children, are eating, but most come here to sample local brews.

"Aramaiti!" a group of eight men and women yell as they clink their green bottles together. Lihing, if I'm not mistaken. They are already red in the cheeks and a couple of them can't even hold their bottles right, and it's only a little after noon. I slink past them and weave my way through the crowd, my eyes roving for that perfect specimen. I take out my DSLR to snap photos of the scenes unfolding around me. Not for any publication or posterity purposes, but because people tend to focus on the camera and not notice my face when I point the lens at them. I also get the opportunity to spot beautiful people without arousing suspicion.

I follow the river of people into the main auditorium when the beauty pageant is about to start. Heavily made-up teenage girls in tribal garb enter the stage in a practiced line. I'm not even interested in pointing *my* camera at any girl, unless it's a commission.

I bump into a cameraman from *The Borneo Post*. It takes him a while to look away, enough time for me to witness his repulsion. This close, even the hoodie cannot hide the acid burn scars that cover the right half of my face and neck. I tug the hoodie to cover my face, out of habit.

One of these girls is bound to have an equally – if not more – beautiful brother or lover. As each contestant comes forward to showcase the garb that represents her tribe and to answer a short interview, I zoom my telephoto lens at the people who cheer the loudest. It's unfair how physical beauty runs in select families. Then again, I inherited my bobohizan gift from my Kadazan ancestors *and* a mystical tome that my mother's ancestors brought from mainland China, so I can't complain.

There are certainly good-looking supporters in the crowd, but none of them are worth an extended second look. I will not settle for any of them. Not when I have only one exposure.

✕

I walk out long before the judges announce the winner. I don't even care which locality wins. Seems that today is a bust, but I'm not willing to give up just yet. I head for the hall beside the main building. Inside, the ethnic groups of Sabah display their own legacies as if they were a circus act. Of the more than twenty different tribes, only twelve are represented in the air-conditioned hall. The Kadazandusun people are dressed in their modest black garb, but the yellow linings and multi-colored beads woven onto their clothes and headdresses lend them a festive air.

The Murut men wear vests and loincloths made from tree bark adorned with vine-and-leaf motifs. Their tall headdresses are made from the same tree bark, but adorned with the tail feathers of great argus pheasants. Their long wooden shields are painted black and red. They walk about and entertain guests with their warrior-like stances and bearing.

That's when I see him.

It's not surprising that among the Murut warriors, he gets the most requests for photo-taking. His face is distinctly Sabahan, with wide-set teardrop eyes, a flat nose and full lips, but with the strong eyebrows and deep dimples on both cheeks and the near-perfect symmetry of his teeth when he grins, he's breathtaking. He is tall, not just by Sabahan standards, and his skin is just the right shade of caramel. His vest is undone, and with good reason too. The sharp curves of his pecs and abdominal muscles refuse to be hidden by clothes. The ladies keep looking for excuses to touch his sculptured arms. I take out my DSLR and snap a candid shot of him grinning while his picture is being taken with a gaggle of giggling aunties. His beauty translates into the photograph well.

He's perfect.

I wait in line to approach him. It takes a while; the aunties refuse to let him go. When I finally get to him, his grin no longer quite reaches his eyes. I don't pull down my hoodie; I don't want to scare anyone away. Especially not him. I offer my hand and he shakes it without hesitation. He has a strong grip.

"Long day, isn't it?"

He scratches his head and readjusts his headdress. He's about my height. Absolute perfection. "Iya bah. But can't complain. It's a paying gig," he says. He sounds like a boy whose voice is changing, and has a flu. Well, not quite absolute perfection, but his voice will hardly matter, anyway.

"You get paid a lot?"

He shrugs. His vest rustles. "Not really. Enough to pay for the bottles of Montoku later."

"You want to get paid more?"

If he's surprised by my question, he doesn't reveal much. I only catch a slight widening of his eyes and the upward twitch of his lips. I take out a business card from my back pocket. The name is not mine, of course.

He studies the front and back of the card, and then returns it to me. "Sorry. No pockets."

"You've done modeling before?"

He nods. "Here and there. Nothing big."

"Want to make a quick 300 ringgit?"

He narrows his eyes and edges a little farther away.

"Just a few shots in your gear," I say. "But not here. Too crowded."

The shadow on his face passes. He nods with enthusiasm, his face bright again. "Boleh bah. I'll be off in a bit. Meet me at the back of the hall in half an hour. My name's Felix Gaising, in case you can't find me."

"I'm Luis Masidin." It's the name on the card. Not mine. But it'll do.

Sometimes I forget my own name.

I wait for him at a bench under the shade of a canopy, and I'm on my third cigarette when Felix approaches me. He holds his headdress and shield in his arms. I hold out my opened box of cigarettes. There are eight sticks left.

He takes a cigarette and I light it for him. He sits down and places the gear between us. "Thanks. I don't normally get to smoke expensive brands."

I offer him the entire box. "Take it. Goes well with the Montoku you plan to get drunk on later."

Felix nods and smiles. "Thanks. Can I get it later after the photoshoot? No pocket."

I keep the box in my DSLR bag. "Sure thing. Are your clothes really made of wood?"

He nods again, this time grinning. "Iya. And they itch. But the elders will have my head if I lose or ruin anything. They've been in my tribe for generations."

"I didn't know Murut people were headhunters."

"Not anymore. But you haven't seen my elders when they're angry."

We both laugh. I wait for him to finish his cigarette. His scent is a mixture of sweat, wood and cigarette smoke. It's a pity I cannot capture his scent as well. Once he's done, he flicks the butt to the ground and extinguishes the smoke by stepping on it.

"Where do you want to take those pictures? At the Murut house?"

A large part of the cultural village is dedicated to traditional houses of the major ethnic groups of Sabah, which showcase the items and cultures of each group. The village is filled with craftsmen and tourists alike today, and I cannot have anyone accidentally entering the frame when I use my other camera. Besides, some of the older equipment and costumes on display have resident spirits, and I don't want any of *them* entering the frame, either.

I shake my head. "Too crowded. And I don't need an authentic background, so we're fine anywhere there aren't people."

Felix narrows his eyes again, just like before in the hall. "This is not the kind of photoshoot where I have to take off my clothes, is it?"

"Only if you want to," I reply with a straight face.

Felix laughs and shakes his head. "Just checking. Almost got tricked into it once, with this cilaka old uncle."

I stand up and pick up my bags. "Don't worry. Just a few shots in your gear and that's it. Shall we?"

Felix leads me to the far end of the compound where several people are lounging at wooden picnic tables. I pick a spot beside a gnarly old tree with twisted trunk and branches. Ants run in equally twisted lines on the ground between its roots. Felix puts on his headdress and straightens his clothes while I fix the 50mm prime lens on my DSLR.

We go through standard warrior poses. Despite his complaints, Felix looks at ease in his ancestral gear. I bet I can even sell some of the photos I take to travel magazines and stock photography websites. Unlike most people who have modeled for me, he takes only a few initial shots to warm up, and he doesn't seem to be distracted by my disfigured face.

"Have you thought about modeling for real?" I ask between shots. "You're a natural."

His grin etches the dimples on his cheeks. "Thanks. My parents say they don't know what to do with me. I'm not smart enough to go to college like my sister, but they don't want me to work the fields like them."

I don't need to know about his future plans or his family. The knowledge doesn't impact my decision in any way, but…no, I don't need to know about his life. "Okay. One last shot using my other camera. You can smoke while I set it up, if you want to."

Felix borrows my lighter and sits on a root as I squat on the ground and take out my flat plate camera from the other bag. I loosen the side screws, lay open the wooden frame, pull out the accordion bellows and then fix it on the base before securing the smaller plate with the lens in the middle. Then, as gently as possible, I take out the wooden back with the film plate inside, and then slide it at the rear of the camera. I then put on the canvas cover over the back.

"Is that some old camera or something?" Felix asks, his eyes glued to what I've just assembled.

I nod. "Made it myself."

Anyone with half an interest in vintage cameras can make one, but what I have that no one else has is the back frame, and the film that I can produce only once a month. The inside of the frame is lined with ancient Daoist containment spells, while the film was spelled under a full moon using the darkest and most secret of bobohizan magic.

I screw the camera on a tripod, and then look through the viewfinder under the canvas cover. The camera is ready. I poke my head out and give Felix the thumbs-up. "Okay. No need to pose or anything. You don't even need to wear that headdress. Just stand in front of the camera and look straight at the lens."

Felix positions himself within the direct path of the lens as I peer into the viewfinder. Once his entire head and the top half of his torso are well within the spell circles of the viewfinder, I give him another thumbs-up.

"Just look straight into the lens, okay?"

"Bah," Felix says, nodding. He looks at the camera, his gaze sharp, the lines of his jaw intense. A perfect headshot.

I press the trigger.

The outer circle of meticulously engraved spells flares green. I usually release the trigger at this point for commissions. But this is not one. My thumb doesn't budge. The second circle lights up. And then the third, followed by the fourth.

When the fifth and innermost circle lights up, the entire formation flares a bright green, burning my eyesight for a few moments. The spell is completed.

Felix wobbles and stumbles sideways to lean against the tree.

"You okay?"

Felix nods. He sits on a root and cups his forehead against his palms. "A little light-headed. Maybe I should have eaten before coming here."

I slide out the back frame with reverence, and store it in the bag. I then dismantle the camera as Felix catches his breath. I take out three crisp 100 ringgit notes from my wallet and walk towards him. He reaches for the money, his hands shaking.

I take out a 50 ringgit note. "Here. Get a good meal and even better booze. Montoku isn't good for your liver."

Felix grins and takes the money. "Bah. Terima kasih."

When I leave him, he's still leaning against the tree bark, his headdress on the ground.

✕

It's almost midnight when I reach home. The apartment building is old and derelict, and the walls are so thin I can hear my neighbors humping and fighting. However, it's obvious that my door is the only one with a state-of-the-art electronic locking system. But this being Malaysia, state-of-the-art just meant a digital pad. None of the thumbprint or retinal scan door locks like they have in Japan. Inside, my home is dark and almost bare. A stale stench wafts from the kitchen; I left unfinished dinner in the sink two days ago, and the dirty plates are starting to reek. I switch on the TV in the living area, partly to wait for the news, which should start in a few minutes, and partly to serve as background noise. Not in a rush, I clean the dishes before they get too nasty to salvage.

While cleaning the kitchen, the newscaster mentions the Kaamatan event earlier today. I perk my ears.

"A 23-year-old man identified as Felix Gaising was found slumped against a tree, dead, at the KDCA Cultural Village in Kota Kinabalu earlier today. While witnesses said he was in perfect health, the police, in their initial assessment, have ruled out foul play. The body has been sent to the forensic department, Queen Elizabeth II Hospital."

Good. No mention of him being with a hooded man. No mention of me.

I head for my room and open the hidden door built into the back of the wardrobe. When I bought this place, I walled off the adjoining room and built a secret entrance. I keep all my mirrors and arcane gear in this smaller space. Most of the identical full-length mirrors I commissioned are covered with white sheets. If I concentrate, I can catch hints of movements mimicking mine.

I hoist one of the unused mirrors and prop it up in the middle of the room, and then set up my homemade camera in front of it. I attach the cable switch before moving away and switching off the lights. Darkness envelops me like a cool blanket. Confident from years of practice that the setup is perfect, I press the switch. The camera flares green, filling the room with an unearthly glow and long shadows. Once the room becomes completely dark again, I switch on the light and rush to the mirror.

Instead of the reflection of an ugly man with acid burn scars, the person staring back at me is a youthful, handsome Murut man. Praise the ancestors. The soul transfer is a success. I unscrew the camera from the tripod and place it on the desk where I keep the ancient Daoist tome, camera spare parts, and unenchanted films.

I stand in front of the mirror, excitement causing my pants to tighten. I've not found a more beautiful specimen in a long time. The young man in the mirror follows my every movement, and I take my time to remove my clothes as I enjoy the view. My naked reflection is glorious. My fingers roam across the expanse of my body. I can almost forget the scars and stretch marks and flabby skin as I watch the Murut warrior trace his muscular form. I gasp slightly when I touch myself.

A padded thud lands behind me, breaking my concentration. I whip around to find the stupid cat perched on a stack of covered mirrors. It keeps making its way into this room using the small gap in the ceiling. I've been meaning to repair the ceiling, but I keep getting distracted whenever I'm in here. I hiss and shoo it, and the stupid beast gives me a dirty look, licks its front paw, and jumps back into the hole. Before I can react, the frontmost mirror falls forward and lands with a sharp shatter.

No! It's one of my commissions. I'd only captured a small portion of the celebrity's soul, so he's still alive and acting, but the buyer has promised RM8,000 for this. Stupid fucking cat. I kneel down to collect the sharp pieces, expecting to find fragments of the celebrity reflecting me, but the shattered mirror has gone dark. Not even my own reflection is present.

Weird.

When I get up to fetch a broom, I notice a difference in the naked figure in the mirror. I stand in front of it, mesmerized. The face staring back at me is that of the Murut warrior, but not quite. I catch hints of the celebrity mixed in, making the face a shade lighter and even more stunning. Even the nose is slightly sharper.

My mind races at the possibility. *This is it. This is what I've been missing.* Excitement making my movements lighter, I undrape the mirrors and select the best reflections in my collection. It takes me over an hour to finally select eight mirrors. I place them in front of my newest acquisition and smash them on the floor one by one, never mind the splinters flying everywhere and piercing my skin. One by one the smashed mirrors go dark. With each broken piece, my excitement grows until my stiffness is more painful than the bleeding wounds. Not bothering to get a broom, I roll one of the sheets and push away the broken mirrors so I can position myself in front of the one left standing.

My reflection is absolute perfection.

The figure is an amalgamation of all the beautiful men whose souls I'd captured over the past five years, all of them dead, all of them mine forever. Deep-set hazel eyes with long lashes and strong brows, a sharp nose, a sharp jaw that I can't stop admiring, and a muscular physique that I can't stop touching. The dick that stands erect is glorious.

A reflection is no longer enough. I want to *be* that man in the mirror.

With trembling hands and a frenzied fervor, I take out the one spelled film I kept for emergency purposes, and then set up the camera and cast the spell on it. Luck has it that tonight is a full moon. After setting up the camera on a tripod, I grab hold of the cable switch. I've never been more sure in my life. I press it long and hard.

I feel a sudden lightheadedness overcome me. It's like I'm drained, fatigued after hours of running. So this is how it feels. I don't have much time left. I place the camera in front of the mirror and press the switch.

Too late, I hear the thud again.

✕

When I come to, I'm surrounded by a weird misty darkness. I can feel my presence, but I'm somehow incorporeal. I stretch my hands in front of me, but I don't see anything.

After wandering for what feels like hours, I make out a vertical rectangular light. I move toward it, which feels extremely weird because I can't see my feet but I can tell they are *moving*. Through what seems like a clear window in this dark formless world, I see my secret room. The camera is on the tripod, its lens staring at me. Sprawled on the floor is the naked form of an ugly, plump man with scars all over his face and upper torso. I can tell that he's dead, from his still chest. *My* still chest. Beside the corpse is another, smaller form. The cat.

No. No. No. What have I done?

The shock and horror hit me like a wrecking ball. Do I have striped fur? Is my figure part cat? Have I become more of an abomination than what I was?

As I watch the two dead figures in disbelief, I see more cats jumping through the hole in the ceiling. How is it possible to have this many cats coming into my room? They land on my corpse and sniff it. Some of them lick the dead cat, reverence clear in their bowed heads.

And then they start biting my body. I watch in rapt fascination. The scene reminds me of lions ravaging a wildebeest in a documentary I once watched. They tear at the skin and rend flesh, biting, gnawing, chewing. I feel pain at the areas where the cats gnaw. Instead of fangs, hands with sharp nails pull at me from all directions, tearing me apart.

Have I angered the gods and ancestors?

I somehow see an angry face staring at me. The Murut warrior. He pulls my arm and rips it apart, even though I still cannot see myself. Others do the same.

I can only watch as the cats eat my corpse, and I can only feel myself being torn apart.

Slave of Mine

✕

Joshua Lim

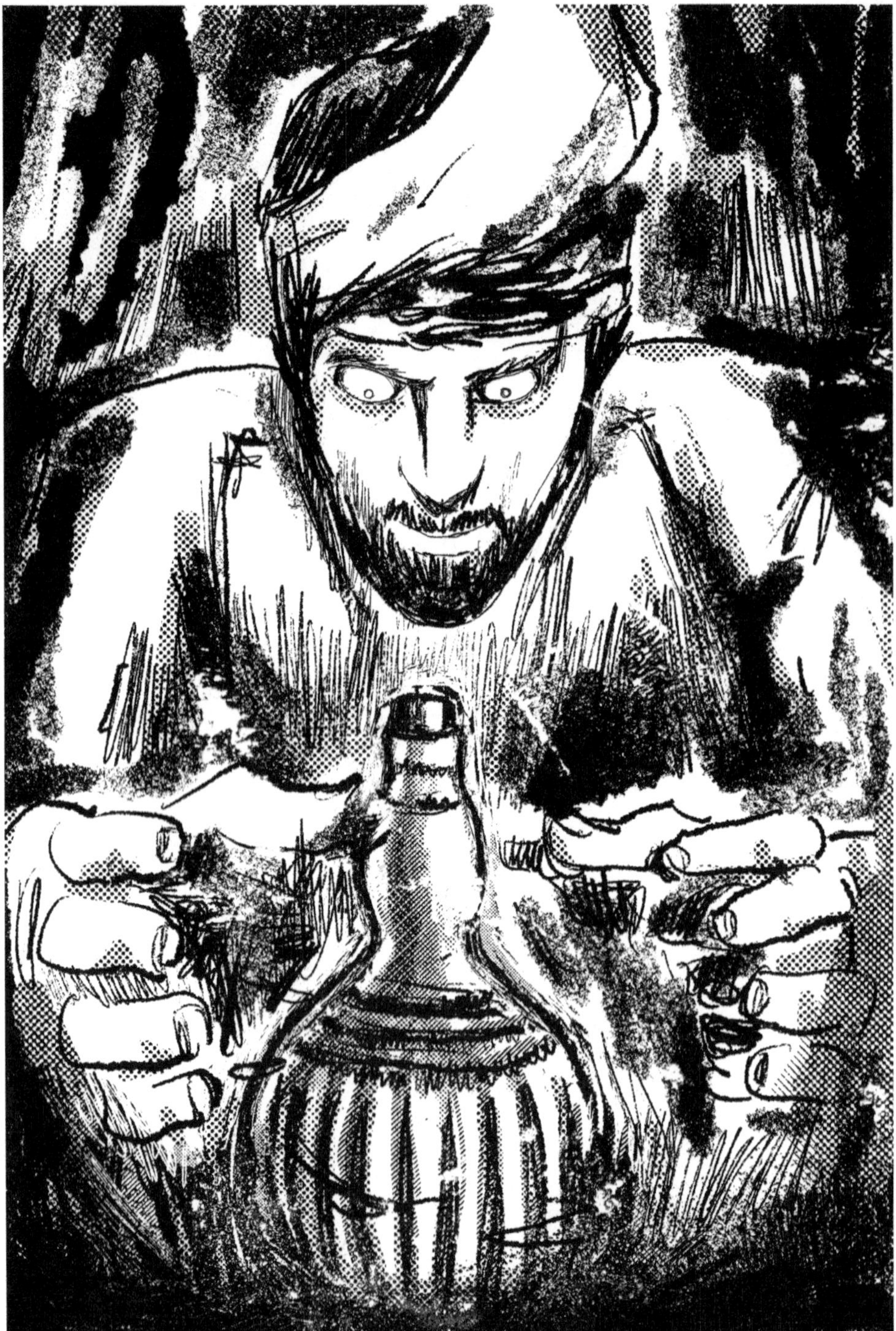

At midnight on the day J.W.W. Birch was killed, Dato' Azman buried an earthenware jar under the mango tree in the jungle behind his house. It was a small jar, barely more than a foot tall, narrow-necked and sealed with a cork. Azman dug the hole himself instead of ordering his slaves to do it, and after he had removed all trace of his activity, he smiled.

"Enjoy, Mr. Birch," he said to the ground.

It was the 3rd of November, 1875.

✕

Birch's murder would eventually bring all of Perak under the control of the British, but Dato' Azman did not know that yet, nor did any of the slave traders and nobles that had conspired to get rid of the loathed Resident. Birch was hugely unpopular with the locals, and he had sealed his fate when he visited the Sultan's palace a few months before.

Azman had stood among the crowd of curious Malays on the riverbank to witness the arrival of the white men, and he had clearly seen Birch stride up to the Sultan's palace and enter without taking off his shoes.

There's going to be trouble, Azman thought, feeling the angry murmurs that rumbled through the crowd. *This can't get any worse.*

He was wrong.

"I have made it clear that slavery is to be abolished immediately!" cried Birch, his voice ringing through the royal hall. "Such a despicable practice should not be allowed to persist!"

Aside from the Sultan and the white men, only the Malay chiefs and nobles were in the hall, including those such as Dato' Azman that had come from neighboring villages. A few chiefs were grunting in disapproval, some narrowed their eyes and one openly shook his head.

This white man will ruin me. Dato' Azman was a rich man, a minor chief among his people in Kampong Gajah, and the slave trade was his livelihood. In fact, he had come to sell some slaves to other nobles on that day. *It is our custom, our right, and Birch is here to destroy it all!*

The Sultan replied, and his words were translated to Birch, explaining how debt-slavery worked in Perak.

Birch's mustache bristled. "I've seen how you people treat the Sakai," he said. "These poor people are treated worse than any of the other slaves. Debt-slave or not, I shall ensure there will be no more slaves in this land!"

Later, as they were leaving the palace, Dato' Azman stole a look at the Englishman's boathouse. There were servants on board, both dark-skinned and light, serving Birch hand and foot.

The chiefs met again when the Sultan summoned them to discuss Birch's impudence. Among them were Dato' Maharaja Lela of Pasir Salak, and Dato' Sagor of Kampong Gajah. The chiefs spoke out strongly against Birch, but none more strongly than Maharaja Lela.

"I will not allow Mr. Birch to set foot in my village," said Maharaja Lela firmly. He and Dato' Azman were key players in the slave trade, and so their hatred for the Englishman ran deeper. "He interferes in our affairs, and he has also been overheard saying that our customs are not worthy of his consideration. I say, this man deserves to die!"

The nobles applauded and roared their approval, and that day, with the full support of the Sultan, the chiefs planned the murder of J.W.W. Birch.

Azman, however, was in a strangely contemplative mood.

"Whatever Maharaja Lela does, I will do," said Dato' Sagor, and he motioned for Azman to do the same. Their village was on the riverbank opposite Pasir Salak, and they would be expected to assist in the murder. Azman pledged his help, but Maharaja Lela's words had stirred up something in his heart.

He deserves to die…?

Uncommon for a noble of his age, Dato' Azman was unmarried and lived alone in a large house. His slaves stayed in a little hut close to the jungle. He was still mulling over Maharaja Lela's words when he reached home that night and sat on his doorstep, staring out to the river. From his position, he could see Maharaja Lela's fortified house in Pasir Salak across the river. One of Azman's indigenous slaves, a young man, came down to draw water from the river.

'No more slaves,' Birch had said, as his own slaves waited in the boathouse.

Azman's eyes grew wide. "That's what he deserves," he muttered to himself.

So he went to visit the pawang.

There was no wilder-looking man than Siputum, the pawang. His hair stuck out and his lips were curled in a perpetual grimace. He protested against Azman's idea from the start.

"It is dark magic, Dato' Azman," Siputum croaked. "Even we pawangs do not play with the spirit realm if we can help it. When we do, we do so with utmost caution. There are rules we do not understand, Dato' Azman, we cannot do it on a whim!"

"It is not a whim," said Azman. "I have given it enough thought."

"Killing Birch is enough, Dato' Azman! Mr. Birch is going to come down the river someday, and Maharaja Lela will greet him with a keris. Once he is dead, the problem is solved. I advise you to follow the plan and do no more!"

Then Dato' Azman came close, and Siputum trembled at the cold fire in his eyes.

"Then you shall tell me everything I need to know, Siputum, so that justice shall fall on Mr. Birch as he deserves. He shall not escape."

"Justice cannot be done in this way," whimpered Siputum.

But the fateful day had since come and gone.

Dato' Azman had walked slowly and stately through the roaring crowd that massed on the beach of Pasir Salak, passing through the forest of spears and kerises in the hands of furious men. Birch's guards had escaped to the boats or were still fighting the Malays, so the bathing house was empty when Azman entered.

The bathing house was a simple log house floating beside the riverbank, with one cloth wall that served as a door. Azman lifted the flap and stepped inside, feeling the cold water rise up to his thighs. The walls inside were splattered with blood, and the river was swirling crimson. There was no sign of Birch.

Azman plunged his hand into the water and groped about. His hands touched something soft and he pulled.

Birch broke through the surface, spitting and coughing, blood pouring from the spear wounds in his pale body and the horrific slash across his skull. Azman let go of Birch's hair in disgust and reached for his parang.

Birch fell to his knees, his head and shoulders left above water.

"N–"

"Die!" Azman swung the parang.

J.W.W. Birch's head fell from his shoulders, and the Resident's body toppled backwards with a splash. Azman caught the decapitated head before it sank into the river. There was blood gushing from the neck, and he knew he had no time to lose. He put away the parang, brought out the small jar he had prepared, and carefully dripped the blood from Birch's head into the narrow opening.

He could hear Maharaja Lela's voice outside.

Azman kept his eyes on the dripping blood. A few drops missed and spattered onto his hand. He glanced up at the head–

–Birch was looking *straight* at him.

Azman's throat closed. He dropped the head and backed away.

Birch's head fell with a plop – and floated upright on the surface of the water. The bloodshot eyes were glowing with an unearthly light, and they did not break eye contact with Azman, staring into his soul, rooting him to the spot in sheer terror. Birch's mouth slowly opened.

"No more slaves."

Azman heard the words clearly, as if spoken from the white man's living lips. Everything faded – Maharaja Lela's voice, the red river, the bathing house – and the world was just Birch, the horrifying, speaking head that froze Azman to the bone.

"No more slaves," hissed Birch's head, baring its red-stained teeth.

Terror turned into fury. Azman groped for his parang.

"No – more – slaves–"

Azman grabbed the parang and hacked and hacked and hacked at the head, churning up the water. It sank instantly and did not reappear.

Azman waited, still clutching the parang with his trembling fingers. Outside, he could hear Maharaja Lela's voice again, calling for someone to send a message to the Sultan. Azman calmed himself down, washed the blood off his hands, then exited the bathing house and headed straight home. No one noticed him.

✕

Siputum caught him that night, as he was returning from burying the jar in the jungle. The pawang was waiting in front of his house.

"Dato' Azman, it is a bad idea."

Azman stopped a few meters away and leaned on his shovel. Digging was strenuous work, he realized. "I heard you were the one who cut Birch across the head, Siputum."

"Yes, and that should have been the end of it," said Siputum. "Dato' Azman, it was a mistake to tell you about that kind of magic. Please don't go any further."

"Siputum, please do not interfere with my affairs."

"A slave ghost is too much!" cried Siputum.

They realized the wind had died. The clouds loomed in the sky, shutting out the moon, and the trees and houses were shrouded in darkness.

Siputum lowered his voice. "The hantu polong is the ultimate slave," he said shakily. "A spirit bound in servitude."

"A slave from beyond the grave," said Azman. He couldn't see Siputum clearly through the gloom. "What better punishment for the white man who wanted to abolish slavery?"

"You shouldn't mess with what you don't know!"

"But I know, because you told me all about it, didn't you?" snapped Azman. "The polong is created when the blood of a murdered man is kept in a jar for two weeks. Every day, I must chant the incantations over it– incantations you have generously provided. On the fifteenth day, the polong will emerge from the jar in the form of a thumb-sized ghost and will obey all my orders. It will call me Bapak." A thought struck him. "Is there something you haven't told me?"

"The pelesit," said Siputum.

A breeze began to blow. The clouds moved, and slashes of moonlight lit up the land for a second. One shaft passed over Siputum, and Azman saw his face: pale, haggard, wilder than before, his eyes lined with terror. Then the light passed, and everything was dark again.

"The what?"

"The pelesit – the pet spirit of the polong," said Siputum. "When a polong is born, it will want to find a plaything of its own. It will search for someone to become the pelesit. Do you want to have the death of an innocent man on your hands?"

Azman frowned. "Tell me how a pelesit is created."

Siputum hesitated. "Some say it is made from a baby's tongue, others say that any dead tongue will do. Once a tongue is cut off, it will become a pelesit and be the pet of the polong."

The wind was getting stronger. It was freezing, Dato' Azman realized, as cold as the river had been that morning. It whistled through leaves of the trees, weaving its multiple notes into a single keening wail, an eerie song of the night. It was singing like the wails of the dead.

"I'll find a way," said Azman. "Good night, Siputum."

Before he entered his house, Dato' Azman turned back to look. The moon came out fully, illuminating the silhouette of Siputum as he shuffled back to his own house, his shadow stretching long and dark behind him towards the forbidding fringe of the jungle.

The next night, Dato' Azman began the ritual.

✕

The British soldiers did not arrive in force for another week or so, but in the meantime, many who had participated in the murder took fright and fled. Among the earliest to flee was the pawang Siputum.

Azman caught him just as he was ready to escape into the jungle. "Tell me, what does a pelesit look like?" said Azman, catching hold of Siputum's sleeve.

"I don't know and I don't care!" cried Siputum. "None of you are scared at all, are you? They are coming for us. Killing Birch will not end well for any of us – the Sultan, Maharaja Lela, Dato' Sagor or myself, mark my words!"

"You're delusional," said Azman. "You don't know what a pelesit looks like?"

"I only know that we have spilled blood." Siputum's eyes were wild with fear, like a hunted beast. "The blood remembers. You wash it off, but it stays on you. We will get what we deserve!"

Azman could get no more out of Siputum, who fled and would be captured by the British in early 1876. Dato' Sagor, Maharaja Lela and others involved would be arrested, tried and executed in the following year, but that was still a long way off and most of the chiefs still bore no fears. So Azman returned to his house, where he was waited on by his slaves, and he continued his nightly ritual.

He was seen on the fourteenth night.

As usual, at midnight, Azman made his way to the trees where his jar was buried. The daily digging and refilling had strained his untrained muscles, so he had resorted to covering the hole with banana leaves. He removed the leaves, drew out the jar and laid it on a patch of sandy ground. It seemed to be getting heavier every night.

He knelt before the jar and uncorked it.

A putrid stench wafted out. It had been faint the first few days, but had become stronger since, filling his nostrils with the air of death every night. *But it is the last night*, Azman told himself, *tomorrow the hantu polong will be mine.*

He sat straight and opened the small parchment Siputum had given him.

"Dengarlah," he said.

He began the incantation.

As he read, there was a faint bubbling from inside the jar. A thin trail of smoke rose out of the mouth, curling and spiraling like it did every night. It blossomed slowly, coiling around the jar like a ghostly dragon in a graceful dance between life and death. In the dim moonlight, it was the color of dead leaves and rotten trees and insect spawn. With each word he read, the smoke grew thicker, and the odor grew stronger.

Azman reached the end.

The bubbling ceased. The smoke faded away, and the foul stench disappeared. A few meters away stood his young indigenous slave, staring at him with wide eyes.

Azman was frozen for a long while. Then he rose, face reddening, and lunged at the slave. "You! What are you doing here?"

The young man dropped to his knees, stuttering. "Pardon, Master – you left the door open –"

"How long were you standing there?"

"You are crossing a line, Dato' Azman."

Azman recoiled. The slave wore the hairy face of Siputum.

"You do not know the rules," croaked Siputum. "It is the last night. It is not too late."

"Siputum, don't – mess with my business," choked Azman. *It isn't real, is it? Siputum is in the jungle far away.* "That's how Birch got into trouble, meddling in others' business!"

"He told you no more slaves," said Siputum, grinning with yellow teeth. "He told you no more slaves –"

"I'll show him slavery!" snarled Azman.

He blinked. The slave was huddling before him, trembling. Azman grabbed the slave's face and stared. There were no beard and yellow teeth, only the Orang Asli's own terrified features.

"How much did you see?"

"Nothing," whimpered the slave.

Azman gritted his teeth and thought quickly. He ordered his slave to sleep across the front door of his house that night, forbidden to speak to anyone for the next day. It was much later, lying in his bed and staring at the ceiling, when Dato' Azman drifted off into a restless sleep.

He dreamt.

He was back in Pasir Salak, and the river was red. A ghostly crowd was on the beach, bearing spears and swords that blazed with white fire. The familiar faces were all there – Siputum, Maharaja Lela – but they were wraiths walking among shifting clouds of mist. One person came towards him.

'Azman,' called Dato' Sagor. His voice echoed as if in a long tunnel. 'You will not escape. The blood remembers.'

Dato' Sagor was growing larger and larger, blotting out the light, a gargantuan shadow looming over him. 'You will not escape,' boomed the voice, now deep and growling, 'not escape…'

Thunder and lightning.

He was in the jungle, under the mango tree. The hole lay empty. Where was the jar?

Thunder again.

He was beside the river now. The jar was balancing precariously on some rocks in front of him, leaning dangerously, and he realized that a single touch would send it toppling into the rushing waters below.

'The last night,' Siputum's voice rang in his ears. 'Not too late.'

He felt blood rushing into his ears – too real, unlike a dream – his heart thumping in his chest, faster and faster. Suddenly he was walking forward, reaching out towards the jar. For a second he saw two visions overlapping one another: one of him grabbing the jar and pulling it to safety, and another of him shoving the jar into the dark river.

'Not too late…'

Lightning.

Azman sat up in bed.

The house was quiet. The mountains in the distance were dark hulks rimmed with silver. Not too late.

Azman realized he was covered in sweat. From the front door came the light snoring of the slave.

"The pelesit," muttered Azman.

✕

Dato' Sagor was in his house when Azman came to see him.

"Was Siputum in the village yesterday?" asked Azman.

"He hasn't been seen since he left. I don't think he'll be back soon. The white men are bringing soldiers upstream into the jungle now."

Azman nodded half-distractedly, but Dato' Sagor posed a question to him. "Do you think they will spare Siputum if they catch him?"

Azman thought about it. "No. If someone had killed a Malay chief, we wouldn't let him go either."

"The white men will come after us," sighed Dato' Sagor. "You might be safe, though – thanks to your own cowardice."

"What?"

"You said you would come to help in the murder, but no one saw you there. Where were you?"

Azman was about to reply but he stopped himself. "My apologies – thank you," was all he said, and quickly left.

The young slave was still sitting in his house when he returned, keeping silent as ordered. Azman took a length of rope, some cloth and a knife. "Come here," he said to the slave, who did as he was told.

✕

Night fell. The moon ducked behind thick stormy clouds and sealed the world in darkness. Nothing stirred in Kampong Gajah, except the two men at the edge of the jungle under a mango tree.

Azman made the slave kneel. The young man was bound and gagged. Dato' Azman uncovered the hole and took out the jar. It was definitely much heavier than it had been two weeks ago.

Azman laid the jar on the sandy ground and stared at it.

Dare he open it?

Memories resurfaced – *of J. W. W. Birch walking into the palace wearing shoes.*

'You will not escape,' echoed Dato' Sagor's voice.

Birch, pierced by spears through the cloth wall of his bathing house.

Curling, twisting smoke, the perfume of rot.

'Do you want a death on your hands?'

The slave whimpered through his gag.

Azman realized that the jar had started to shake. It was wobbling by itself, leaning to the left, to the right – and a crack appeared in the neck.

Azman drew in a breath.

The jar exploded.

Smoke billowed out and blinded him, thick and foul and smelling of old blood. Azman backed away, waving his hands in front of his face, gagging and coughing. The air slowly cleared enough to see the polong.

It stood amidst the shards of clay – a thumb-sized figure.

"Polong," blurted Azman.

The polong turned towards him. It had a face.

"Polong, I am your Bapak," said Azman. His voice trembled on the last word. *Remember, you are the master here.* "Here is the man for your pelesit." He unsheathed a sharp knife and pointed to the bound slave.

The polong moved closer. It was walking unsteadily on two legs. The darkness made it hard to see, but it seemed vaguely humanoid.

"Come," said Azman with an encouraging smile.

"No more slaves," said the polong.

Azman's blood ran cold.

The polong took one tiny step at a time, tottering like a toddler. It smelled terribly like the smoke.

"No more slaves."

Lightning flashed.

Azman screamed.

The polong wore the likeness of J.W.W. Birch. Whitish hair, black spiky mustache, wrinkled white face – but it had no eyes, only gaping holes that yawned like open mouths, and its wide grin was lined with bleeding gums. The body was a clotted red mass of gore.

"No – more – slaves!"

"You – you want your pelesit, right?" Azman stammered, the knife almost falling from his shaking hands. "That's what you want? Here it is!" He grabbed the slave by the hair and slit his throat. The young man cried out, a muted gurgle, but he quickly fell silent.

The polong kept advancing.

"You want the tongue, right?" Azman yanked open the slave's mouth and tried to grab the tongue, inserting his knife between the dead jaws. "I'll cut it for you, yes?"

The polong took a step closer.

"Answer me! You belong to me!"

There was a familiar laugh from below. Dato' Azman looked down, and all the blood drained from his face as he beheld the grinning face of Siputum in his hands in place of the slave's.

"You did not know the rules," snickered Siputum, showing yellow teeth stained with red. "The blood of a *murdered man* – not the blood of *a man that you murdered*. The polong always goes after its killer first."

All the strength left Azman's limbs. He dropped the knife, let the slave's body fall to the ground, and turned to run. His first step got tangled in the legs of the slave and he fell hard, knocking the breath out of him. Pain shot up from his twisted right ankle.

"I told you, you will never escape," giggled Siputum. "It is now too late."

A tiny cold hand touched Azman's foot.

Azman screamed and kicked. The polong's head flew off and landed upright in the sand. The head of J.W.W. Birch stared at him from empty eyeholes and opened its mouth again.

"NO MORE SLAVES!"

Lying on his back, trying to catch his breath, Azman became aware of two cold feet tip-tapping up his legs, balancing like on a log in a river, making their way up his body. The polong reached Azman's left hand and gave it an icy touch.

"The blood remembers!" chortled Siputum.

The headless polong stood on Azman's chest, stretched out its little arms and pried open his jaws with unearthly strength, reaching for the tongue that lay within. Azman tried to resist, but it was futile. His own words rang loud in his ears as lightning flashed and rain began to pour around them.

I'll show him slavery.

Siputum was laughing, but Birch's shriek was louder than the thunder. "No more SLAVES – only PETS!"

Dream Home

✕

Yanna Hashri

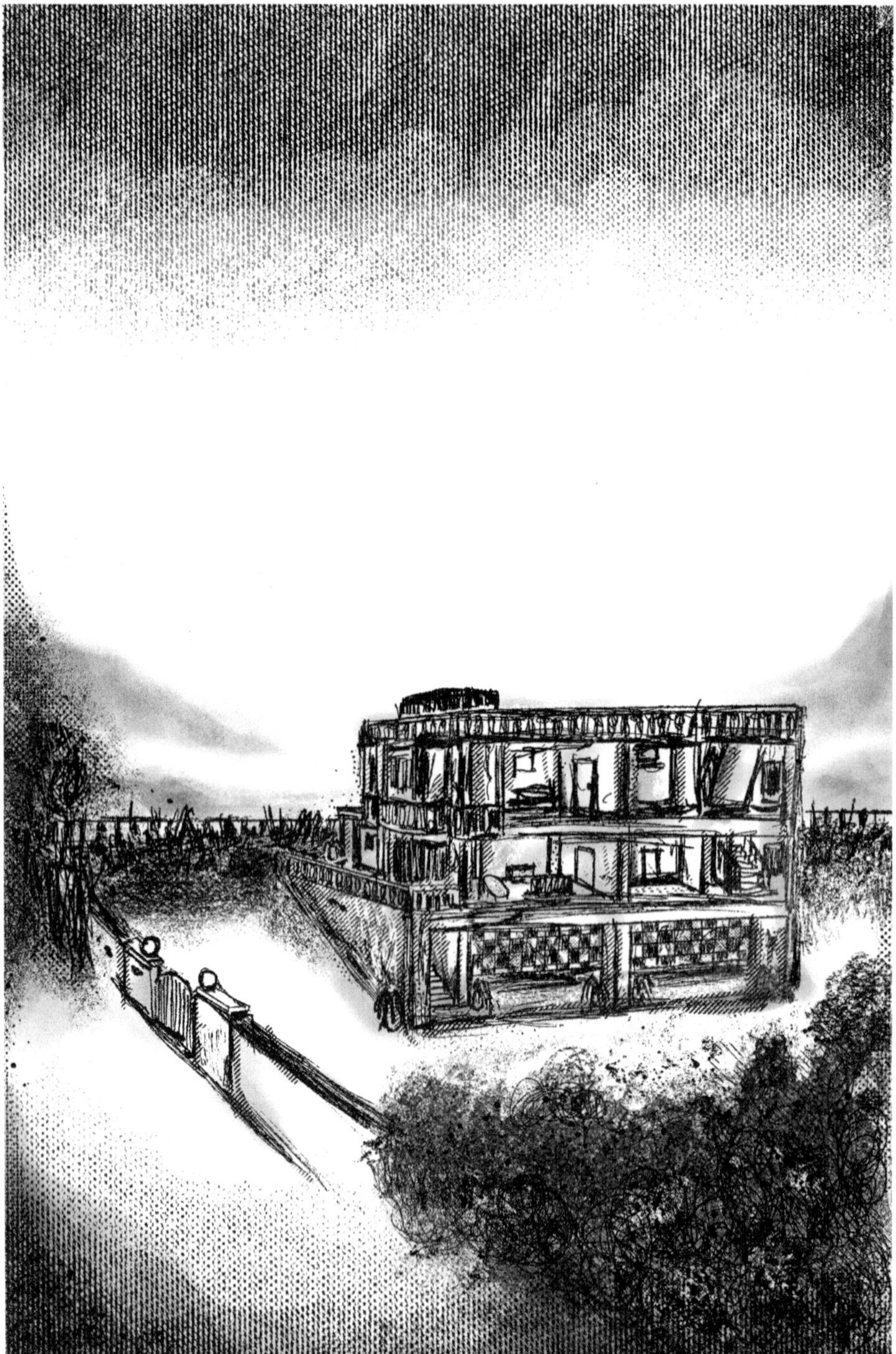

THE first group of prospective buyers smells like artificial sunshine, like someone had created a perfectly smooth and round orange but forgotten to add its texture and smell. You watch as the trio flounces up the road where their car is parked, stopping to inspect the rusted sign that separates the end of the road from the start of the hill slope where you stand waiting.

"Kampung Mambang Bertatap," the shortest of them, a young man wearing a green beret, impossibly thick glasses and skinny jeans, reads.

"Shit, that's some *Silent Hill*-type name," the other man laughs. He has a high-pitched, wheezing sort of laugh, the kind that goes on and on until it chokes off like a rabbit's dying squeal. "'Bertatap' means roof, right?"

"That's 'beratap' lah, bodoh," the only woman in the group sighs. She is already walking ahead of them, arms stretched out slightly on either side of her body as she navigates her way up the slope. Her wedges tap, tap, tap against the earth. Behind her gold-rimmed sunglasses, her eyes light up when she spots you. "Oh, hello there, hi! Are you the house guide? We spoke on the phone with your associate earlier?"

You nod once. Smile back. It's been a while since you had to smile.

"Thank you for meeting us on such short notice," she continues, the last few words coming out in pants as she finally reaches you. "When we heard about the property, we just knew we had to come and see it."

"Not a problem," you say. Each word comes out cautious and precise, like beads being placed on a string. You gesture at the looming structure behind you. "Shall we see the house?"

Beret Boy and Hyena Laugh appear at the top of the slope as you push open the black wrought-iron gates. It protests loudly, stiff and creaky from long disuse. "These are the original gates from when the house was built in 1963," you explain. "Imported from Italy."

The silence is loud as the group takes in the sight of the three-story brick house. Despite the evidence of time and neglect, it is a spacious structure, with floor-to-ceiling windows wrapped around all sides. A blue-

and-white wall of patterned tiles off the side of the driveway breaks up the monotony of the once-white facade, now mottled with brown creeping plants. Dead plants droop sadly inside blue and white porcelain vases of various sizes, as if the previous owners had left them in a hurry. Beyond the house, a garden stretches wild and abandoned.

"See, I told you this is a great set-up. So much space for such a great price!" the woman is telling her companions. "There's enough space in the driveway for a photo booth. And the garden can easily fit, what, 400 wedding guests, Faris?"

Beret Boy nods, crinkling his nose. "It's nice, but it's in the middle of nowhere. Sure people want to drive all the way out here ah?"

"If you can find rental this cheap in the city, let me know," she huffs back as they all step into the foyer. The woman's shoulder brushes yours as she walks by, and you have to make an effort not to crinkle your own nose. There's that smell again: processed, fake, all form and no substance. It swirls in the blood of all three of them.

The house tour goes smoothly, for the most part. The woman coos over the skylight – "Natural lighting, one of God's greatest gifts" – as the men discuss studio set-up options, renovation, decoration. It's clear they are keen on snapping up the house. And yet…

On the way back down to the first floor, you are the only one to notice the black crow perched silently on the marble slab outside the house. It tilts its head to one side, its beady gaze fixed on you, as if to ask: "Are they the ones?"

No, not them. They're all wrong for this place. We'll wait. Like we always do.

✗

The second group smells more appealing, but only slightly so. The middle-aged man wears his arrogance like a second skin as he steps through the front door. You don't have to try hard to catch the scent of overripe durian left to fester in the sun, of rotten fish mixed with crisp ringgit notes and curdled blood.

The rot is already deep in this one, the house whispers. The others only hear the words as creaks on the stairs and a gust of wind outside.

The rust-haired woman clinging to his arm is a more interesting study. Under the heady scent of one too many sprays of knock-off Victoria's Secret perfume is the surprisingly crisp scent of pears. They spill down her chin, past the back of her sundress, trailing down her legs like sticky invisible chains. It had been the favorite fruit of her childhood, the one her mother used to cut into perfectly symmetrical slices for her, before she moved to the city, before her name became Tanya—

"Excuse me? Are you listening?"

You draw back instantly. Wait for the shadows to curl back behind your eyelids. Your teeth ache from the effort of suppressing the rattling.

"My apologies. What was the question?"

The man glares at you like you're a piece of tissue stuck to his expensive leather shoes. "I *said*, which room is the master bedroom?"

Up the stairs you go again, placid even as your client mutters grumpily behind you about incompetent salespeople. His companion shushes and soothes him, and by the time you reach the first-floor landing, they are already talking about how this beautiful countryside home will be the perfect place to start a family, away from the prying eyes of his actual wife.

You remember when a man not so different from him used to live here. Better looks and manners, but rot is still rot wherever it goes. In the dark, it is easier to recall the finer details of his demise. The sound of glass shattering. The wet splats of blood coating the furniture. His eyes, black as ink, boring into your dead ones. Another, smaller set of handprints digging a helpless trail along the floor near a mess of upturned toy cars.

A long, low moan ripples through the rooms. You've upset the house. A few rooms away the couple continues their chatter, oblivious to the change in atmosphere.

For a moment, you press a finger to the blemished wood of the staircase railing. *I'm sorry. No rot. We'll keep looking.*

✕

When the third group drives up, you feel unmoved. The family of three walks up the hill slope like they are being sent to the gallows, the daughter lingering behind her parents.

It's always the same, this kind of family. You don't need to come close to know the stale, sour tang of a match long expired. The mother hides her stress and exhaustion behind nervous smiles and an endless string of questions about the house: How long has it been vacant, how far is it to the nearest town, why is the price so below market value—

"My wife has a big mouth. Likes to ask so many questions. Sorry," her husband offers with a tight smile, gripping his wife's shoulder in a pantomime of affection.

You don't miss the way she opens her mouth to say something more and shuts it when his grip tightens like a vice. The bruising will start soon and stay for weeks. You've played this song and dance before.

You turn to get away from the tension when you suddenly catch a glint of light from the corner of your eye. A sliver of warm afternoon sunlight is peeking through the skylight and spreading itself like a blanket over the teenage daughter's hair. She has not uttered a word during the tour, hasn't so much as acknowledged your presence. She stands there in her sneakers and jeans and her too-big shirt, her gaze fixed resolutely on a crack in the wall before her. But when she hears your footsteps, she half-turns to you.

The saltiness of the tears pricking her eyes nearly leaves you winded. She is a tiny, innocent thing, yet her pain is so immense it flows on your tongue like thick globs of barbed honey. She smells like a thousand lilies crushed and mingled with blood, like an orange pricked of its sweetness. She smells like a cry for help. And the house always wants to help.

You stare at each other for a heartbeat, before turning back to the adults. The husband has gone off on his own to explore one of the bedrooms. The mother opens her mouth again. If you see the way she covers her shoulder with one delicate hand, you don't comment on it.

"My family…we're looking for a fresh start. We wanted a quiet place away from the hustle and bustle of the city, but also not so heavy on our savings. Is this a good place for families?"

Hope wars with pain in her eyes, and it's painful even for you to look at.

So you don't tell her that in six weeks, her crumpled body will be found in the living room. That the patterned tile wall in the driveway will be splattered with her daughter's blood. That the neighbors will find her husband teetering on the edge of the roof, a knife gripped tightly in one hand, mumbling about voices in his head telling him to do it.

Because rot is always rot, and houses always remember what has been done within them.

"It's perfect," you assure her.

✕

They depart half an hour later, leaving a trail of salt and copper in the air. Despite everything, you know they will come back. They are the ones. Your work is done, and now you need to rest.

Alone in the darkness of the living room, you press your forehead against the cool brick wall and caress it. Something caresses you back and tugs you forward gently until the rest of your body is flush against the wall. Your face melts into the dusty red brick with a sigh before the rest of your body follows, skin sucking into stone until finally all is quiet in the old house on a road in a corner of the countryside.

Gunik

✕

Collin Yeoh

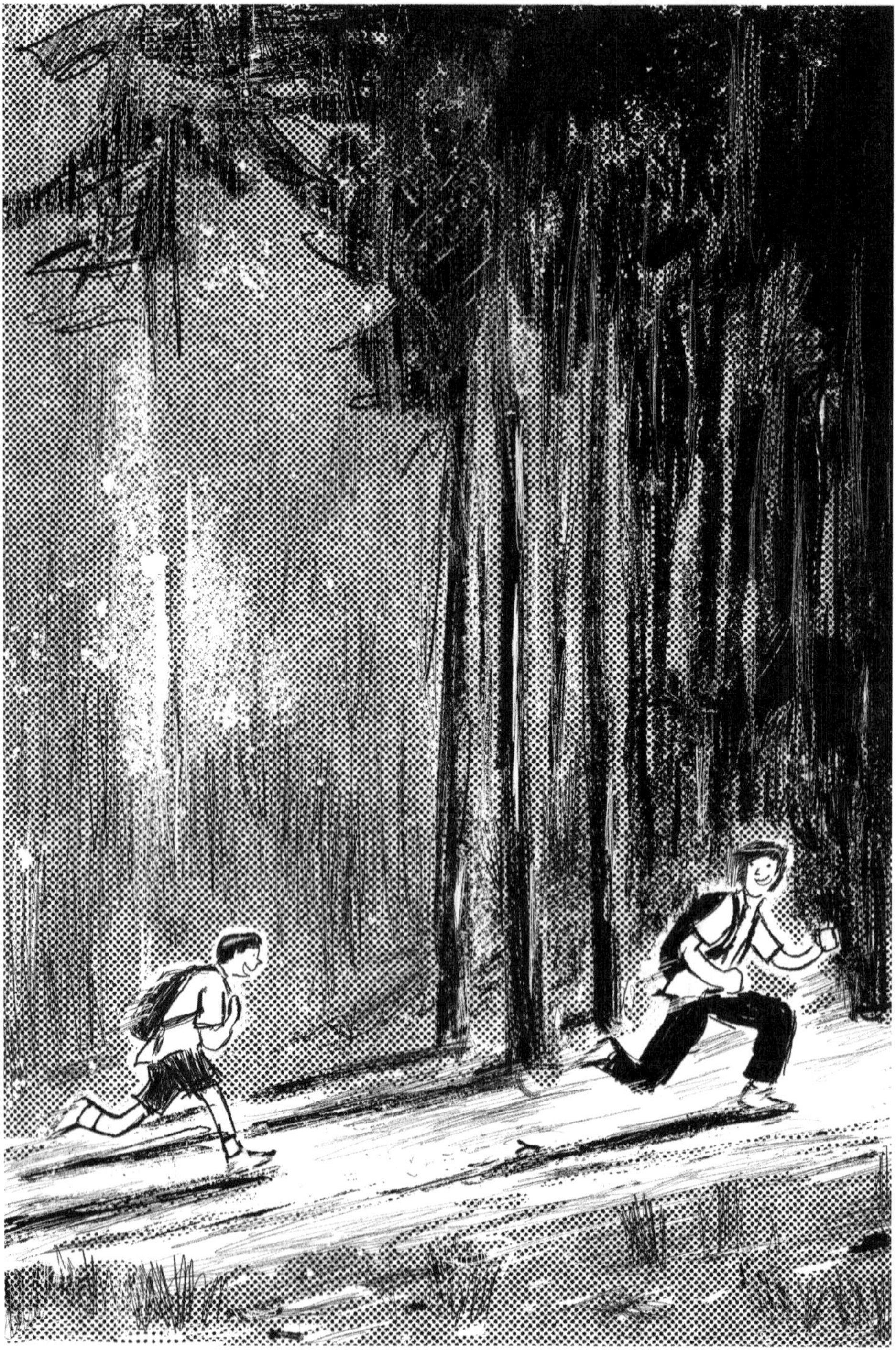

"Muhammad Hisham Haidar Ali, you stand accused of crimes against the Sungai Ong river, the Semai people of Kampung Ong, the environment, and human decency and humanity. What say you to these charges?"

Muhammad Hisham Haidar Ali squinted, both because of the harsh spotlight on his face and the swelling bruise above his left eye from the punch he had received earlier. His hands and ankles were tied with raffia string to the wrought-iron frame of the cheap wooden chair he had been placed in. He couldn't tell where he was; other than the blinding white light, all else was shrouded in darkness.

He sneered. "Mr. Daniel Trevor, isn't it? You bloody fool. You're about to find out what it's like to rot in a Malaysian jail."

The electronically-disguised voice spoke again. "You have no proof that I'm him. You don't recognize my voice. You can't see my face. And Daniel Trevor is, at this moment, having dinner with three Semai tribesmen who will testify to that alibi."

Hisham blinked. He thought he could see a vague blur behind the spotlight, possibly indicating a person. Two blurs, as a matter of fact. "So you've shown your true colors at last, have you? Filthy American so-called 'activist.' Terrorist, more like."

"The only terrorist here is the one sitting before us. And your destruction of Sungai Ong is the true terrorism."

"'Us,' eh?" Hisham grinned. "Who have you got there with you? One of those poor ignorant Semais? Mat salleh ni pergunakan kau jelah, bodoh!"

"You think they'll listen to you if you call them 'ignorant' and 'bodoh'?"

"You think I care about them?" Hisham chuckled and shook his head. "I've got a 60-million-ringgit development project on my side. That means the police, the state government, the courts, even their own Welfare Department are all on my side. Nothing the Semais or you can do to stop me. You arrogant white boy, you think you can just waltz into this country with your fancy Western ways and teach *us* a lesson?"

"Silence!" The artificial bass of the disembodied voice rang in Hisham's ears. "Do not think your crimes will go unpunished. You face your reckoning this very moment. Sungai Ong was once a healthy and thriving river, full of fish that fed the Semai people. Juling falls was a site of pristine natural beauty, and the tourists making the hike there were another valuable source of income for Semai guides. Now the waters are brown and full of silt, the fish are gone, and no one goes to the waterfall anymore. All because of your hotel project upriver that will benefit no one but yourself. These are your crimes, Muhammad Hisham Haidar Ali. And before this night is over, you will answer for them…one way or another."

Halfway through that speech, Hisham had started convulsing with silent laughter. By the time it was over, he was giggling audibly, and soon progressed to loud guffaws.

"Something funny?" asked the electronic voice.

"Oh, plenty," Hisham replied, making a show of holding back another chortle. "Did you minor in Theater at your prestigious American university? Is that where you learned to talk like a comic book villain? And that ridiculous Darth Vader voice? No, not Darth Vader…more like that evil robot from *RoboCop*. What was it called?" He started giggling again. "You expect me to take that seriously? You're trying to be scary, but you fail because you're too *over the top!*"

Despite more exaggerated mocking laughter from Hisham, the voice seemed unfazed. "Laugh while you still can, Mr. Hisham. You are entirely in our power, and no one is coming to your rescue. We have all the time in the world to enact justice upon you. That's right…haven't you realized what this is about yet? Justice, Mr. Hisham. Justice for your crimes. Tonight, it has come for you."

The spotlight went out, plunging his surroundings into a blurry gray afterimage. He heard the sound of a door opening but saw no light from any adjacent room. Then the door closed, leaving him in complete silence and darkness.

✕

Daniel Trevor and Anjang removed their ski masks in the adjoining room. Daniel was smiling; the Semai was not.

"Well, I think we're off to a very good start."

"I don't know, Tuan Daniel. He doesn't seem afraid at all," replied Anjang.

"I told you, he doesn't have to be," said Daniel with the boyish grin that had charmed the pants off many an American co-ed, and that had a not dissimilar effect on many Semais. "He's already hinted at bribing the police, the courts and the JHEOA. He obviously doesn't know we've got a camera on him. We just need him to incriminate himself and get it all on video. In fact, his little defiant act back there is playing right into our hands. I'll just lay on the theatrics a little thicker, get him even more worked up, and he'll be singing like a canary!"

Daniel had it all planned out. The hardest part was to get Hisham to admit to bribery and malicious intent on video, which is why it was crucial that he did not know about the camera set up on a tripod behind the spotlight. That video could either be used to blackmail him into halting his project, or simply released anonymously onto the internet, resulting in public anger that would be a PR disaster for the development company and accomplish the same goal. And with the ski masks, the voice changer and the alibi, Hisham could cry to the police all he wanted, and nothing could tie the kidnapping to Daniel or the Semais.

Which wasn't to say that no one would know who the mastermind was. Once this was all over, Daniel was going to let a particular group of people know. A group with whom he had been arrested for attempted vandalism of an in-construction oil pipeline back in the States. A group that had once been raring to go at defending the land rights of a certain Native American tribe, who then developed an acute case of the chickenshits when that same tribe disavowed their actions. A group that, after their wealthy parents got the charges dropped, went on to form a much more respectable environmental activist group, focusing on perfectly respectable activities such as making awareness-building online viral videos. A group that had won some advertising awards for their videos, which then enabled them to win some generous grants.

A group that – once they saw proof that Daniel's radical methods could bring about real change and real victories, such as actually stopping a major construction project that was harming an indigenous tribe – would regret excluding him and beg him to come back into their fold, where he too would have a say in how to use that generous funding.

Unlike the inner room where they held Hisham, the outer room had windows through which some faint moonlight shone. In that light, Daniel could make out Anjang nervously hugging his blowpipe, a slender bamboo instrument longer than the Semai was tall. If Hisham got too stubborn, Daniel would have Anjang step out of the darkness and make a show of threatening to shoot him with one of the poisoned darts they famously used for hunting wild game. It would be a last resort, of course, since it wasn't a threat he could follow through with, but it was good to keep in the back pocket. And all the better if hanging on to the thing helped Anjang calm his nerves.

The hardest part of the plan was convincing at least one of them to join him in this scheme. Semais were guileless and trusting, which had unfortunately led to decades of them being cheated and abused. They were also famously pacifistic: Their culture had no concept of competition even in their children's games, parents would never dream of physically punishing kids, and for generations they didn't even have any leadership structure in their tribe. Only recently had they appointed a village committee to represent them in their dealings with the outside world, spurred by the plundering by Hisham's company of their ancestral lands. It was among this committee of de facto tribe leaders that Daniel had broached the idea of taking more drastic measures than pleading for help from the JHEOA, or hiring lawyers, or holding peaceful protests at the construction site that were inevitably broken up by the police. Kidnapping was a step too far for them, however, and they had all – politely – refused to help. All but one.

Daniel had been worried that just two of them wouldn't be enough to overpower Hisham when they ambushed him in the parking lot of his office, but Anjang possessed surprising strength for someone supposedly non-violent. Maybe it was because of that dream vision he had, or some such mumbo-jumbo that Daniel had only half-listened to the Semai telling him about.

He pressed the illumination button on the dirt-cheap digital watch he had bought at a night market in town. It was just coming up to 15 minutes since they left Hisham alone to stew in the dark, which Daniel guessed was enough to feel like much longer. He picked up the electronic voice changer that he had also bought at that market, a child-sized megaphone made of bright orange clear plastic. "All right, shall we get this show back on the road?" he said to Anjang while pulling down his ski mask. Staying behind the spotlight would keep them out of sight, but it was good to have an extra layer of precaution to make sure they couldn't be identified. He congratulated himself once again on remembering to bring the masks from the States; they were virtually impossible to find in tropical Malaysia. And they were a good deal cooler-looking than the voice changer.

✕

All Hisham had managed to figure out was that he was indoors, that it must be a relatively old building by the faint musty smell, and that he was likely in a rural area by the lack of any sounds of traffic. Other than that, the pitch darkness and silence did a good job of making him feel completely cut off. He still had hope of escape, but he was beginning to wonder what he could do if he got himself free from the chair and the building, only to find himself miles from help in the middle of the night.

His thoughts were interrupted by the sound of the door opening, and he closed his eyes in anticipation. Sure enough, his eyelids were seared once again by the glare of the spotlight.

"Are you ready to resume your trial, Mr. Hisham?" boomed the distorted voice.

"ED-209," said Hisham.

When the voice didn't reply, Hisham spoke again. "That's the name of the evil robot from *RoboCop*. ED-209. That's what you sound like," he chuckled. "But maybe a millennial like you wouldn't get the reference. It was a popular movie from the '80s, you see."

"Nobody's laughing at your jokes, Mr. Hisham."

"What I can't figure out is, what are you up to exactly?" Hisham asked with a casual air. "What do you mean to accomplish? Because I sure as hell don't believe you'd actually harm me. Even you aren't that stupid."

"Muhammad Hisham Haidar Ali," the voice boomed again with a touch more imperiousness. "Graduated 2006 with a Bachelor's in civil engineering from University of Westminster, London, on a MARA government scholarship. Prior to that, a diploma from Universiti Teknologi MARA, completed secondary school at Victoria Institution Kuala Lumpur, primary school in Sekolah Kebangsaan Haji Hasan…in Tapah. Born 1983, right here in Tapah.

"You're a hometown boy, Mr. Hisham. This town raised you. But you left it the first chance you got, first to the big city of KL, then to London, and then back to KL to work in fancy high-rise office buildings. And now you're back with a fleet of bulldozers to destroy the environment where you grew up. Are you proud to be doing this, Mr. Hisham? Are you what your people call 'kacang lupakan kulit?'"

Hisham was silent for a moment before muttering, "I've forgotten nothing."

"Speak up, Mr. Hisham."

"I said I've forgotten *nothing!*" Hisham snarled, all his insouciance gone in an instant. Daniel's play to get under the skin of his innate Malay traditionalism had paid off. "You think you're so clever because you know how to Google my name and look up my LinkedIn profile? You know nothing about me. *Nothing!*"

"You are here to be judged. If you wish to defend yourself, now's the time."

"I have no intention of defending myself to you or to be *judged* by you." He stared straight at what he thought was the blur from which the electronic voice came, despite the spotlight. "But if you want to know who I really am, I'll *tell* you. A little story, if you want to hear it. I think you and your Semai friend will find it interesting."

"Tell your story then."

With a feral grin, Hisham began.

✕

I was eight years old. My brother Haziq was 13.

Tapah isn't my hometown. My hometown is Kampung Cengkerik, a village just outside of it. I grew up surrounded by the kind of nature you claim to be a protector of. Forests, rivers, creeks, the sounds of dozens of different birds and insects, all of which I could identify – this was my childhood. I knew them better than you ever could.

Haziq was my hero. He was the best older brother a boy could have. He was the strongest, fastest, smartest, and wittiest of all the village kids. And I was his younger brother, whom he protected from bullies, whom he always brought along on his games and adventures, whom he never teased or made to feel small.

I had the best childhood a child could ever have. And it was all taken away from me in an instant.

He said he wanted to go to the waterfall. This was before it got the 'Juling' name, before it became a day-trip destination for city folk. Back then it was just 'the waterfall' to us – a nice enough place to swim and play, but a long hike away. There were smaller, shallower streams nearer to our village. Haziq invited the other kids, but none of them wanted to walk that far. Of course, I went with him.

I don't know how he found the energy after that long walk to run the last few meters to the waterfall. But he did, jumping into the water fully clothed. I ran after him, stopped by the riverbank, and began taking off my clothes – and then I realized that Haziq hadn't come up for air. It must have been only a few minutes, but it felt like an eternity of calling my brother's name before he resurfaced.

And then … he said there was a beautiful woman down there in the waterfall pool. He said she wore a dress of red silk and gold brocade, like a princess. She was the most beautiful person he had ever seen. She brought him to her banquet table filled with food, sweets and drinks. They were delicious, the most delicious things he had ever eaten. She allowed him back up to the surface so that he could bring me with him and feast at her table. He said she was waiting for us, and that I should hurry and jump into the water right now.

I didn't. I couldn't. There was something frightening about the look in my brother's eyes: a dreamy, almost intoxicated look. He asked me once, twice, three times, and each time I refused. And after the third time…he didn't reply, didn't even say goodbye, he just dove into the water again.

And this time, I waited till I was sure he wasn't coming up.

I tried to run back home. But it was a long journey, and I was already tired from making it once. So I ran till I got a cramp, then I walked fast for as long as I could with that cramp, then I switched to walking slow. My sides were in agony by the time I reached my house.

And I still had to face my mother and father, and tell them what had happened to their eldest son.

All the men of the village, young and old, set out for the waterfall. They dove into the pool and downriver as far as they could, but found no trace of him. The next day, policemen and the army got involved, searching even further along the river with their scuba diving gear. They finally found my brother on the river bottom, a short distance from the waterfall. I didn't see his body, but people told me he was pale and swollen, particularly in his belly, to the point he was barely recognizable as a human being.

And I only know this because I was hiding behind a corner of the hospital hallway and overheard the coroner telling it to my weeping parents: when they autopsied my brother, they found hundreds of live, wriggling worms and larvae in his stomach. I suppose that was what he ate at that princess' banquet.

I don't expect you to believe this story, and I don't care if you do. But you can believe this: Everything I have done in my life, I did because of what happened at that waterfall that day. I applied for and won scholarships to secondary school and university here and in the UK. I worked days and nights for years at my career till I could lead my own development projects. I studied civil engineering for the sole purpose of coming back to this place and building something that would destroy that waterfall and that river.

You think yourself a protector of nature. What do *you* know of nature? I'll tell you what nature is: It's home to forces you and I can never comprehend. Forces that aren't just content to mind their own business, oh no; they come for us. Prey on us. Pick some poor unlucky soul to carry off and eat. Or someone's child to be their plaything for a while till they tire of him. They've done this for thousands of years because they have power over us. Well, not anymore. Not now when we have bulldozers and excavators, when we can reshape the very earth they dwell in. We can get back at them, destroy them even, and we will – *I* will. I'll gladly ruin a hundred sites of 'pristine natural beauty' if it means those filthy things never harm another human being again.

Mark my words, Daniel Trevor. I don't care what you do to me. I don't care if you ruin me or even cripple me. I'll haul soil and mud and sewage by the wheelbarrow myself to that river and dump it there one load at a time if I have to. That 'princess,' whoever or whatever she is, took my brother from me – murdered him for nothing more than her own amusement. My whole life has been dedicated to my revenge on her, and neither you nor a bunch of half-naked, hut-dwelling savages are going to stop me. Unless you kill me.

Let's see if you have the balls to do *that*, you cowardly fucking mat salleh.

×

Daniel contemplated what he had just heard. It was a hell of a story, but he needed to focus on the task at hand. He had gotten it all on video; what could he do with that? Could it paint Hisham as mentally unsound? Hell, he thought, it might even win Hisham public sympathy; it hadn't escaped his notice how credulous Malaysians, even the supposedly well-educated ones, tend to be about the supernatural. No, no, he had to stick to the plan of getting Hisham to admit to legal malfeasance. There had to be a way to poke at Hisham's crazy supernatural vendetta – which he believed in whole-heartedly, as the fierceness and vehemence of his telling had made clear – in order to trick him into spilling the dirt. Daniel would edit out the spooky ghost-story parts la–

His thoughts were interrupted by a slender, cotton-fletched dart suddenly appearing on Hisham's chest. A shocked Hisham gaped at it, and at the slowly growing blood stain on his white dress shirt.

"*What did you do?*" Daniel screamed at Anjang, forgetting the voice changer, as the Semai lowered his blowpipe. "Why did you even bring darts? Are they…are they *poisoned?*"

He turned back to Hisham, who had already begun to convulse and froth at the mouth, and knew the answer to that question.

"Gunik," said Anjang calmly. His expression was inscrutable as he looked from his victim to Daniel. "For our gunik."

All his plans for a glorious return to the States and a hero's welcome by his former activist friends turned to ash before Daniel's eyes, replaced by visions of a scandalous murder trial and a squalid prison cell. Then suddenly, preoccupied though he was, he realized he knew the meaning of the word Anjang said. The Semai had explained it to him before. It meant 'guardian spirit'.

As Hisham stared sightlessly, and as the poison in his bloodstream caused his heart to fail, his mouth curled into a little smile.

Janice

×

Nurul Hafizah

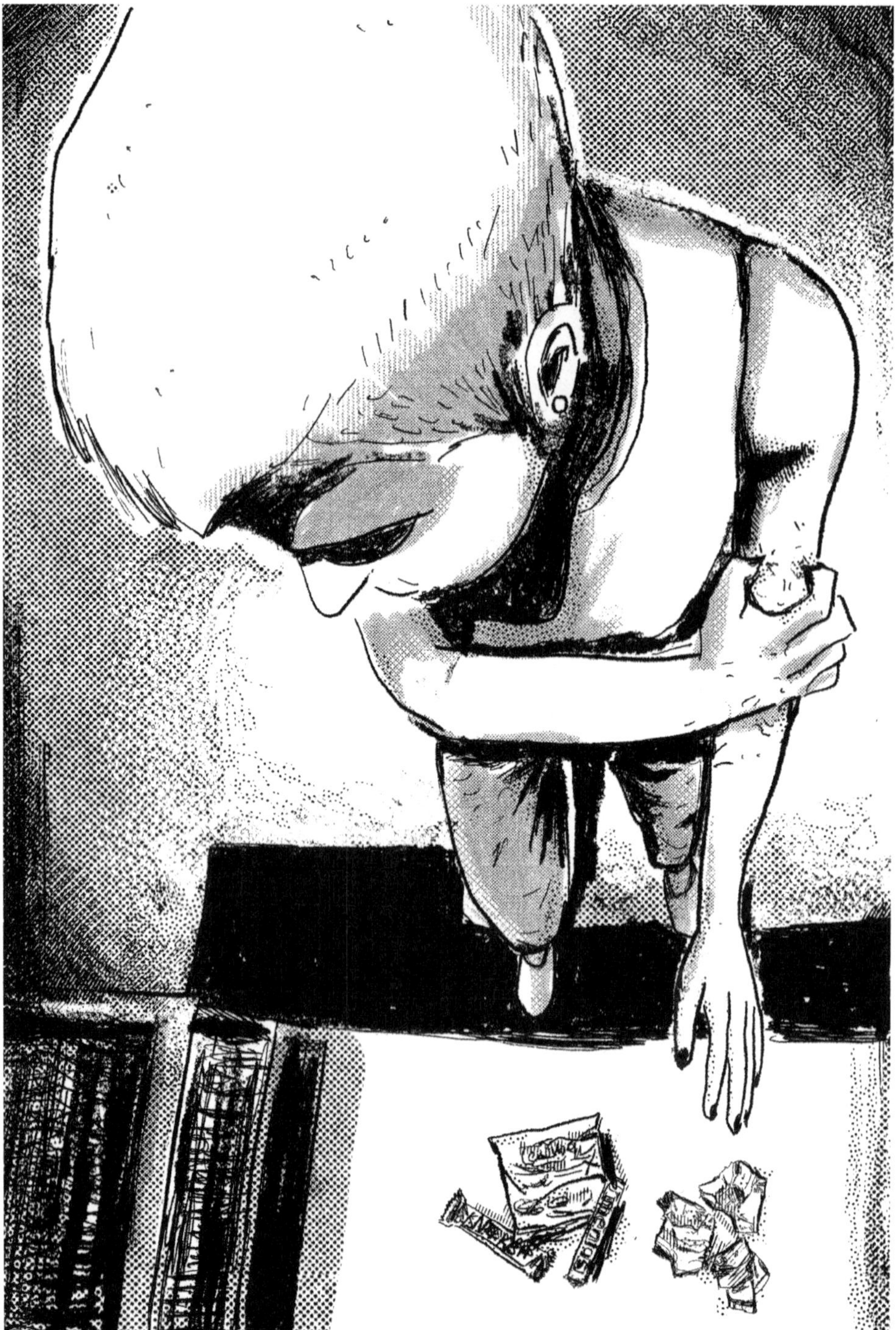

"We're all afflicted with something. Everyone's sick in one sense or another."

If anyone ever asks me about Janice Lee – and I sure as hell hope no one will – this would be the first thing to come to mind. Strangely not the bugs or everything that happened after, but this very moment. The two of us sitting by the roadside in the dead of night, me clutching a cold Ramly burger that was well beyond unappetizing at this point, and her with a cigarette she mostly only allowed to burn. Her gaze wild yet unfocused, as if she wasn't quite existing in this world despite occupying space in it. She may as well have not been, given the rant she had started spouting.

I glanced up from my soggy half-eaten burger in time to see Janice take a puff of her cigarette, and then slowly exhale. Tendrils of smoke danced in the air, forming wispy curlicues as they faded. For a moment it was all I could focus on; my brain struggled to process her statement and how abruptly the words seemed to spill from her lips.

She had always been the kind of person whose conversation topics jumped from one random thing to another, although if someone paid enough attention, they probably could figure out how her mind formed the connections. I thought I understood enough to get how she ticked. But this sudden leap from a personal anecdote about getting lost to what sounded like the beginning of a philosophical rant was out of left field even for me. I could only manage a half-hearted: "That's cynical even for me, chief."

"Much as I enjoy metaphors, I actually meant it in a more literal way." Another drag from the cigarette. Chesterfield this time. The ones with the charcoal filter. Not that I had much of an idea what that meant, despite my job requiring me to handle various tobacco products on a daily basis. And I was almost certain Janice never really knew what she was smoking either. To her it was more about the novelty of trying something different each time – if choosing among the meager selection in the store counted. But in a sense it didn't matter. I wasn't sure if anything really mattered to her.

I waited for her to elaborate on the statement.

The look on her face was pensive, and her dark eyes were distant. She twirled the cigarette between her fingers. The smoke haloing her form gave her an almost ethereal look. It intensified that feeling of unreality.

"We're not just masses of flesh that house a consciousness, you know," she said finally, running her tongue along her bottom lip. "We're also home to billions upon billions of tiny little things. Tiny little voices that thrive both on and within us, and we don't even know it." A pause. "Well, not really. I suppose biologists have some of the bits figured out. They call it a *microbiome* or something like that. Not that they can fully grasp the whole scope of it." She wrinkled her nose.

"Isn't it kind of a stretch to call our gut bacteria a sickness when they actually serve a purpose?" I tilted my burger slightly to lick at the mixture of sauces that had started to seep through the wrapping.

Janice's laughter was so unlike her it was jarring. She generally had a loud, raucous laugh that most would find obnoxious. The noise that escaped her then was more of a subdued titter that conjured up an image of crickets. "They don't *serve* anyone," she argued. "And least of all us. We, the ignorant fools who like to make bold assertions about things we cannot even begin to comprehend." There was no mistaking the hint of disgust in her tone.

I had thought it absurd, how she seemed so offended by the notion that simple single-celled organisms were working for us. In hindsight, I should have left her to be the madwoman she was. But I still wanted to see where she was going with this. Maybe I was a fool. Maybe she had some hold on me that wasn't entirely natural.

"There is only one thing that matters: survival. Any living creature to have ever existed knows this. The fact that what they – *we* – do to persist ends up aiding in some other being's continued existence is just a side effect. Most of the time, the selfish drive to stay alive just ends up killing what we leave in our wake. That's what sickness is, really. A side effect of something else gaining something from us." Another pause. This time to take one final drag from the Chesterfield before deftly flicking what was left into the air. The cigarette butt, stark white in the dark of night, ricocheted off the asphalt once. I didn't see where it ended up. "But sometimes," she muttered, slowly turning to face me, "we adapt. We learn to live with what we get. We learn to coexist with what makes us ill. And together, we make something new."

"So your point is..."

Janice shrugged. "I actually forgot where I was going with that." For a moment, she seemed a bit more like her usual self. Relaxed and present in the real world. "But." She bit her lip, and that same distant look crossed her features again. She tilted her head to the side to stare off into space, breaking our eye contact. "We're all sick because we have yet to accept what needs to happen. And how can we, when we do not yet know what's happening? What burrows and writhes under our skin, just waiting to emerge. We don't have the slightest clue. But...maybe we do. Maybe deep down, we all feel it. Hear it whispering to us."

There was something in the way she spoke, that odd conviction. It sent a prickling chill down my spine. I opened my mouth to ask what she meant, but the words remained floating in an unreachable part of my brain.

"They call to us. Some nights I can even feel them crawling." She scratched her shoulder. "How they squirm just under the surface."

I flinched at the sound of fingernails scraping against skin.

Janice's voice was barely above a tiny whisper. "It. Itches."

✕

I didn't see Janice much in the weeks following that night. It was probably a good thing, even though I missed her. I had met different kinds of people while working: Young and impressionable office interns looking for their early morning coffee fix, disgruntled ustazes who made a point to rant about the sad state of youths nowadays, confused mak ciks who needed help to navigate their e-payment apps. But very few people held my interest in the way Janice did. Maybe it was because we both didn't really fit in. Janice was a nonconformist in a far more obvious way – or at least she made it a point to be that way. She wore her idiosyncrasies like a badge of honor. I envied her for it. I loathed how disconnected I felt from my own country, and tried to downplay anything that marked me as an outsider.

Studying overseas had been a mistake. I was naive enough to think home would always be home, no matter how long I stayed away. Meanwhile the world moved on. I returned home a stranger. Any optimism was crushed by the fact that I was 'overqualified' for the jobs I applied to. Well, I'm technically overqualified for working a dead-end job at a convenience store, but I had the excuse of my expertise not being applicable in this field. The pay sucked, but I had to do something. I needed to feel like I belonged.

Did Janice sense that? I don't have an answer for why we gravitated to each other. All I know was that one day a petite Chinese girl with messy pink hair strode into the store and asked for a pack of cigarettes. Said it didn't matter which, just sell her whatever I felt like selling. *Rich brat*, I had thought. She didn't bat an eye when I slid the most expensive brand across the counter. She came back a few hours later to buy more cigarettes. She also had two packets of nasi lemak with her. She offered me one.

My stomach was at least still Malaysian enough to be won over by food gifts.

She swung by regularly after that. I had made it a point to avoid letting customers into my personal life. Janice became the exception. We hung out after work almost daily. She made time to talk to me when my shift ended. Even when she didn't, we still bantered as she made her purchases.

She didn't show up for three days after her weird ramblings about sickness and creepy crawly things. She didn't try to strike up conversation on the fourth day, when she finally made her appearance. Her gaze remained glued to the floor while I rang up her purchases – snacks with an obscene sugar content – and tried to get a read on her. Her expression was blank, but her hands were fidgeting. Every now and then her fingers would curl against exposed skin, and I would hear the scratching.

I should have said something. If I had, maybe I could have saved her. Or perhaps it was already too late. So I kept my stupid mouth shut. Not a word, not even to tell her how much she owed. RM18.70. Don't ask me how I can remember that. The mind works in odd ways. Sometimes it plays tricks.

I was sure that was what it was. What I saw. Just my imagination.

A few seconds of silence passed after I set down the scanner. I drummed my fingers against the counter. The sound was drowned out by the steady whirr of the Slurpee machine. I briefly considered speaking. Yes, things were awkward. But this was technically work. And had there been other people waiting in line, it would have been necessary to speed things along.

But Janice moved before I managed to say anything. She fumbled for her purse, fished out a couple of crumpled notes and counted them out. She dropped the money onto the counter. Her clammy fingers brushed against mine when I reached over to collect the cash.

Smoothing out wrinkled plastic RM5 bills was irksome, and I was preoccupied with the thought of having to fold and unfold the things repeatedly just so they could lie flat in the cash register.

Some nights I wished that had kept my attention more. Other times I regretted being so distracted. Either way, I'm still not sure if I would prefer to have seen it in great clarity or not at all. Anything would have been better than a glimpse from the corner of my eye. A blink-and-you-miss-it instance.

The flesh of Janice's hand *rippled*. Like the bubbly surface of boiling water. Like something was moving underneath –

Janice cleared her throat.

My gaze shot back to her face.

She wasn't looking at me. She raised her arm to cover her mouth, turning away from the counter. She bent over slightly and coughed. Once, twice. Or at least I thought it was coughing. It was an awful hacking noise that was more like choking. I didn't have time to dwell on that. Janice had straightened up and was still for a split second. And then she bolted right out of the shop.

I didn't chase after her. My shift was far from over, after all. I simply stashed her purchases under the counter. Thinking she would come back for them later, and I could ask her what was up when she did. I began to walk away from the register. There were plenty of chores I could get done while there were no customers. And sorting and arranging products was just the kind of mindless monotonous task that could give me some sense of normalcy.

There was a sickening crunch as my foot made contact with something that was most definitely not the floor. I fell back a step, tilting my head. A half-crushed insect lay there, its bright scarlet coloring a stark contrast to the gray tiles. Its limbs flailed in the air. Its antennae swayed slightly. I couldn't tell what kind of bug it was, especially since a part of it was smeared against the sole of my shoe. But something told me I wouldn't recognize the species even if it were whole. Entomology is not my field of study. And pests of any sort were bad news for any store. So I raised my foot and put the sad specimen out of its misery.

It didn't cross my mind that I had found the bug where Janice had stood when paying for the snacks she did not take. At least, not at that moment. The realization only hit me after I kept finding more and more of those wretched red creatures. Most of them lingered where Janice had been.

I had my manager call the exterminator. And I was glad Janice didn't come back for her things.

✕

"Cockroaches again. I thought we already had the exterminator over." Hazri brandished the can of bug spray and sighed. "And I'm pretty sure I'm on my third can of Ridsect. I know we don't exactly keep the backroom super tidy, but come on…"

I peered over my co-worker's shoulder to look at the pile of writhing insects. I had mostly tuned out what the poor boy was saying. It was normal for bugs to turn up shortly after pesticide use, either dead or on their way to being dead. So there was no point in complaining about creatures making a futile last-ditch effort to flee the poison. I absentmindedly brushed past him to grind my heel into the still-twitching bodies. They crackled beneath the soles of my work shoes. "Some bugs are just tough cookies. Chemicals don't really do anything to them. You gotta smash 'em to make sure they—" I stopped. My mind finally registered what I was seeing.

Those were definitely not cockroaches.

I didn't know what the hell they were, other than bad news. I recognized the blood-red carapaces, though. The bugs I found after Janice left the other day. That had been almost a week ago, and I had not seen any more of the things after that. I was beginning to think my eyes had been playing tricks on me. That there had never been any red bugs. Only cockroaches.

But they were real.

I stamped my foot down on the insects. Again and again. And again. I didn't stop until the bugs were reduced to a pulp. Hazri ended up pulling me away so he could actually clean up the mess. He did a fairly good job. No evidence of the bugs remained. Except for that crimson stain. There was no washing that out.

Janice showed up the week I had the graveyard shift. It was around 3 a.m. or maybe later. I had locked the door and brought out the cleaning supplies. I was partway through dunking the mop into a bucket of soapy water when the irritatingly upbeat door chime caught my attention. I spun on my heel automatically, my mouth already forming the well-practiced greeting. "Hi, welcome to Sev—"

My gaze fell upon the figure at the entrance. The first thing I realized: No one was supposed to be in here. *I had locked the door.* The key was still in the lock. I could see the metal glinting in the fluorescent lights.

And then I recognized the wild cotton candy-colored hair.

"Janice?" I cautiously approached her. Something felt off. My grip on the mop tightened.

There was a vague putrid stench of rot, wafting in waves.

"A pack of cigarettes, please. Whatever you feel like selling." Janice's head was bowed. She remained at the front of the store. She was standing still, yet there was something ... shifting. Like the subtle waves on the surface of a body of water. Movement that pooled at her feet, spreading outward.

I squinted, trying to figure out what it was. All the lights in the store were still on, but somehow the world seemed darker. The air grew heavier the closer I got to Janice. My instincts screamed at me to turn and run, that nothing good would come out of anything else. But I kept moving forward. I was drawn to her like a moth to a flame. Like an insect – no. What was I doing? I shook my head, and started to back away instead.

My retreat was halted when I felt something skittering along my leg.

I yelped, dropping the mop. My foot caught on its handle, and the next thing I knew I was on the floor. I put my palms against the tiles to push myself up.

That was when I realized I was surrounded by the bugs. There had to be hundreds upon hundreds of them. Coming closer. Swarming me. I flailed my limbs, swatting at the ones that came near enough. I scrambled to my feet.

And found myself face to face with Janice.

If what I saw could even be counted as a face. That mass of meat didn't resemble anything that might have once been a person's visage. It had no eyes, no mouth, no discernible features. Only an impossible number of regular, vaguely hexagonal holes. They covered every centimeter of flesh. Some of them were occupied by more twitching red insects. Others housed slimy silvery grubs that writhed in a sickly rhythm. The spongy body that housed the creatures throbbed in a twisted mockery of human breathing.

This close, I could easily tell that the reek of death and decay was coming from the thing that used to be Janice.

I wanted to run. But I remained rooted where I was.

The thing that was no longer Janice spoke. No, 'speak' is not the right word. There had been no sound. It was more of a feeling. Something that sank deep into my bones. I understood the message as though it had been put into words.

Why do you reject what calls to you? This is how it should be. We can create something beautiful. We belong together.

It was the voice of a thousand chittering insects. Crawling all over me.

The scream that tore its way out of my throat was a guttural cry I couldn't recognize as my own. I pushed Janice – *that thing* – and broke into a run. My hands came away sticky. I wiped them against my pants and dashed to the backroom. I slammed the door shut. Pushed the lock into place. Shoved as many unopened beer crates as I could to act as a barricade. I slumped against the cartons, barely even registering the shuddery whimpers as my own.

I'm not sure how long I stayed there, teeth gritted as I tried to block out the angry screeches coming from the things that hollowed out Janice and made her their home. Some of the red bugs managed to slip through my makeshift fortress. I stomped on them until they turned into mush. It felt like I was trapped in that hell forever. I could no longer tell if it was sweat or tears that slicked my skin.

I must have passed out from exhaustion at some point. I woke up to missed calls and irate messages from both Hazri and my manager. I didn't tell them about the bugs. Or Janice.

That was the last time I ever saw her. Assuming that was her. Assuming I hadn't dreamt up the entire scenario. I wish that was all it was, a nightmare. I may even be able to convince myself that it must be the case. But a bad dream doesn't explain the bugs. How they keep turning up everywhere. How they don't seem to match the description of any local species. I want to remain skeptical and say it could be nothing. They're just a type of regular insect that researchers have yet to discover. Or an invasive species some random sod inadvertently unleashed upon the area. But I think deep down I know the truth. I can feel it. The crawling and burrowing.

I'm starting to itch.

Faceless Portraits

×

Joni Chng

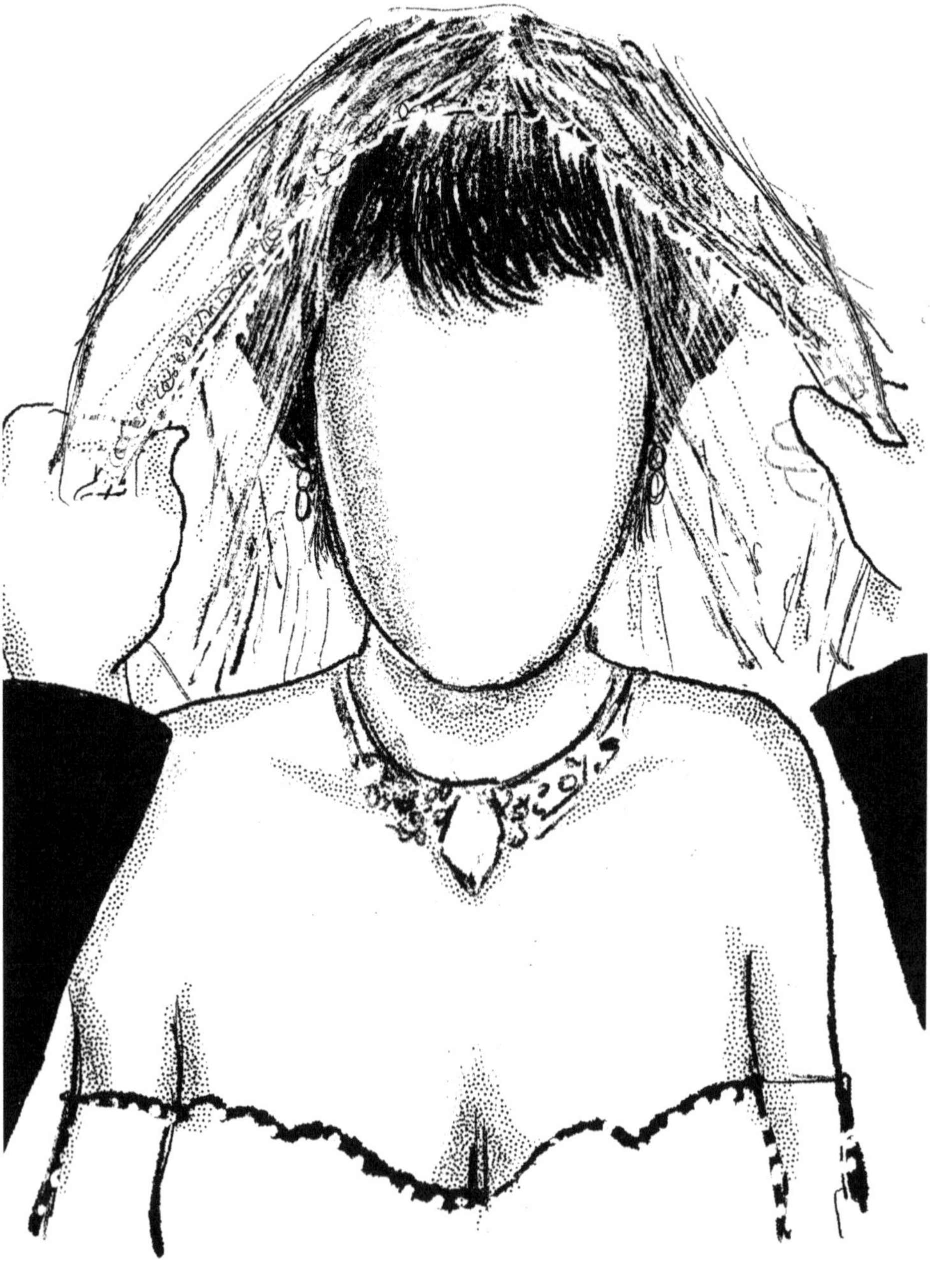

This was *not* how Robert Yen envisioned the pinnacle of his career as a photographer. He had just launched the exhibition for his *Extraordinary Portraits of the Ordinary* series at the National Art Gallery less than an hour ago. In a while, he would be making a six-hour drive from the capital city to the rural northern district of Padang Terap with his nine-year-old daughter to see his ailing mother – probably for the very last time. Having stepped away to the next hall after entertaining questions and posing for pictures with admirers of his work, here he was, face to face with the subject of a recurring childhood nightmare.

The painting that made his blood freeze was big enough to occupy a whole wall, rendered in black and white, with very subtle shades of gray in areas. The wraith-like figure of a bride stood a bit off-center to the left against a solid black background, a bouquet in one hand. Her long trailing veil, pinned on the top of her head, flowed rightwards to complete the asymmetrical composition. The wedding dress was a very conservative kind, with long sleeves and a headscarf wrapped snugly around the head and neck that would leave only the hands and face exposed. These parts were painted as black as the background with white outlines, as if the bride was an invisible entity floating in a dark void. Her head was turned at a three-quarters angle. Where her face was supposed to be, there was just a solid black oval.

"That's so creepy," a girl's voice remarked. Robert looked sideways to see his daughter standing next to him. Rebecca made a face and feigned a shudder in an exaggerated show of dread. "She looks like a ghost."

Robert nodded in agreement. He would not have made portrait photography a lifelong mission, had it not been to conquer the unsettling effect that human figures without faces had on him since he was 10 – when the faceless demon first visited him in a vivid dream.

✕

He could not forget that night, because it was the eve of the field trip to the Kedah Royal Museum. Robert went to bed looking forward to a whole day of being out of the classroom. He was so excited that he wasn't even aware when he crossed the threshold between sleep and wakefulness, into dreaming.

He remembered finding himself standing in a meadow under the twilight sky, where the tall grass was dried and brown. At a distance ahead stood a lone figure in a flowing white dress, with long black hair framing a face that wasn't there. It extended a slender arm with long twig-like fingers, beckoning him. He wanted to run, but his legs felt heavy, like they were rooted to the dry earth. The entity just stood there, arm outstretched, as if it could pull him into the dark void where its face should be. Then – he was awake in bed, momentarily paralyzed and drenched in cold sweat. Whatever enthusiasm he had for the day was gone, replaced with a foreboding he couldn't quite explain.

If Robert learned anything at all on the field trip, it was that museums were not about to become his favorite places. Being among old things in an air-conditioned building, with creaky wooden flooring and a low ceiling, gave him a sense of being watched by the hundreds of invisible eyes of those who once owned those things.

In the middle of the museum's main gallery was a diorama displaying royal court attire, draped over mannequins with no faces. Suddenly, Robert was back at the meadow from his dream. His legs were trembling, his stomach was in knots and his body felt numb. He would have peed his pants had he not run out of there to hide in the garden. The whole class had to organize a search party to look for him when it was time to go.

Whatever it was that came to him that night, he would have no peace from it throughout his adolescent years. This entity would visit his dreams at random, meeting him in different settings that were both familiar and unknown to him in waking life: his classroom at school, by the riverside where he used to play with his friends, on a lonely road in the middle of nowhere, in the woods, and even outside his bedroom window. Robert was convinced he was haunted by a demonic entity inhabiting the 80-year-old family home he had lived in all his life.

"There's no faceless evil spirit in this house, alright?" his mother said when he finally told her one morning over breakfast. "You see things in your dreams when you think about them a lot."

"The more you keep thinking about it, the more you let that nonsense keep replaying in your head, and you end up scaring yourself," his father chimed in, briefly exchanging what he thought was a knowing look with his mother.

"It's all just dreams, my dear boy," his mother said. "It's all in your head. It cannot hurt you. Try not to think of it and it'll go away."

Except it didn't. Relief only came when Robert moved out of the old family home to Kuala Lumpur.

✕

"What time are we leaving, Dad?" Rebecca asked, taking Robert out of his memories.

"In an hour or so, after we have lunch. You can go have a look around. Just make sure to meet me back at the main hall at 12.30, okay?"

Seeing his nine-year-old going off on her own little adventure in an art gallery filled Robert with so much pride that he was smiling to himself. Such curiosity at her age; her mother would have been proud. Instantly, his smile faded.

The thought of his ex-wife – the mother of his only child – never failed to dredge up the guilt he felt over how much he had failed the woman he loved. She was his muse, his first subject for the series of photos on exhibition today, and the one who from the start believed in his vision to shoot stylized portraits of regular people. *Extraordinary Portraits of the Ordinary* was as much her project as it was his, and yet she didn't live to see how far it had come.

If only he had stood up for her when she was being picked on by his mother. Being a man in the crossfire of a feud between his wife and mother over how his daughter should be raised, Robert should have intervened and put his foot down when his mother was overstepping her boundaries. Instead, he chose to step aside and turn a blind eye to it all, leaving the two most important women in his life to their animosity. If only he had fought for their marriage when his wife told him she couldn't take it anymore and decided to call it quits.

As he turned to leave the hall, Robert took a quick glance at the painting from the corner of his eye once more. His palms were cold and his heart rate elevated. That damn painting had caused the suppressed memory of a dream he had about two years ago to suddenly resurface.

In that dream, it was his wedding day all over again, but all the guests had somber expressions as if they were at a funeral. His bride was standing before him at the altar. When he lifted the bridal veil, she had a featureless slab of flesh for a face.

Robert now recalled that in his waking life at that time, he was in the midst of a messy divorce and custody battle with his then-wife. Despite his mother's objections, they had both agreed to amicably negotiate a shared custody arrangement. Three days after he had that eerie dream, on her way to meet him at the lawyer's office, she died in a car crash.

✕

The dusty storeroom beneath the staircase reminded Robert of museums; it reeked of old, abandoned things. The stuff in here probably hadn't been touched since the day his great-grandparents moved into the house. It was a surprise the florescent light bulb still worked when he flicked the switch. He had only ventured in here a few times as a child, and hadn't stepped foot in it since he moved out. He would have gladly ignored this part of the house, had his mother not sent him down here to get her a small wooden box.

Holding up a hand to cover his nose and mouth from the dust, Robert cautiously stepped inside and looked around. There were at least three generations' worth of possessions chucked in here, forgotten. It didn't take long for him to find what he was supposed to get. On top of a shelf was a black rectangular box, the only item not covered in a thick coat of dust, as if placed there just last night. It appeared to be a jewelry box with some kind of script he couldn't identify – ancient Chinese, perhaps – scribbled in red paint across the top of its black matte lid.

When Robert brought the box upstairs to his mother's room, she was seated up in bed, having a violent coughing fit and wheezing with every breath. He sat down on the edge of the bed beside her and proceeded to gently pat and stroke her back with cupped fingers. When she saw the item he was holding, the coughing subsided and she managed to catch her breath. Her sickly face brightened up with a smile as she took the box in her trembling hands, stroking its lacquered top. "Ah, the heirloom from my grandmother. When I am gone, it will belong to Rebecca."

"What's inside it, Ma?" Robert asked. He had to wonder what was so valuable in a box meant for his daughter that he'd only found out about now.

"When my grandmother – your Ah Chor – arrived in Malaya from China to marry my grandfather, she didn't expect her husband would turn out to be a philanderer, until her second child, my uncle, was born blind. He had given her a disease he got from fooling around with one of the hostesses at a nightclub. Little did *he* know," the ailing woman smirked, "she was no simple-minded fool. He had married a woman of the ancient ways. Your Ah Chor wouldn't have come all the way to a foreign land, to marry a man she never met, without some kind of insurance of her own."

Robert watched his mother open the box. Inside it laid a crudely carved wooden human figure, coated with some kind of yellow powder. A piece of folded red paper was tied to it by a red string. "Do you remember the faceless demon you used to see in your dreams when you were a child? You thought this house was haunted?" She chuckled and shook her head.

"That's no demon and this house isn't haunted. What you saw was our family's guardian spirit that watched over my grandmother." She paused and looked at Robert. "Do you remember the story of how your great-grandfather died?"

"It was a freak accident at the construction site he worked at, right? A beam collapsed and fell on his head..." *His head was so badly disfigured, his face was beyond recognition*, Robert remembered what his mother had told him. He felt his stomach knot up as his mother dug her fingers into the box and carefully pulled out a red envelope from underneath the wooden figure and handed it to him.

"You must understand, son, the spirit that protects our family is not inherently evil," she said. Robert proceeded to open the envelope and pull out an old photograph, one of those taken in a portrait studio in the early days of photography. It was a wedding portrait, bride and groom in traditional Chinese attire. The bride was seated on a chair, hands on her lap, looking straight into the camera with a neutral face. The groom stood beside her; his face was erased from having been scratched off with something sharp, leaving a white blank oval. Something that was stuck behind the photo fell off onto the floor beside Robert's feet. It appeared to be a lock of hair. His mother spoke again, "The spirit acts on its master's command. It can remove from her life those who have, or intend to, wrong or harm its keeper."

Robert looked up from the photo into his mother's spotted and wrinkled complexion; her eyes were cold and barely recognizable. Suddenly, the old woman's face before him looked nothing like the loving and reassuring presence he'd known his whole life. It was the face of someone nefarious...evil even, and he was scared of her. Scared to ask about the photo in his hand. As if reading his mind, she said with a smile, "That's my grandmother and grandfather."

He didn't need to know any further, but she went on, "This guardian spirit has been with us for five generations, passed down to female descendants. It needs a master, because its nature is such that it will latch onto and feed off the life essence of the males in the bloodline, if it is not contained and controlled. You saw it in your dreams and it tried to get to you, but it can never hurt you because I am here. I won't be for much longer."

She grinned a wicked grin. "Fortunately, before I was bedridden, I completed the ritual of binding the spirit to my successor. It will lay dormant for the next few years, until she's able to take control of it as its keeper, when she comes of age."

Robert shook his head. "Ma, what are you talking about? This is –"

"It's okay, son! Like I said, it's not an evil spirit. Rebecca will have it at her beck and call. It could protect her and help her attain whatever she wants throughout life, as it has done for me and my mother before me, and it will do the same for her daughter in the future. It is her birthright, you see! It's how we women who follow the ancient ways ensure our legacy lives on. All the spirit demands in return is a few drops of blood, shed on her monthly cycle."

His mother closed the box and held it out to him. When she spoke again, her voice was strained, "Otherwise, it will be your own life that's in danger! This spirit can cause you a lot of misfortune. It's going to feed off your life force until you become weak and ill, and waste away. You now understand why I insisted you must gain full custody of your daughter when that bitch filed for divorce. I couldn't stand that woman. She always had to be at odds with me, questioning everything I do for you and my grandchild. I only put up with her because of you, son. She didn't deserve Rebecca. I could not let her take away my only successor."

Robert was about to say something in protest, but his mother had another coughing fit and spat out blood, her eyes rolling upwards in their sockets.

✕

"Dad?" Rebecca called from behind him. "How long are we stopping?"

"It's just going to be a few minutes, girl," Robert replied. "Go wait for me by the car."

Standing by the Kedah River, holding the cursed box in his hands, Robert contemplated tossing it into the currents, sending whatever it contained far, far away from him and his daughter. He had not seen the box since his mother passed on two weeks ago. He thought he never would again, and that he could assume whatever his mother had revealed on her deathbed as nothing more than ramblings of a decrepit mind. That was until earlier today, at the reading of her will, when the lawyer handed it to him.

The old woman had left everything in her name to Rebecca, including that nearly century-old family home and the land upon which it stood. All these would pass on to his daughter when she turned 18, but she could only lay claim to her grandmother's estate if she had the box in her possession, which Robert as her sole guardian would have to hold on to for safekeeping, for the time being. In the next three to four years, or whenever her menstrual cycle began, the entity in the box would be bonded to her for life. The very thought of it made Robert sick to his stomach.

He lifted the lid, picked up the wooden figure and turned it in his hands. With his thumb, he pushed open the folded piece of paper tied to it. There, written on it in bold brush script, were the three characters that spelled out his daughter's Chinese name. He could feel the blood drain from his face. There was another unopened red envelope in the box. This one looked new; even the scent of the paper was fresh. Setting the figure back inside, he picked up that envelope, opened it and pulled out a photo.

It was one of his wedding photos – his favorite, in fact– taken with the Botanical Gardens as backdrop, by a fellow photographer whose work he admired. The smiling face of his then-wife was scratched off, rendering it a blank spot. There was a graininess to the surface of the photo, as if some kind of powder was rubbed over it. Robert turned the photo over to find a lock of hair, stuck to it by a dried yellowish paste.

He recalled his ex-wife's funeral; it had to be a closed casket wake, because her face was disfigured beyond recognition in the accident.

Covet

✕

Tina Ishak

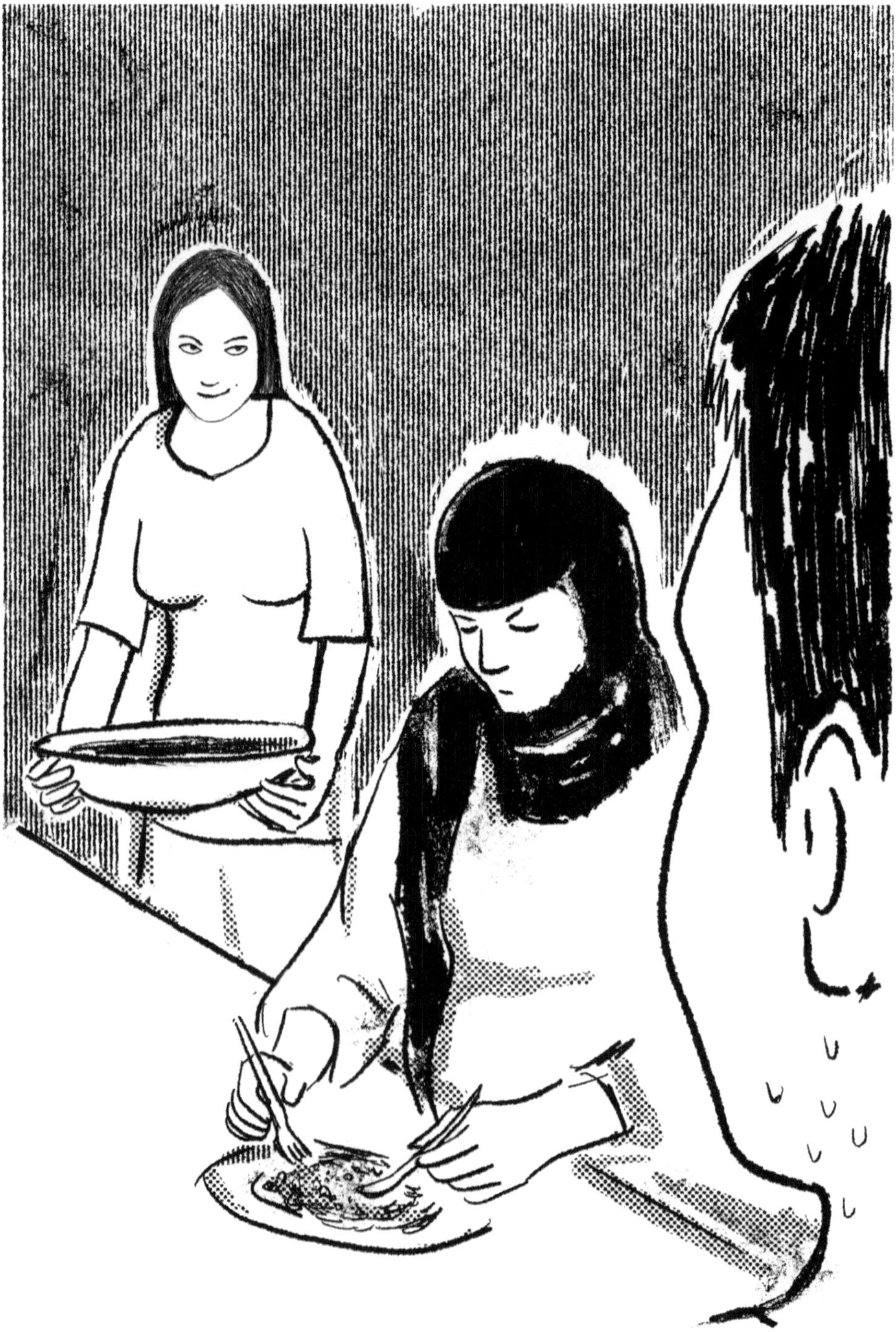

I never thought it was possible that everything I held true could be thrown into doubt in a matter of hours. Every smile, every loving gesture, every piece of encouragement. Lying on the sofa on my Sunday off, I couldn't believe the scene before me.

Two women stand in our living room. The woman screaming on my left – the one with the large protruding stomach – is my dear wife, Farrah. The girl shouting back at her on my right – dressed in a T-shirt over wraparound batik is our domestic maid, Lestari.

The two are going head-to-head while I sit there in a daze.

"It's a misunderstanding, Madam." Lestari's brown eyes are wide like a kancil frozen by headlights, her voice shaky. "I'd just finished showering. Then realized I'd left my clothes behind. And the towel. I was just making a quick dash to my room."

As if detached from my body, I observe Lestari's ordinarily well-kept hair has become a tangled bird's nest, her clothes sitting crooked. In contrast to our maid's dishevel, my wife looks great. Pregnancy certainly agrees with Farrah because she is radiant. In fact, she looks better now than she did on our wedding day eight years ago.

Still, I knew by now not to be fooled by Farrah's apparent calmness. When my wife gets pissed, she scares even me. And I have never seen her *this* pissed.

"Liar!" Farrah shoots back. "Walking around naked, showing your wares like a bitch in heat!" My wife shakes her head. "You were lying in wait for my husband to pass by, weren't you? You think I never noticed your behavior all this while?!"

"It's not true, Madam!" Lestari's voice is beseeching, her lips trembling. Her cheeks are red and blotchy. She looks back and forth before her eyes settle on me, as if I would step in and save her.

Not a wise move on her part.

As I anticipate, this only serves to escalate Farrah's rampage. "Don't!" she screeches, stepping up to block me from Lestari's view. "Don't you dare look at him."

"No!" Lestari shrieks, "I didn't mean anything by it, Madam." Lestari takes a step back, palms upturned towards my wife, a feather trying to hold back a tsunami wave.

Their screaming is incredibly loud. It's good that our bungalow in Tropicana is at the farthest end of the gated community and our nearest neighbor at least 20 meters away. I pray the sound doesn't travel across the expanse of the golf course which borders our home, that the words can't be made out by residents of the condominium across the green.

And thank God that Sofea, our seven-year-old daughter, is at her grandparents.

Farrah is not to be deterred. "Owh-oh…" my wife replies in a sing-song fashion, "you're saying you didn't have seduction in mind?!" Farrah tilts her head, looking the girl up and down. She releases a dry laugh. "An innocent girl shaves her privates as smooth as a baby's slit?" Her fingers make a double-hooking motion as she said 'innocent'.

I shake my head, trying to clear the image my wife's words conjure. Good thing that by the time I had arrived at the scene, Lestari was already dressed. My attempt to calm them down is interrupted when I was suddenly thrust backwards onto the sofa. I hadn't even seen anyone's hands move.

When I had tried to rise from my fall, a crippling headache wracked me, forcing me to collapse in agony. Even trying to concentrate my sight on the two women was a huge undertaking. The image seemed to waver, my eyes as if weighed down by a 20kg kettlebell. And my arms were as useless as limp noodles; I couldn't even wipe at the pool of sweat forming on my forehead. I could only observe the scene in disbelief.

"You think I don't know what you're up to? You think I'm a naïve Malay madam with no knowledge of what you young girls plan when you come to work here?" Farrah's voice rises. "You think I don't see you making eyes at him?!"

Lestari falls onto her knees, her hands clasped in supplication, her head swinging left to right. She is a sobbing, whimpering mess.

I push past the sounds and try to recall when things started going south.

Lestari has only been with us for two months.

It's been years since we'd had a domestic maid. Our last one, Mustika (we called her Kak Mus), an older lady hailing from Jogjakarta, had been with us for a few months after Farrah gave birth to Sofea. Despite her brief stint, Kak Mus had been a Godsend.

You see, Farrah had not been much of a homemaker nor a cook when we wed – clearly, this was a criterion no one considered important in selecting my bride. I had been a 34-year-old doctor with a relatively successful practice. My parents had grown tired of my reluctance to settle down and decided to take matters into their own hands. An arrangement was struck with Farrah's parents who they knew from their social circle. Although I had been upset with their scheming, I was besotted by Farrah as soon as we were introduced at a Raya Open house. We were wed within a year, and Sofea was born a year later. And despite our ups and downs, I grew to love my sweet Farrah.

We hit a rough patch when Sofea was born. Farrah was melancholic during confinement, taking some time to regain her good spirits. Kak Mus became the answer to my prayers during our family crisis. She took charge of our household, and I was able to head off every morning reassured that Farrah and our baby Sofea well taken care of. With my busy work schedule, it was a relief to return to a home that was spick and span and be served tasty meals.

I was more than a little bit sad when, just after Sofea celebrated her first birthday, Kak Mus had to leave under bizarre circumstances.

We had awoken that fateful morning to sounds of a commotion from downstairs. I initially thought we had a home intruder, so I left Farrah with Sofea upstairs in our bedroom, ensuring I heard the *click* of the door lock before I went to investigate. I found the outer door locked and Kak Mus all alone in the kitchen. The floor was strewn with broken crockery, and her hands were bleeding. She looked at me funny as I guided her to her room to clean the cut, and when we walked by the mirror lining our dining hall, she started screaming the house down. She grabbed my arms, shaking me, shouting "Apa ni, Abang?" to my face. It sent goosebumps all over my body – *I mean, how weird is it when your maid calls you "Abang", when she'd always called you "Encik"?* But it also felt *right*, strangely.

I couldn't comprehend what caused Kak Mus's hysterics. *Was it something I did?*

My interactions with our domestic maid were minimal. Mostly I just greeted her before heading out for work or thanked her when I ate her cooking. Otherwise, it was Farrah who spent all day with her.

Her grip on my arms was strong; it took some effort to extricate myself without hurting her in return. I called out to Farrah to fetch my medical kit, yelling loud to reach her in the bedroom. And, when Farrah joined me downstairs, Kak Mus's actions became eerier.

It is a moment that remains vivid in my memories: witnessing the kind lady who had been a boon to our household, tears streaming like rivulets down her leathery cheeks, rocking herself in the corner the rest of the day. "This can't be right, this can't be right," she kept muttering. It was heart-wrenching.

I called my contacts and soon got hold of a psychiatrist, Dr Wang, who was gracious enough to visit our home (for a fee) and examine her later that evening. Farrah revealed to Wang that she had seen Kak Mus acting erratically a couple of times in the past. I was livid that my wife hadn't confided in me sooner, and then Farrah got choked up, worrying about the harm that would befall Sofea if Kak Mus were allowed to remain in our household.

With the doctor's help, we kept her sedated in her room that evening. By the next morning, our six-bedroom bungalow became overrun with extended family, who insisted on being on hand to help "monitor" the situation.

Wang theorized that a mental switch must have flipped, triggering a psychosis in Kak Mus's mind. Apparently, according to the good doctor anyway, this happened sometimes when some women reached menopause. *Ya right,* I thought, giving the doctor the side-eye, but didn't have time to check for a better explanation because Farrah – and then her parents and my parents as well – started to lose their shit too.

After no improvement over a couple of days, it was with a heavy heart that I instructed the maid agency to return Kak Mus to her family in West Java. *Maybe they could do something for her?* The agency director shared our perplexity at her behavior. The older lady had been a strong, dependable, stalwart employee, treasured by all her previous employers, not prone to any problems, physical or mental, until then.

And imagine my surprise when Farrah turned down the agency's offer to get a replacement. My wife declared that, a year postpartum, she was ready to manage things herself.

I tried to dissuade her. My work schedule was busy – the medical practice was picking up; by then I owned eight GP clinics – which meant Farrah would be left alone with Sofea for long hours. And, after being coddled by Kak Mus' excellent housekeeping and cooking, I also worried Farrah would be overwhelmed. But as Farrah seemed so sure, I eventually relented.

And my wife proved me wrong when day after day she kept the house tidy and even started cooking surprisingly delectable dishes. I thanked my lucky stars for Kak Mus, who must have imparted some of her Nusantara-cooking skills before her unexpected departure.

I guess Farrah must have also felt she had something to prove, because she turned into a firecracker in the bedroom, evolving from the timid bride I remembered into an insatiable siren. Suddenly, we were trying things we had never attempted even when we were newlyweds. Things I had only seen women do in porn.

Without my realizing it, I began passing evening patient consultations to my colleagues, rushing through the workday and driving like a madman to get home. My weekend pursuits with my mates were substituted with family time. Even the medical conference getaways I used to love didn't interest me anymore. My colleagues were relentless with their teasing. *What could I say?* I was overcome with desire for my newly-improved wife and life.

Our household was a picture of contentment until, a couple of years later, Farrah suffered a miscarriage. She was morose for months, spent whole days asleep, and passed off Sofea's care to a babysitter. Over four years, she gained weight, her hair and appearance became haggard, the devastation clearly took a toll on her physical and mental wellbeing. She took to muttering Indonesian gibberish to herself – *Kak Mus's influence maybe?* – and I was at a loss as to how to help her. Even visits from her mother proved useless; in fact, Farrah seemed to withdraw further into herself when dealing with anyone except Sofea and I. It wasn't until Sofea started kindergarten that Farrah's mood really picked up again. My wife eventually signed up for rigorous gym classes, juggled in between household chores and ferrying Sofea to school. I also noticed her increased consumption of Indonesian herbal jamu – *Kak Mus's influence too, no doubt* – to help regain her figure.

When Farrah got pregnant a third time, I couldn't help but worry. "I'm perfect, Abang," she would say, throwing bright smiles my way. We had a medical scare in the fifth month when Farrah began spotting. We couldn't afford the past to repeat itself, so I put my foot down and did what any rational man in my position would do: I contacted the employment agent, demanding a new domestic helper ASAP.

I just never expected anyone so…*so young.*

Lestari's records said she hailed from Aceh and was 21, but she looked barely older than Form 5. The agency madam said it was the best they could do at such short notice. Their promise of a suitable replacement in a few months' time was useless because Farrah was already in her third trimester by the time Lestari arrived.

The moment Lestari stepped a dainty foot into our home, I knew she was going to be trouble. She was kinda a looker with straight, jet-black hair and porcelain skin. If she had come from better circumstances, I had no doubt she could have become a model or an actress.

I'm in love with my wife, but hey, I'm not *blind*.

And I also didn't miss the sly looks Lestari threw my way when she thought Farrah wasn't looking, eyeing me like I was a delectable piece of ikan bakar.

Maaannn…I felt violated every time.

I did everything to avoid being alone with her, making excuses to *not* be at home until late night, by which time Lestari had retired to her room.

I'm not sure if that change in my behavior was what triggered Farrah, but about two weeks ago, I noticed my wife's interactions with Lestari became increasingly tense.

I am knocked out of my reverie when I hear the two women start growling – yes! like harimau! – and I immediately notice the increasingly aggressive body language that accompanies their growls; their faces are so close, they are almost kissing.

"You think you're so great," I am amazed to hear Lestari say. There is a cruel sneer on her face, a 180° transformation from the submissive behavior she exhibited just a moment earlier. She pushes hard against Farrah's chest and turns away, as if an argument with Farrah is not worth her time, heading in the direction of her room – then pauses beside our baby grand piano and makes an about turn. "It's *you* who doesn't deserve him!"

I guess the girl is resigned to the reality that her jig is up.

"He wants me. You're blind if you don't see that," she continues, her voice dripping with disdain. "You're the worst kind of greedy, you know that? Who's to say Dr. Umar can't take another wife? Why can't you learn to *share* like so many do? He can certainly afford it!"

Puh-leez! I roll my eyes, hoping Farrah won't be persuaded by this girl's delusions. I mean polygamy is a thing with some Malay men, but she knew I'd never been a subscriber to that ridiculous way of life. *Farrah knows that, doesn't she?*

Looking at the disbelief on Farrah's face, I can't say I know for certain.

I was so preoccupied with this thought that nothing prepared me for when Lestari raises her left hand, sweeping it in my direction.

An excruciating pain hits me in the chest. It feels like a burning cattle-rod is being shoved into my heart. I groan, doubling over and slide off the furniture. I knock my head against the marble floor, barely missing our living room carpet, and taste copper on my tongue.

Suddenly, there is a booming roar: "No!"

I don't know if I hear it in my ears or in my head, but the sound reverberates in my cranium, rattling my jaw. The brutish tone seems to come from Farrah's mouth – *but this voice couldn't be my wife's, could it?*

In a flash, Farrah's hands whip out in the direction of the girl. I swear there is a distance of at least eight feet between the two, but somehow Lestari is struck. A gust of wind picks up the girl, slamming her into the wall. Then Lestari collapses into a heap on the floor like a broken doll, her limbs askew.

"I found the perfect man. The perfect life. Something I've always coveted," the booming voice continues, its pitch lilting. Then Farrah turns to face me. "Umar is…kind and caring."

I eye my wife with dread but am surprised to see that she now looks normal.

Gentle.

Loving, even.

"This beautiful house. The clothes and jewelry he buys me. All our luxuries. The way he holds me at night." Farrah's head swings back toward the girl. "And I've paid my dues. I deserve it! You think I want to return to Jogja? Have to scrimp and save every rupiah to pay off debts?! I gave up my old life. So that I could have *this* life!"

Wait. What?!

"You think *you* have powers?" Farrah's head tilts to the side and, even though her back is turned to me, I imagine her sizing up her enemy with disdain. "You're barely out of diapers. You dare covet what I have?!"

Then it's as if Farrah's shadow expands, looming over the body of the girl at her feet. "You dare challenge a master?"

Lestari's eyes become large as it dawns on her that she's met her match.

The monster inhabiting my wife's body begins singing a lilting but haunting tune. The sound flows and mesmerizes, and I have to struggle to prevent my eyes from drooping. I see a whirlwind building up in our high-ceilinged space, causing a furious whistling to accompany the deafening voice. The combined chorus amplifies and echoes around the living room. The curtains shake and billow, the chandelier in the stairway swings, the legs of our furniture rattle.

Farrah – or the *being* that resembles my pregnant wife – swings her arms a second time. Gashes form against Lestari's pale left cheek, from ear to nose. The girl's body slumps to the side, blood trickling out of the cuts, darkening the collar of her white T-shirt. The crimson stain spreads until her clothing hangs heavy over her form.

I see my wife's lips quiver as she mutters furious incantations at a low timbre. Then in a flash, everything becomes silent.

It's so quiet, you could hear a paperclip drop.

After a few moments, I realize I can hear the soft patter of rain outside, stark against the quiet. Then, another soft sound breaks the stillness. It's the weak mewl of a small creature.

And then I see it.

A tiny orange kitten is rolled up on the floor, sitting among the heap of blood-soaked clothing where Lestari once lay. The kitten mewls again, stands on unsteady feet and trots over to the threshold that separates our living room from the garden.

Farrah rushes forward, a bounce in her step, to open the sliding door, and the kitten obediently exits while I stare on in disbelief.

Then, she pulls the door shut and turns toward me.

I recoil when she stalks towards me. Farrah reaches down to the floor and grabs my stiff body. I must have at least 20kg over her – but, as if I'm no heavier than our daughter, she lifts me and gently lays me sideways on our sofa.

My eyes sweep over her face, now serene and gentle – the Farrah I knew from yesterday – but I am gripped with a fear so incapacitating that I am a trembling, panting mass of muscle.

This…this *being*, this monster, isn't my wife. *It is nothing but a fraud.*

I draw back as she climbs beside me, settles her soft and small body half atop, careful to angle her rounded stomach to the side. I'm too frozen in fear, I don't even react when Farrah reaches a hand to sweep my sweat-soaked hair back from my forehead.

"You see, Abang, there's nothing I wouldn't do to keep you all to myself," she says, her voice velvety again, "Not now I've *finally* got you."

I don't even dare shake my head at her, I am beyond horrified.

Her gaze is intent, reaching into my soul, while she takes my hand and places it over her pregnant belly. "We made this beautiful baby together, and we *will* be happy, just us…"

It is then that my brain plays catchup and I realize *when* I had lost my wife to this terrible creature. *My God!* I shake my head vigorously. My wife – my *real* wife – had asked me for help, but I had just stood by – let myself be instrumental even – in the substitution!

There is a shrewd look in the being's eyes, and then she grabs my jaw in her strong palms, angles her head, and presses her lips against mine.

I don't even have time to struggle.

Before I can take another breath, my mental and bodily aches clear like a smothering blanket snatched away from a suffocating child.

I blink, moving my sore neck, and look around the living room. I notice the cushions are strewn all over the floor. The curtains are akimbo, and carpet askew. There is a crumpled mess of some red cloths near the adjacent wall.

"What happened? Did I fall asleep?" I turn and look at my wife, who is awake and lovingly curled up against me on the sofa.

I find myself searching the space for answers. There is something I need to remember, but I don't know what. My heartbeat is galloping, but I can't be sure if it's from a dream or reality.

"Yeah," Farrah says, a twinkle in her eye, "I think I must have wiped you out with our morning activity." She gives a saucy wink as she reaches over to push my hair from my eyes. "And you never could resist an afternoon nap during the rain."

That vague whisper of a memory dissipates. It occurs to me I have no worries. No troubles. I live the perfect life with my perfect wife, my perfect family in our perfect home.

I pull her soft body close, inhaling the floral scent of her shampoo. "You're insatiable, even now, so late in pregnancy," I say, rubbing my palm over her stomach.

Farrah laughs aloud and I capture her lips again. "Shh…" I whisper against her rosy cheek. "You wouldn't want Lestari to hear us, would you? You'll scare the girl all the way back to Aceh or she'll go crazy like Kak Mus."

For a moment I see Farrah's eyes narrow, and then the expression clears so fast I'm not even sure it had been there at all.

My wife releases a gentle laugh. "Abang, actually, you're not wrong. Did you know she was not in her room this morning?"

"What?!" I exclaim, springing to sit upright, settling Farrah's body beside me on the sofa. "You mean she ran off?"

"Iya, Abang, I thinks so la," Farrah gives a nonchalant shrug, "Told you I saw her flirting with the golf caddy the other day. Dah agak dah. That girl is so miang! I'm surprised she lasted this long," my wife quips, her face a mask of disappointment.

"Astagfirullah…" I rub my palms down my face. "This is beyond ridiculous! Why can't that agency give us someone decent for once?"

"I already said, tak payah lah, Abang," Farrah says. "Fed-up lah. Would it be okay if I just go to my parents when the baby comes? I'll be fine, I promise," she juts out her bottom lip. "It's so leceh lah, having to train these Indon maids."

I release a fatigued sigh and respond with a reluctant nod as I lean my head against the sofa back. Maybe life is simpler without any outside help. "I guess I have to call the agency to report the runaway."

Farrah rises and, with a sprightliness that surprises me given her advanced pregnancy, snatches the fallen cushions, settling them back in place on the sofa. "You do that. I'll start on lunch. But…" she sends another wink over her shoulder, "You know…there's at least an hour before Sofea returns."

I make a rumbling sound in my chest and rise to chase her to the kitchen, beguiled by her enchanting giggles.

I marvel and thank the Almighty for granting me what most men covet: an amazing wife. And a marriage that seems to improve over time.

What can I say? *Happy wife, happy life.*

Death in the Power Station

✕

Muthusamy Pon Ramiah

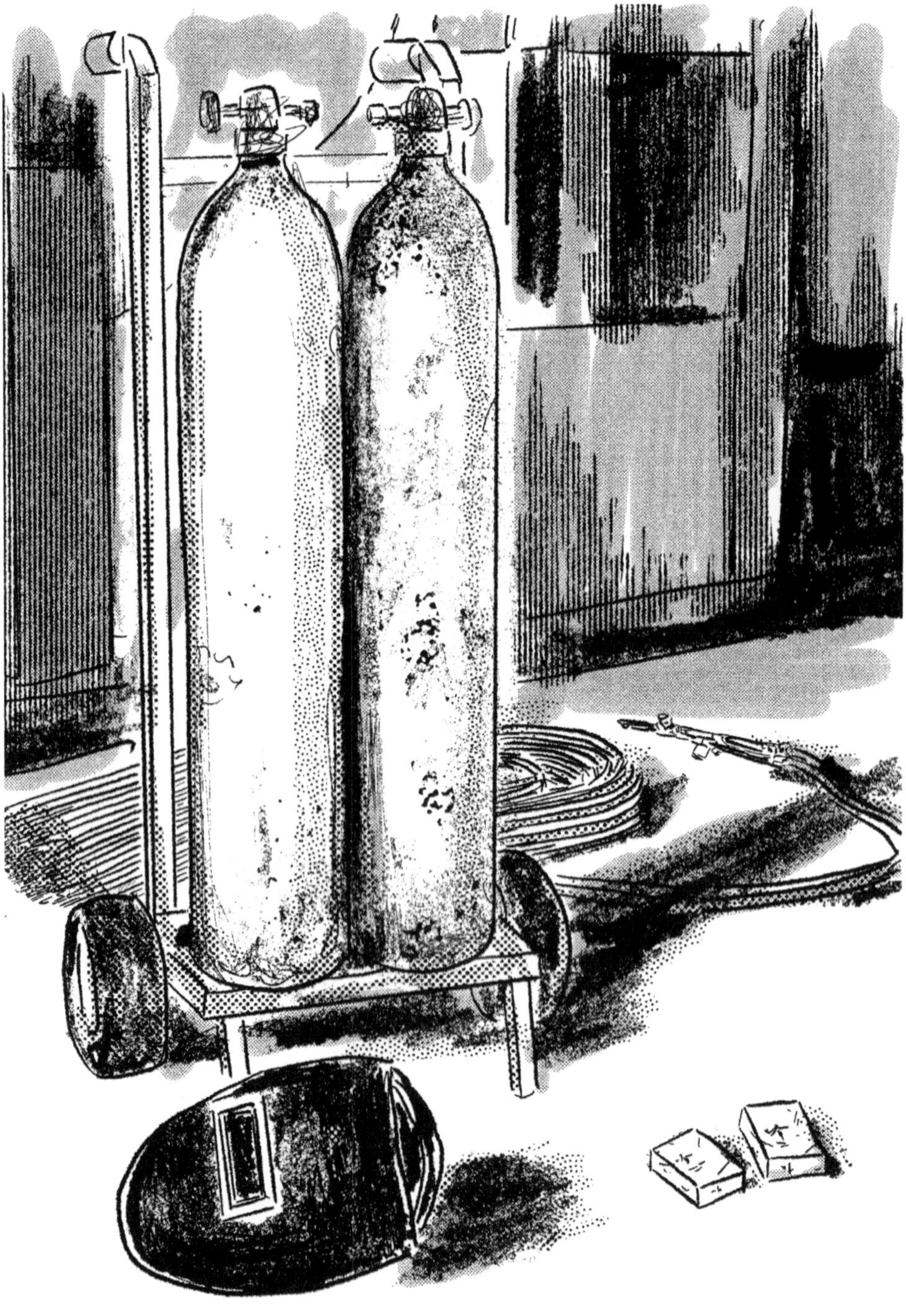

On the third day of Peter's one-week training and familiarization stint at the new power station, a man fell to his death. He missed Peter by a few seconds, a few feet.

After following Jamal Polytechnic on the morning rounds, Peter was tracing the feedwater line of Unit One when he heard the heavy thud close behind him. He scrambled away, his arms over his head, shoulders hunched, thinking it was one of the heavy sacks of asbestos slabs that were used for insulation. The dust rising from the impact was getting into his nose and eyes.

Standing at a safe distance, he rubbed his eyes and looked up. Nothing else was falling. Then he looked at the floor. A man was lying there on his back. Peter expected him to struggle to his feet, look around to see if anyone had seen, shake off the dust and walk away. But he did not move. Peter went closer.

It was the samurai, lying on the dusty floor, face up, his bloodshot eyes bulging. Peter had last seen the samurai about an hour earlier at the boiler drum level of Unit Two which was under construction. The samurai was leaning against the beam behind him, smoking a cigarette and smiling sardonically like he was amused at the way Jamal Polytechnic and he were going about their daily routine. Peter was holding a 555 notebook and noting down things.

Jamal Polytechnic said the man was Japanese. He was an expert high-pressure welder. The company that manufactured the boilers had sent him to weld the massive pipes that would carry the high pressure feedwater and superheated steam between the boiler and turbine once the unit was commissioned.

Like a samurai, thought Peter and the word stuck. Tall, broad-shouldered, the samurai wore a gray overall and a pair of black leather boots. He had combed his long hair back and tied it in a ponytail, a little high on his head. He sported a sparse mustache. He wore a black headband. His goggles rested on his head, above the headband. All the man needed now was the traditional samurai clothing and a sword in his hand, thought Peter.

Peter had turned and looked at the samurai as he followed Jamal Polytechnic to the steps, making his way between the massive pipes lying on the iron grill floor nearby, waiting to be welded together. Asbestos slabs in sacks were staked on one side by the railing. Knocking and scraping noises came from all directions. The place was swarming with construction workers, already sweating in the morning, their clothes covered in dirt, dust and grease.

Now Peter looked up at the boiler drum level. It was more than twelve stories high, just below the roof. The samurai must have fallen from there. Blood was flowing from his ears, nose, mouth and from under his head, soaking his ponytail. His legs were twisted below the knees, the fractured shin bones jutting under the overall leggings. The black leather boots were still on his feet, filling with his blood.

Peter felt faint. He was going to vomit. He placed his palms on his knees and bent down until the spell passed. He began to step backwards, his eyes glued to the body, expecting it to move one last time. It didn't. Soon the construction workers came shouting and running from all directions. There were so many of them, strong, hardy men. He could feel the strength of their arms as they brushed past him and surrounded the samurai. He could not see the samurai now, but the image of him lying on the dusty floor, the blood oozing out, his eyes bulging, was etched in his mind.

He went to the turbine side and sat on the steps and held his head between his knees, his heart pounding. He had taken a liking for the samurai in the short time he saw him up there on top of the boiler. It was the way he smiled, the ease with which he stood leaning against the iron beam like he had all the time in the world and how he smoked. The amount of blood oozing out of his body and spreading on the floor was unbelievable. Then Peter thought of himself, of what would have happened to him if the samurai had fallen on him. The sweat on his body began to turn cold, sending a shiver down his spine.

After a while, he walked up the two flights of stairs to the operating floor. From there he watched the crowd, the body sprawled in the center, the blood around the samurai's head looking black. The engineers from the power station and the construction companies came running and waved the workers aside and bent over and looked at the samurai. No one touched him.

After some time, a police patrol car entered the station. The construction workers began to struggle away. A policeman snapped photos of the samurai from different angles. Peter hoped none of the construction workers would remember seeing him alone with the samurai, looking at him at close range. He did not want the trouble of going to the mortuary to identify the body or to the police station to give his statement. He was a stranger in the power station and the two-street little town where he had rented a room in Eat First Restaurant and Hotel.

An ambulance entered the station without the siren on, its lights flashing. The samurai's body was placed on a stretcher, covered with a white sheet and placed in the ambulance and it left as it had come, silently, its lights flashing, like mourning for the samurai. The spot where the body had spattered had been marked and cordoned off. Peter stared at the bloody spot for some time before he went into the unit control room.

There, the other operators were all talking about the samurai and his death. The cold, air-conditioned room appeared too small for their loud, excited voices. Peter stood by the door and listened.

"He didn't make any noise as he fell. I only saw after he hit the floor!" said Senior Unit Operator Leong, his Mao forehead gleaming under the fluorescent lights.

"Pity lah, coming all the way from Japan and dying here like this. Good fellow, always smiling! In the canteen he would open a cigarette packet, take one for himself and then pass the packet around."

"Yes, a pity but I tell you, it was going to happen sooner or later! Then what? They are simply building power stations all over the place. After this station, I hear they are going to build another one on the east coast and send the electricity back to the west coast. Isn't that stupid? What big industries do they have there except fishing and now, oil?" asked Unit Operator Rajandran.

The others looked at him without saying a word. To them, it didn't matter where they built the power stations. The more power stations they built the better the chances of promotions for them.

"You see, they get permission from the state government for the land, borrow money from the banks or wherever and straight away start building", said shift laborer Mahmud. He was a local, from the nearest kampung by the sea. "Did they talk with the kampung people? No. They also did not ask permission from the dato who might be living in the trees. There may be a dato in the sea also. Not one tree or bush was left standing. They flattened the whole place like a football field and started piling work! All in a hurry. And now one life is gone!"

The humming of the turbine outside was a notch louder in the silence that followed.

"True lah. There may be a dato or djinn living in this place now! The station superintendent should call a bomoh to say some prayers. Must slaughter one or two goats and make the dato happy. Better if the kampung people are invited."

"The Kampung people say we always must ask permission when we enter other people's houses. Same with the dato. We must ask permission. Even to pass urine we must say sorry and then pass urine. The dato may be sleeping on the ground or resting against a tree trunk. You cannot go and pass urine on him! Once a big branch fell on a man as he was passing urine against a tree trunk. People suspect he didn't ask permission or say sorry! The man was bedridden for life!"

"I remember, many years ago in the old station, the first thing the contractors did was call some priests to say prayers and slaughter a few goats for the dato and called the people from the nearby estate to eat before they cleared the earth and started construction. Nothing bad happened. Even now the small tokong is there behind the workshop. It's a Chinese dato with a long white beard," SUO Leong said. "But I hear nowadays the fellows go to him and ask for four-numbers!"

Someone laughed.

"Whatever it is, we are very lucky lah! It was not one of us."

"Yes, but we don't know whether it will stop with the Japanese man or look for more lives!"

"Now, come on lah! It was just an accident," said Peter. "It happens. Do you all still believe in all the dato-datin stories in this time of science and technology? When Jamal Polytechnic and I went up, we saw him. He looked okay. He was leaning against the iron beam and smoking his cigarette happily. Maybe he fainted and fell through the side railings."

They, the ones who had been in the newest, biggest power station in the country for more than a year, regarded him skeptically.

"I think the dato or djinn waited and waited, but nobody did anything for him", said Mahmud. "Nobody showed any respect or said sorry. So now he is showing his anger. See from what height the man fell! I think the dato waited for him to keep going up, welding the pipes floor by floor until he was right at the top!"

"Leong, you better talk to the station superintendent. Tell him to talk to the contractors and make them sacrifice one or two goats for the dato. Then the dato won't cause any trouble."

SUO Leong raised his eyebrows.

"If the SS tells, the contractors will listen! Chinaman to Chinaman can kowtim! The money won't be a problem for them. Sap sap sui!" said Rajandran.

"Better to get them to do it fast, before the construction work is over. Once over, the contractors may not do anything!"

"True, what do they care? They will collect their money and go away. But we will be working here until we retire. And we got a new assistant operator. Peter is going to walk up to the boiler drum to check the gauge-glasses until he gets his next promotion or retires!"

"Hei, don't talk like that! Peter, you don't worry lah. Nothing will happen. The dato has already taken one life. He won't disturb anybody anymore. But better to be careful. Wear your helmet. This new power station is not like your old one."

Peter wished they would stop talking about it. He didn't tell them that the samurai had just missed falling on him. He didn't want them to think of him as a man marked for death, the one next in line.

The next morning when he went to work, there was no sign of the blood. They had covered the blood with sawdust and scraped it away. The remaining sawdust was in a sack by the steps. The cordon was still there with two **DILARANG MASUK** signs. People kept looking from a distance as they went about their work.

In the unit control room Jamal Polytechnic said he was not well. He looked pale. Fever, he said. They laughed at him and asked whether he was afraid. He ignored them and left for the dispensary. Later he called and said he was on medical leave for the day. Leong, instead of calling someone to work overtime, told Peter to take over Jamal Polytechnic's place. Peter felt he was not ready, especially after what had happened, but he went out of the unit control room without saying a word, a piece of rough paper and a ballpoint pen in his shirt pocket, the small hook spanner in his hand and the piece of cotton rag half-hanging from his trouser pocket.

After checking all the motors and valves in the basement and noting important readings from the gauges, he walked up the steps. When he reached the boiler drum level, his knees were unsteady. Sweat was running down his hairy legs and his khaki uniform shirt was sticking to his back. He found the samurai's oxy-acetylene gas cylinders and the welding equipment and welding rods where he had left them. Two empty cigarette packets were lying on the floor. Japanese brand. Peter felt like the samurai was there with him. His heart began to pound. He felt dizzy. Moving away from the side railing, he squatted, his eyes closed tight. More sweat.

A while later he felt better. When he opened his eyes he saw the dirty, safety shoes first. Then the faded jeans, frayed at the knees and then the sweat-soaked singlet. He looked up. A Malay construction worker was standing in front of him. His wrinkled checker shirt was tied around his hips. He had long, unkempt hair.

"Brader, you oright?" the man asked. There was a lit cigarette between his fingers. The smoke smelled of incense and clove.

Peter got up slowly, wiping his face.

"Felt a little dizzy. I think I walked up the steps too fast," he said.

"You should take the lift lah brader."

Peter pointed at the lift. It was switched off for the day shift because construction workers were not supposed to use the lift. They were loading their heavy tools and things in the lift, leaving dents and scratch marks on the doors. They also left rubbish and urine inside. There was graffiti on the walls and doors.

"Brader, you want me to walk down with you?" the man asked

Peter shook his head. After the man left, Peter wondered whether he was real or a dato. The smell of incense and clove lingered. Then he realized he was standing alone on that floor with the samurai's welding equipment. He quickly glanced at the drum gauge-glasses, noted the water level and walked down the steps, holding the railings tightly.

$$\times$$

Wednesday. The last day of the one-week training period. At the end of shift Jamal Polytechnic handed over the hook spanner and the locker key to Peter. Jamal's days as assistant unit operator were over at that moment. He was not going to walk up to the drum level anymore or do any work outside of the air conditioned unit control room unless there was an emergency. Peter would take over the duties of checking the meters and valves and going up to the drum level two day later, starting at midnight on Saturday. Nothing to worry, he told himself as he added the locker key to the Vespa key and the room key.

He left for home that evening to spend the two off-days with his family. The news of the samurai's death had already reached them. He assured his worried wife and daughters that it was just an accident. It was safe for the station staff as long as they kept out of the cordoned-off areas where construction was going on. But his heart was heavy when he thought of the samurai and how he had died. The next evening, he went to church with his family and prayed. Father Sabestian said a special prayer for him and blessed him. The Lord will be with you, the priest said.

Peter left for work late Friday evening after an early dinner, riding his old Vespa slowly along the narrow road winding through palm oil estates, kampungs and jungle. There was no other light along the road except for the dim yellow light from his Vespa.

He had not expected to take over duties in the midnight shift. But he was proud of his long work experience, his flawless service record. He was proud of the fact that he was one the few workers who never slept during the midnight shift. He felt he would do the same here in this new station, do his work well, dato or no dato. The promotion had been long overdue. He had been promoted after ten years and four grueling and demoralizing interviews.

After the third unsuccessful interview, he decided to fight. He went to the local union branch secretary. The union secretary, a young fellow who was new to the position, accused the management of discrimination against the rank-and-file, less educated workers on whom the old station had been depending all through the years. He knew that a batch of young fellows from the polytechnic would be reporting for training in the station soon. They had paper qualifications but no experience, the union secretary argued.

The twenty fellows from the polytechnic descended on the old power station one morning in a group, all of them riding motorcycles. Like it was all pre-arranged, like they were a gang. The older shift workers felt uneasy. They suspected that the boys from the polytechnic were there to learn work from them, then grab all the future promotions and gradually lord over them. One morning the boys were assigned to the three shifts. Jamal Polytechnic was assigned to him. Jamal Polytechnic was so different from what he thought. He was friendly and respectful. Soon Peter and Jamal Polytechnic became friends.

There was a fat, balding Ceylonese man on the panel at the fourth interview. He asked all the questions in pasar Malay and roared with laughter every time Peter answered a question, leaving him confused. Peter felt all the questions were aimed at finding out how much he did not know, and use that to not promote him. The personnel officer from headquarters, who was not an engineer, kept looking at him under his eyebrows. At the end of the interview, he asked Peter whether he was willing to go on transfer to the new power station if promoted. Peter felt that was another ploy to deny him the promotion. Although in his twenty years of service he had never been transferred to any other station, he said he would go. It was now or never for him.

He did not hear anything for a month after the interview. Then his shift engineer gave him the letter and told him to report at the new station in a week's time. His colleagues who had not expected him to get the promotion discouraged him. They asked Peter why he wanted to go so far away when he was past forty and all his children were still in school. It might be difficult to get places in the new school in the small town in the middle of the year, they reasoned. They also pointed out that although he was going to be a technician, he would be third in rank in the new station whereas he was already second in rank at the old station.

Peter felt they were jealous. For him it was a matter of pride. Besides, it was a double jump, from junior technician straight to technician. He would be equal in rank to the polytechnic boys. And the maximum salary was so much higher.

✕

When Peter first entered the new power station, he felt he had made a big mistake. He felt lost. The concrete floor was vibrating under his feet as he stood looking at the turbine and up at the boiler. He had not imagined the boiler and turbine would be so huge. The turbine was like a few mammoths lying together on their stomachs with the smallest one at the end, all painted in light blue. To his left was the boiler. Peter could only see the three burner galleries. The rest were blocked from view by the row of huge pipings.

He hesitated to walk into the unit control room and introduce himself. Standing outside, he looked at the big control panel inside. It was three times bigger than the one in the old station. A schematic diagram covering the entire top portion of the panel was littered with tiny green, orange and red lights that blinked now and then. It appeared like a spaceship. But he told himself that if others, some of them from the old station, could do it then he with all his experience should be able to do better. His wife and children would be disappointed if he backed out. He would lose face with his former colleagues who he thought were waiting for him to fail.

Just then he saw Jamal Polytechnic, formerly from the old station, walking down the iron steps from the top burner gallery. A shift laborer was following him. Jamal Polytechnic led Peter into the unit control room and introduced him to the other operators. The shift engineer was in the room. After reading the appointment letter he gave Peter a week to follow Jamal Polytechnic around and learn the work and then take over from him. Jamal Polytechnic had been promoted to Unit Operator.

Peter realized he was going to work under Jamal Polytechnic who had learned work from him just two years ago. He had no choice but to swallow his pride and carry on. Being a technician and getting a hundred and thirty ringgits extra in salary immediately was a big thing for him. There was still a chance he would be promoted to unit operator like Jamal Polytechnic if he did well in the new position. He could retire with a bigger pension.

As he entered the control room just before midnight, he found the evening and night shift operators talking excitedly about the samurai and how he had died. Some of them were talking as though they had seen it happen. He felt like telling them that he had seen the samurai before he died and moments after he hit the floor but it was something he didn't want to even think about. He learnt from their crossed-line conversation that the police had determined the samurai's death was an accident. The post mortem confirmed it. There was no eyewitness to prove otherwise. The case was closed and the samurai's mangled body had been flown to Japan that morning.

"But remember, he has left behind his blood," someone said.

"But the contractor's workers covered the blood with sawdust and let it soak and then scraped it and put it all into a box and took it away."

"Yes, I heard that, but don't tell me they sent the box all the way to Japan. It must be buried somewhere here. "

May his soul rest in peace, whispered Peter, as he stepped out of the unit control room to go on his round. The electric clock on the beam showed thirty minutes past midnight. He looked above. The rows and rows of fluorescent lights from the high roof of the turbine hall made the place look like a lighted arena waiting for the crowd. Only he was standing outside. The other shift staff were inside the control room. They appeared to be moving in slow motion as they went about their duties, checking the meters, preparing new log sheets and changing the charts on the panel. Leong was putting on his old cardigan.

Peter whispered a prayer and turned to the other side and crossed himself and walked down the steps on the turbine side, away from the stairs near where the samurai had fallen to his death. He checked every meter, every valve, and noted down important readings on the piece of rough paper with an unsteady hand. Then he heard the horn. He went to the telephone by the iron pillar and called the unit control room. Leong told him to go up. Load was going down. He had to take off a burner. He felt so relieved as he walked up the steps. He felt he may not have to climb up the stairs to the drum level, after all.

Jamal Polytechnic was reducing load, his eyes darting from indicator to indicator, the flowcharts and the meters on the panel. Peter went to the bottom burner gallery with Mahmud and switched off a burner and watched as Mahmud cleaned the smoking burner and left it on the burner rack. The load was stabilized. Peter hung around watching Jamal Polytechnic do his work. Leong told Peter there was no need to take off any more burners. Peter knew he was being told to go on his round.

There is nothing to worry, Peter told himself as he climbed the steps. There is no dato, there is no djinn. He paused on the second landing. There is no dato or djinn. It was an accident. He walked up two more flights of stairs and paused, not because his legs were tired but his heart was cautious. At the fourth landing he felt he could turn around and walk down the steps slowly, hang around in the middle burner gallery for about half an hour and then walk down and enter the unit control room with enough sweat on him and write down the usual things on the bottom of the log sheet and sign it and pretend he had gone right up to the boiler drum level and checked the drum gauge-glasses. No one would know. But what would happen if someone was observing him on his first day? And how long was he going to cheat on his job and keep the fear in his heart? Whether he liked it or not he would have to work seven nights a month. He chanted a religious song that used to come on the radio on Sunday mornings and evenings in those days before it was discontinued. But after a while even that felt difficult. His mouth was going dry.

There was a sharp hissing sound as he passed the superheater area at the seventh landing. Steam was shooting out of a pinhole leak on the joint of a pressure gauge. Luckily we came, he thought but he didn't go too close to the gauge. He noted the name of the pressure gauge on the rough paper and continued to climb. He felt he was sweating more than usual, the extra sweat from something other than the heat. He walked up another flight of stairs, now breathing through his mouth. No dato, he muttered. Sweat was running down his legs. Holding the railing with one hand, he looked down at the ground floor briefly to see if anyone was watching him. He couldn't see a soul. The huge wooden crates looked like discarded shoeboxes. Some parts of the dusty floor were in the shadows. He continued to climb.

He was three landings below the drum level. He kept his eyes away from the boiler under construction to his right and continued to climb. Before he reached the next landing he felt a crawling feeling on his feet, spreading up his legs. He stomped on the steps, trying to kill it off. The crawling stopped but he felt there was something inside his trousers, waiting to crawl.

He paused one landing below the boiler drum level. It was very bright now. Two headlights had been left on above the boiler drum. The beams and scaffoldings around him threw strange shadows. No dato, no djinn! He didn't feel any better. He decided to turn around and walk downstairs and go back to the safety of the unit control room. Holding the railing tightly, he turned around. Something caught his eyes. Instead of walking down, he stood still for a moment and then looked up. The samurai was standing on the landing above and looking at him.

Dead Men Don't Close Calls

✕

Ethan Matisa

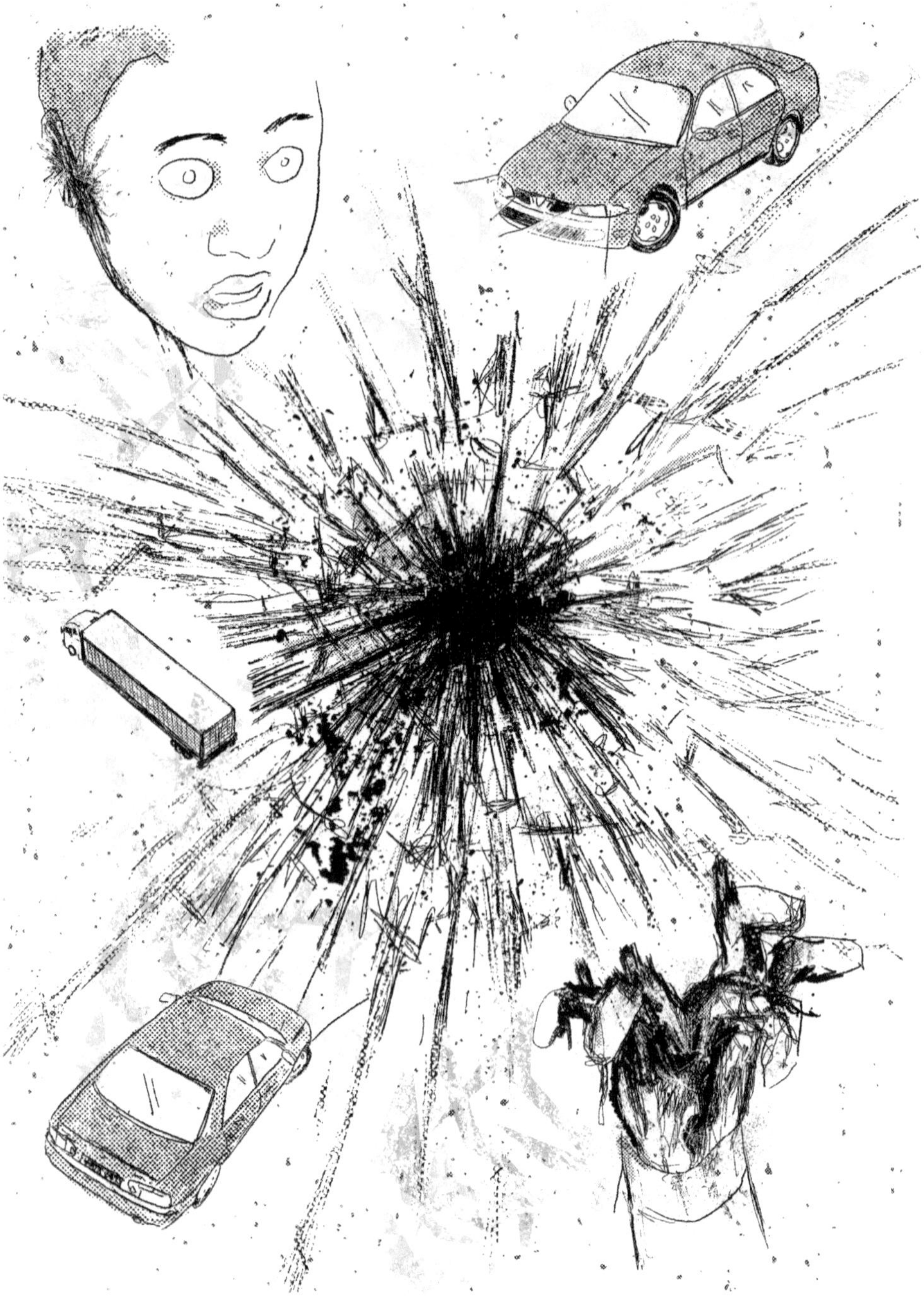

It was a blue Proton Wira that nearly hit Spencer Lim that morning – a sickly, cerulean blue, a color he soon grew to resent. In his mind, Proton Wiras should be dull rustbuckets, not this youthful, almost naive-looking thing he saw out of the corner of his left window. Spencer had his foot flat on the gas pedal, trying to pass the Wira on the right. He'd already put his signal light on; you had to give him credit for that. Up ahead was a red light, and just twenty yards in front of Spencer was a parked trailer.

The Wira, goddamn him, was speeding up, too – and with the trailer getting nearer by the second, Spencer sucked in his breath, kicked down harder on the pedal, and swooped to the left.

He narrowly missed smashing into the tail end of the trailer –

And then he kept going. *Lucky that trailer was sitting to the right of the lane*, he thought, in a frantic haze, conscious of nothing except his need to get into the left lane. In his rearview mirror, he saw that the Wira was right on his ass, so close that its headlights were obscured from view.

If he slammed on the brakes now, he'd get rear-ended. The bastard in the Wira was matching his speed and didn't seem to give a damn.

Cursing, he gently pumped the brakes, gradually bringing himself to a halt at the red light. Behind him, the blue Wira slowed and stopped, still too close for comfort.

Spencer let out a sigh, and then grinned to himself. Now that that heady moment of adrenaline was over, perhaps he could congratulate himself on, oh, being alive. Jeezus, did he have to be such a hothead all the time? He'd made it into the left lane, and he'd avoided becoming a Wira-and-trailer sandwich by inches. Hell, it was a miracle he was still alive and breathing right now. The trailer had given him just the barest amount of space to squeeze past, so small it was almost nonexistent. God, he was lucky to be alive…

He had a sudden image of himself smashed face-first against his steering wheel, blood trickling down his chin, his forehead pulverized and bits of skull leaking out into an inflated white airbag – and blinked it away.

"It didn't happen," he said. "Knock it off, Spence."

He laughed to himself and snuck a look at the Wira driver in the rearview mirror. The driver's face was washed out in the morning sunlight, barely visible. No matter. Spencer noticed that his fingers had begun to feel awfully sore, probably from gripping the steering wheel too tightly.

It was 7.49 on a Wednesday morning, traffic was starting to build, and now his goddamned fingers were aching, too. It was going to be a swell asshole of a day.

✕

There are no good days in customer service. Spencer's senior, a grizzled older guy named Ravi, had told him that on his first week – no good days, only good callers. And that's something you make for yourself. Well, it had been two years at WX Banking, and he still had no idea how Ravi did it, but he was trying, wasn't he?

On his way up to the office, he passed a monitor that showed the number of employees in the walkway. Right now, it was fixed at "0." Probably a glitch. The photo-sensitive trackers were prone to alarm. Like everything else that went wrong at this Cyberjaya office, it was just another thing that didn't need extra attention.

Spencer settled into his desk at 8.03 and flipped his laptop open, hurriedly typing in his password while he bit back the pain from his fingers. Three minutes too late. No, four. A shadow fell over him: Murali, his colleague and occasional coffee-mate.

"Keep up this tardy timing, and the boss is going to chew you out," Murali said in a low whisper. "You know he's been chasing you, and even I'm beginning to hear about it. Why you gotta piss him off?"

"I don't do this on purpose." Spencer didn't take his eyes off the screen – the database was loading, loading, loading. "I can close three deals before lunch, I just know it."

"All right, man. Whatever you say." Murali clapped him on the shoulder before walking off, and added in a low whisper, "Just don't crash and burn."

Whatever that meant.

The database finally finished loading, and long scrolling lists appeared, white and blue. A red flag near the top flashed: **3 CALLS PENDING.** Already, a massive headache was rumbling to life in his skull.

He put on his headset.

✕

"Well, ma'am, I'll file a closing on your protection account this afternoon and transfer the remaining balance to your main, but it will take at least two working days till we get confirmation from the system."

"Why can't you get back to me by the end of the day? It's a Wednesday, young man. If it were the end of the week, I'd understand, but as it is –"

She'd gone into what Team B called the Dissatisfaction Rant. Spencer nodded, barely listening as the woman on the other end – probably an upper-class rich lady with two kids in a private school, one attending piano classes in the evening and the other enrolled in football and archery and running – gave him a right piece of her mind. He made a few noncommittal "yeah" and "uh-huh" noises (this was a great way to let the customer know you were on their side, that you sympathized, and in many cases, it made the Dissatisfaction Rant wrap up faster, saving valuable call minutes).

His eyes flicked upward to the frosted glass screen of his cubicle. A large yellow bumblebee flashed a thumbs-up. A speech bubble proclaimed: "THE DAY IS NOT GOOD OR BAD, IT'S WHAT YOU MAKE OF IT!"

Wise words to a rookie, maybe, but now it was little more than office-cubicle decoration. Spencer winced. The talons of his headache now felt like actual fishhooks digging into his brain.

"Ma'am," he cut in, against his better judgment, "may I ask when the protection account was set up? If I know, I could probably get it processed faster."

"Last October. Honestly, young man, I didn't even want to, I was just talked into it by another one of your…"

A pregnant pause of someone who is clawing around trying to find something that isn't a curse-word.

"… office boys," she said at last.

Spencer raised his eyebrows. "Well, if you recall his name, I could check with him and –"

"Raza. No, wait, Riza. Khairul Riza."

Khairul Riza had jumped ship two months ago for a supervisory role at RHB.

"I'll work with him to close the account ASAP, ma'am," he said, biting back his frustration. "Is there anything else I can do for you?"

"If you can get me a reply before today evening, that would be great."

Of course she would say that. Of course.

"I'll do what I can." He ended the call – it had lasted twenty-six minutes and forty seconds – and sighed.

Right on his left, his cubicle-mate Albert turned to him, flashed a thumbs-up, and tilted his head upwards: *Close it?*

Spencer made a slicing motion at his throat: *No. Didn't manage.* He mouthed: *Riza.*

Albert gave a knowing grimace – and without missing a beat, went right back into his own call, while scrolling through a page of stock-investment graphs on his Huawei. In a practiced drawl, he said: "Actually, Miss, we have various investment packages which you could take a look at…"

Spencer jotted a note down on a nearby scrap of paper: *Terminate the Yong acct.* His headache was getting even worse. He put a hand up to his forehead, massaged it, and felt something warm and sticky.

Spencer pulled his hand away and looked down. His fingers were coated with blood, dark crimson and drying – and best of all, they were smashed into crooked, misshapen shapes that looked like twigs with splinters of gray bone sticking out of them.

But that was crazy, he couldn't be –

A sharp, ululating cry pierced the air – his desk phone was ringing.

He blinked, looked back down at his fingers again, and breathed a sigh of relief.

Sweat.

Nothing but sweat. That was all the warm, sticky feeling had been – just a build-up of sweat on his forehead, from all the stress.

In an air-conditioned office.

Yeah, that was perfectly reasonable. It was half past ten in the morning, and he'd only managed to close one case. Of course he would be sweating a little –

His desk phone let out another ringing cry, this one seemingly sharper than the last. A devil-red light was flashing on the device. He snatched the receiver up, and as he did, he was sure he saw flecks of blood and brain matter sticking to his fingers.

"WX Banking Customer Service, how may I help you today?" he said automatically, without thinking.

"In fact, Spence old boy, I was thinking about how I may help *you*." The voice on the other end hissed like an ancient snake: it sounded gritty, full of earth, like something that had been buried. Spencer felt a chill, and a fresh wave of pain rolled through his head.

Prank caller. I've got a prank caller. It wouldn't be his first. Hell, it wouldn't even be his fifth. All he had to do was blow it off and he'd be back to regular calls, calls that could make him actual money.

"Sir, I'm not sure who you are, but this kind of thing isn't funny, and I have other clients to see to. I'll hang up now." He reached out and thumbed the switch. It sank with a satisfying click.

Yet the earthy voice on the other end continued to speak.

"That's not a very nice way to say hello, Spence." The guy, whoever the hell he was, spoke in a mock wounded tone that pissed Spencer off to no end. "Aren't you wondering how I know your name? That's the first question they usually ask, ya know. *'Oh, how did you know my name?'* You're not even a little bit curious?"

Spencer depressed the call switch again. It poked out of the well where the earpiece of the receiver would usually sit, looking like a plastic tongue, and was very much real and not streaked with dried blood from his thumb (which wasn't broken, by the way).

"Don't try that shit around here." The voice was suddenly stern. Spencer sat up straight. "Don't you know that dead men don't close calls?"

"What?" His voice was shaky, spooked, cold, despite knowing that this was just a nobody trying to sound tough, a nobody who probably still lived with his parents.

"Ah, questions, questions. Soon, you will have answers – but the answers you seek may be closer than you think. How about we start with the one right in front of your caved-in face? Look up. That's right, look up from your screen right now, and maybe you'll see."

Already, the sheer force of his own curiosity was tugging his head upward. "No," he breathed hollowly. "No, no." He fixed his eyes on his laptop's webcam-hole, anything, anything to stop from looking up.

In the end, his curiosity won, and his gaze flicked upward, with the ease of someone slipping on a warm and well-loved shoe.

The frosted-glass surface of his cube was a long, shattered pane, spiderweb cracks radiating outward from a hole punched through the center. Sunlight glittered on shards of glass, giving them a glazed, sugary appearance. Spencer could see blurred movement through the broken glass – and he was sure it wasn't the guy sitting on the opposite end of his desk. Far too colorful. Far too many shining reflections. They were moving like –

Like cars, dear God, they're moving like cars.

Air was coming in through the hole in his windshield. He wouldn't let it. Couldn't. He'd kill himself before he ever –

Spencer squeezed his eyes shut, and felt blood pounding in his ears with the force of a thousand drums. His headache was splitting now.

When he opened his eyes, the prank caller was cackling.

"Starting to get it now, are you? Starting to piece it together? Oh, Spencer. Nobody who's ever gotten into an accident is ever proud to admit it, not even to themselves – something as stupid and careless as this, believe me, I can understand why you –"

"Shut up," he said flatly. "Shut up, shut up, shut up." He pushed the switch, and his shaking finger slipped off.

Why were his fingers still hurting, dammit? He hadn't done anything to them. Not a damn thing. In fact, the only thing he'd been doing was –

"– starting to wish you'd never tried to race that stupid blue Proton, huh? I bet you 're starting to wish you'd driven slow and steady this morning. Well, it's hard to shake off old habits, Spence, old boy, but let me tell you this, you won't have a problem anymore, now that you've been –"

– gripping the steering wheel tightly at the traffic light, after his near-miss with the blue Proton. A little tighter than usual, but nothing that would have injured his fingers, for goodness' sake. Hell, the pain he was feeling now was the kind of pain he'd feel if his fingers had been –

"– shattered in the crash, you know? Come on, let's not pussyfoot around this. It's simple physics, old buddy – if you're hit from the back by some crazy fucker who's racing you, that's going to slam you forward, really hard and REALLY fast, and when that happens in such a short time, the whiplash is incredible. That's the reason your body is –"

– bent backwards and flexed and broken, then left to hang. Nothing else would explain the pain in his fingers, which had started as a strange soreness out of nowhere, and had grown to absurd proportions. Then there was the question of his headache, which now felt like it was extending beyond the confines of his skull. He remembered having headaches like these on odd Saturday mornings in college, after drinking seven shots of Jack and somewhere around a dozen glasses of semi-warm, somewhat stale Heineken the night before – waking up with his jaw pooched out on his pillow, his arms splayed out, his knees –

"– buried all the way up in your chest, yes, that's the way it is, and you really have to face it now, Spence, because if you don't face it there's nobody else to face it for you, nobody except you, yourself, and the Great Yawning Judgment beyond. Here's the kicker, though: Your kneecaps were so badly shattered that they turned into jagged little rocks of fragmented bone, sharp as icicles, and when they punctured your ribcage, well, they… not to put too fine a point on it, Spence, but they pierced your heart so bad that blood –"

– splayed out on the mattress, and the early-afternoon light streaming through his window feeling like daggers against his skull. This headache was just like those college-day hangovers, except he'd never felt one quite as horrible. This felt like actual icepicks had sunk into his scalp, digging deep and pulling up freshets of blood.

Oh, what the hell. It was just a grand asshole of a day – everyone working at this armpit of a company had at least two each year – and today, the grand wheel of misfortune had shuddered to a halt and made him the victim. Spencer only wished it had happened a couple of hours earlier, so that he could have called in sick.

And now this smartass was trying to pull a fast one on him for cheap laughs. *Wasting valuable company money – and any chance of me closing an ACTUAL commission.* The thought inflamed him, and he found his voice rising through his crumpled throat like wildfire:

"I don't know who you think you are, and I don't care about whatever script you had prepared for this." He licked his lips and swallowed, hoping the guy on the other end couldn't hear how terrified he was, and his saliva went down his dry throat like a ball of chewed-up paper. "But I don't have time for this. I've got real clients to get to."

He reached out for the switch in the earpiece well one last time.

"What do you mean, you don't have time? You have all the time in the world now, Spence. You're no longer bound to the earth of mortals, time isn't a dimension that defines you. You're beyond. You're transcended. You're OUTSIDE."

Spencer rested his finger upon the switch-button, felt its cold, reassuring weight.

"I'd advise you not to feel bad, though, old chap. Why, just last Saturday, we received a guy eaten by wild boars up in Terengganu, when his Nissan crashed into a side-shoulder and the engine caught fire. An ugly way to go, but don't worry, he was cooked to death long before the pigs found him. A tasty meal he did make –"

"That's it." Spencer depressed the switch-button, felt it sink all the way and clack down in the well. "You're not funny."

Nothing.

Silence.

This time, the sound of the Caller's voice was like a roaring flame in his head, in both ears, in the entire world around him, flooding everything he knew with awful, earth-shattering volume:

"I TOLD YOU. DEAD MEN DON'T CLOSE CALLS. AND YOU ARE DEAD, DEADER THAN DOG-SHIT, DEADER THAN OLD WOOD FALLEN IN THE FOREST AND FORGOTTEN FORTY THOUSAND YEARS AGO, YOU'RE DEADER THAN FOSSILS WASHED UP IN THE DESERT AND KEPT IN AN OLD OBSCURE MUSEUM, YOU DENY IT ALL YOU CAN BUT YOU'LL BE –"

Now Spencer realized what he'd been doing wrong the whole time. *Bastard can't get me if I don't have my ear to the earpiece.* He yanked the receiver off his ear – the entire side of his face seemed to cry out in relief – and as he slammed the receiver down, seemingly in slow-motion, he thought he could hear the punk's voice, shrill and pathetic, crackling out of the receiver:

"– just another statistic, Spence, deny it all you want but you're just as dead as they are –"

Sad, really. Not even worth feeling frightened over. Spencer almost felt sorry for him – a faraway man with no future, no goals and dreams, not even the grit needed to commit to something and crawl out of whatever hole he was in. A guy who could do nothing better than those stupid Gotcha calls you heard on the radio.

He put the receiver down, and there was nothing in the office but the clitter-clatter of keyboards, and the unified hum of everyone else's voices blended in a rash mix: each one trying to open new accounts, resolve tallying errors, and round-up balances. Just another regular day.

He sucked in a deep breath through his collapsed lungs, and let it out slowly in a dry, shaky whistle. The pain in his head was beginning to lessen and fade away.

It's over, then.

Spencer Lim didn't take any calls for the rest of the morning.

✗

Not even two hours later, he was heading down the stairs for lunch with Murali and Nick Kumar, who was so new that he rode a motorcycle to work. Lunch hour, glorious lunch hour, when you could get away from your troubles for a blessed slice of the day.

"I'll drive," Spencer told his friends, as they walked out into the sunny parking lot.

He walked up and down the rows of cars…then, bowing apologetically to Murali and Nick, moved in the other direction. That was funny, he was sure he'd parked it in this spot…

It happened to everyone, didn't it? You pulled into the parking lot at eight every morning, so used to the motions that none of it registered… and ended up forgetting where you'd parked.

"Sorry." He gave his friends a sheepish grin and tucked his hands into his pockets. "Can't seem to find it. Murali, can you drive?"

And so Murali brought them to a nearby Chinese food stall they ate at nearly three times a week. As he was turning in, a motorcycle shot out of a corner and nearly came end-to-end with Murali's grille.

"Crazy shithead," Nick remarked.

"Son of a bitch," Murali said.

They continued talking about the idiocy of motorcyclists even after their food arrived, piling on verbal abuse as they piled chicken onto their plates of rice.

"You want to know what's really screwed up?" Murali said. "GrabFood drivers."

"Oh my God." Nick shook his head. "Tell me about it, cha."

"The worst type of motorist is a GrabFood motorist. These asshats will weave through moving traffic without a care, never sticking to one lane…and at red lights, who do you think is shooting through and crossing intersections? GrabFood motorcycles. Them, and the Foodpanda guys."

"This is why the number of motorcyclists killed on the road is going up." Nick made an emphatic stab in the air with his fork; a chunk of chicken nearly flew off the end. "They drive the way they do, and then when the statistics rise, they're all, *'Oh please spare a thought for us motorcyclists.'* Then they blame their bosses."

"Not to take a swipe at them, but yeah," Murali said. "All they think about is being in front of anyone else, and if they die, it's someone else's fault. That's why I always say, I hate motorcycles."

Spencer's head was full of thoughts, but he found himself unable to say anything. The words had caught in his throat and choked him. His chicken rice smelled of smoke and petrol, and the meat tasted charred and burned, like ash. And Nick would never say stuff like this – Nick rode a motorcycle to work, for goodness' sake.

He looked down at his own plate and saw that it was sprinkled with broken windshield glass, clumps of hair matted together with gore and flesh, and streaks of blood.

No matter how hard he tried, he couldn't blink this vision away, couldn't ignore the smell of smoke and petrol – and the sounds of sirens wailing in the distance.

"Spence?" Murali turned to him. "Thoughts?"

Spencer forced a smile. A single tooth fell out of his mouth and onto his plate with a plink.

"I have no regard for anyone who races in traffic and denies responsibility when they're killed," he said.

They finished the rest of their food, but Spencer couldn't bring himself to eat any of what was on his plate. You couldn't eat glass. Anyway, most of his teeth had been knocked out, smeared across his airbag.

There was no denying it…but if he could just enjoy this moment a bit longer…

Murali tapped his watch. "Let's go. Spencer?"

"Just let me finish this coffee."

Spencer raised his glass to his friends, looked around, and as he sipped the Nescafe, he told himself he had never felt more alive.

✕

When he was done with his coffee, the medics scraped what was left of him off the seats and the windshield.

DON'T GO FAR-FAR

✕

HADI M NOR

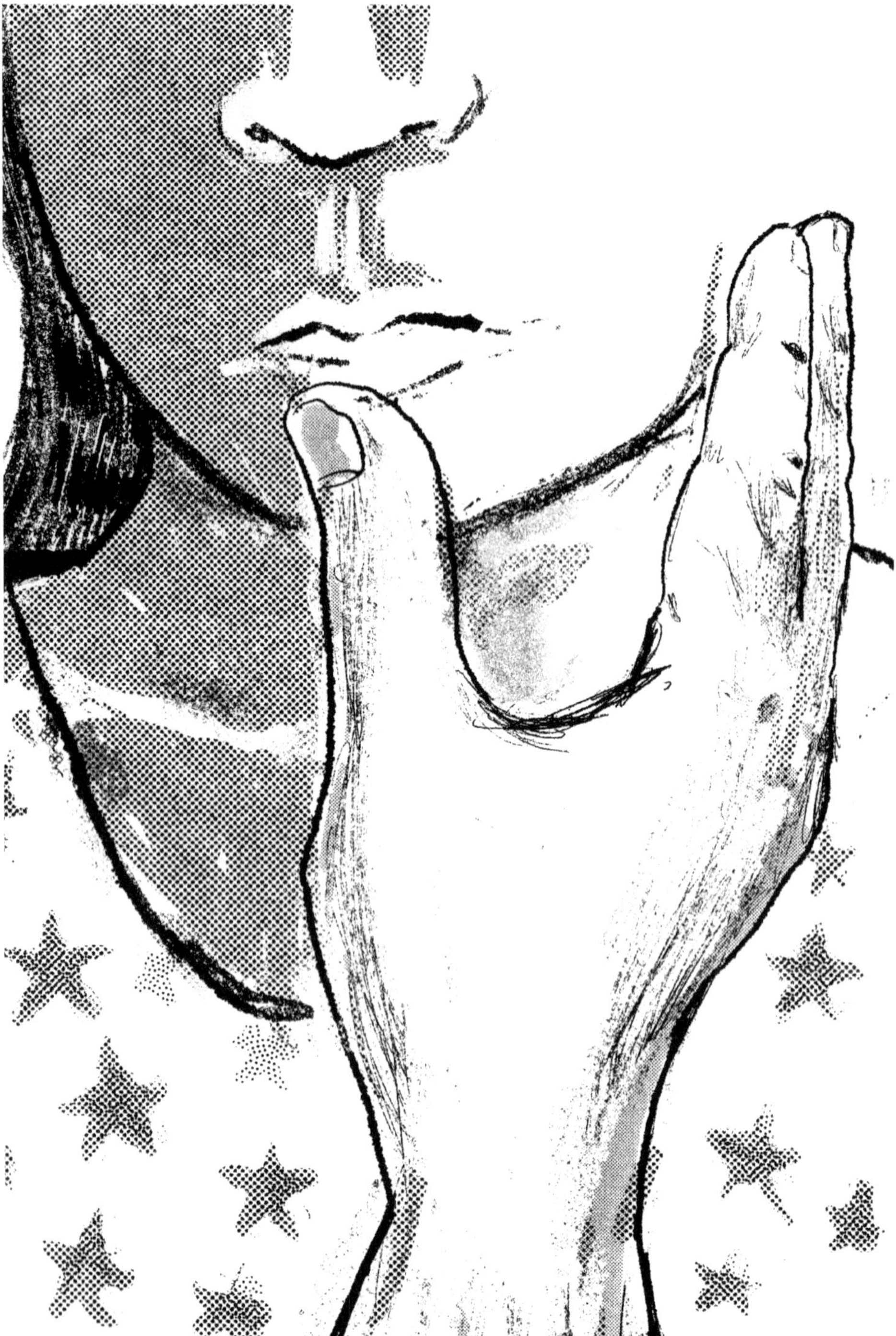

Kila had just turned 5 when Mama stopped holding her hand in public. It was fine. She preferred to wander off on her own anyway. With all the energy she had, how could she slow down to match Mama's pace? Mama was not old, but she was very slow. And it wasn't due to her weight either. She was not big. She was just slower than other mothers.

"Come, Kila," said Mama as they crossed the underground parking lot into the big complex.

Kila was already restless when they went up the escalator that was moving painfully slow. She wanted to climb to the top as soon as possible, but she had learned the hard way that the edges of escalator steps have teeth. When you hit them with your shin, they will leave a painful mark.

From the dark, smelly stuffiness of the parking lot, they finally arrived at the bright, open, and lively complex. Kila was ready to dash as soon as she reached the landing. She took two big steps before stopping herself. She turned to Mama. Mama cocked her eyebrow as if to say, *What do you think you're doing?*

Kila smiled apologetically.

They walked to the supermarket. Mama took her temperature at the digital scanner. Kila wanted to do it too, but she was too short. She liked the machine. She liked the tech. As she was admiring it, Mama called her while pulling away a trolley.

The ceiling of the supermarket was high. She looked up and saw the exposed vents, pipes, and the lights. They reminded her of her favorite video game that she played on Papa's phone – *Among Us*. In *Among Us*, she played an astronaut working in a spaceship. The pipes and vents above resembled the game's cartoony spaceship that she loved. And in *Among Us*, each player was given tasks to complete all around the different parts of the ship. The players had to wander alone, all the while avoiding the dangerous impostor: a murderous alien posing as a human.

She imagined she had tasks to complete here in this supermarket. First on her list: to fix the wiring in the electrical room.

"Kila!" called her mother. "Don't go far-far." Her mother was picking up some cans from the shelves.

For a moment, she was taken out of her imaginary world. But it was easy for her to get back into it. She went down the aisle, skipping a little bit just like the astronauts in *Among Us*. She found herself standing in front of a shelf full of brooms and mops and buckets. Here was where the electrical panel was located. She poked on a sponge that was still in its package as if she were punching a sequence of numbers, making "beep-beep, boop-boop" noises as she did. Task completed.

She skipped to the other aisle for her second task. Destroying meteors.

There was a price checker machine attached to the wall. This was the ship's radar, and she held up her hands like she was holding a control stick. She aimed at the meteors and fired, clearing a path for the ship. Task completed.

She turned to attend to the third task, which was scanning her body for a health inspection. And she knew where the scanner was: at the entrance. The temperature checker. But as soon as she turned around, a young man blocked her way.

"Hey," said the young man. Twice her height. Bespectacled. Dressed in shirt and jeans and sneakers. "What are you doing?" He spoke with a gentle high-pitched voice. Like the voices adults always used when they spoke to her.

She didn't answer. She had always been shy with strangers. Her parents usually did the talking for her. They were her shield against these people.

The young man crouched so that they were at the same level. He had a friendly clean-shaven face. His hair was a little long, combed to the side. He looked younger than her parents and he smelled like powder. "Where's your mother?"

Kila looked behind. Her mother was no longer at the shelf with all the cans. Or was that a different aisle? She wasn't sure anymore. The young man asked, "What's your name?"

This question she could handle. She had answered it a million times before. "Kila," she said.

"Kee-la," repeated the man, nodding, liking the sound of it. "That's a pretty name. My name is Fuad. You can call me Abang Ad." He paused. "Can you say it? Abang Ad?"

"Abang Ad," she said. She liked the sound of that. It was fun to say.

"Clever girl," said Abang Ad, smiling widely, flashing his teeth. "I like your dress. Did you pick it yourself? Or did Mummy?"

She was wearing a white cotton gown with pink stars on them. "I picked it myself."

"What?" Abang Ad looked shocked. "Wow. So young but already so good at fashion. That's amazing, Kila," he said, sounding very impressed.

Kila smiled. She swung her body from side to side, flattered by the compliment.

"Such a nice dress." He pinched the fabric. "And soft, too."

Kila stopped smiling. She was used to head pats and cheek pinches, but no one had touched her clothes before and she didn't know what to feel or how to react. The polite thing was maybe to just say, "Thank you." She said it softly. Unsure.

"Pretty dress. Pretty hair." He tucked her hair behind her ear. His lips quivered. "Pretty face."

His fingers were now on her cheek. They were damp. Sweaty. She froze. She felt her jaw clench. She wanted to pull away but decided against it. Once, she had pulled away from an adult who wanted to touch her face, and Mama snapped at her for being rude. So she stood and let it happen.

His face changed. He wasn't smiling like before. He looked like a different person now. And his eyes were focused on different parts of her face. Her body.

"Big eyes. Cute little nose…" His voiced softened to a whisper. His fingers still on her cheek, his thumb caressed her lips. "Soft lips."

She whimpered a little and stood frozen.

"Kila!" Her mother's voice. Abang Ad quickly stood up and disappeared behind the rack. He was gone in a flash. "Kila." Her mother finally saw her. "There you are," she said, breathing a sigh of relief. "I told you not to go far-far. Come. Let's get nuggets. Your father finished the bag we had."

✕

"Why are you so quiet?" asked Mama on their drive back home.

Kila didn't answer. She didn't know why, she just didn't feel like talking. She just wanted to go home now. She sat in the passenger seat looking out the window, feeling things she had never felt before. Whatever she was feeling, it wasn't good.

At the traffic light, while the car stopped, it suddenly jolted as if the ground shifted. Mama gasped and, in reflex, threw her hand in front of Kila. She yelped a bad word before asking Kila, "Are you okay?"

Kila's heart was thumping. She looked around, not sure what was happening.

"A car hit us from behind," said Mama. "Idiot."

Mama unbuckled her seatbelt and got out of the car. Kila called for her mother but was ignored. Mama was already outside, yelling at the driver of the car that had just hit them. She turned to look at the driver.

It was Abang Ad.

She couldn't hear what her mother was saying, but she saw that she was yelling at him as he held his hands out in apology. He crouched down, disappearing from her view, to check the damage on the bumper. He emerged again, talking to Mama. Kila sat back down in her seat, looking straight ahead. Her eyes wide. Her breathing rapid. Her face hot. She was close to tears. She wanted to call her mother again to get back into the car, but Abang Ad might hear her.

Mama got back into the car after what seemed like an eternity. "What an idiot," muttered Mama.

Abang Ad's car passed them. He was driving an old, beat-up car. She couldn't help but stare at him. He didn't even look in her direction. He drove off, disappearing out of sight. Did he know she was in the car?

"I couldn't bear to ask him to pay for the damage. Look at his car." Her mother was talking to herself now. "Poor guy. Sometimes you feel sorry for these idiots, you know?"

✕

Her parents had a minor argument when Mama told Papa about the accident. And she roped Kila into the argument by asking, "I was not moving, right Kila? I was stopped at the traffic light and the car hit us from behind, right?"

Kila nodded, siding with her mother because it was the truth.

"I believe you," said Papa. "I'm not angry at you. I'm just pissed off. We don't have money to send it to the shop."

"Do you think you can fix it?" asked Mama. "It's just a little dent on the bumper."

Papa sighed. "I'll do it tomorrow." Papa looked at Kila. "Or maybe you can fix it," he quipped.

Kila tried to smile.

✕

That night, Kila couldn't sleep. She lay on her side, knees close to her chest. The ceiling fan was squeaky but it was comforting. A noise that told her she was safe.

Her bladder was kind of full. It had been a hot day, so she drank a lot of water as per orders from Papa. After a long contemplation, she decided that she couldn't hold it in any longer. She got up and went out of her room.

Her parents' room was just beside hers. She could hear them snoring. Papa was not much louder than Mama. Both of them were window rattlers. She didn't want to wake them up and ask them to teman because previously, her father had given her a long lecture about being brave. She badly needed company, though.

No. She told herself she was going to be brave. The bathroom was not that far. Just pass the living room and the kitchen. It was a small house. Not nearly as big as the spaceship in *Among Us*.

Her feet padded on the cold floor as she got into the dark hall. Her head, straight. Eyes, focused. She told herself not to let her gaze wander. If you ignore hantu, they will leave you alone.

She raced to the bathroom and closed the door behind her. After relieving herself, she went out and back into the dark hall that did not seem so scary now.

She was about to make her way back to her room when she noticed that the kitchen was a little brighter. The lights were not on but it was just a little different. She squinted to see what was going on. Then she realized that the back door was open. Light from the street lamps was pouring in.

There was a movement in the shadows. She gasped.

A man was standing in the corner.

Before she could scream, the man pounced on her.

She grappled, squirmed, doing her damnedest to escape, but to no avail. Her attacker was overpowering her. Her small hands and legs were no match against the strength of whoever was holding her. The attacker cupped her mouth with his hand with a piece of wet cloth on it. When she inhaled and tried to scream, she felt moisture entering her mouth. It smelled strong and foul. And it was making her dizzy. Her energy was draining. She couldn't breathe. She tried to pry the fingers off. Her vision was already blurry. Her head felt light.

And then she heard Mama, screaming for her.

She was whisked away, toward the back door. The attacker was making a run for it. Then she felt yanked, Mama was screaming, pulling the attacker. Now Papa had come out of the bedroom, yelling in his loud booming voice. He got close really quickly. There was hitting, and screaming, and yelling. She was slowly losing consciousness.

Her attacker finally let her go.

The man ran out the back door. Papa kept chasing him, determined to catch him. Mama held Kila close, hugging her, asking if she was okay. Kila was half-conscious, but she managed to put her hand over Mama's shoulder and hug her.

✕

The next morning, a couple of police officers came by the house and asked her about the attacker. She told them about Abang Ad and the incident at the supermarket. Mama was shocked. "Why didn't you tell me about this, sayang?" she asked. Kila didn't answer.

The police assumed that 'Abang Ad' (they were sure it wasn't his real name) probably followed them home.

"It might be that guy," said Mama. "He drove an old beat-up car. But he looked like a nice boy. He looked smart."

"You can never tell with these types," said the older police officer. "They could be anyone – teachers, guardians, or even uni students."

Like impostors in Among Us, Kila thought. She would never play that game ever again.

Her parents thanked the police officers a few times after they promised they'd go around the neighborhood to make sure it was safe.

That afternoon the house was quieter, but the air sure was tense. Kila sat with Mama on the sofa. Mama kept her as close as possible, like she was a baby again. Kila held her mother's hand.

Papa came back in after looking at the dented bumper of their car. He held up a small black box in his hand.

"What's that?" asked Mama.

"I found it underneath the car," said Papa. "It looks like…"

No one dared to say it. Perhaps to avoid scaring Kila. But she knew what it was: a tracking device.

Sio Bak

×

Wong Jo-yen

It occurred to me, as I stared at the disembodied head, that Chinese people have a thing for pigs.

A fly landed on the rheumy half-lidded right eye, and a corner of the dead boar's lips was pulled up to reveal ghastly yellowed teeth with jagged edges. The hide was pink, tinged with the gray of death, the skin thicker and coarser than I expected. There was a red stamp on its left rump, boldly proclaiming **Hock Heng 01285**. They had branded the *'o'* right over a wart with a single long hair growing out of it.

I was jolted out of my reverie by a booming laugh and a loud slap. My second uncle had smacked the pig right across its butt, making it jump half a centimeter off its throne on the red-clothed table.

"Big one, right? Almost 35 kg! But I got a discount, only RM20 per kilo!"

Our neighbors around him nodded in approval and began discussing pig vendors. Prices were going up again, they complained, but thank goodness not as much as during the last Chinese New Year. Those figures were daylight robbery.

It felt as though the whole village had gathered here under this large striped canopy, and that was probably because it had. I read the embroidered banner hanging over the ritual stage, recognizing barely enough Chinese to make out the words for *'Kampung Anyi'* and *'festival.'*

"Twelve years since the last one! You were what, twelve last time? I bet you don't even remember it anymore."

I tried to hold my shoulder up against the weight of my uncle's hearty clap. He was a strong man. "I was twelve, Shushu, but I didn't attend. UPSR, remember?"

"Really?" My uncle scratched his stubbled chin. "But I thought—"

He seemed to freeze, vaguely startled for a second, then he smacked himself across the forehead with a sound so sharp it made me wince. "Aiya, forget it, whatever! You should just enjoy this one. Winter Solstice of the Tiger Year, only once every round of the zodiac, you know. Very rare. And look at this spectacle!"

He waved around the venue with a flourish. There were 158 tables lined up in the field outside our local temple, with twenty of the largest tables standing in front of the stage. Ours was Table No.18, and the donor signs behind the makeshift counter said that Shushu had paid RM1,888 for this privilege.

"At least a duck, a chicken, and an entire pig for the first twenty tables! No side of sam chan or just the pig's head, not for us! Not this time! No, the whole pig!"

Shushu had bought an entire pig for my grandfather's funeral two years ago, too, while the rest of the family pitched in for one more. In the end, he made a fuss about two not being a round enough number and bugged the in-laws into sponsoring another. It had taken the family months to finish up three roast pigs, and I even got half a rack of ribs to bring back to university. Not that I could get it past Customs.

The fly flew off the right eye and landed on the snout instead, helping itself to a speck of dried blood in the hairy left nostril. It seems that Chinese people associate pigs with prestige.

A memory stirred in the back of my mind, of watching *Mythbusters* at my grandfather's house during a school holiday years ago. They used a lot of pigs in their experiments on that show, because—

"Wah, is this Jason? You've grown so big!"

My grandfather's second-door neighbor's youngest niece ("Don't you remember? She used to take care of you when you were a baby!") interrupted my train of thought and I did not find it again for the rest of the morning.

Most of the village was here…and then there was me. I had many memories of lazy afternoons spent wandering around this little village during primary school holidays. Even though all the wooden houses had been replaced with an eclectic mix of mismatched one-story bungalows, this was still a village, not a suburb. The key to that lay with the people.

Was I one of them? My name was listed in the ancestral registries, controlled by a 90-year-old woman who had outlived all her children and half her grandchildren. She knew me by name, too, as did what felt like a good quarter of the village. But I did not know theirs, and I had spent most of the first day at the festival standing awkwardly behind my uncle's elbow. My father was not feeling well, so my mother stayed with him back in KL, sending me here instead as the family rep.

It was now noon of the second day. Three more days and five hours to go, and I was feeling slightly hungry despite standing in the middle of a beastly mortuary.

It had been more than ten years since I had been back for any extended period of time. At some point, my parents just stopped bringing me here for the holidays. We only came back for the eve and first two days of Chinese New Year, and for no more than three days for any given funeral, except Grandpa's. Each trip was filled with a flurry of activity, and I had not had time to walk around like I used to as a kid.

The more I looked around, the more I remembered. And the more I realized this place had not changed much at all.

The same voices, aged by tobacco. The same faces, lined with time. The same crunch of the gravel under my feet…

I looked at the side of pork belly on one of the smaller tables and tasted salt on my tongue.

"Hey, Shushu. Do you remember a type of sio bak that I really liked?"

The low hum of conversation around me, punctuated by the occasional roar of laughter, fell abruptly quiet.

I glanced around, confused. "Shushu?"

The big man turned to me slowly, his grin crinkling at the corners. "Sio bak? Do you mean your Hua-yee's?"

"Ah, yes, Ah Hua! Her sio bak is the best in the village."

My grandmother's best friend's oldest son hastily agreed. "She uses a special blend for the seasoning, you know. I always ask her, but she says she won't tell anybody her recipe, not even her husband."

"Her husband, that Ah Foo? Bah, he would just sell it to the first bidder—"

"Not Hua-yee's." I shook my head. I just had Hua-yee's sio bak rice yesterday. My nostalgia was craving something else, a flavor long forgotten. "I remember an uncle…"

"You must be remembering wrong." Shushu's grin turned even more pained, wrinkling at the seams. "Don't let Ah Hua know, or you'll get it! Besides, you know me, I always prefer char siew."

That was a lie. Shushu had eaten an entire leg of the largest pig at Grandpa's funeral.

But that was not the taste I remembered either.

That ghost of a memory plagued me for the rest of the day. The niggling thought wriggled into the recesses of my brain, eating me from the inside out. That tingling sensation, of not just a taste, but also a smell, floated just a hair above my receptors, just out of reach. It was torture.

But no one would tell me. After a while, I was certain that they knew what I was talking about. Yet they averted their eyes and changed the topic.

Why? It was just some sio bak.

Or was it?

Now that I was actively looking, I noticed an undercurrent of uneasiness permeating the festival and its attendees. There was something they were avoiding. And somehow, they avoided it more aggressively when I asked.

I was not getting anywhere like this. I wandered away from my family's table, toward the side stalls where there were smaller lots allocated to newer families, households that could only afford the poultry and maybe a large-ish fish for their little square tables. The faces grew increasingly less familiar, until I reached a corner where I could loiter inconspicuously in front of an industrial stand fan, pretending to hog the ventilation as I eavesdropped on the conversations.

"…never seen so many whole hogs in one place before. There must be, what, ten thousand ringgit in pigs here?"

"Tsk-tsk, what a waste. What are they going to do with all those pigs anyway? So much meat, no way they can finish."

"Lots of cai boey, I say. Tau yew bak, with plenty of five spice and at least four hours in the slow cooker."

I was really starting to get hungry. My eyes drifted over to the nearest table, where there was a large slab of raw pork belly, complete with two neat rows of half-dried teats.

Still hungry. The sinew of the red meat, the even layer of cloudy fat, even the stubborn dirty hide, all of it could become a delicacy with the right skill, the right hands, the right heat—

"Too bad we don't have Ah Huey anymore. His sio bak was the best."

I stiffened, the name opening yet another lock in the safe of my memories.

...Ah Huey Shushu. It was the same sensation as when I stumbled across a primary school classmate on Facebook friend suggestions and suddenly remembered a childhood love for basketball in the flooded courts under makeshift hoops during recess. Chains of dusty memories were unlocked all at once, a part of my life that I had compartmentalized neatly in a corner of my mind and then promptly forgotten for a decade.

Ah Huey Shushu had lived in the house at the end of my grandfather's street, through a wooden fence that was low enough for me to climb over. Not that it mattered – he never locked it anyway. He drove a lorry and lived alone, so I went to play with him often and he let me watch him work. I sat on the smooth concrete floor outside his warehouse door, breathing through my mouth to avoid that smell...

The smell of the pigs in his backyard. Right?

But...I would get scolded when I went home. Why?

"Shh! Don't mention him now."

Why? Since when had the name become taboo? Ah Huey Shushu was as much a part of the village as everyone else, until...until...

Until what?

That answer was locked under yet another layer of security, and as much as I hammered on the door, I could not get through.

Ah Huey Shushu…and his sio bak. Was that the taste I was missing so badly?

I wandered back to my family's table dazedly, where Shushu was on his phone.

"…Yeah, yeah, we didn't tell him. I don't think he remembers…No lah, we won't tell him!"

When he caught my eye and immediately hung up, I made up my mind. I was going to get to the bottom of this.

✕

No one was going to tell me, so I had to go back and find out myself. I told Shushu that I was feeling tired after the long morning and that I wanted to head home for a nap.

"But what about lunch?" Shushu gestured at the packets of chicken rice stacked up at the counter. "The festival committee sponsored some. You wanted sio bak, right?"

I wanted Ah Huey Shushu's sio bak, now more than ever, but saying that would probably call my investigations to an abrupt and final halt, so I shook my head. I could eat after I solved this mystery.

Most of the villagers were gathered at the festival, so the roads were relatively empty. I walked down the street toward my grandfather's house, now inherited by Shushu, and waved at the second-door neighbor, a hearty woman in her eighties who was feeding an adolescent pig in a tiny pen in a corner of her front yard.

"Hello, Ah Sun!" she greeted me with my childhood name. "Not at the festival ah?"

"Came back to get something. You, Ah Po?"

"Just feeding Oh-mor here, then I'll go back and join them."

"Weren't you supposed to slaughter Oh-mor for the festival?"

She shrugged. "I'm thinking of keeping him for Ah Ping's graduation at the end of the year. That should be grander."

Ah Ping was her oldest granddaughter and, if I remembered correctly, a bit of an environmentalist. All those newfangled liberal ideas she gained at university, apparently. If you ask me, the trouble began the moment they decided to give their piglet a name.

"Good luck with that," I said, and I meant it.

Chinese people and their pigs. Then again, they did taste sublime.

There was a rattle of metal as Ah Po went back inside. Once I was sure she could not see me, I went past my grandfather's house and made a beeline for the abandoned house at the end of the street.

I had always known it was abandoned, but the fact never seemed to properly register with me. Now I was aware of two realities in my head: One where the house was warm, and another where it was empty. But there was a missing link between the two.

The wooden fence-gate was even shorter than I remembered, and it hung off its rusty hinges. I pushed it away gingerly, wary of splinters. The yard was smaller than I remembered too, the jambu trees shorter. Leaves had piled up on the ground, forming a layered carpet of rot. My feet squelched slightly on the wet matter, but at least I could still feel the hard packed dirt of the land underneath.

The dirt had been compressed by the wheels of Ah Huey Shushu's lorry. Not big, four wheels with a black tarpaulin. I had jumped into the front seat once and he'd scolded me for playing with the Guan Yin amulet hanging from the rearview mirror. The lorry had smelled like…sio bak.

That was right. Ah Huey Shushu's corner house smelled bad, because he kept pigs in the yard, but it smelled good at the same time, because of his sio bak.

I walked up to the main building – his house tucked deeper inside his compound – beyond the yard. There was no front door, just a large opening leading to…

The furnace.

The walls of his living room were bleached from the sunlight streaming in through the holes in the attap roof. There were rust-covered clasps on the pillars, with a few tools of his trade still hanging there. A cleaver the size of my forearm. Meat hooks that spelled tetanus and death, their gruesome tips caked with the red-brown blood of thousands of pigs, from where they had pierced through the top of the hogs' mouths and re-emerged on either side of twitching snouts...

My footsteps were muffled on the floor as I approached the furnace.

I remembered now. Ah Huey Shushu did not rear pigs. Unlike Hua-yee, he did not make his sio bak in a charming oven, either. No, he was a roast pig supplier.

My mind flashed back to Shushu's prized festival pig, Hock Heng 01285, still raw and soft. Ah Huey Shushu could have made a feast out of it, if he had not—

With every step closer to the giant metal furnace door, the smell intensified. Crisp, aromatic. Salty. Generous amounts of five spice, with a strong hint of star anise too. More salt, enough to make me salivate. Ah Huey Shushu did not believe in low sodium – and besides, roast pigs were by nature an indulgence.

The secret ingredient, of course, was the heat.

The heat had to be turned up just right to baste the skin, turning it from a foul leathery hide into crunchy heaven in a bite. The flames melted down the fibers and teased apart the fat underneath the dermis into translucent goblets of tissue, absorbing the flavor from the seasoning slathered freely along the lines of glistening flesh.

I put my fingers on the edge of the furnace door and pulled. It was heavy. I put my back into it.

Slowly, it moved.

In my mind, I saw the inside of the furnace as it was more than a decade ago. Lined with a veritable forest of dead pigs, all their eyes open and staring blankly as the fire licked off their eyelids. Death turning into delicacy as I watched in fascination. Oil and fat dripped from their hanging hooves, forming a puddle on the furnace floor that bubbled and wafted a meaty aroma. It was almost good enough to lick off the ground, overwhelming the smell of dirt and excretion. The flames burned bright and roared viciously, loud enough to drown out—

I opened the door and looked around the empty iron walls. No pigs here.

Then I took a step and looked down.

There was a shape in the soot on the floor.

The furnace door creaked to a close behind me. I turned around.

There were streaks of a now-familiar reddish-brown running down the underside of the door.

Ah. I remembered now.

The last festival, twelve years ago. I had attended it, after all. It was after my UPSR, and I was excited to attend the first village festival in my living memory.

And it was great. The problem was what happened after.

Ah Huey Shushu made the best sio bak in the village, and everyone knew that. So the orders poured in. Everyone wanted him to roast their pigs after the festival. And well, there were many rounds of mahjong and beer on the last night.

Everyone slept especially soundly that night. Except Ah Huey Shushu.

I looked down at the floor. There was a shape in the soot from where he had curled up, the fat melting and dripping off from under his skin.

I was there when they opened the door. My throat felt constricted.

His eyes had been rheumy and open, his mouth agape and his tongue burned to a char. His clothes had been seared off, his skin bubbling and roasting into crunchy golden crackling. There had been a large wart on the small of his tanned back, right under the waist of his trousers, and even that had crisped up nicely. The memory of fear and blood and salt and spices coated my tongue. I gulped again…to swallow the saliva building up in my mouth.

Shit. The particles settled on my tongue. This was the taste I remembered.

The one my family wanted me to forget.

All of a sudden, the last piece clicked in my mind. On my grandfather's crackling TV speakers, the Mythbusters cheerfully said:

Pigs are the best substitutes for human bodies. Everything from their skin down to their flesh.

Guess I was never going to taste that nostalgic sio bak again.

Skins

✕

Nadiah Zakaria

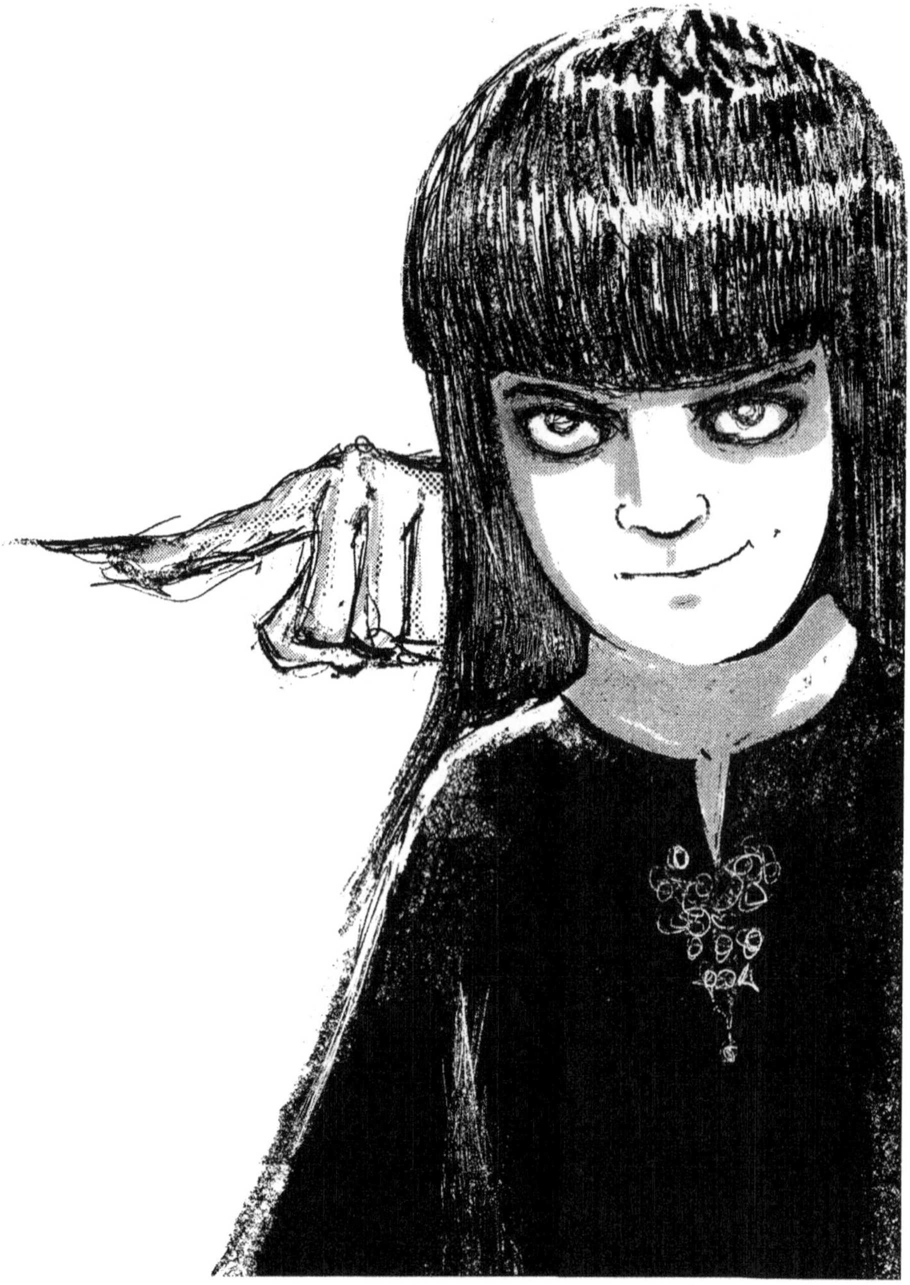

Quiet nights never bothered Mahirah. In fact, quiet nights like this made her work easier. When it was so silent not even a low whistle of late-night breeze could be heard, that's when she knew it was perfect.

The 24-year-old made her way down the vacant street of Taman Nuri, a neighborhood she lived in but was never fond of. Her black velvet dress was wrapped around her body like second skin, matching the dark of her long hair cascading down her back. It was a pity, not hearing the usual whistles and snarky comments from boys on motorbikes tonight. She would've loved the attention.

Mahirah walked past the line of terraced houses, the gravel beneath her feet the only sound. She glanced at a mango tree in front of her neighbor's house and let her gaze linger at the dark mass hanging from a branch. When she turned the corner to reach her own house, she glared at the figure wrapped in kain kapan, watching her from a distance.

"Jangan ikut aku," she said.

Mahirah held a recycled bag that failed to contain the pungent stench of its contents in her right hand. It had led to her asking the taxi driver to drop her off at the entrance of the neighborhood instead of her house. Besides, walking made her less visible.

When she reached the house at the end of the street, she pushed past the gate and stopped in front of the door. Placing the bag down, she unlocked her front door and was greeted with pure darkness, just as she liked it. She had been renting the small house for a little over six months. So far, no one had bothered to get to know her, and she would like to keep it that way.

Alor Setar wasn't as small as she remembered, but everyone seemed to know everyone around here, and Mahirah definitely didn't want anyone knowing *her*.

"Finally," she muttered to herself once inside. She picked up the bag and silently shut the door behind her.

Walking through the pitch-black living room was as simple as breathing. A single ray of light peeked through the curtains, and that was enough. Mahirah opened the left drawer of her wooden cabinet, situated just beside the doorway to the kitchen. She felt for a lighter and let the small, dancing flame illuminate the features of her face.

One by one, she began lighting candles that were placed around the house. There were seven of them, situated in unique spots which allowed her to see well in the now dimly-lit space. The seven flames danced with no wind, casting elongated shadows on the walls.

Mahirah reached into the bag she had abandoned by the couch in the center of the living room. It was the only piece of furniture there, save for the wooden cabinet and a full-length mirror hung where a television was supposed to be.

A smile dripping with malice slowly formed on her red lips as her fingers grazed the material of the items in the bag. She gave a low laugh, pulling them out one by one and holding them up for admiration. A large shadow swept over the room right then, and the air turned frigid even with the fan off. The shadow stood in the kitchen doorway, watching intently.

"You're late," said Mahirah. She lifted the paper-like items and waved them around with pride. "But look what we got today," she grinned, "fresh from the boy who couldn't keep his eyes off me at the market yesterday morning."

The shadow moved forward, the air got colder as it got closer. Light from the nearest candle made the dark figure more visible – its long hair swept across the floor, framing a wan face with graying skin and hollow sockets for eyes. Its body was nothing but a dark mass, floating in the air behind Mahirah as she proudly showed off her newest possession.

She presented the item before the figure, letting it bow its head to inhale the sour, rotten smell. Another sinister laugh escaped Mahirah's lips when she sensed the satisfaction that the figure exuded.

"Let's add it to our collection, shall we?"

The hour had inched past midnight by the time Mahirah was done pasting her new wallpaper. It still wasn't enough: There were several empty spaces left on the wall, showing the chipped beige paint underneath. She sighed and took a step back, hands on hips as she let her eyes rake the wall in satisfaction.

"One more person should be enough, don't you think?" she asked. Her eyes were fixated on the wall as the dark entity behind her groaned. Mahirah turned around at the deep sound with yet another grin. "We'll complete our collection soon, my friend. Then you shall be free from me."

The figure faded into thin air without a trace, and Mahirah stared at her four walls. Her smile grew bigger as she took in the sight of the skins she had managed to take. With every layer of skin her eyes landed on, the sound of their agonized screams echoed in her ears. She laughed at the look on their faces when her knife first tore through their flesh; she laughed at the warmth of their blood that she bathed in.

24 different skins from 24 different men, adorning her walls like medals. She sprayed them with chemicals that kept the smell at bay, and went to the storage room with the remaining contents of the recycled bag.

It was a small room, with only some cleaning appliances put up against the wall beside a wooden chest. Mahirah pulled the chest that she kept locked and opened it with ease. Another wave of pungent odor hit her, yet she brushed it away with the same disinfectant chemicals.

"Join your new friends, Aiman," she said mockingly as she held the bag above the chest, dumping Aiman's remnants along with the twenty-three other sets of bones. "Just one more friend to go, boys," she smiled as she closed the chest and wiped her hands clean.

"Just one more."

×

"Look at her," a woman said, voice laced with jealousy. "Gatal. I bet she flirts with every other guy she sees."

Mahirah strolled past the vegetable stalls and pretended not to hear the mockery. It was her routine, scouting the markets to find eligible bachelors no one would remember, and lead them into her trap. If it meant buying ingredients she'd never cook and listening to middle-aged women badmouth her, so be it.

Wherever Mahirah walked, a strong scent of mandrakes and white mistletoe wafted along with her. It was enough to turn every man's head in her direction, though all they saw was a beautiful young woman, and not the demon behind her.

"Tengok tu," another woman whispered. "Who is she? I feel like she's here just to show off her assets and leave."

"You should protect your husband from girls like that," someone replied. "She probably practices black magic to look that pretty. Maybe she has a hantu raya following her around and we don't even know."

Mahirah turned her head slightly at the comment, making sure not to show she had been actively listening.

Her friend groaned behind her, letting her know it was still there, and that was enough to keep her walking. She put on her winning smile once more and visited one stall after another, looking for the last boy.

"Eh, where's Aiman? Tak kerja?" a woman asked the fishmonger Mahirah was walking past.

"Tak tau. Haven't seen him in a few days. Maybe he's sick," answered the boy as he put two siakaps on a weighing scale.

Mahirah nonchalantly strolled past these stalls with fake interest at each one. She heard several more names that perked her ears. *Rahim. Imran. Faizal.* Biting back her laugh was a challenge as she pretended that those names meant nothing to her.

It's not like their skins were hanging on the walls of her home.

It took her 20 minutes to finish walking around the entire pasar, but Mahirah was not about to go home just yet. As if on cue, she found a group of boys – probably in their early 20s – hanging out on motorbikes underneath one of the trees beside the road. Usually they'd be there in the evening, when it was dark out.

Luck must've been on her side today.

She stood several feet away, eyes scanning the faces of the boys catcalling every single girl who walked past.

Mahirah scoffed. "Which one do you want?"

The demon lifted one graying hand with long black fingernails and pointed at the boy in the middle. He was doing most of the catcalling. The words left his mouth so easily, as if he'd been repeating the same things like a mantra every day. He turned to see Mahirah slowly walking towards the group, and his eyes widened.

"Look! That marka is coming towards us."

The four boys around him began sniffling and pinching their noses the closer Mahirah got. The chosen boy, however, was smiling sheepishly in a hopeless flirting manner when he realized Mahirah was walking towards *him*.

"What's up, young lady? Like what you see?"

"What's your name?" she asked, feigning innocence.

"Kamal. You?"

"Doesn't matter," Mahirah smiled before leaning forward to whisper in Kamal's ear. "Meet me at the playground after Isyak. Can you do that?"

Her lips were an inch away from Kamal's earlobe, tickling his skin with her breath. He felt goosebumps rising on his skin at the sound of her melancholic voice and found himself staring into her eyes intently. They were a dark shade of brown, almost black. He nodded before he could process what he was agreeing to, and didn't seem to notice his friends had taken several steps back due to the growing stench.

"Great," Mahirah grinned. "See you later."

✕

Kamal was sitting on a bench at the playground around 9:30 p.m. His right leg fidgeted in anticipation while his eyes darted around the dark area. There was only one nearby lamppost, where he'd parked his motorbike.

The other streetlights were either too dim or not functioning at all, and the 22-year-old boy wasn't as brave as he was when he was with his gang.

He found it weird when his friends backed out, not wanting to join him to meet the woman. A myriad of thoughts had gone through his mind when Mahirah invited him. What was it for? What could they do at a playground?

It was a very dark place, situated behind a daycare center. Nobody ever hung out at the area after dark, and vehicles seldom drove past as a new road had been constructed on the other side of the building.

He was starting to panic. Whatever sinful things he had wished to do with the woman disappeared from his brain. After another 10 minutes of waiting, Kamal wanted to get up and leave, but he jumped instead when he found Mahirah standing right behind him.

"Going somewhere?" she asked with the same fake smile on her face.

"I…No, I was just looking for you."

Mahirah chuckled as she shook her head at the boy trying to keep his cool. Anyone could look into his eyes and know he was afraid. If only Mahirah had brought along a mirror, just so she could let Kamal see how stupid he looked.

"So, where do you want to do this?" Mahirah asked as she took a step forward, forcing Kamal to take a step back. "We can do it here, for all I care."

Kamal stammered for the right words, but his mind couldn't form any coherent thoughts. He sized up Mahirah, taking in the curves of her body wrapped in a black satin blouse and matching skirt. He gulped as he backed into the wall of the daycare center, his uneven breathing louder than the dry leaves crunching under his feet.

"What are you…What are you doing?"

Mahirah's fingers were skillfully tugging at the hem of his shirt, which she ripped off in an instant. It would've turned him on – if he'd missed the split second where her pupils turned blood-red.

"Why are you shaking?" she asked. Her fingers felt for the zip of his jeans. "Cold?"

"Are we really doing this here?"

His voice was small, a contrast to his confidence when whistling and catcalling girls. But Mahirah didn't answer his question and continued to undress him like a doll.

She could see onlookers, especially those hanging from the tree branches above them. There were dark shadows in the drain beside them, and the same figure wrapped in kain kapan standing several feet away near a tree. Her friend waited behind her, sealing her off from the possible view of human eyes.

Mahirah pushed Kamal onto the ground, which was covered in leaves and dirt and yellowing grass. She straddled his waist, letting her skirt ride up her thigh as she stared at the naked man beneath her.

"Do you do this often?" she asked. He seemed taken aback, but she didn't give him time to answer. "You should've listened to your friend's advice. Faiz, right, his name? 'Never follow a woman who smells like a graveyard,' that's smart."

"How…How did you know that?"

"Well," Mahirah smirked, "my friend told me."

Just as the words left her mouth, the demon behind her showed itself to Kamal. It hovered above them, its long hair tickling the boy's feet.

Kamal screamed.

His eyes were bulging from their sockets as Mahirah laughed. She took the knife she had kept on the ground before Kamal arrived and held it high above his head.

"You're not bad-looking, Kamal," she said. "I hope you taste as good as you look."

It was impossible not to hear the screams when Mahirah began slicing the skin off Kamal's arms. But luck wasn't on his side, as not a single person walked by to save him.

Mahirah shut her eyes, satisfied with the taste of Kamal's flesh and blood that warmed her mouth. She continued to peel off his skin until he was only flesh and bones, then left him for her friend to devour whole.

The witch moved to the side with the folded skins in hand and watched the demon crouch over Kamal's lifeless body. It began to swallow the flesh in large bites, licking each bone clean. It was a risk, doing the job so close to her home, but Mahirah was getting impatient. She *needed* to have her wallpaper collection complete by tonight – the night of her 25th birthday.

None of the 25 boys were going to be missed, and certainly no one would suspect they were eaten by a hantu raya, unless those nosy women from the pasar got involved. Who would believe them?

Mahirah wiped the blood off her face and hands before cleaning the skin and putting them in her usual recycled bag. She waited until the demon was done and collected the bones, clearing the area of any signs of them. Kamal's clothes would be burned, his bones put away, and his skin displayed as her final trophy.

That was all Mahirah needed.

×

The neighborhood was extra quiet tonight.

It was already 11:30 p.m. when Mahirah reached her house, carrying the bag full of Kamal's remnants. She lit the seven candles and prepared for her ritual while she pasted the new skin onto the wall. The last of the beige wall could no longer be seen once Kamal's skin covered it.

She sighed when she was done. She wasted no time, going into the storage room and dragging the wooden chest out into the living room. It was placed in the center of the small room, the couch pushed against the wall to give her more space. The pungent odor of chemicals invaded the air once the chest was opened, revealing the bones inside.

Kamal's bones soon joined the rest.

With the same knife she had used to skin all 25 boys alive, Mahirah bit her lip as she sliced her own palm. The thick crimson liquid streamed down her wrist as she made a fist, letting the blood trickle onto the decaying bones. The droplets seeped between the crevices, and the whispers began.

"You shall be free of me," Mahirah said.

The demon appeared in front of the full-length mirror, bigger than it was before.

"All this for eternal youth?" it spoke for the first time. Its voice was hoarse and deep, sending a chill down Mahirah's spine.

"Are you judging me now?" she scoffed. "You and I devoured 25 young men for this. Your work here is done. I will send you back where you came from."

The demon didn't reply, so Mahirah proceeded with her ritual.

She retrieved her mandrakes and poisonous white mistletoe from the cabinet before throwing them into the chest of bones. The demon hissed in pain, its groans booming through the house. Mahirah kept chanting spells she had learned almost a year ago from a well-known bomoh in Kulim, her hometown.

Her voice grew louder as she recited the spells. Smoke was coming off the demon while its body grew smaller with every word that escaped Mahirah's mouth.

"I condemn you back to where you came from!" Mahirah shouted and slammed the lid of the chest shut.

The demon's screams pierced her ears, a shriek so high it could've shattered the windows and peeled the skins off the walls. The silence that followed was even more deafening. Mahirah, however, was satisfied.

She would live without ever looking a day older than she was then, and that's all she wanted.

"Happy birthday to me," she said.

The chest was pushed out of the house several minutes later through the back door. Mahirah's backyard wasn't large, but it was enough. There was a tree in the corner, with fresh soil she'd ordered a fortnight prior.

Perhaps the neighbors thought she was going to plant a garden, which was exactly what she was going to do.

Mahirah would plant a garden of bones.

She rolled up the sleeves of her blouse and began to dig, making as little noise as possible. Three holes were visible under the tree less than fifteen minutes later, and she opened the chest before tipping it over so the bones would fall into the holes. Mahirah made sure the bones were spread evenly, the soil covering every inch.

The truth was simple: she couldn't wait to get out of that godforsaken house. She washed her hands clean once she was back inside. The chest would be destroyed in the morning, and she would paint nice patterns on her new wallpaper for the next owners to admire. Maybe some flowers or butterflies.

Mahirah blew out the candles in the living room one by one. The last to extinguish she took with her as she walked toward the full-length mirror. A smile seemed to never leave her lips, her eyes scrutinizing every feature in the reflection.

"I will look this beautiful forever," she said to herself.

25 skins taken just for her own to last. Mahirah was going to be envied until the day she was buried. Her dark eyes stared back at her in awe, but they failed to see the long-haired demon that still lingered behind.

The Desired One

✕

Malachi Edwin Vethamani

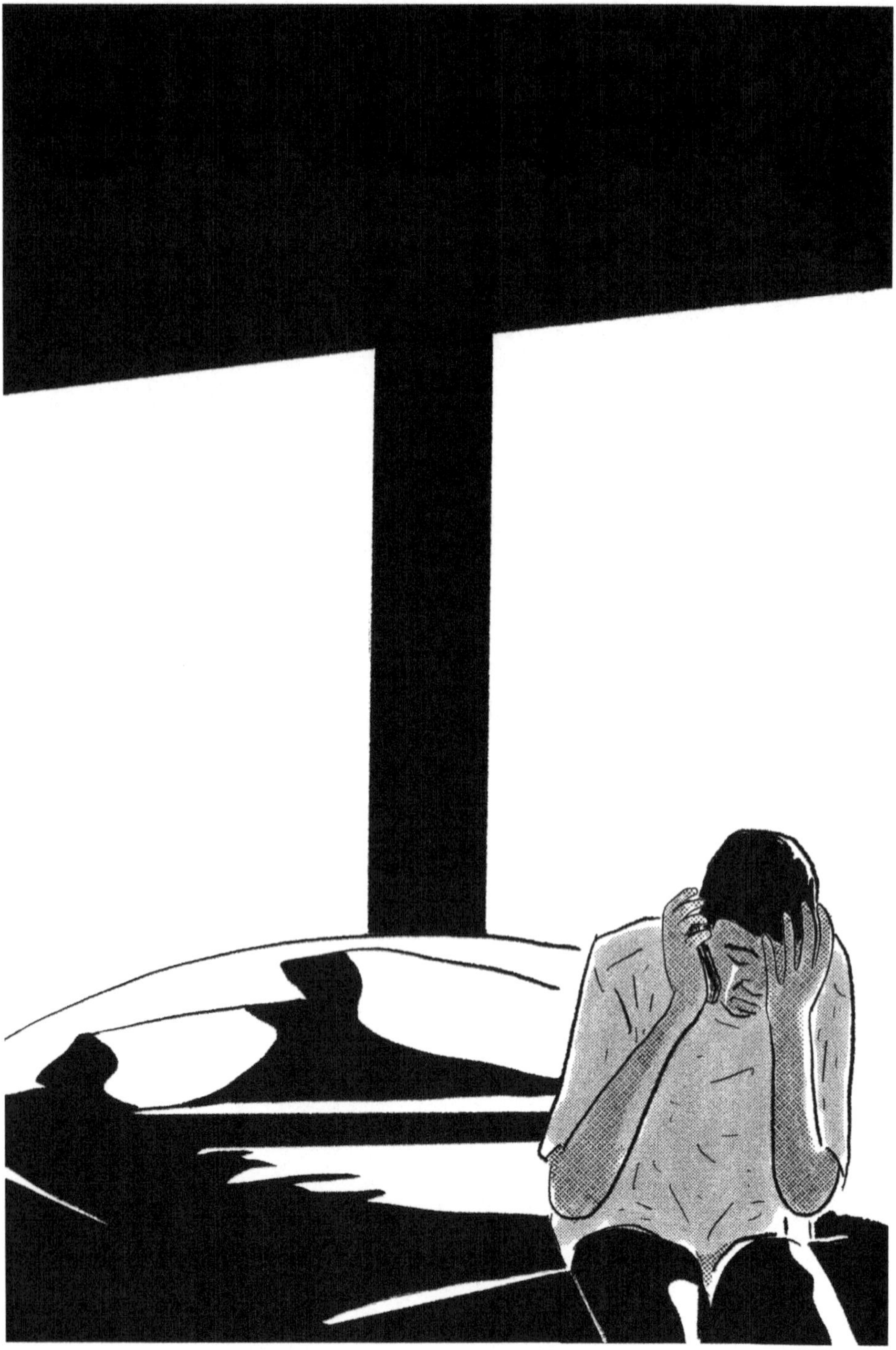

As he entered his lover from behind, the beloved cried out *Avven*, howled, turned around and bit deep into his neck. The loving embrace turned violent. Blood spurted out from the neck and he convulsed so violently that it broke the light body beneath him. A terror-struck spirit looked on from a distance. His earlier efforts to do good had all gone awry. The God of the Dead had his day. When their bodies were found, they were still locked in an embrace, one with the head of a dog.

×

It was a time of lockdown and social distancing. Everyone was staying indoors and neighbors who had generally been strangers now kept their distance even more. Kannan and Nandan shared a two-room flat in one of the less affluent Kuala Lumpur suburbs. It had a mixed group of residents: Malaysians, migrant workers and some of dubious origins. The two men kept to themselves and had no friends among the flat dwellers. It was mostly a head-nodding casual relationship, as they saw each other in the lifts or corridors. They kept everyone at a safe distance: Not too friendly a smile, and the fewer questions the better. Now with everyone wearing masks, Kannan and Nandan could not actually recognize most of them anyway.

Kannan drew closer to the sleeping Nandan. They were still facing each other. Nandan had dozed off in mid-sentence as he often did. Kannan gently laid his lips on Nandan's. He pressed a little harder. Nandan moved closer and his lips gently parted. Kannan, encouraged, gently pushed his tongue between his lover's parting lips. He felt Nandan's hand draw him closer into an embrace. In the warmth of their pressing bodies, they slipped into an undisturbed slumber.

When Nandan awoke towards the morning, he watched Kannan's gentle breathing. The snores of the night seemed to have subsided. Over the last three years they had become immune to each other's snoring. His throat was dry, and he felt a sore throat coming on. His body felt slightly warm and was aching. He got some water and decided to take two Panadols. Nandan began to panic, thinking of all the symptoms of the dreaded disease spreading across the world. He had been carefully following all the guidelines.

As usual, last Monday, he had met Mark and got him the week's groceries. Mark had seen him through his university days and Nandan was happy to be of help to him. Mark was elderly and not very mobile after a stroke, but seemed to be in general good health otherwise. They had spent time chatting and worrying about how things were going. Mark's dog, Ben, sat by his master as they spoke. Neither wore masks as they felt they were in their own private space. Later, as Nandan got up to leave, he hugged Mark and asked him to take care and be safe. Nandan remembered what he and Kannan had done together the night before. He hoped he had not picked up anything from Kannan. Or he had not picked up the virus at his workplace. It had been safe, and no positive cases had been reported in the places they visited.

Around 7 a.m., Nandan began to panic. His body ached more. He wasn't sure if he was just imagining it. Kannan was still asleep. Nandan called Mark. The phone went to voicemail. Nandan waited a few minutes and called again. Voicemail. Now Nandan was feeling ill and guilty. Nandan called Mark again. This was the fifth call that went to voicemail.

Kannan walked into the hall around 10 in the morning. "Thought we were going to have a Sunday lie-in," he said.

"I was thirsty and then couldn't get back to sleep. Thought it better that at least you had a good rest."

"Ready for some roti canai?"

"I'll make coffee. Can't wait till lunch?"

"Think I worked up an appetite after our workout last night. I need food."

"You tapau for us lah. I'm suddenly tired and don't feel like leaving the flat."

"Lazy bugger. I get the food first then shower when I get back."

Kannan left with his mask on. Nandan was feeling unwell. The Panadol did not help. His body hurt and his breathing was labored. It had been a while since he had an asthmatic episode. He went to the drawer and took out his Ventolin inhaler. He took three puffs. He had been constantly hearing about the symptoms and he couldn't tell if what he was experiencing was the real thing. He called Mark again. This time there was nothing on the other end of the line. No voice message even.

Nandan did not know Mark's family or friends. Nandan had met Mark at a charity event Nandan had organized with his Form 6 schoolmates. He had caught Mark's attention. Nandan struck Mark as intelligent. Mark was rich and wanted to help young deserving Indians. They kept in touch and when Nandan applied to a local university, Mark helped pay his fees. Mark supported Nandan from a distance, making no impositions. When Mark suffered a stroke a year later, his movements were impaired and Nandan began to visit him more regularly. Soon it became a weekly routine, when he helped with the dhobi and grocery shopping.

Kannan was taking an unusually long time. It should not take this long to pack roti canai and return. *Must be a long queue. Social distancing, MySejahtera, taking temperature*, he thought to himself.

Kannan appeared almost an hour later. "The bloody Mamak was closed. A worker tested positive. They are sanitizing the place. I had to walk a bit before I found a coffee shop. I got two packets of nasi lemak instead. That was the fastest and there was no queue for it."

Nandan sat opposite him. He was beginning to panic. He didn't want to say anything and hoped he would feel better soon. He drank plain water and gargled with salt water. He hoped that would help. It did not.

"I'll go catch up on the sleep I lost this morning."

"You want to go to bed at midday?"

"I'm feeling warmish. I've taken a couple of Panadols. My old asthma seems to be acting up. I used the inhaler. Let me sleep it off."

Kannan did not think much about it. They had been together most of the week. He had forgotten Nandan's weekly visit to Mark's earlier in the week. Kannan knew of Mark's kindness to Nandan. He liked it that Nandan was caring towards Mark. "Hey! Gratitude is a virtue. Send my regards to your Mark Mama," he had said to Nandan that Monday.

Nandan tossed and turned, trying to sleep. He was feeling more and more uncomfortable. Finally, he was worn out and fell asleep. Kannan checked on him around 2 pm. It was an odd Sunday. But then again, in the last two months everything had changed so drastically; today was not so unusual. Kannan got tired of playing games on his computer and watching sports on Astro. The daily statistics soon appeared on the news. This virus was not going away.

Nandan awoke and made his way to the hall. He did not look as if he'd had any rest. He looked unwell. Kannan began to worry and took Nandan's temperature. It was 40 degrees Celsius. Nandan got up to get some water and fell to the floor. Kannan carried him to the sofa. Nandan was lying unconscious as Kannan called 999. Within an hour, three men in full PPE came and took Nandan away. They wrote down Kannan's mobile number and said they would keep him informed. They asked him to do a test the next morning.

He tested negative and was asked to stay home for the next 10 days.

Kannan never got to speak to Nandan again. Four days later, an unlisted landline number rang Kannan's mobile phone. *Not another sales pitch*, he thought. "Hello, Mr. Kannan?" a soft-spoken female came on the line. On hearing his confirmation, she introduced herself as Sister Kwan, a staff nurse from the COVID ICU ward. "I'm sorry to inform you that Mr. Nandan Balasubramaniam passed away. He died a few hours ago. His family has been informed. We are letting you know because you had called the ambulance and we have your contact details. I'm sorry for your loss."

"Is there any way…I can say my goodbyes to him?"

"No, sorry. It's strictly family."

I'm his family, he wanted to say. *I've been his family for years,* he wanted to add. "I understand," he replied. Kannan looked at the empty side of their bed.

"I called you because in his delirium, he called out your name. He said, 'I will come back', those were his final words," the staff nurse said.

"Oh, Nandan!" Kannan lay on Nandan's pillow and wept. Kannan wept for his friend and lover. The last few years were bearable for both because they had each other. It was almost midnight when he awoke. The pillow which was often drenched with their sweat was now soaked with his tears.

Kannan prayed. "Please come back to me. In any form you choose, come back and love me again. I cannot live without you. Show me a sign and I will find you. Dear God, please let me find him."

Alsa, a good-natured but bumbling spirit, heard Kannan's plea. "Here's my chance to make amends," he said to himself. Alsa took pity on Kannan. He granted Kannan's wish.

✕

A dog stood forlorn and lost in a house. His master had gone away unexpectedly, taken away by strangers. He feared those men whose faces and bodies were fully covered. Ben had hidden under his master's bed. Once they left, he came out and lay on his spot on his master's bed.

Soon, the food his master had laid out for him ran out. He now drank water from the pails in the bathroom. As the night drew on, Ben lay on his master's bed. He missed Mark. He whimpered quietly and occasionally howled. In the dog's heart, he made a wish: *Give me a companion like Mark who will love me. I don't want to be left all alone.*

Alsa heard Ben's plea. In these days when people were dropping dead like flies and many hearts were being broken, he felt sorry for this creature, and granted Ben's wish.

A few miles away, a broken-hearted young man yearned for his dead partner. Alsa, seeing these two sufferers, used his powers to grant their wishes. They would all find each other as the desired one. This was the third and final wish he granted. Nandan's distressed face flashed in Alsa's mind as he recalled granting Nandan's dying wish.

Alsa vanished, having bestowed the three wishes required of him at his first level of spirit internship.

Ben felt a little peculiar when he woke up on his master's bed. He felt stretched and naked. In an unfamiliar fashion, he stood up. Saw his reflection in the mirror opposite. There stood a tall and handsome young man looking back at him. He heard a voice. Ben looked around. There was no one. "Ben, it's me. Nandan, your master Mark's friend. I'm not sure what happened. We are in this body together."

Ben let out a yelp which only Nandan heard.

Ben was familiar with Nandan's voice. It was a kind voice. Ben started to whimper. Nandan was confused and Ben's whimpering didn't help him. Nandan said to Ben, "Don't worry, I'm with you. We will figure this out." Ben slowly calmed down. There was an eerie silence. Two minds both lost in thought. It was unclear to Nandan how they could co-exist. He remembered he wanted to live. Now he was alive.

Nandan remembered his human body had died and he had desperately wanted to come back to Kannan. He just could not work out how Ben had a human body and they were both sharing it. It was mind-boggling. He felt glad to be alive. He remembered Kannan. He wanted to go back to him. That certainly posed a problem now. They were in Mark's bedroom. The voice in his head was screaming: How did he and Ben get into this human body? He did not think Ben had transformed into a human. And where was Mark? He could sense Ben's presence. And he was glad he didn't feel anything really doggish. They were in a human body together. Nandan was mostly in control. Ben tried to be calm in an unfamiliar body. Nandan sensed Ben's occasional whimpers. Nandan thought Ben was missing Mark or was confused. *I'm confused,* Nandan thought. Nandan remembered not being able to get in touch with Mark. It dawned on him that Mark had probably passed the virus to him and was also dead.

Nandan found Mark's clothes that were two sizes bigger than his own. A belt solved the pants issue. They were about the same height. He would go with a baggy look until he figured out what to do. Nandan began to think of some practical matters. *How will I explain my presence in Mark's house and Ben's disappearance?* Having looked after Mark the last few years, he knew where the supplementary debit card was. He had used it to buy the weekly groceries and sometimes get cash at the ATM for Mark.

Nandan felt a hunger. He wasn't sure whose hunger it was. He wanted biscuits. He knew that was Ben. He decided he would have a meal and both of them would have their hunger sated.

✕

At the ATM he withdrew 3000 ringgit – the maximum in a single day, Mark had told him. He felt a guilty pang; he was taking Mark's money for himself. He quickly left. *The security cameras would have recorded my transaction but how would they trace me?* he briefly worried. *No more "illegal" and risky activities,* he decided.

Nandan and Ben had a light Indian meal. Nandan wasn't sure how Ben would react to it. He also bought cream crackers, just to be on the safe side. Ben seemed quiet. *I'll watch what I eat and drink. Will have to give chocolates a miss.* Nandan made sure he didn't look suspicious. *How do I now make sense of this before I talk to anyone, especially Kannan? It's too early to go and sit in a park.* He decided to go to a café he had never been to. *I have to sort this out before I go anywhere near Kannan.* He ordered fresh apple juice and a slice of butter sponge cake. *Safe options.* Nandan was so preoccupied with his own thoughts that he did not sense any agitation Ben was feeling.

Nandan decided to gather his courage and call Kannan. His voice choked when he heard Kannan's voice: "Hello…Hello…Hello?"

Nandan replied, "Hello, I'm sorry to disturb you. I'm a friend of Nandan's. My condolences to you. I'm sorry to disturb you. I'm trying to contact his friend Mark and there's no answer on his phone."

"Mark died three days ago at GHKL."

"Oh God!" Nandan replied.

Kannan thought the voice suddenly sounded familiar. "Who is this?"

"I'm Mark's former colleague. Thank you." Nandan put down the payphone before Kannan could ask another question. "Kannan, sweet baby," Nandan said to himself. Ben was quiet. Mark's silence began to make sense.

Nandan returned to Mark's house. He could sense an excitement in Ben. When they were in the house, Ben quieted down. Mark was not in his regular chair in the living room. Mark's living siblings were abroad and certainly would not be back over the next few days. Nandan knew where to find their contact details but wasn't going to contact them. Nandan's mind was racing. He had quite forgotten about Ben till he heard some sounds. *It will be okay, Ben. Don't worry. You are with me. I will take care of you. We won't be seeing Mark. I will be with you from now on.*

"All-right," Ben replied.

"Did you just say *'All right', Ben?*" Nandan asked incredulously.

"Yes, I can talk," Ben replied.

Nandan needed to sit down. There was a talking dog with him in another man's body.

"It's not another man's body, Nandan. I woke up this morning and I had changed into a man. *You* are in *my* body."

"Thank God you didn't change into Kafka's monstrous insect," Nandan laughed almost hysterically. This was the first time he had laughed in a while and soon he broke down. The reincarnation and body-snatching were too much for him. He dozed off in the living room. Ben remained awake, watchful.

When Nandan awoke, Ben said he needed to pee. Nandan decided to sit on the toilet bowl to avoid anything untoward, not having done this before with a dog in him – or him in a dog, as Ben thought.

The rest of the day, Nandan talked through his plans with Ben. Nandan did all the planning. It was all very new to Ben, who grew restless; this was not his idea of being a man's best friend.

✕

Over the next two days, Nandan went back to his neighborhood. He watched Kannan from a distance. Kannan returned home at the usual time after work. Unlike before, he was alone. Nandan ached to be with his grieving partner. Ben was silent, sensing Nandan's emotions. Ben remembered sitting at Mark's feet. He yearned for his master's comforting voice and the treats Mark gave him.

Nandan bought the cheapest mobile phone he could find. He got a prepaid account. He remembered that Kannan and he had an account on Grindr they still used to chat with other gay men. He hoped Kannan would see his message and that way, he could find out Kannan's state of mind.

Nandan called his profile Nanben21, which was close to the Tamil word 'nanban' which means 'friend'. He did not want to freak out Kannan with a profile name like "Nanban' which was too close to his own name. Nandan sent a condolence message to Kannan. Said he had heard of Nandan's passing from a university mate. He asked Kannan if there were any prayer sessions he could attend, with lockdown SOPs of course.

The next day, Kannan replied thanking him for his message and informed him that Nandan's family was not doing any prayers during these pandemic days. Nandan thought of the next plan of action. He decided the direct approach would be best. A face-to-face meeting at a convenient place. Nanben21 asked Kannan if they could meet for coffee. Nandan was a long-time friend he had lost contact with and he wanted to meet Kannan just to catch up to talk about Nandan. He gave his mobile number and signed off as Ben. After he pressed SEND, he wondered why he had used Ben's name.

Kannan read the message on Grindr. He had not spoken to anyone about Nandan's passing. Nandan's death weighed heavily on him. Here was someone who knew Nandan and would not judge them. He thought about it and the next afternoon, he texted a message inviting Ben to a café near his flat. He added: 'please send photo so I can recognize you.' Kannan thought this would deter any imposter. Kannan and Nandan's photo was already on their Grindr profile.

The thought of seeing Kannan again set his heart racing. Ben seemed to make no demands on him. Ben had heard Nandan's thoughts and this made Ben miss Mark even more. Nandan thought he heard a howl. He wasn't sure, as Ben had earlier spoken to him. Nandan tried to be attentive towards Ben. Nandan was grateful that Ben was not difficult. That a man and a dog could occupy a single body, he didn't think it possible. He imagined he had a sleeping dog within him. Ben sensed Nandan's thoughts rather unhappily.

Nandan had less than 24 hours to decide how he would reveal himself to Kannan. His main worry: How do you tell your grieving husband that you have returned in another man's body with a dog in tow?

The café was quite empty. Nandan did the necessary MySejahtera registration and found a table at the furthest end. Nandan, true to his nature, had arrived early. He sat strategically looking at the entrance. He saw a familiar face approaching. Nandan's smile was hidden under his mask. Ben made no sound. Kannan saw him and nodded. It had been nearly two weeks since Nandan was so close to Kannan. He feared his voice would choke. Ben whimpered, Nandan moved in his seat. He stood up. For the first time in years, he was shaking Kannan's hand. The hand which already knew every part of him.

"Hi, Kannan."

"Hey, Ben."

"Thank you for meeting me. I wanted to see how you were doing."

"Managing."

Nandan's eyes welled with tears. Kannan was a little surprised.

"This is a horrible time. So many deaths," Nandan said.

Kannan thought he heard the same voice that had called him a few days after Nandan's death. A waitress interrupted them and took their orders.

"Kannan, when you received the news of Nandan's death, did the person say anything to you?"

"Why?"

Nandan hoped the hospital had informed Kannan of his dying words. "I was wondering what he might have said before he died."

"The nurse who called me said…Nandan mentioned my name and said he will come back to me. She said he was probably in delirium."

"What did you say when you heard of his death, Kannan?"

"I was heartbroken. I cried. I cried and prayed. I begged God to send him back to me. I begged God to send Nandan to me in any form. I wanted him back so badly."

"Kannan. Avven…Avven, naan terippi vandrikaren, Avven, I have come back to you, just as you prayed. I have kept my promise to you."

Kannan stared at the man sitting before him. The only person who ever called him *Avven* was Nandan. He only called out *Avven* during their most intimate moments. No one else knew this but Nandan.

Nandan's excitement grew on seeing Kannan's recognition. Ben moved uncomfortably in their body.

A Kulit for the Shadow King

Ismim Putera

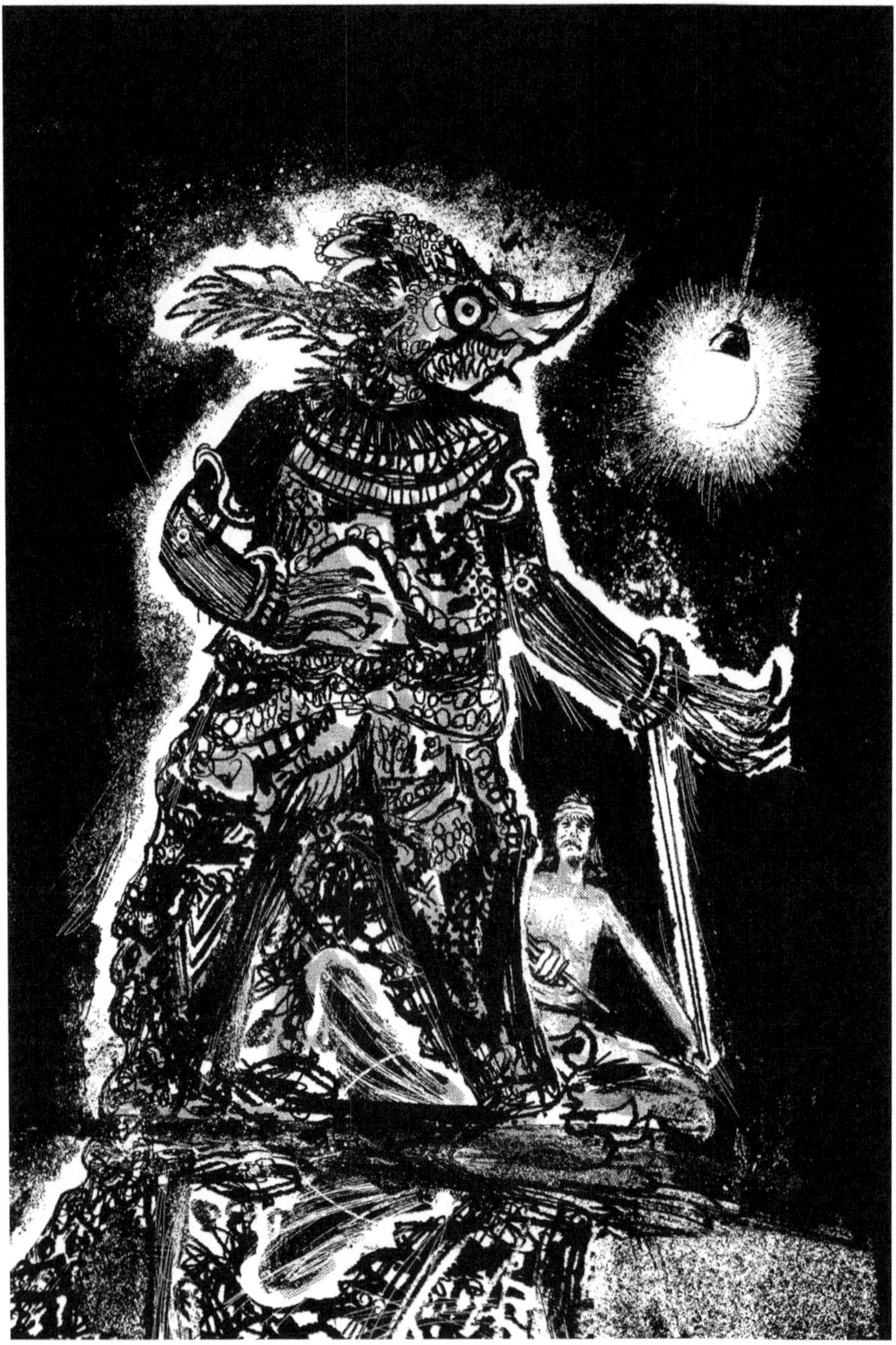

Rawana took off the Mask of Ten Demon Faces. A smudge of pale blue blood crusted the right half of the porcelain relic, down to his fangs which had just pierced the enemies' bones. The left half was shattered into pearly shards by a spear thrown at him at the speed of moonlight. The pieces flew in all directions and the poisoned tip nearly gashed his eyebrows. His celestial reflexes seized hold of the metallic bar, which was only a few inches in front of him. And with his aura alone, the spear burnt and splintered like a wet stick.

✕

The wayang kulit was in progress, and had just completed the first of four scenes. The play narrated a memorable scene from the epic *Hikayat Seri Rama*.

The performance was held once a month in the panggung. Despite the hot and humid atmosphere, the audience squeezed onto the wooden benches. The seats in the first three rows were fully occupied. Children sat on the laps of parents, and some on their parent's shoulders, to get better views. Some older people dirtied their sarongs by just sitting on the muddy ground. Outside, a crowd of shirtless youngsters stood along the perimeter of the panggung, peeking through the holes in the walls towards the stage. The ticket for the two-hour show were RM1, free for children under 12.

During the 20-minute break, the gamelan musicians calmed the restless crowd with deep beats from the gongs, metallophones and gendang. Some cheered and clapped. A few paired up to joget and ronggeng simply to enjoy themselves.

Tamin, the dalang, wiped the dust off the muslin screen and shone it with the brightest of light. He oiled the nuts and screws, swiftly unknotted the entangled strings and polished the puppets' faces. Being thin and fragile, they were about half the thickness of average human palms. The arms and legs were fastened with strong strings connected to control rods, to make them movable. He provided the shadow puppets with intense motions, memories from the distant past, tones, voices, breaths and magical essence. He gave them his *life*.

The puppets seemed eager to be re-animated back into the world by the artist. They waited for their turn, standing motionless on the gedebong.

✕

"Are you sure you want to do this, Tamin?" Azri, the chief gamelan musician, with a gendang in his hand, asked.

"Yes. This will be our final show. The Islamic department has issued the warning letter explaining the wayang kulit is forbidden and blasphemous because it portrays demons and gods other than Allah."

"But this is our culture. Our kampung has been doing this show for generations."

"Good point, you can tell them to their faces. I've told them that the show is just for entertainment purposes. They don't believe it. They don't want villagers involved in un-Islamic activities."

"Un-Islamic? It's just a cultural show!"

"Yes, we conjure spirits and demons and those villagers like the idea very much. They fear that we're spreading some sort of deviant teachings to them." Tamin exhaled a deep, remorseful sigh. As the oldest living dalang tonight, he was prepared for the last show

Tamin's great-grandfather, along with the pioneer musicians from the gamelan group, had collaborated to set up the panggung thirty years ago. The secrets of the art flowed into their veins and thus passed down to his grandfather then his father. The panggung was a small open-air theater, built on a barren field at the outskirts of the kampung. It was equipped with wooden chairs and bamboo benches for the audience. Thatched layers of intertwined nipah leaves formed the roof, strong enough to repel wind and rain.

Ever since the Islamic Department fortified certain sharia laws, almost all traditional arts and dances were strictly prohibited. Mak Yong, Ulik Mayang, Kuda Kepang were slowly disappearing. Apart from the invocations of spirits, those performances had also encouraged the mingling of men and women. The use of tight and revealing clothing would eventually lead to carnal sin.

"It must be his work, I knew it! That man has never liked us anyway." Azri put his gendang down next to his gong.

"Don't blame him. He's the new imam in this kampung and he needs to do his job. Anything that is against Islamic teachings will be penalized."

"I like the old imam, Haji Berawi. He was nice and open-minded. He watched and supported our show."

"No point remembering him now. He's in the land of the dead and can't help us anyway. Like him, this panggung is also going to be buried." Tami averted his gaze towards the blank screen.

"What are we going to do now? This wayang is the only way we earn for our living. I don't know where else to do our gamelan."

"Well, like the officers said, 'You have both hands and feet, why don't you get a more respectable job?'"

"Easy for them to say! All they do is conduct raids, patrol every now and then, and fine anyone that doesn't follow the rules. Then they spend their hot afternoons in air-conditioned rooms. Many days ago, I heard they fined a few men who'd purposely skipped Friday prayer. This is too much! It's none of their business if anyone wants to pray or not."

"This is an Islamic country and the state has been funding them. I guess I'll become a farmer or a fisherman. Better don't waste your time arguing with them. You still have your gamelan. Maybe you can do your performance in some private functions."

"It's difficult to get invitations these days," Azri said. "God! I feel so helpless."

✕

"Is this the house of Tamin bin Jali who worked at the panggung playing wayang kulit?" asked one of the officers. Other officers strolled among the puppets in the living room.

"Yes, I'm Tamin bin Jali."

"We're officers from 'you-know-what' department and we'll give you our final warning. This is the letter, read it carefully. The department wishes the activity to cease immediately. Otherwise we'll take serious action."

Tamin sat on the sofa while his eyes latched onto the letter, extracting the vital information. He had received a similar-looking letter a month ago.

"Assalamualaikum!"

A man entered his house. He was the new imam, Haji Budin, the most respected man in the kampung. He sat next to the officer.

"Ever since the gamelan group joined the panggung, the wayang has doubled its audience. The mosque is abandoned! They no longer do solat sunat or recite the Quran. Youngsters spend most of their time in the panggung, and even children no longer run around the mosque," the imam explained.

"It's true, Encik Tamin. We as Muslims are forbidden to get involved in activities clearly against our teachings. We cannot conjure any forms of spirits. Look at these puppets. Don't you think they resemble demons and monsters!" The officer with the long curly beard pinched the puppets.

"I understand." Tamin put the letter on the table.

"I want you to collect all your puppets and put them away. We'll close down the panggung for the sake of the villagers' aqidah. We'll turn it into something else, like a market or something."

The imam got up from his seat. He gave him a snide smile before leaving the house.

"I hope we don't have to come here again next month."

✕

"Help me, Rawana!" Tamin mumbled with his eyes shut tight. He sat in a magic circle inscribed with Sanskrit runes.

"How can I serve you, my master?" Rawana the puppet moved its head and opened its mouth.

"Give me strength."

"What kind of strength?"

"The strength you use to defeat Seri Rama."

"Haaaarrarr!" roared Rawana. The mouthpiece opened widely, stretching the strings sewn along the lips and face. Tamin could see its hollow body.

"I don't believe it! A dalang, the God of the wayang, asking help from an ugly puppet?"

"You're not ugly and you're not a demon! You were once a warrior. I know that you learnt the art to become a divine spirit. I conducted the ceremony to welcome you to our shadow world and then return you to your spirit realm. So, you must help me."

"What is it you wish for?"

"Give me strength to fight those men! I'm the dalang, protector of the puppets, conjurer of the spirits and defender of the wayang. They'll close down the panggung. I need your power."

"It's easy! We move out from here and find a new place. The earth is vast."

"There's nowhere to go. This state and also other states forbid ritualistic performances."

"Then we go to other countries!"

"We won't survive! Listen, I'm not a warrior who lifts swords or spears, but I want to protect the wayang. I've sacrificed everything for wayang kulit! Help me now!"

"And what do I get in return?"

"Anything! What do you want?"

Rawana paused. He could see Tamin's true intention, like a flame sparkling on a pile of raw coal.

"A new kulit," Rawana stated his wish.

"Kulit?"

"I'm a spirit, this puppet is my vessel and the shadow is my soul. I do not need anything else. The kulit is the only thing that allows me to walk in and out from our world to your world."

"So, you want to become a man again."

"That will be the payment for using my power."

"That can be arranged."

✕

The surging crowd clamored for attention. The wayang continued with its play.

Tamin let out a howl of amazement. Gradually the screen vibrated and the ground cracked as if suffering from an intense earthquake. Blinking lights twirled from side to side. He pulled the lamp closer to the screen, telling the audience the sun was engulfing the universe in its brilliance. Chaos had regained its ultimate purpose.

"Dunia langit dunia bumi, gegarlah!"

At the far-right corner of the screen an unworldly tree, Mahameru, skyrocketed from the plain earth. It was said the flower of the tree bloomed only once every 400 years. The flower bore the Mahameru fruit.

The tree was the bridge that linked the earth and sky. Tamin directed colored lights towards the screen, red then orange then green then sky blue. With images prancing on the screen, he pulled the string and the surface of the earth flickered again.

Droplets of glassy sweat condensed on Tamin's forehead. Slowly they trickled down and wet his neck.

It was time for the next scene. Tamin signaled the musicians to hit the gong ibu five times.

Kooom, koom, koom, koom, koom!

A strain of serunai stood out and alternated with the gong ibu. The dark air became a cacophony of innate musicality.

Tamin moved his right index finger vigorously, pulling on the string that instructed the puppet to extend its arm and plunge the miniature sword forward. The strings, as fine as a maiden's hair, were bow-string taut. The puppets reacted to very small and subtle shifts as if they could read the puppeteer's mind. The vocal work: blaring shouts and melancholic whispers, rhymed and unrhymed syair prose-poems, masculine war cries and feminine wails…

Hands and minds synchronized. It was indeed a superhuman task.

"Don't worry my friend; I'll let you win tonight. You'll be the king! I'll change the flow of the folklore." Tamin placed the Rawana puppet next to him, because the Shadow King deserved to sit next to the God. A faint smile glinted on the puppet's face.

Tamin delivered a breathless and effortless spiel about the epic. Flying monkeys, curses and mantra, keris and daggers, all weaved into a kaleidoscope of light and shadow. The portals of both worlds opened and merged into a singular bridge. Rawana, the Shadow King, rode his armored horse onto the screen.

Tamin moved the figures, expertly drawing the curves of confrontation between a naga and Rawana.

×

"I shall fight you, guardian of the tree!"

The naga uncurled and raised its hood. Two lupine eyes leered at Rawana.

"Another useless spirit! You want to fight me with those small bows and arrows? Look at yourself, even your mask is broken in half!"

"Haaaahaaa—" The audience hooted while clapping joyously.

"Yes, Naga Mahameru, I will slice your kulit and give it to the audience down there!"

Rawana was about one-fifth of the size of the naga. Bouts of arcane power amplified in him and he drew Taming Sari from the pocket. He gripped the hilt and chanted the mantra kuasa.

Three overlapping circles of red, golden yellow and green lights shone on the screen. The epic scene was diaphanous. The youngsters cheered in excitement, squeezing their heads through the holes in the wall.

He had only the right half of the Ten Demon Faces mask, but Rawana could stab his keris at the naga repeatedly in its slimy belly and back. The mask granted healing to him, each time a substantial amount of magical damage drained his energy.

The naga opened the cavern of its wide, fiery mouth to singe him. The battle seemed endless because both protagonists were immortal. The audience was as enthralled as the musicians. The troupe beat and percussed louder, adding acoustical suspense to the story arc.

Rawana divided his shadows into five forms and each figure attacked the naga at different spots simultaneously —

✕

When Tamin lifted the naga puppet, his soul shrank to the size of a tick.

"Argh—" Tamin pressed one hand over his chest, sensing pain gnawing his ribs. Both hands were slippery and uneasy. His breathing was short. The other fingers lost their grip on the remaining strings, and the puppets slowed to a trot before they completely froze, unanimated.

"What—no! Not now! We had a deal!" Tamin complained to Rawana.

The shadows on the screen blurred. The lamp before him was a fuzzy orb of golden fire. Tamin breathed deep and slow to maintain consciousness. Tears encrusted his eyes. A cold shudder made his body sway like coconut leaves against the black wind. Then a sharp call of the hypnotizing night-piercing serunai punctured the dreamy darkness. Unaware of his sudden ailment, the musicians continued their gamelan.

He wanted to continue but the piercing coldness pervaded his senses. Something lurked within his ribs, attempting to push his windpipe out. The puppet of Rawana slipped from his hands and fell next to the gedebog.

The screen remained bare for over a minute. The audience gaped restlessly at the bare screen, a world without living inhabitants.

"Tamin! Tamin! Are you okay?" a musician called to him.

Behind him, the other musicians murmured to each other.

Tamin was unresponsive and did not flicker a muscle. Azri put his gong ibu aside and rushed towards him.

"Tamin?" Azri pinched Tamin's shoulder to wake him up.

"What happened to him?" Another musician approached them.

"Shhhh! You're starling the God-Spirit!" Azri warned them. "We need to address the God-Spirit."

"What?"

"The God-Spirit is here! Look, he's not himself anymore. He…he smells different and…"

"What should we do?"

"Do nothing…nothing…" Azri removed his hand from Tamin's shoulder and knelt beside him, awed by the mystical phenomenon before him.

"Oi! What's happening back there?" shouted an angry man from the audience. "We paid for this show!"

"Oi!"

The musicians had stopped the music. Confused and irritated audience members talked to each other, voicing their disappointment.

"Sorry, but we have to end our show," Azri said, standing up to face them. "Please go back now."

"What?" The villagers voiced their frustration with harsh groans and jeers. The restive crowd went up the stage, trying to see behind the darkened screen. Some bystander surged towards the back of the panggung to steal a glimpse at the dalang.

"Stop! Stop! Please get off the panggung. It'll collapse!" Azri pushed some men down from the stage.

"The dalang is possessed by spirits!" a man shouted after jumping down from the stage. "Run! We must leave this place. The spirits might possess us too!"

The villagers bustled out from the panggung, taking their children with them, buzzing like hundreds of bees. Some lingered in the nearby bushes, eager to see the aftermath of the pandemonium.

"Get some help!" ordered Azri, frantic with worry. His face was as pale as a corpse's. "Go get the imam!"

On the stage, Azri sat next to Tamin, wiping the sweat off his brow and face. He murmured some incantations to wake him up.

"Stop this show now! I want everybody to get out from this place!" shouted Haji Budin angrily from a distance. He charged into the panggung along with a few religious officers. The musicians abandoned their instruments and rushed down from the stage immediately.

"Please don't harm my friend, Haji Budin. This is just an accident!" pleaded Azri.

"Accident? This is what happens if you disobey my warnings. He is possessed by the demon!"

Red-faced, Azri was silenced by the scolding.

"Now leave this place at once! I don't want to see your face anymore. Tell the villagers to evacuate!"

On the stage, Tamin stood facing the screen, talking but to no one in particular. Occasionally his hands twisted and his body twirled in a stance resembling a Mak Yong dance.

"Astaghfirullah! Tamin! What is this? Tamin!"

Tamin continued to dance along the edge of the stage, ignoring the men who tried to grab his shirt from behind.

"You've nice skin, my friend," Tamin greeted the officer once they caught him. They laid him prone on the stage, spreading his arms and legs. Tamin breathed heavily as his chest pressed the floor.

"This is not how you treat a king, my friend," Tamin smirked as the officers slapped his back many times to 'wake' him up.

"You've been possessed by the demon! It's using your body! Wake up!" Haji Budin's resentment had reached boiling point. He then kicked his legs.

Tamin remained stiff. His body was as rough as stone.

"Shall we perform the exorcism?" queried the young religious officer.

"Let him be! I'd love to see him suffer. We warned him many times. Let him taste his own medicine!"

"Take all the puppets and burn them now! The demon will leave his body once these puppets are destroyed!" instructed a senior religious officer.

They snatched the puppets from the control rods and piled them up behind the panggung. A fire was lit, slowly engulfing the entire set along with the spirits.

"Stop! My skin is burning! Stop!" Tamin shouted from the stage. That was not his voice. It was deep and dark. He rolled on the floor, as if to douse an invisible flame on his body.

"Leave his body, you ugly demon! Return to where you came from!" Haji Budin recited the verses while two officers restrained Tamin on the floor.

"Is this how you treat the Shadow King?" blurted a croaky voice at them.

"Shut up, demon! Get out from this body! You don't belong here!"

"No one tells me where I belong. I've lived in this world of yours and now I've conquered the shadow realms!"

"Silence!" Haji Budin continued chanting verses from the Holy Quran to torture the Shadow King. Tamin giggled and screeched in delight, deriding the team further. Only the sound of a sizzling flame chewing the puppets formed a slight background noise.

"You've burnt my kulit! I demand a new kulit!"

"You'll get nothing! Leave his body now!"

Tamin struggled fiercely. The officers tried their best to pin him down.

"Let's end this show now!"

As the men chanted their prayers, Tamin threw a violent fit. The unexpected jerk pushed the officers a few feet away from him. In an instant he was howling on all fours. He then stood straight, eyeing the men resentfully, and levitated a few inches from the floor. The main lightbulb exploded and glass rained down on them. It was pitch black on the stage. Only the flickering flame illuminated them from afar. A red crescent moon shone weakly at them.

"I'm the new King and I'll have all seven layers of your kulit!"

"Tamin! Tamin! What are you doing—"

"Help! Noooo! Noooooo–!"

Words were replaced by ear-piercing screams as Tamin buried his claws deep into the men's chests and necks. Their skins were peeled off their bodies like a tree shedding its old bark. Fatty tissue was discarded. The floor was a sea of red where the men were wriggling like fish out of water. The Shadow King pasted the silken skins all over his body, in many layers, covering his face, arms, torso, back, legs, palms and soles.

After a few moments of quiet, a black shadowy smoke exuded from the white screen and swirled into a circular portal. Amidst the raging flame on the stage, Tamin walked into it…

✕

The panggung was unexpectedly filled with people thrilled to spend their weekend in an air-conditioned hall. It could accommodate at least 500 people. The old panggung had been burned down by a great fire three years ago, killing five people in the tragedy.

Dato' Azri welcomed the audience with a brief speech. He was the president of Mahameru Wayang Kulit Club. The wayang had a few new dalangs. Enthusiastic youngsters had volunteered to indulge in the art of drama and music. The kelir screen was larger, and sophisticated equipment had been bought to augment the lighting effects during the show. Shadow puppets were designed from high quality materials, and new musical instruments, scripts and heroes were introduced.

The audience was waiting for a particular pairing: Maharaja Rawana, the Shadow King with his new radiant golden kulit, and his partner Maharaja Tamin, the God of the Sky. Both kings shared the kingdom of Langkapuri. Together they rode their sun-powered vimanas leading fleets of wingless nagas into the human realm…

The Gift

✕

Bissme S.

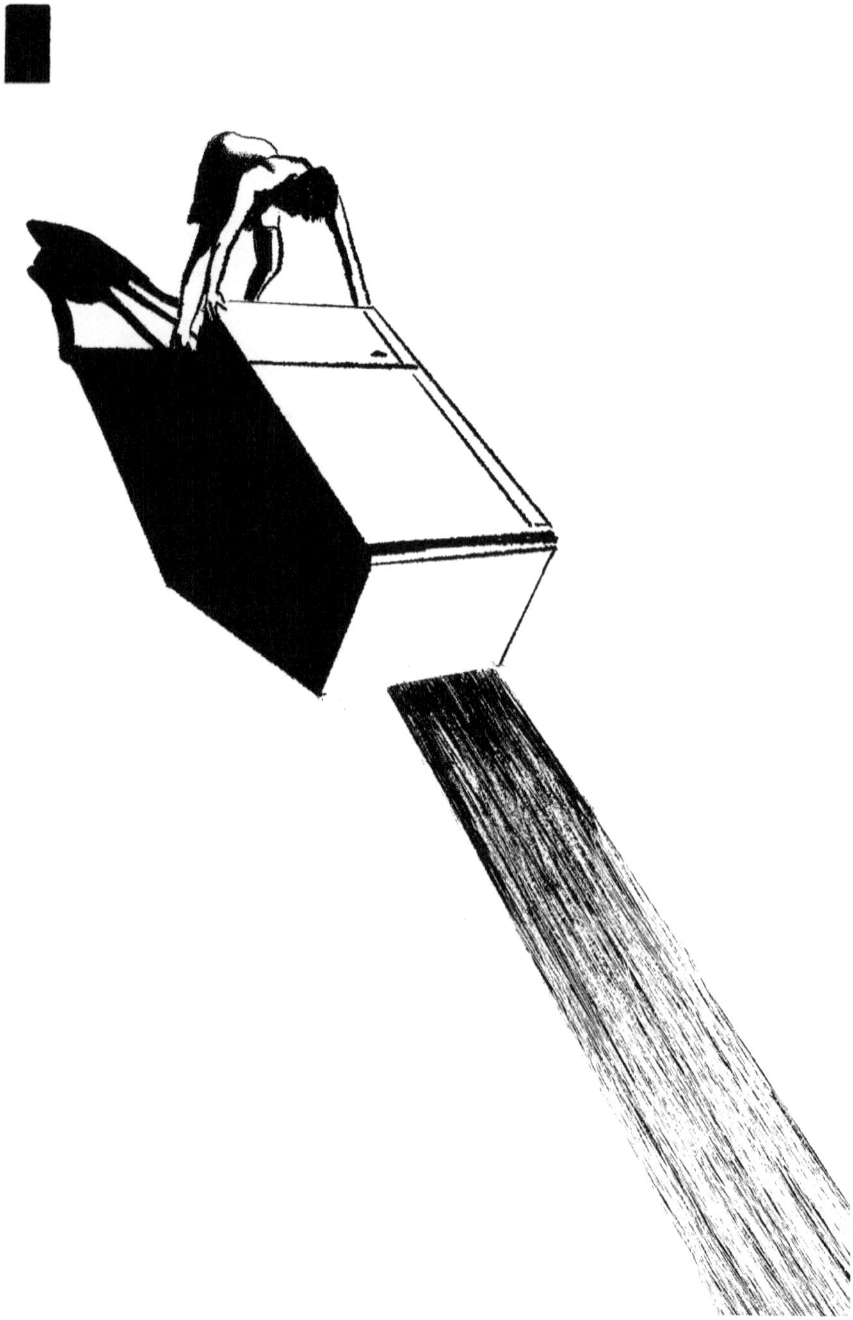

I did not need a mirror to look at my reflection. I just had to look at my sister. She looked like me and I looked like her. People had a hard time telling us apart. But as we got older, things changed.

People could easily differentiate us then. Physically, we still looked the same. We had the same long black wavy hair and green eyes. Emotionally, we were different. I was sane and she was not.

×

"I can see ghosts. I can talk to them," my sister kept saying.

My mother shouted, "Ghosts do not exist! You cannot see ghosts. You cannot talk to them. You are just making up stories. You just want attention."

My mother desperately wanted my sister to be cured.

The preacher said: "God cures everyone."

My mother said: "I just want the madness to end. I want everything to be normal."

My mother enlisted the help of a preacher who dabbled in exorcism. My sister was tied to the bed. The preacher recited words from the Bible while splashing holy water on her.

"God and the angels from the heavens, please have mercy on this child and save her soul from the devil and hell," the preacher said.

Spitting at the preacher's face, my sister said with laughter: "My darling preacher, I have news for you. There is no God. There are no angels. There is no devil. There is no heaven. There is no hell. Only ghosts exist."

×

"Are you afraid of the ghosts that you can see?" I asked.

Smiling at me, my sister answered: "I used to be afraid of them. Not anymore. What I have is a gift. Not everyone can see ghosts. Not everyone can talk to ghosts."

A gift is supposed to enrich your life. A gift is supposed to make you happy. What my sister had was not a gift. It was a curse. Her gift had ruined her.

✕

God was not kind to us. God failed to cure my sister. Reluctantly, my mother had to put her in an asylum.

Down on her knees with tears streaming down her cheeks, my sister begged: "I do not belong here. Take me home."

My mother turned a deaf ear to her. "This place will cure you," she said.

"You will regret this!" my sister shouted.

A week later, my sister was found hanging from a ceiling fan. She left behind a strange-looking painting on the wall. The painting had a woman who looked like my mother, dragging a refrigerator.

On the wall where the painting was, my sister wrote:

Dear Mom,

Jason has forgiven you. I am not as kind as Jason.
I will never forgive you.

"Who is Jason?" I asked.

My mother said, "Your sister was mad. She was talking gibberish. I do not know any Jason."

Later that night, I saw my mother at the backyard of our house, burning the painting to ashes and crying her eyes out. My mother was hiding something sinister.

✕

At my sister's funeral, my mother never stopped crying.

Dramatically beating her chest with her hands, she kept repeating: "I killed my daughter…I killed my daughter!"

My mother kept hugging the coffin, refusing to let it be buried.

My relatives were busy consoling her. "You have to let go. You have to allow your daughter to be buried. You have to let her soul rest in peace," they kept saying.

I had a totally opposite reaction from my mother. I stood like a mannequin, no tears, no emotions and no tantrums.

One of my cousins said: "You should cry. You should not bottle up your emotions."

I answered: "My sister died a long time ago. Today, we are just burying her."

✕

The truth cannot be hidden, not forever. On her deathbed, my mother finally confessed who Jason was. The strange painting that my sister had done finally made sense.

My sister and I were not her only children. I had an older brother named Jason that I had never met. When Jason was seven, my mother killed him.

"For me to be happy, Jason had to die," my mother said.

✕

My mother had hated every moment of her pregnancy…the morning sickness…the swollen feet…the strange cravings. She was constantly irritated. Tears flowed for no apparent reason.

"When Jason was born, I thought my misery would end," she said.

But she was wrong. Her misery was just beginning: "Jason drove me insane with his cries and his tantrums."

She hated motherhood as much as she had hated pregnancy. "With pregnancy, your misery ends after nine months. But with motherhood, your misery lasts as long as your child lives."

My mother could no longer tolerate her misery. She took a kitchen knife and mercilessly slit the throat of the son she was supposed to love.

Holding his lifeless body in her arms, she said: "No more tears. No more tantrums. Finally, some happiness."

✕

My mother stuffed the lifeless body of her son in a refrigerator. She had dragged the refrigerator to the porch of her house.

She then called the police. She told a story of a clown she had encountered on her porch a week before Jason was killed.

She said: "The clown was trying to sell me a refrigerator. I was not interested. The clown got angry."

She tried to convince the police that the clown had murdered her son and stuffed his body in a refrigerator.

She said: "I can never forget his last words to me."

"What did the clown say?" the police officer asked.

"A sad clown is a cruel clown."

✕

The police intensely searched everywhere for the sad, cruel clown.. But they never found him. The police never truly believed the ridiculous clown story my mother had fed them.

They were certain that my mother was the murderer. But they did not have enough evidence to apprehend her.

She said: "God loves me…Perhaps God loves all murderers."

Unlike the police, my father believed my mother was absolutely innocent.

He said: "No mother would be cruel enough to kill her flesh and blood."

My father failed to understand that some mothers are not meant to love their children.

"Why did you kill Jason and not us?" I asked her, out of the blue.

I was surprised when my mother did not leave my question unanswered.

She said: "I was very young when I had Jason. Perhaps I was not ready to be a mother yet. When I had you and your sister, I was older. I was more mature. I was more prepared to be a mother."

After a long silence, my mother spoke again.

"Perhaps I love daughters more than sons. You can never really know why a mother kills her child."

Sometimes, I wish it was my throat that my mother had slit… Sometimes, I wish it was my body that my mother had stuffed in the refrigerator…Sometimes, I wish I could switch places with Jason. Death can be beautiful. Death can be the end of all misery.

"Your sister was not lying to us," my mother said before swallowing some bitter pills with a glass of water.

After the pills were inside her body, she continued: "Your sister could really see ghosts. The only way she could know about Jason is if she saw his ghost. Jason probably told her the horrible thing I did to him. Only a heartless mother would kill her child."

There was a long pause before she asked: "Do you think Jesus will forgive me for killing my son?"

"Jesus is kind. Jesus forgives everyone," I said.

"Do you forgive me?" my mother asked.

Some sins cannot be forgiven. I believe my mother should rot in Hell for what she did to Jason. A mother is supposed to love her child, not kill him. But I did not want to torture a dying woman.

"All children forgive their mothers," I lied, while hugging her to my chest.

She died with a smile on her face.

✕

What motivated her to reveal the secret she had kept in her heart for years? I wondered.

Perhaps she did not want to go to her grave carrying the heavy burden of her sin. My mother was looking for redemption, and I was her ticket to it.

Like my mother, I have a secret in my heart. But I will never confess my secret to anyone. I will carry my secret to the grave.

I am no different from my twin sister. I can see ghosts, too. But I do not want to be labeled as mad. I do not want some priest reciting words from the Bible and splashing holy water on me while I am tied to a bed.

I do not want to spend the rest of my life in an asylum. I want to remain sane. I do not want my life to be a carbon copy of my sister's. Our faces may be the same but our lives would be different.

I do not pay heed to what I see. The ghosts try to talk to me, to tell me their stories. I turn a deaf ear to them.

I keep whispering to myself: "Ghosts do not exist…Ghosts do not exist…"

✕

Since her death, my sister has been haunting me.

She keeps whispering in my ears: "You have to tell the world I was not mad…You have to tell the world you can see ghosts, just like me…You have to tell the world that ghosts exist…Ghosts walk among us."

I refuse to acknowledge her presence.

She says: "I will keep talking to you till you speak to me. You cannot ignore me forever."

I am determined to not give in to my sister. The dead should not be talking, roaming among the living. The dead should remain dead.

✕

I am on a blind date. I am enjoying myself. Our conversation is lively. My sister followed me on my date. She sits in front of me, right next to my date.

She says: "You can't shut me out of your life. I am your twin sister. I am a part of you. Talk to me, you stupid fucking bitch."

I ignore my sister and her harsh words. I focus on my date. I only pay attention to what my date has to say.

Looking at the pendant of Jesus Christ at my neck, my date says: "I do not believe in the existence of God. I am an atheist. But you seem to be religious."

Clutching the Jesus pendant, I say with a smile: "I am not religious. This crucifix is just a decoration. There is no God. There are no angels. There is no devil. There is no heaven. There is no hell. Only ghosts exist."

My date laughs loudly. So do I.

The Original Mother

✕

Atikah Wahid

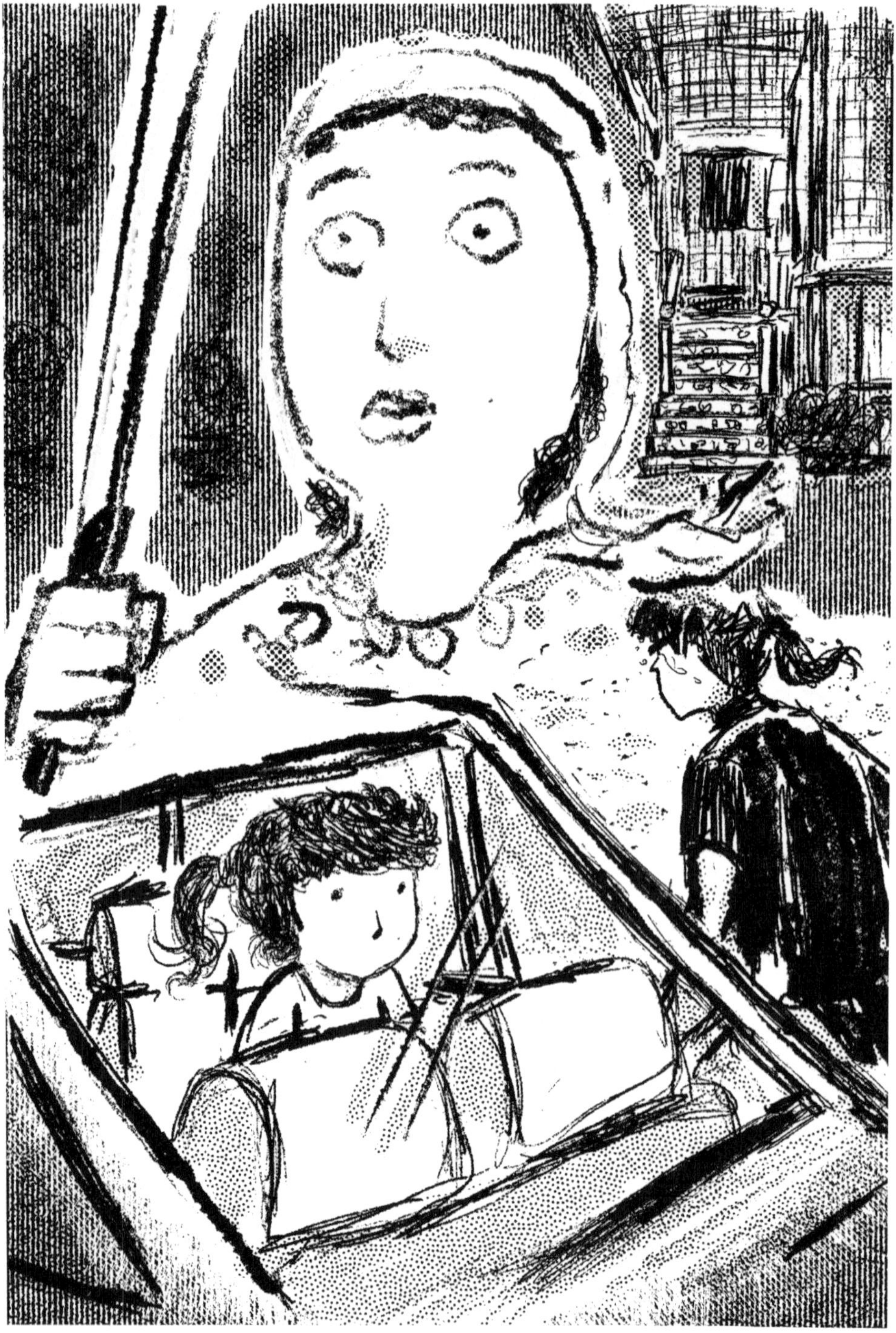

Sometimes when Balqis wasn't careful, her mind would wander back to a particular memory of Ibu: the first time Ibu let her ride a carousel.

It happened during one of their special Aidilfitri traditions together. Ibu and daughter, hand-in-hand, traipsing along with other tourists in Genting Highlands. She was much younger then, when she could be distracted by the bright lights and had Ibu's undivided attention. Balqis had once loved that it was only the two of them during this special occasion, and she used to brag about her theme park escapades. That was before she learned why the hills became a sanctuary during a holiday dedicated to families.

The carousel towered above her in its startling blazing colors, and the rush of the horses thundered by her in their perpetual circular track. Despite her unblinking gaze, Balqis did not want to ride the carousel that day. Yet, when Ibu led her by the hand through a crowd of other families, the child found herself clambering onto her own personal horse. Balqis remembered how tightly she held onto the pole skewering her horse while she tried to return Ibu's enthusiastic waves with her own reluctant ones. Then, the world began to spin. And Ibu disappeared from the crowd.

Balqis couldn't remember much of what happened next. Years later, Ibu would tell this to anyone willing to hear: that the theme park employees had to peel Balqis off the ride. That she would not let go nor stop screaming. The ride was stalled for half an hour as an inconsolable child held it hostage. Until Ibu came to save the day.

"Oh, Qis, I should've never left you there."

It was this memory that came unbidden to Balqis as she drove through the empty kampung lanes in the dark. She had been on the road for two hours with no stops and she was about to reach her destination. At least, that was what Google Maps told her. In her handbag was the catalyst for this forbidden trip. A pink wedding invitation card decorated with faux pearls—Balqis' name emblazoned on the front along with the name of the man she was going to marry in a month. Its envelope was left bare with nothing to indicate the guest. The term "Nenek" lingered in her mind, but they were strangers, not even acquaintances. But the wedding would change it all.

It was Balqis' turn to abandon Ibu and she wasn't leaving until it was done.

Over the course of one year, the wedding had become an unmanageable yet inevitable mess. The pink card had been a problem. The white and gold color theme for the wedding hall had been a problem. The venue was too small, the date not suitable. Balqis' mother had decided that she would twist and turn the threads surrounding this wedding, unfurling ugliness until the day arrives. An early marriage? Vulgar in Ibu's eyes.

"Ibu, this is what I want. You always told me that you'd support my dreams." Balqis could not conceal her disappointment when she and her boyfriend informed Ibu of their decision to marry.

"And being tied down to a man at 23 is a dream?" Ibu countered. Amir, the man in question, nervously laughed. For a moment, Balqis felt as though she was in a scene in one of Ibu's plays. Ibu always had a flair for being the center of attention.

"You got married at 19!"

The older woman brandished her arms out as though taking a bow. "Welcome to your cautionary tale. Haven't you been paying attention?"

Balqis knew Ibu would object; marriage was not a word in her vocabulary. Ibu had only married once, to Balqis' father, and she skittered around the topic since then. Ibu loved men – Russian roulette-style. There was Uncle David, perpetually smelling of smoke, a gold chain tangled in a carpet of chest hair. There was Kai, the young and waif-like understudy at Ibu's last theatrical performance. Men would come to their doorstep like mail, some light and meaningless as junk mail while others were hefty packages that needed to be undone carefully. They all called her "Dewi", her stage name. Goddess.

What was it like to be the daughter of a goddess? When she was younger, Balqis felt like an extension of her mother, tagging along as part of the "Dewi the C-list celebrity" package. She would follow Ibu to casting calls and television commercial sets, trying hard to blend into the background. At other times, Balqis was another face in a bewildered but amused audience. There was no moment where Ibu did not snatch attention to herself. Her appearance was loud but her voice was louder. Balqis used to dread parent-teacher events at school because, unlike other parents, Ibu assumed her appearance on those days was far more important than her child's school performance. She would totter to Balqis's classroom in her six-inch heels, her bronze-tinged coiffed hair gleaming in the morning sunlight.

Balqis met her father sporadically – when funds ran low, Ibu would remind him of his Islamic duty to provide for his daughter. Apart from bearing his name, Balqis could not relate. Balqis did not mind this absent relationship. Despite Ibu's haphazard CV of television and theater gigs, Ibu somehow made it work for them. Her usual mantra: *I am all you need.*

"Don't you worry about it," Ibu would wink and slip a RM50 note into her daughter's hand. "You got me, remember?"

But all Balqis did was worry. Worry that Ibu's never-ending charm may run dry. After all, wasn't it Balqis who prepared the meals at home, a skill she learned due to Ibu's unpredictable working hours? Wasn't she the one to brush the tears from Ibu's face each time Ibu confided about her relationship troubles? While Ibu would drop off gifts and money to Balqis like a benevolent fairy godmother, Balqis felt as though she was the one responsible to patch the empty spaces in their lives. At times, she wondered if a father figure would make their lives better. But it wasn't enough. She was homesick for a different sort of blood tie.

Come Aidilfitri, the television commercials would instill a piercing longing: boisterous families arriving in droves to the huge yards of kampungs for a long-awaited reunion, with gleeful children running into the arms of grandparents. It was the allure of a welcomed return, the seduction of collective forgiveness, the mirage of a happy family, extending through generations. Balqis would watch these ads in a cold hotel room in Genting Highlands, their own special Raya tradition. Ibu thought distracting Balqis from filial poverty with noisy roller-coasters would do the trick – and it did. For a few years, at least. But she couldn't help wondering what it would feel like to run into the open arms of a woman called her grandmother.

✕

"Qis, sayang – don't. This is a bad idea."

She sighed, even though she expected this answer. She rolled over in her bed and switched her phone to another ear. She knew Amir too well, he would err on the side of caution. It was part of his appeal – he could keep her grounded where everything else in her life was up in the air. But not at the very moment.

"Oh, come on –"

"*Come on*? Qis, this is not a decision you make on a whim! We have to think this through."

"Well, I've thought it through, and I need you to be okay with this."

For a second, Amir balked at her answer but composed himself. "Qis. You're planning to meet your crazy grandmother who you haven't seen in *years*. She might not even remember you! And what will Ibu say?"

Balqis stiffened. "Well, she will just have to deal with it. Somebody needs to be the adult in this family and if I have to be that person, so be it! Also, my grandmother is *not* crazy."

Amir's silence hinted otherwise.

"Amir, I need to do this. I need to fix us."

"Look, Qis…" Amir's words trailed into a long-suffering sigh. Balqis could just imagine the resigned look on his face. The two fell into silence but they knew the argument had been settled. Another sigh. "All right, let me know when you're going. Might as well introduce me too."

"Wait – you're coming?"

"Of course. I'm your fiancé now, so wherever you go, I go."

Balqis squeezed her eyes shut. "I think – I think I'm doing this alone."

"Qis –"

"Look, you might be right. She might be too old to remember me. The last thing I want to do is overwhelm her. I need her to know me for me, sayang. I need her to know me first. Not just as Ibu's daughter. Not just –"

"My future wife?"

It was Balqis' turn to be silent.

"Balqis…you're a lot more like your mother than you think."

<hr>

The car moved slowly as Balqis peered at every house on the street like a predator; her phone had indicated she was close so it could be any of these houses. Lying under the wedding card in her bag was an unsent letter Balqis had found in an old shoebox. A letter with the address of the kampung house. The notes felt fragile as though they had been refolded several times, the splotchy ink implying shed tears – perhaps of guilt, or even relief. It was in Ibu's handwriting, announcing she would never return and that she had found a savior in a husband. Balqis couldn't recognize the woman in the letter.

Suddenly, excitement gripped Balqis' heart. A wooden house came into view and somehow, she instinctively knew she'd found it. She had been here before. But most importantly, Balqis could see light within: her grandmother was home.

<hr>

Another memory floated into her mind: Balqis at six, feet dangling above her seat, half-listening to the talkative man driving. Balqis could not remember what he looked like, but he was the only person who managed to waver Ibu's conviction of remaining a single parent. A traditional Malay man, he wanted the whole nine yards: meet the future in-laws, engagement ceremony, grand wedding reception, et cetera. His enthusiastic nervous ramblings only highlighted the unfamiliar silence emanating from Ibu. Years later, Balqis would recognize it as a sign of her intense fear. They were visiting Nenek for the first time.

When Nenek's house came into view, Balqis realized how big it was for a single occupant. The house stood on stilts, the windows and doors open like maws. Only the concrete staircase, with rows of colorful floral tiles, felt welcoming. The entire house dwarfed their two-bedroom flat. "Wait here." Ibu stepped out of the car before the man could protest. She hesitated on the steps but quickly disappeared into the open door, calling out, "Ibu!"

Curtains raised and Balqis would never forget the scene that unfolded.

The house was still at first, the only noise Balqis could hear were grumbles from the driver's seat. Suddenly, a wave of rising voices emanated from the house, angry and relentless. Then, a crash made them sit up in their car seats. A second later, Ibu appeared at the door, scrambling down the stairs, with a tear-streaked face. She slipped as she thrust her feet into her slippers. That was when Nenek came to the door frame, brandishing a parang.

"*Useless child!*" the older woman spat. "I will make you *learn*. How dare you come to my house after –"

Anger was displaced by shock. Nenek never finished her sentence. Her gaze fell on Balqis, shy and shivering in the backseat. A tiny mirror image of her own daughter. A granddaughter she never knew existed. For Balqis, fear intermingled with awe; the matriarch figure was stunning in the child's mind. The sharp cheekbones, the fury in her eyes, the compact strength in her petite figure. As the man frantically reversed the car out of the yard, the hope of a wedding dissolved. And after that, he stopped coming to their flat.

Through the years, words lingered unspoken between them. Balqis always tried to dig deeper, to trace the hurt back to the old kampung house. But Ibu, for all her eagerness in diving into life blind with arms wide open, had kept that one secret. Conversations stunted before they began – Ibu would glower so fiercely that it felt as though Nenek had burst forth from her body. Finally, she relented but the words were as transparent as smoke:

"When I was born, my mother already knew how my life was going to turn out. The women in our family…are different. We have specific rules to live by. Responsibilities," Ibu continued as tears spilled down her cheeks. "I proved her wrong, I could escape. I won't inherit their hell. And I won't let it happen to you, too."

The answer was disappointing. For years, Balqis raked over these words, trying to interpret them. Balqis continued to ask Ibu as time went by, tugging that fragile filial thread from herself to her grandmother.

But one day, Ibu made a misstep. After a long day at work, Ibu came home delirious with fatigue. Balqis was helping her tired mother to bed when she said: "She would've loved you."

Balqis froze. Ibu continued, unperturbed: "She always wanted a good daughter. I was bad. Very bad. Never listened to anything she wanted. It was her fault though…" Ibu yawned, rambling as she turned over: "Her fault. Shouldn't tell me. I didn't mind about it all. The stupid rituals. The feeding… *But it was so ugly.*"

"Ugly? What's ugly?" Balqis held her breath.

But Ibu started to snore softly and the magic was broken.

Balqis pondered at these new words, another clue to a world she had been excluded from. For all her life, Balqis felt untethered, like a forgotten item slipped underneath a sofa. Learning that their family might have a dark secret did not push her away. Ibu could be wrong. Wouldn't be the first time.

Balqis was aware that the emptiness that had been steadily built within her began with a choice made by someone who was not her. In a few months, she would find herself married – would she simply repeat the cycle? Continue the trail of broken families and damaged children? No, she would take the reins that Ibu had long abandoned.

✕

Balqis drove into the wide kampung yard. She absentmindedly slammed the car door shut behind her, her eyes never leaving the bright fluorescent light within the house. Then, a small figure appeared by the doorframe: *Nenek*. Balqis clutched her phone closer to her heart, almost wishing someone would call. Amir, or even Ibu. One last plea for blissful ignorance. But every step closer to the house felt foretold. Balqis was meant to be here. Hadn't she witnessed a younger Ibu making the same pilgrimage? It was her turn now, and Balqis would not return until she got her grandmother's blessing for her marriage. Balqis was not Ibu, no matter what Amir said. She was her own person, looking for her own place in the world.

You can't keep me to yourself anymore, Ibu, Balqis thought as she stepped onto the cold, muddy tiled staircase. *I can take care of myself now.*

Yet her heart felt as though it was being wrested out of her ribcage. Even in the shadow of the night, she could tell her grandmother's gaze was following her every move. Balqis swallowed her fears and stepped onto the wooden foyer of the house, the home of Ibu's childhood.

"Nek?" Balqis' voice rang out in the silence.

Years of absence had created a fearsome image of Nenek in Balqis' mind. Balqis imagined her as a force of reckoning, one that she should never cross. Ibu's sparse details certainly did not help. Balqis did not know what to expect. An invitation to a long-denied hug? A parang just like what Ibu faced? But standing before her was anything but that person.

Nenek 's bulging eyes blinked at Balqis' voice, dull and lifeless. Underneath the light, Balqis could see how skeletal she had become, her skin sallow and mottled with veins, wisps of her remaining hair fluttering in the wind. Was this the woman they had feared all their lives? All Balqis could see was a wretched elderly woman. Balqis' heart clenched now, but for a different reason.

"Nenek, it's me." Balqis tried again but this time she stepped forward and held out her hand. Then, she kissed the hand of the woman who gave birth to Ibu with the reverence she deserved. "I'm Saleha's daughter."

Finally, a flicker of recognition in Nenek's eyes of a name long buried. A croak escaped from her lips: "Saleha?"

"Yes, Saleha." Balqis nodded. "I'm her daughter, Balqis. We… met once."

As Balqis stepped into Ibu's childhood home, all she saw was further evidence of Ibu's abandonment. A strong smell of mildew and dust permeated the air. Furniture, possibly in their prime decades ago, was scattered about the space. Balqis tried to imagine the fantasy kampung house of those Raya ads that lived in her mind, but this fell short. Apart from the foyer and living room, the rest of the house was enveloped in darkness. Balqis wondered if she had interrupted Nenek's sleep.

For a while, they sat on the wooden floor in uncomfortable silence as Balqis struggled to cross the years of separation. Balqis hadn't thought this through. Nenek's face was as blank as slate but her eyes remained fixated on her granddaughter. Those same eyes widened as Balqis placed something between them. The pink wedding invitation card.

"Nek, I'm getting married soon. Next month, in fact. I would like… for you to be there. I want you to meet my future husband."

Nenek extended a bony trembling hand to the invitation card, softly fingering its faux pearls.

"And I want you to be there, not just for the wedding but – our whole lives. You don't have to worry about money or transportation. I will handle everything. I know you and Ibu –"

"Ibu?"

"Yes, Ibu. Saleha?" Balqis wondered if Nenek even knew who she meant.

Then, an almost childlike smile brightened her grandmother's face. She cradled the invitation card in her hands. "Ibu," Nenek began to coo, almost absentmindedly. "Ibu."

Balqis parted her lips, speechless. She had expected Nenek's wrath or indifference, perhaps even toyed with the idea that her grandmother might be dead. But senile? As she watched Nenek giggling by herself while repeating the same word, new emotions took over Balqis. Disgust. Hatred. Disbelief. What did Nenek do to Ibu to deserve this? Through the years, Ibu had been a lot of things to Balqis, but never cruel. Yet, all she saw now was evidence of neglect.

A familiar cry rang from Balqis' side. *Amir*, Balqis thought as she fished her phone out of her handbag, until she saw the name on the screen. Whatever fear she had felt about her grandmother earlier shifted to a new owner.

"Ibu?"

"Qis, where are you?"

The question hurled at her as sharp as a knife. "Ibu, I –"

"Please don't tell me you're in Melaka. Please don't tell me you're doing the single most dum –"

Shock floored Balqis into silence. How did she…? Then the answer popped into her mind: Amir. Betrayal stacked on betrayal. Now, she knew she was truly alone in her crusade to end the curse that haunted three generations of her family. Balqis stood up and walked outside to the darkened foyer, preparing for a fight that was years in the making.

"And what if I am?" Balqis' retort was just as sharp.

"Come home *now*. Is this some kind of a sick punishment because of what I said –"

Balqis' grip tightened on her phone. "This has nothing to do with you! It's about *me!*"

"Give me a break! There is nothing there *for you!*"

Balqis looked at the "nothing" sitting in the living room, still holding onto the invitation card lovingly. "If only you could see what I see now, Ibu. You wouldn't –"

"What are you talking –"

"Ibu, I'm at the house. I met her."

Silence from the other side of the call. For a second, she wondered if they had disconnected but Balqis pounced on the rare opportunity.

"It's over now, Ibu. I'm bringing her back home to us. You should see the state she's in. Nenek can barely take care of herself, and if you won't do it, I will!"

Balqis expected another yelling match or even an ultimatum. Anything but the timid voice that followed: "Y-you *met* her?"

"Yes, she's right here," Balqis huffed, slightly confused. Ibu couldn't possibly still be afraid. "Like I said –"

"No. That's not… *how?*"

"Forget about *how!*" cried Balqis, annoyed that Ibu was focusing on the wrong thing. "I'm in the house –"

"Qis, listen to me…"

"No! I should've come here sooner! Then Nenek might even –"

"*She's been dead for two years.*"

Tears pricked her eyes. "Stop it, Ibu! Just stop it! She's *here…*"

Suddenly, an ear-splitting shatter of glass stunned Balqis silent. In a blink, the entire house plunged into darkness, save for the weak glow of Balqis' phone. Balqis could barely hear her mother yelling her name. *The living room's lightbulb had exploded,* Balqis reasoned. Yet her reasoning could not stop the shiver running through her, the fear gripping her body rigid. Because in the darkness, she could still hear her: Nenek's soft giggles as she repeated the words:

"*Ibu… Ibu…*"

"Nek?" Balqis cried softly now. Logic would demand her to get into the house and bring her grandmother home.

But logic could not explain why the figure in the darkened house stood taller than Balqis remembered of the woman she met minutes ago. In fact, as Balqis peered into the dark with the help of her phone, Nenek was almost eye level with Balqis. Logic could not explain why Nenek's face was now hidden by long tendrils of black hair. Most importantly, logic could not reason why, as Nenek began to coo the same word again and again, her voice had changed. It was not the weak croak Balqis heard earlier. Instead, it was something familiar.

It was Balqis' own voice.

She's been dead for two years.

I won't inherit their hell.

Ibu's words echoed in Balqis' mind now as Balqis slipped down the tiled staircase, running away from the house. It was Balqis now who was trying to escape as fast as she could. But she could not escape from the cry of the creature she left behind.

Ibu! it wailed as the car careened out of the yard.

Ibu! it screamed as the house began to shrink away in the rear-view mirror of the car.

Yet, even in the stark lights of the highway leading home, Balqis could still hear the voice. Giggling in the shadows inside her car. It was her own voice, spoken by another.

Balqis had returned to her kampung, seeking a family she could claim. One that would be hers forever. She did not realize she had inherited a child, passed down from generation to generation. She was its mother now.

The Talisman

✕

Eileyn Chua

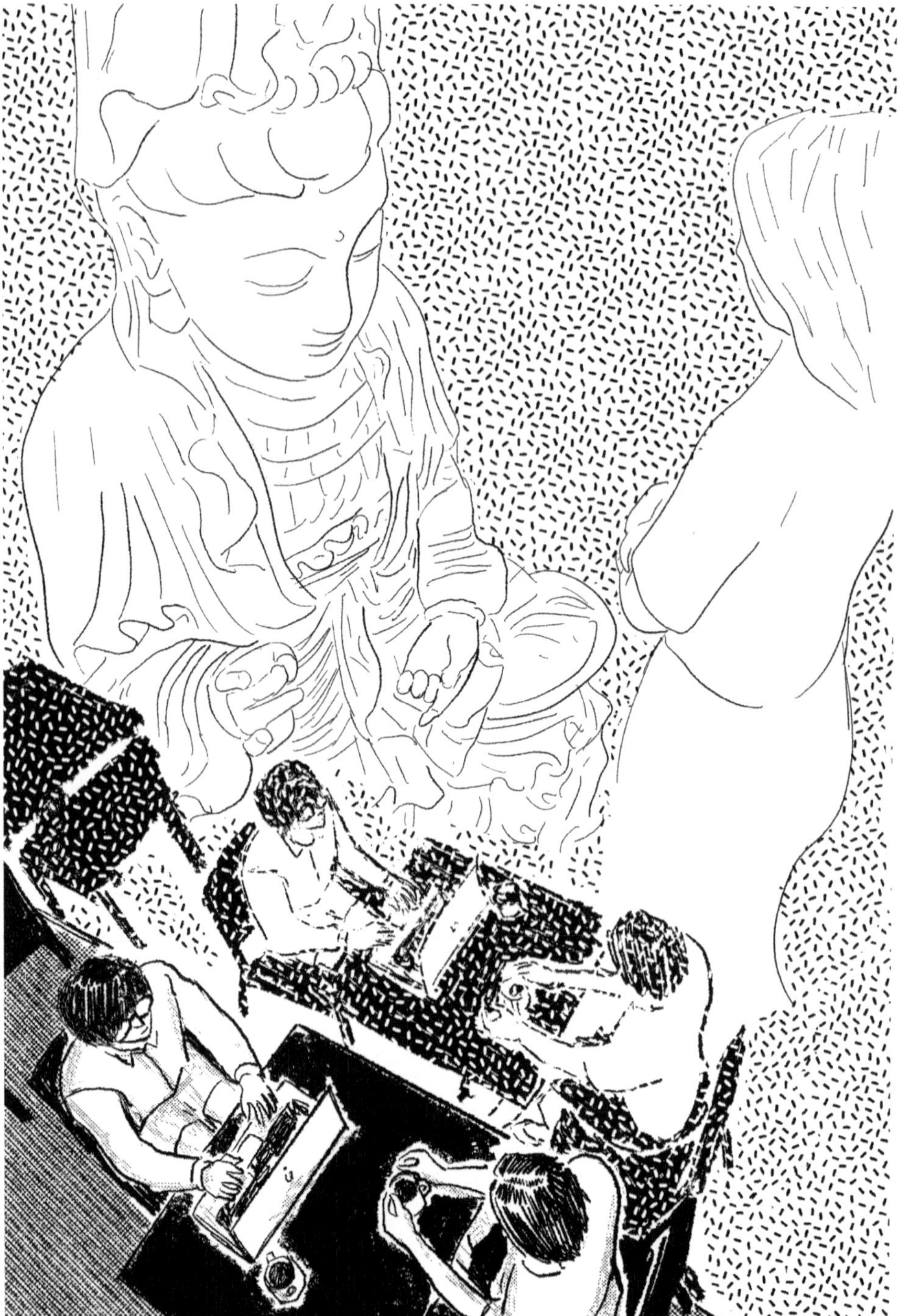

Her fingers typed furiously on the keyboard. Once in a while, she looked up from her laptop and stared at me. Behind the frames of her glasses lay piercing, dark brown eyes that seemed to penetrate my soul. Then, just as suddenly, she would close her eyes in deep contemplation. A petite young woman with a smooth and fair complexion. To an outsider, she would look like a college student on an assignment.

Upon her suggestion, we met up at Starbucks. I found it strange she would propose to meet at this location. I was hoping for a quieter place for what we were about to do. Then again, for safety reasons, it was indeed a better idea to meet a stranger at a public place instead of somewhere secluded.

She introduced herself as Carmen. I have to admit, upon meeting her, I was skeptical. *Can she really solve my problem? Does she have the necessary experience for this task?* Her youthful appearance somehow bothered me.

"Hi. I am Mei Ling," I introduced myself as I sat on the chair facing her.

The smell of freshly brewed coffee was overwhelming. Coffee was something I rarely drank; the aroma wasn't pleasant to me. I fidgeted with the plastic table menu holder, looking at the latest coffee promotions. None appealed to me. I was growing restless. *How long will this take? Her cup's nearly empty.* I took this opportunity to calm my nerves.

"Would you like another drink?" I asked.

"Erm…ya. Thank you," she said without looking up.

"What would you like to drink?"

"Anything is fine with me, except coffee," she replied.

I chuckled. *Another person who doesn't drink coffee, and here we are at Starbucks. The irony.*

Looking at the menu at the counter, I ordered two Signature Hot Chocolates. While waiting, my mind wandered and drifted to the events leading to today's meeting.

Examining the yellow talisman closely, I could see some Chinese characters in red ink on it. Characters I could not understand. The talisman reminded me of those Hong Kong movies from the 1980's, where the Taoist priest in full traditional costume would paste them on the heads of ancient vampires to stop them from jumping.

Oh well, as long as a good night's sleep is within reach, I'm willing to try just about anything. Following the instruction of the Taoist priest, the talisman was adjusted and pasted above the headboard of my bed. That night, I slept like a baby. No interruption. Just continuous deep sleep. I had not slept like that in a long time.

For years, I detested the prominent dark circles under my eyes. They seemed to be my permanent feature. Sustained by a few hours of sleep every day, tiredness was my constant companion, along with grumpiness, moodiness, and crankiness. Yet sleep eluded me. On those rare occasions that Mr. Sandman decided to make an appearance, good dreams were hard to come by.

The most disturbing dreams would be of my mother. She constantly appeared in them, going through her daily activities as though nothing had changed. It had greatly grieved me when she passed away, yet I had not been close enough to her when she was still alive. Many words were left unspoken between us upon her death.

"It worked!" I called to inform the Taoist priest.

"Of course it works," he said.

"How long do I leave it there?" I asked.

"As long as you want. Nothing can disturb you anymore."

Feeling elated, I thought I could finally sleep peacefully after years of restless nights. Unfortunately, I was wrong.

A few weeks later, during dinner: "I had a strange dream last night," my sister said.

"Oh, what about?" I asked while taking a spoonful of soup.

"I dreamt that Mother was so sickly. She was thin and haggard like how she looked before she passed away. She also told me she was bored."

I nearly choked on the soup. "She what?!"

"She said she was bored," my sister repeated. She probably thought I didn't hear her.

My mother had never appeared in my dreams looking sickly and haggard before. As far as I could remember, she always looked healthy.

Suddenly, I feared for my sister's life. Before I could say anything else, my father interrupted.

"That's strange. A few days ago, I thought I saw a glimpse of your mother sitting on the chair at the office, waiting for me. When I looked at the chair again, she was gone."

"Are you sure it was not your imagination?" I asked.

Annoyance briefly appeared on his face. "I know what I saw."

My sister rarely dreamt of my mother, and this was the first time my father saw her make an "appearance".

Tapping on my mobile phone at the dinner table, I swiftly messaged the Taoist priest on WhatsApp. Fortunately, he was quite technologically savvy for someone from his profession.

Taoist Priest
Don't worry, I will do a ceremony to appease your mother's soul

Me
Why is she haunting them now?

Taoist Priest
Your mother can't approach you anymore, so she is disturbing them. Must have taken a lot of energy, that is why your sister saw her as sickly

Me
Why does she easily appear in my dreams?

Taoist Priest
Most probably your spirit is 'low'. Life force is weak

His explanation makes sense, I thought. The Chinese do believe that if a person's spirit is low, they tend to see or feel a ghostly presence.

Thanks to the talisman, daily life continued as usual for me. The only difference was that I finally had enough sleep to function normally. It felt good. The dark circles under my eyes were beginning to lighten up and my face didn't look so dull and lifeless. And then tragedy decided to strike.

My father had a stroke. He was hospitalized and had to undergo surgery. Fortunately, his surgery was a success. Never had I seen my father look so pale and frail. He had aged considerably.

"I dreamt of your mother yesterday," he said in a low and barely audible voice.

"What happened?" I asked, unsure of what he was about to say.

"Your mother was standing beside your stepmother. She was asking me to choose between them."

My blood ran cold. She was still around. *How can this be?* Fearing for my father's life, I quickly called the Taoist priest.

"I thought you said you performed the ceremony for my mother's soul?" My voice sounded shaky; I was trying very hard to sound respectful.

"I did. Twice."

"Then why is she still around?" *Breathe and keep calm,* I told myself.

"I can conduct ceremonies, but whether the spirit wants to go or not, that will depend on them," he explained.

"What?! Can't you force them to go?" I lost my cool. There were lives at stake.

"Young lady, it doesn't work that way…"

"Miss…Miss….your drinks are ready."

I smiled sheepishly as I snapped out of my daydream. Feeling embarrassed, I quickly thanked the young man at the counter and took the tray.

Sitting at my seat, I placed one of the cups near Carmen.

"Thank you," she said, without lifting her head.

After typing a few lines, she looked at me. Then closed her eyes for a short period and continued typing.

Curiosity got the better of me. *How long will the report be?* It was curiosity that had brought me here today anyway. I hoped it wouldn't kill me one day.

It was a week ago that I shared the 'my mother is haunting us' problem with my friend William. I was trying to make sense of things. That was when he suggested I see Carmen.

"Who is she?" I asked.

"She did a life and chakra reading for me. She has dealt with ghosts before too, assisting people with ghostly problems."

I was skeptical; if a Taoist priest couldn't help me, would she be able to? I tried to Google her, but I couldn't find much information. However, William was adamant that she could help with my situation.

"I used to have an ingrown toenail problem," he said wriggling his big toe on the left foot. "I was told it was connected to something I did as a child. Nothing I did helped. It only got more painful over time. After she helped me to resolve that past issue, amazingly the problem went away by itself," he said enthusiastically.

His big toe looked perfectly fine to me.

Was he exaggerating? The feeling of desperation kicked in. *What if something bad happens to my family again?* I couldn't bear it. They must be protected from harm. I did consider getting a talisman for each member of my family; unfortunately, they laughed at the idea.

I decided to throw caution to the wind. *Heck, why not? What's the worst thing that can happen?* It was certainly better than not doing anything at all. I decided to kill two birds with one stone by having my life and chakra reading done as well.

So here I was, in front of Carmen, waiting for her 'report'. So far, the only thing that could be viewed was the sight of her typing furiously, staring at me and closing her eyes. I began to wonder whether this was actually a good idea. *Shouldn't she at least look the part by perhaps wearing something more mystical, like a gypsy costume or something?* A feeling of uneasiness crept in.

As if she had read my wandering thoughts, she suddenly looked up and asked, "Can you tell me more about your mother?"

I had always found it difficult to talk about my mother.

"Er… well…she died years ago, leaving two teenage children and a husband. Since then her husband, my father, remarried."

"What about her funeral?"

"She was cremated, and her ashes are currently at a temple. During her funeral, we conducted prayers, burned joss papers and paper effigies, and followed the normal Taoist rituals."

"Was your mother unhappy before her death?"

The image of my mother's sunken and sickly face suddenly surfaced in my mind. "Well, she did suffer painfully from cancer. My sister and I were still young at that time."

I had grieved for her in the first few years after her death, but life had to go on for those still living. Sometimes, I felt guilty for feeling this way.

Carmen looked at me thoughtfully. "Was there any particular deity your mother prayed to when she was alive?"

I had to dig deep into my memory for the answer, recalling burned joss sticks in urns, thick smoke stinging my eyes, and difficulty in breathing. "She was not particularly religious, but she would pray at the Goddess Guan Yin temple every year on Chinese New Year, and refrain from eating beef."

Carmen's eyes suddenly sparkled and she made a surprising request.

"I want you to call your mother's soul."

"Huh? What?!" Unsure whether I had misheard her, my doubts arose as to the sanity of this woman.

She looked at me and continued, "Don't worry, before you call her, I will call out to Goddess Guan Yin to assist us in sending her soul to heaven."

I was still hesitant. We were, after all, at Starbucks, a public place with other people around, chatting with family and friends.

As though reading my mind again, she added, "It doesn't matter where we are, as long as we concentrate, our external surroundings will not disturb us."

Mixed emotions – fear, doubt, embarrassment – were fighting inside me. *She has probably done this before in public places,* I assured myself. Trying hard to muster enough courage, there was suddenly a strange feeling of reassurance. *Don't worry, trust her. Everything will be all right.*

"OK. I will give it a try."

She continued, "Good. Just set your intention to call her. I will prepare myself first. When everything is ready, I will inform you to call her."

Carmen shut her eyes and folded her legs together. It looked like she was meditating. With coffee in one hand, a middle-aged man passing our table stared at her curiously. I pretended not to notice and looked down at my mobile phone instead.

After a few minutes passed: "OK. You can call your mother now," she said with eyes still shut.

I closed my eyes to concentrate on my mother. Her name and her appearance, the last time I saw her. Calling her from my mind to be present here and now. A heavy sensation and a sudden sense of grief hit me. I felt a presence. I initially thought it was my own emotions, yet part of me knew that it was not coming from me.

Opening my eyes slowly, I looked at Carmen. "Is she here?" I asked, even though I knew the answer in my heart.

"Yes, she is here," she said with her eyes still shut. "Don't worry, Goddess Guan Yin is talking to her now."

I was curious. "What are they talking about?"

"I will tell you when it is over."

So many questions came into my mind. I decided then to just go along and close my eyes; maybe I might see something?

A few minutes later, there was a sudden shift in the air. I felt it. Like dark clouds had finally been lifted. My heart was peaceful and calm. Somehow, I knew that my mother had gone to heaven. I slowly opened my eyes.

"She has gone?"

"Yes." Carmen smiled at me.

"What happened?"

"When your mother came, she was unhappy that you were trying to send her away. After talking to Goddess Guan Yin, she is more at peace."

"She was angry with me?" I asked, feeling a bit guilty.

"Yes, at first. Don't worry about it. Her place is not here anymore. She understands that it's time for her to leave. Goddess Guan Yin has led her to heaven."

"Did you hear what Goddess Guan Yin told my mother?"

"I'm sorry. I was not able to catch their conversation," Carmen replied.

I felt relieved that my mother was gone. "It's strange," I told Carmen. "I was not able to see her, but I could feel her presence. Somehow, I knew she was truly no longer around. No longer haunting us."

✕

Carmen finally saw Mei Ling smiling back. She seemed more relaxed, less tense. Her aura brighter now compared to the first time, when she entered through the door with patches of dark energy. It was really unpleasant that Carmen had to concentrate and focus on removing the dark energy that latched itself to Mei Ling like an octopus.

Doing this work could be exhausting, but it felt good to be able to help others. Seeing her clients free from the clutches of dark spirits made her feel that all the personal sacrifices she went through were well worth it.

Carmen replied, "Yes, she is no longer around."

This is a good time to tell her. Take this opportunity!

Now? Carmen asked the voice.

Yes, now.

Clearing her throat slowly, she asked, "Mei Ling, did you often feel your mother's presence?"

"Er…well, only in my dreams. This is the first time when awake. I am surprised myself," Mei Ling replied.

"Mei Ling, as you know, I was doing your life and chakra reading before we called your mother," Carmen said, suddenly feeling unsure of how to proceed.

It will be OK. Just tell her.

"I have discovered something about you. Hope you can take this with an open mind."

"Yes?" Mei Ling looked curious.

"You are actually a clairsentient. It just means that you can feel things, including other people's feelings and emotions," Carmen said.

"A what? Hmm…I have never heard that word."

"If it is not managed properly, you tend to absorb other people's negative emotions, thinking it is your own," Carmen continued.

"Oh? I do? I never realized this."

"Mei Ling, not everyone would have felt your mother's presence. What more her emotions and feelings. That was why she came to you. Because you could feel her."

"I thought it was because my spirit was 'low'?"

"That can happen too. However, in your case, it is because you have psychic abilities," Carmen explained.

"Hmm…I don't think so. Wouldn't I know if I have such abilities?"

"In this modern time, people are often distracted by many things; mobile phones, TV, work stress and more. Even people with abilities do not realize they are psychic. Some even suppress their abilities."

Mei Ling looked deep in thought.

"Most of the time, we tend to not listen to our inner voice. This can only be heard when we calm ourselves, meditate and listen. From what I see in your life reading, you are supposed to do more in this life. To use your abilities to help others."

"I am? Er…how?"

"You won't need the talisman anymore. You can be your own talisman and much more."

Confusion was written on Mei Ling's face. "I don't understand."

"If you'd like, I can teach you how to harness your abilities."

Mei Ling paused, seeming to ponder the proposal for a few seconds – and suddenly Carmen could feel fear arising from deep within Mei Ling.

"Thank you for your offer. There's currently a lot on my mind. I think I will decline for now."

After a few minutes of further discussion on her report, Mei Ling left.

As Carmen was left alone packing her things, she wondered if Mei Ling would ever contact her again.

Don't worry, you have done your job. It is up to her now.

What is the point of telling her when she is afraid? She will only run away.

She can't run forever. She will have to face it soon enough.

Carmen sighed; it was not easy being psychic. Something Mei Ling would learn soon enough.

They Came from the Sea

✕

Nathaniel Sario

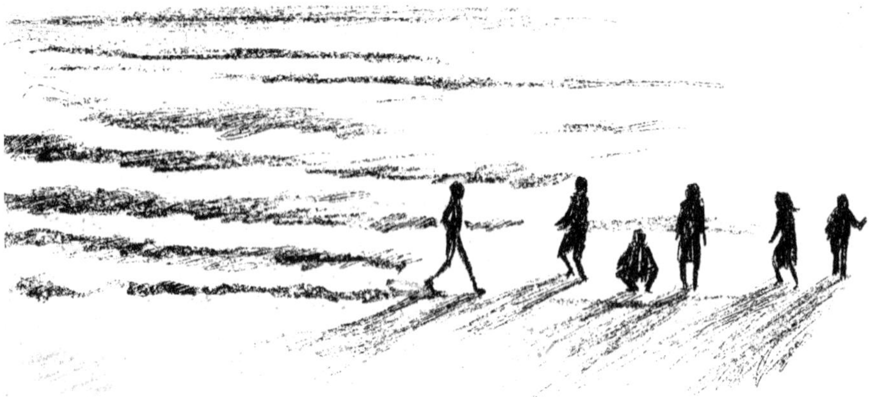

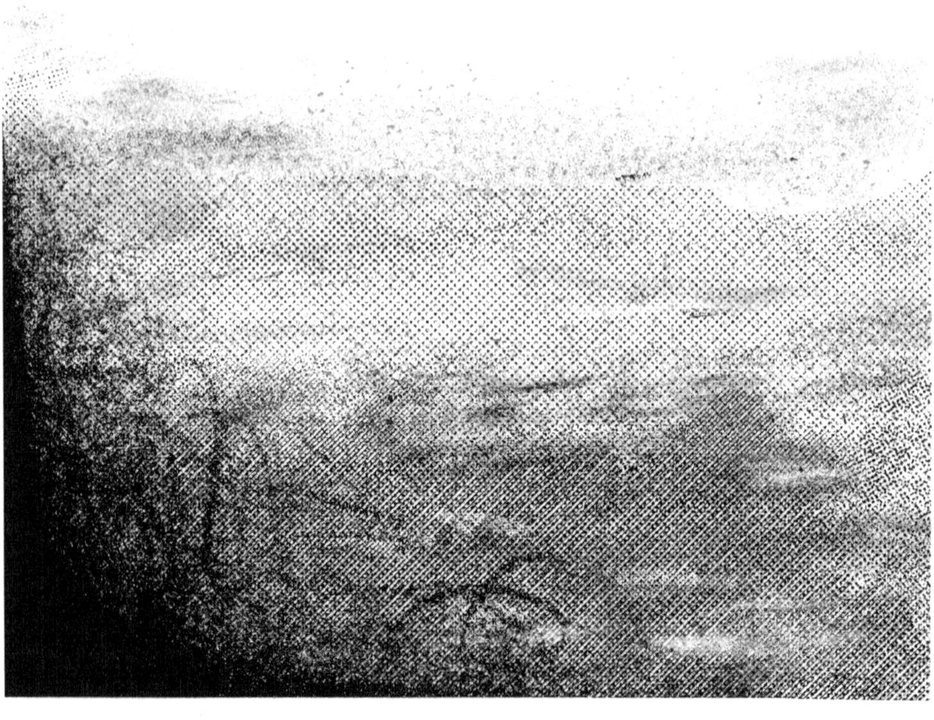

So y'all wanna hear about the orang bunian?

We'll get to that in a bit, this is just a mike test to make sure everything is running fine.

Oh, okay, okay. How am I sounding? Like a million bucks?

Close, sir. Lan, how is it? Good? Great. We can begin whenever you're ready.

It's your show. I'm just the talent.

✕

Can you introduce yourself? Tell us your name, a bit about yourself.

Sure. My name is Raymond Luther Lunsingan. I'm a journalist and a true crime writer. I just published my second book, *Reddest Depth,* which can be found in Kinokuniya or wherever you get books. But of course, since it's October and Halloween is just around the corner, you guys want the truth, right? That's what this "short video" is about?

This is actually a documentary about…we're thinking of calling it "The Big Documentary of Malaysian Horror Stories."

Sounds catchy. Maybe shorten it a little so that it rolls off the tongue better. All right, so a big documentary, need the right people.

Yes.

Ah, I see you bought my book. I'll sign it after.

Thanks. Uhh, anyway, we're thankful that you could come because from what we've read, you changed profoundly after what happened in Darat Kumut, right?

You could say that, yeah.

Because in the preface, you wrote that you've always been a skeptic towards the supernatural.

True. I never believed any of that stuff about apparitions, exorcisms, pontianaks terrorizing suburbia. Any of that weird shit in *Mastika*. I decided to use my platform as a journalist to prove that the supernatural is us, as people, clinging on to some weird belief or another because that makes us sleep easier at night.

But that's changed lah?

…

Mr. Lunsingan?

Yes. The events that transpired while I was researching *Reddest Depth* in Darat Kumut made me question my own beliefs. That, uhh…uhh, maybe in a place that's in tune to the supernatural, like Sabah, there are things that go bump in the night.

Could you tell us a little more about what happened there in Darat Kumut?

A child went missing. Eight-year-old Aliyah Supian.

But she wasn't the only one?

No, there were more. If the evidence that I managed to uncover is correct, then a total of 23 children have been taken by the orang bunian.

Were they stolen?

It's a little more…complicated than that.

And this has given you a change of perspective?

Yeah. Until today, there aren't any plausible explanations for what happened there. And there's a reason for that. In this day and age, with information just a Google search away, why bother believing in something as far-fetched as ghosts, or in this case, orang halus, as they are referred to in Sabah, or orang bunian as they are called here?

It's a hard pill to swallow because it's easier to believe that these children were kidnapped or ran away. It doesn't apply to Aliyah. Especially when her body was found.

But hers wasn't the only one found?

Yes. She and six other victims were found some time after they were reported missing. But this story requires a little context. So, should we start there?

✕

How were you alerted to the story?

A friend of mine in KK, Sarah Robin – also a reporter – emailed me an article when I was there trailing the Prime Minister and his gang during the Sabah State Elections. It was a little story from *The Borneo Post*, buried on page twenty-something, about this small town west of Tawau. Darat Kumut. Not as popular as Pulau Kumut, its sister town, which everyone knows as a rival to Sipadan.

The town sits at the edge of the sea. Most of the people there are fishermen. It's a small place. Around three, four hundred people? It's more of a stop before you board the ferry for Pulau Kumut. The town is pretty. Its main street leads to the jetty and on both sides you have buildings which were erected in the late seventies when the town was incorporated. And nothing is rundown. The place is, as the old saying goes, pretty as a picture. Though I wish the same could be said about the people living there.

Why do you say that?

The people there didn't match with what the town was offering. Everything was bright and cheery except the people. They seemed like the least friendly bunch in the entire state.

Sabahans are the nicest people. Which is probably why they got duped and had their status changed from "partners" in forming the country to just a state. One that economically sits at the bottom rung, but that's a topic for another day. These folks, they were more salt than salt of the earth. I smiled at this one auntie and she spat sirih juice inches from my boots. At the time, I guessed they were still in rough shape over that girl.

But that wasn't the case?

No. Years of children going missing did that. But like I said, we'll get to that part as the story goes on.

Okay. What I don't understand is, an eight year-girl went missing. Why wasn't it big news?

Number one, there was an election happening when she went missing, which was the day before people went out to vote. I won't lie, the fact that the media prioritized the politicians and elections over the disappearance of a child still baffles me, but like some of my contacts in the press say, it's no big surprise.

She was a child.

Yeah. But what was more important? The party that looked to cinch a victory over the state election, or a broken record that's been playing since the eighties? And here's another fun factoid. Outsiders believe that these kids were runaways. The ones before Aliyah were between the ages of 14 to 17.

Teenagers.

Yes. They could have rebelled, ran from home and started anew in some other district. Or barring that, ended up sniffing glue or smoking meth. Toss of a coin really.

Things were a little different with the girl. Her mother, who was living in Semporna – her parents were divorced, the dad worked in Darat Kumut and Aliyah lived with him – did everything. She called the police, pressured them. They worked hard. Day and night. But those TV shows are right. The first 72 hours, or three days, are the most important. I got there on day six.

Which means her chances of being alive were slim?

To none. By then, the investigating officer and his team were not looking for a girl. They were looking for a body.

Which they found?

Yes. Three days after I arrived.

Can you tell us about it?

Do you want the details?

We'll put in a disclaimer or edit it during post-production.

All right. Well, she was discovered floating in the sea not too far away from the jetty. A fisherman found her.

She was…well, I'd say even the medical examiner would have had a hard time explaining how a girl who died of drowning looked like she had been left to dry under the sun. Aliyah had chubby cheeks. She was a little round. But the girl they pulled from the sea…she was sucked dry. Emaciated. Withered away, wasted. I saw some of the pictures and I was just shocked.

The locals must've had a theory?

They did. But I only learned that after…a week in Darat Kumut? Getting them to trust me was one thing. Getting them to talk…well, the first to point me to a lead was the owner of the hotel I shacked up in.

Darat Kumut Seaside Villa, owned by Pauline Talip.

Chatty old lady that one. Loved the color green and drinking Sprite. She said it when I asked her. 'Urang halus tu yang ambil tu budak parampuan'. Need a translation for that?

It's okay. She believed the girl was taken by spirits?

In a way. She said it with just a faint trace of humor. Throwing me a bone and seeing if I'd bite, I guess.

And you did?

No. Not at first. She was just doing that local thing where they say something silly and expect you to brush it off. But I asked her about it. Told her I was curious. She didn't say much. But she directed me to another person in a more…secluded part of town.

This was the bo…the bobo, sorry…the bo-bo-hi-zan?

I like how it flows so naturally from your tongue. In old parlance, you could call Ransuma a bobohizan. But she isn't. She just knows the right vegetables and fruits to eat if you're constipated. At the same time, she also believes in the old practices.

Animism?

Yes.

Do you think that influenced you or your writing?

In what way?

Because it's animism –

Nothing about Ransuma's beliefs influenced me when I left Darat Kumut or the contents of the book. What I saw…what I experienced there…

Mr. Raymond?

Listen, can we take a short break?

Sure.

There are these places, or spots called 'tempat karas'.

Hard places.

AKA haunted places. Or places with reverence. You don't fuck there. Certain trees you don't piss on. And if you do, you ask permission. Ask nicely. Plants, flowers, even the shrooms. Don't touch. Don't pluck, and if they look, smell, or even have a funny name, you zip it and carry on. Most of the time, it's in the jungle.

In Darat Kumut, it's a little strip of beach far west of town that the locals warn people away from. It even became part of the town's unspoken law back in '89 after a white kid went there and became victim 12.

And Ransuma's shack sits at the border. Her shack is a little DMZ. Inside, she burns incense to appease the spirits. Keeps everything in a certain balance.

This is me speaking in hindsight, of course. At first, I couldn't believe in something so silly. When I sat and spoke to her, this hunched old crone, it felt like I was in a silly horror movie. Not real life.

Why?

She gave me an exposition dump about what was going on in Darat Kumut.

And what was that?

All 23 kids had played at the west beach. This was before the beach was designated as dangerous. The oldest case, Ransuma said, happened in the early '80s. A group of kids. Six of them. They were the first six to go missing.

And no one made a connection?

Teenagers, remember? Cops believed that they made a pact to run away. Ransuma said that while they played around...while they enjoyed themselves, something was watching. Waiting. For the right moment. While the kids were playing, they were being marked. And when the time was right, they were taken.

One thing I don't understand is that the previous victims were teenagers. Why would an eight-year-old be taken instead?

I asked Ransuma. The gap between Aliyah and victim number 22 is five years. Between then, a few interesting things happened. The fishermen recorded the lowest volume of fish caught. There were several horrible murders that downgraded the town name. COVID happened and killed tourism in the town. And just as the inter-district ban was lifted, seven people were killed when a truck lost control near the town entrance.

Between 2015 and 2021, the town suffered. Some believed that 'they' were hungry.

The orang halus?

Yeah. When they're hungry and unhappy, bad things happen. When they're fed, the town prospers.

The people were desperate, so what did they do? Someone told Aliyah's mother about a little beach west of town. The woman isn't from Darat Kumut, so she wouldn't know about the beach being a tempat karas.

So she took her daughter to this beach?

And not too long after, her daughter went missing, only to be found several days later bearing the same marks as the other victims who were found.

Jeez...this forbidden beach, you checked it out, right?

Is the Pope Catholic? Of course I did. The trail is right behind Ransuma's house. Followed the trail. Walked for about...ten minutes. Found myself in this beautiful little cove. Quiet. Peaceful.

But after some time, you stop feeling that way. The silence you thought was peaceful turns eerie. No birds in the sky. No crabs scrabbling about on the ground. Even the lapping of the waves sounds disturbing.

I walked around for a few minutes before I felt it.

Felt what?

Eyes. Watching me. Hiding behind the box-sized rocks dotted along the beach. In the trees. The thigh-high grass bordering the white sand. The day was nice and cool but I was sweating.

You didn't turn back?

Told myself that my brain was just making it up. That Ransuma's story was getting to me. Freaking me out. I won't lie. I was very uncomfortable on that little beach. But I opted to do my work.

In your book you were very brief about what happened next.

Yeah. The first incident. I wanted to add in more details as I was writing that part. And I did, but most of it ended up on the cutting room floor after a friend read it and said that it sounded like a horror story.

Do you mind telling it now?

I found a sea cave not too far away from where one of the bodies was found. Took off my shoes and socks and waded into the water. That cave… huge, like a…like a cathedral almost. In the deepest part of the cave was a flat bed of rock that rose up from the sea. Think of an altar.

I took some pictures of it and…well, deeper in, in the spots where the sunlight from the holes in the roof of the cave could not reach, I heard something.

This was not mentioned in the book.

It got cut out.

It's been a while since then…are you sure what you're telling us is the truth?

I've got some proof I brought with me today that you can see in a while.

Okay. What did you hear in that cave?

It sounded like…chittering. With a little clicking and clacking thrown in.

More than one?

Could have been two of them. They…*talked* a little more, and then I heard something drop into the water from the end of the cave. I didn't find anything at first. Just…an empty cave. But then, the deeper I went, and the darker it got, I bumped my hip onto a little alcove that was carved into the wall of the cave.

Which was where you found the skull?

I almost got a heart attack. Thought it was a piece of rock, but as I was telling myself that a rock couldn't be that smooth, I flipped it. The upper half of a human skull. Only two teeth left.

Two things happened immediately after. First, this odd sound coming from behind me and to the right. I turned. Nothing there, but I swear I saw some rocks fall into the water.

And?

Something bit my thigh. Thought I'd bumped into a bit of rock, but a bit of rock doesn't cling onto your leg.

Do you think that we could —

Sure. Why do you think I wore loose jeans today? Hold on, lemme just…

My God. Aliff. Zoom in on that, get as much as you can. The bottom part as well. You don't mind, do you?

Nope. Of course not. Go crazy. It's something, isn't it? Two fangs at the top, a row of smaller, serrated teeth at the bottom. The doctor who treated me said that it'd cut deep. Needed stitches and would leave a scar. Didn't feel so bad as I was running out of that cave. But halfway back to town, though…

Anyway, I got my pictures, went back to the beach and found out that one of my sneakers was missing.

Did you try looking for it?

I did. Couldn't find it. I was already feeling the burn in my thigh so I rushed back to town.

Someone could have taken it. Played a prank on you.

Crossed my mind. But the locals avoid that strip of beach for good reason.

You then met the doctor.

Yes. Dr. Alan Jisol. He isn't a local there either. Lives in Tawau, but doesn't mind the morning drive. Didn't go into detail, but he told me that he'd examined two of the victims found. Said the state of their bodies wasn't too far off from Aliyah's body. 'Drained' was the term he used.

I asked him what he thought could have caused it but he declined to speculate. Said that it was beyond his understanding. He did a full physical examination of the bodies. The worse thing he discovered was this hole-shaped mark, about an inch in diameter stuck into the victim's lower back area.

Was that injury found on Aliyah as well?

Yes. No explanation for it. An odd place for a wound.

I thought that was it. That I would be done for the day. But that night…

The second incident?

Another incident I was pretty vague about in the book. I was feeling a little feverish and doing my best to fall asleep. And I was nearly successful. If not for the chittering and clacking.

Above the headboard of my bed was a wide window. The sounds came from there. But it wasn't one or two. There were more. Ten, fifteen. Could've been more.

I thought I was dreaming so I pinched myself. They were still there. I got up from bed and went to the front door, opened it, expected to see them there in the flesh, but instead there's my sneaker. Sitting on the Welcome mat. Torn up. The upper canvas ripped. The toe cap shredded. Laces chewed up. And there were stains on it. Must've been their saliva. There were streaks of it along the sides of the shoe. In the places that were chewed on.

Then I heard the chittering close by, to my left. I turned and for a fraction of a second, under the dim lights of the hallway, I saw one of them.

The orang bunian?

Or orang halus…whatever you wanna call them. I did a little research on them at the beginning when Pauline threw that little bit at me. They've been described as forest people, that they were beautiful and dressed in pretty clothes.

These creatures were about waist height. Like toddlers. They had tough barrel-shaped bodies and spindly limbs. Mean faces. Dark eyes. Pointy ears. Looked like goblins. Blue-skinned goblins chittering and clicking away.

Were they there to torment you?

Maybe. But once I opened the door and went out, they were running. I wasn't able to sleep after that. They left the shoe, I suppose, as a warning.

To an outsider, the idea of these creatures seems preposterous. If you told someone, they wouldn't believe you.

Yeah, but here's the thing…they've been doing this quietly for years.

If you look at the state government's annual statistic report, you'd see that of all the little burgs in the area, Darat Kumut is the one that stands out: a small place that flourished when many others died out. Put that economic growth track next to the timeline of the teenagers going missing and you start seeing patterns.

Fishermen were catching a ton of fish. Hotels saw an uptick in visitors. Shops recorded record sales. Families made money for years. That's the small price that the town is paying for its survival, and those who know it wouldn't mind allowing more outsiders – the kids – to actually wander off to the west beach.

What about the people in town, those who lost their children?

They had other kids. Like the town, they made a few extra bucks. Pauline was related to victim number five, but she was still benefiting. A couple days before I left, tourists from Sandakan came, she welcomed them. Told me the town was expecting a rise in visitors.

She wasn't wrong; people were streaming into town. Some were there for the fish market. Others went for the shops. Some stayed at the town but took the ferry over to the island so they could gamble.

I was shocked. But I had a book to write. So I left, went home to KK for a while and began writing.

What did your editor think of the first draft?

Amir said that it would have worked better as a horror novel. Too far-fetched to be a true crime book, so we edited. Made it a two-for-one story.

But it still says here that the kids were stolen by cryptids that came from the sea?

Says the locals. Like I said, we put both narratives in. The kids going missing, a crime that hasn't been fully solved, and the idea that these sea goblins could have been involved. There isn't a logical explanation that everyone will believe where the victims were runaways or that there was a serial killer.

But there's a bigger truth to it?

A race of sea goblins that take and devour these children and for that 'sacrifice', they give back to the town. A simple case of trading favors. It would have been laughed at. If anyone else had written it, I would have buried their career. But I've changed teams and become something of a laughing stock as well. The guy who saw shadows and cried ghost.

But you seem unfazed.

People can say whatever they wanna say. I'm just gonna do what I've decided to do and start looking for more ghost stories to write about. Become the thing I once vowed to expose.

Any upcoming projects?

There's a few rumors about a house in Hulu Langat I'd like to write about. A couple construction workers doing renovation work there saw some stuff. Almost burned the place down. I can't tell you more other than that, of course.

Interesting. Well, that's it for the interview, I guess. Lan, can you get the lavaliere mike off of him?

Turbulence

✕

Izaddin Syah Yusof

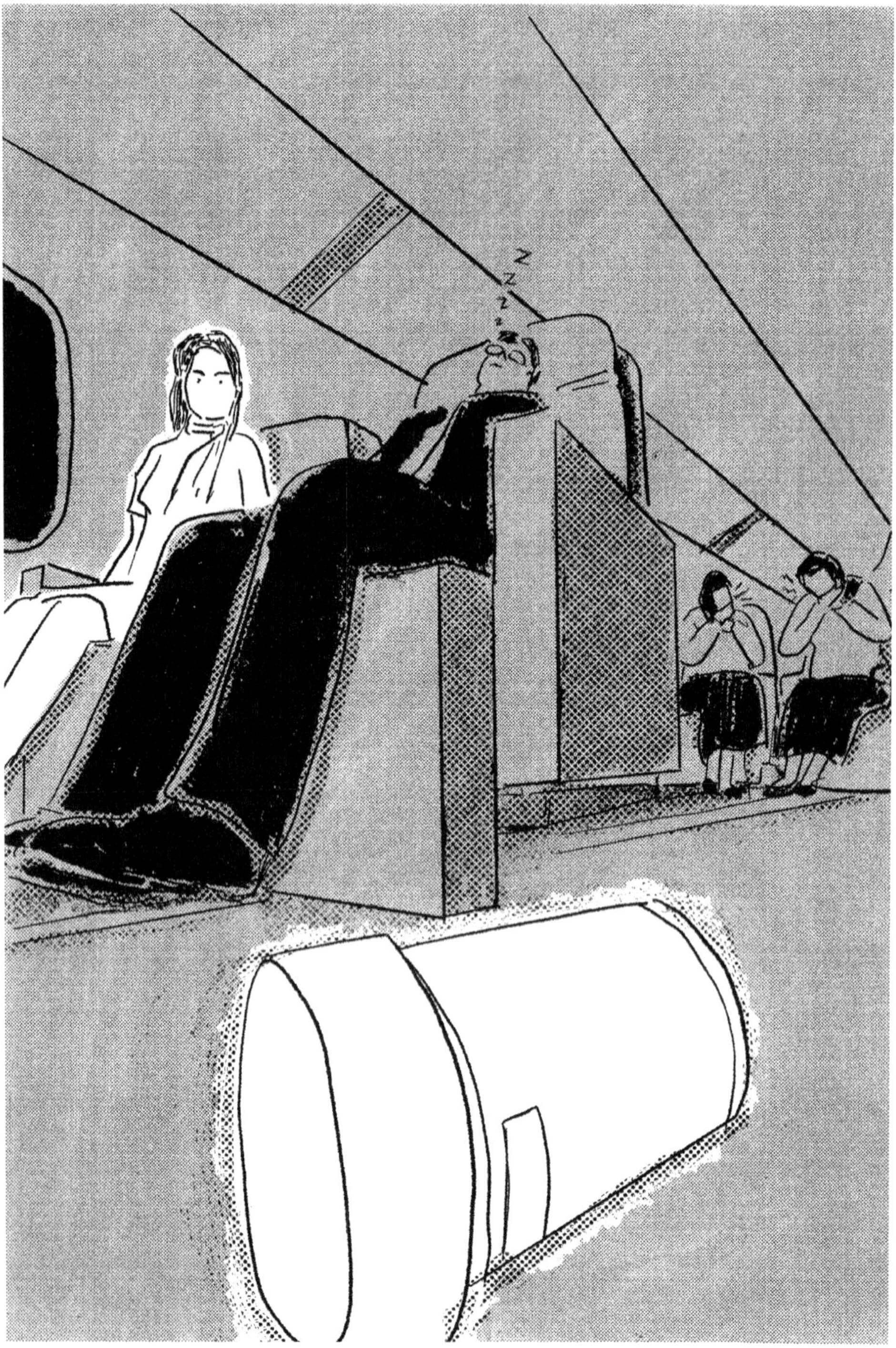

"So it turns out, Siti's husband has been seeing this Indonesian girl for several months now. It's so typical nowadays lah...sundal macam tu will always look for rich Datuk like that. Bloody gold-diggers. Poor Siti. I can't imagine..."

I couldn't help but heave an audible grunt of disgust. Apparently having a seat in Business Class did not spare me from having extremely chatty, xenophobic neighbors. I wished I had a pair of earplugs so I could stuff them in. I could still hear the two Datins giggling in their seats behind mine, happily gossiping away.

The night flight had left Kuala Lumpur International Airport less than an hour ago, but my head was throbbing madly from all the mindless chattering. It was a red eye flight, but I was hoping to at least get some decent rest before arrival. I just hated it when people had loud conversations in public. It's plain rude. Even in the cinemas I can't stand whispered conversations, what more conversations from talkative makciks when I was trying to get a short respite from the hectic week I just had.

I summoned the flight attendant, who graciously came over and smiled. I requested for some warm tea and she asked if I wanted anything else, to which I candidly responded, "Perhaps a little peace and quiet?" while cocking my head to the loud women at the back. The attendant let out a slight snicker, gave me a knowing look, winked at me and said, "I'll be back with your tea, Miss." I could honestly feel the two Datins' glares burning through my seat. I smirked to myself and softly tightened the scarf around my neck. Ever so slowly.

Flying off to China wasn't really what I was looking forward to, but business called for it. At the same time, leaving KL was probably what I needed too. Recent happenings back home did nothing but conjure up dark memories that I wanted to permanently erase.

Deep breath in. Slow breath out. I tightened my scarf further until I could feel it throttling my own neck. Tighter and tighter, until eventually I couldn't hear either of the women's voices.

✕

When I was a little girl, I knew I was different. I was constantly teased in primary school for being a chubby kid. It wasn't as bad as it sounds. I wasn't traumatized, didn't become a recluse. Verbal mocking by little children was normal back then. We weren't snowflakes. I was quick to brush them all off. I'd like to think that helped build character. However, the day Kelly maliciously crumpled a piece of chewing gum in my hair, something inside me just snapped.

I cried as I cut pieces of my damaged hair in the school toilet. Kids had called me many names and I wasn't bothered, but I drew the line when someone went out of their way to be that cruel. Self-pity was soon replaced by anger. Anger was soon followed by rage. I started tugging my hair violently until several strands came out, while wishing ill on that nasty little bitch. Kids could be cruel. But most kids back then did not know how cruel I could truly be. Even I didn't know back then how cruel I could truly be.

✕

"Miss, here's some chamomile for you."

The flight attendant was a blessing, but I doubt the chamomile tea was going to put my mind at ease. It wasn't just the chatterboxes that were giving me a headache. There were too many other things weighing on my mind.

The attendant dropped to her knees and whispered to me, as if to share a private joke, "It's strange, but the ladies seem to have lost their voices. I think you'll feel much better now." I nodded and we both exchanged a naughty silent smile before she got up and left. Strange? Not if you know what I'm capable of.

In their seats, the two ladies were rubbing their necks, as though trying to soothe sore throats, as they rather ineffectually tried to engage in wordless conversation between themselves.

✕

Kelly didn't come to school the next day. I didn't notice it at first. I didn't care about the horrid girl. After recess, news started circulating among my classmates. Something unfortunate happened to Kelly on her way back from school yesterday. She fell victim to a snatch thief, reportedly a drug addict, who tried to steal her necklace.

I didn't know who the bigger fool was: the addict who thought the necklace was real gold, or the girl who proudly wore and displayed jewelry at school. Someway or somehow, the necklace got entangled in her locks of luscious hair. That, however, didn't deter the thief from tugging and yanking at the necklace until it eventually broke free. The necklace was gone, along with a good handful of Kelly's tangled hair, literally torn from her scalp.

Strange as it was, I wasn't shocked upon hearing the news. I was wistfully listening and twirling my short hair, all the while thinking that she got her comeuppance. I started to wonder if I unconsciously did that to her. Did I suddenly have supernatural powers? Was I a living and breathing voodoo doll? But I didn't care. After what she did to me, I was laughing on the inside.

She came back to school two weeks later, fully recovered. I did notice, though, that she maintained a good distance from me. She probably felt I was directly or indirectly responsible for her misfortune. She wasn't wrong, and I absolutely didn't care.

✕

The plane jerked suddenly and I almost jolted out of my seat. Turbulence. The passenger next to me was knocked out ever since the flight took off. He got nervous every time he flew, so he told me beforehand that he would be popping some sleeping pills. A small wry smile surfaced, as I thought to myself about those sleeping pills.

The flight crew made an announcement, sounding ever so apologetic for the minor turbulence. At least I was no longer hearing the irritating loud conversations anymore. However, something else was on my mind. The thoughts were going hundreds of miles per hour, rivaling the Boeing 777 jet itself.

I eyed the bottle of sleeping pills which had dropped out of the gentleman's pocket due to the turbulence. I unbuckled my seatbelt, got up and swiftly picked it up before it could roll away. I went back and slumped into my seat with the bottle of pills firmly in my hand.

The chamomile tea didn't help as expected. Perhaps these will? I thought before popping a handful of pills down my throat. *Fuck this and fuck you, Daud.*

✕

The incident with Kelly was the first time I realized I had something special within me. An unholy ability to make things happen. Over the years, I learned how to hone this to my advantage. In school, I was no longer a shy, chubby little girl. I became a much more confident young lady. No one got in my way – if they knew what was good for them.

However, this gift has a way of coming back at me. It may not be swift, it may not hit me hard, but just like the Monkey's Paw, things had a way of turning against me. By the age of 25 my hair was already thinning – the problem was not hereditary, so I instinctively knew it had something to do with what I did to Kelly all those years ago. But, meh. Nothing a simple weave or extensions couldn't help.

I started working as a pharmaceutical sales representative for a multinational company. The tricks I'd learned over the years helped me get to where I am today. I was very careful in what I did, so that the worst didn't hit me hard in the face – but just enough to get me what I wanted. I managed to reel the curse in to a certain extent.

I was able to clinch several major sales away from the leading sales executive in my company. A vigorous rubbing of my eye, plus a little ill intention, resulted in the said executive getting a sudden eye infection and having to excuse himself from major dealings. And sure enough, there I was, rather conveniently, to swoop in and seal the deal. It didn't matter that I had to eventually get corrective eye surgery. I had considered it a very small price to pay. And this went on at every sales pitch, after sales pitch, after sales pitch.

The only drawback to this was I could never tell when the unholy retribution would come knocking back on my door. I could somewhat control *when* I wanted the unfortunate incidents to befall my victims (normally instantaneously), but I can never tell when, or how bad, the curse would affect me. It could be after several days, weeks, months, or years even. I was living in the present, but the dark karma waiting game was definitely not fun.

✕

I woke up, slowly massaged my neck a little, as I gazed out the plane window. It was almost pitch dark outside. The night sky was clear, but not enough to allow stars to shine through.

I looked at the time. It turned out the sleeping pills were only good at putting me out for a mere 15 minutes. The cruel night sky above seemed to stretch all the way to the horizon below, which I deduced must be the South China Sea.

I let out a disappointed sigh. 15 pathetic minutes. What a waste. But at least the cabin was quiet now as it seemed everyone else had nodded off, including the two annoying makcik bawang.

✕

I met Daud three years ago. The love of my life was only five years younger than me. He was a promising sales rep, just like I was when I first started. At the time, I was recently appointed as the new Assistant Regional Head of Sales – quite an achievement for someone who had just turned 30.

Our attraction was immediate and led to a torrid love affair. We were, after all, working in the same company, and he was my subordinate. That had people talking. It didn't bother me in the slightest. I showed him no preferential treatment when it came to his job, but it bothered him greatly. As a result, he left the company after we got married – a mere 6 months after we first became intimate.

Seeing that I had the financial means to support the both of us, Daud decided to launch his own startup. He had the luxury of working from home - our lavish condo in Mont Kiara – while I continued to go to meetings, pitching sales in and out of KL. Whenever I got home, Daud would be there waiting on me hand and foot - ever so ready to fulfill my every whim and desire.

My work commitments soon had me traveling a lot throughout the Asia-Pacific region. Trips to Singapore, Bangkok, Hong Kong, Beijing, and Tokyo soon became routine. Sometimes I'd be gone for days, and sometimes weeks even. One would think that would put a strain on my relationship with Daud, but it didn't. He was constantly in his loving and charming mode whenever I got back from my trips. And I didn't even have to use my so-called powers to keep him in check. I almost forgot I even had the powers. Life was good. For a while.

✕

The plane shook rather violently and jolted me from my seat for the second time. Turbulence again? *It's not unusual,* I thought to myself. Then more turbulence. This time, there were no announcements from the cabin crew, which I thought was a little strange. Normally they'd be making reminders that we should stay in our seats when these things happened.

Something was amiss.

More turbulence. This time, hard. Hitting turbulence was normal in any flight, but something was wrong. I noticed there weren't any reactions from the other passengers. I looked around. Everyone seemed to be in deep, full slumber.

In a normal situation, you could expect attendants walking the aisles and trying to pacify passengers who might be stressed out, or even offering them some drinks to calm the nerves. I needed one. Where were they? The entire cabin was unusually still. I buzzed for the attendant.

My heart started to race a little as I felt the plane start to dangerously swerve in different directions, as the haunting silence in the cabin grew even louder.

$$\times$$

My brief marriage with Daud was a fairy tale on the outside, but deep down inside I knew things were just too good to be true. My suspicions were confirmed by a private eye, who found out he was constantly cheating on me with different women every time I was out of KL. And in our matrimonial bed too. That ungrateful babi.

It broke my heart. Sadness and rage melted into one, but I never let the emotions disrupt my steely facade. I tried to forgive him, but it was too painful. I was being taken for a ride. The marriage was a sham. The little chubby girl inside told me to just do it.

Eventually last Sunday, when Daud went to the clubhouse for his weekly swimming session, I laid down in my bathtub with a glass of red in hand. As I cried and wallowed in self-pity, I slowly popped some pills that would leave me dead in the tub. The betrayal was too much. Life was meaningless. I wanted it to end.

Death was supposed to embrace me, but it had other plans. I woke up several hours later, only to see several missed calls on my mobile from an unknown number. A few minutes later, it rang again. I was greeted by a police officer who told me of Daud's unexpected passing. I was informed he had lost consciousness while swimming, and drowned. They tried to resuscitate him but failed. I wasn't surprised. I guess I forgot I still had that power to destroy others. I had forgotten about the curse.

✕

So here I was. Deep down I knew we were not going to make it to Beijing the following morning. How could I have been so foolish to think the damned ramification of the sleeping pills would've ended with only Daud? I realized the pills I had just taken must have rendered everyone in the plane unconscious too – the passengers, cabin crew, pilots, everyone but me.

In my head, I was screaming as the plane started to plummet several hundred feet at an alarming speed. Oxygen masks dropped like sad sagging yo-yos from the overhead compartments. It was a bizarre and silent chaos. I was the only one fully aware of the doom that would soon occur, while everyone looked so, dare I say, peaceful in their sleep.

I peered out the window one last time and saw thick black smoke billowing from what was possibly one of the engines. The plane crashing into the deep black abyss was imminent, but I was strangely calm. I managed to utter, "So this is how it's going to end," before visions of my lovely Daud appeared, welcoming me and the rest of the ill-fated flight into the dark watery grave below.

*Author's Footnote: This story is an updated revision of a submission for **KL NOIR: BLUE** back on 31st December 2013, two months before the MH370 tragedy occurred. Even though it is purely a work of fiction, needless to say, I was horrified when the actual tragedy struck.*

Bad Spirit of Google Translate

✕

Saat Omar

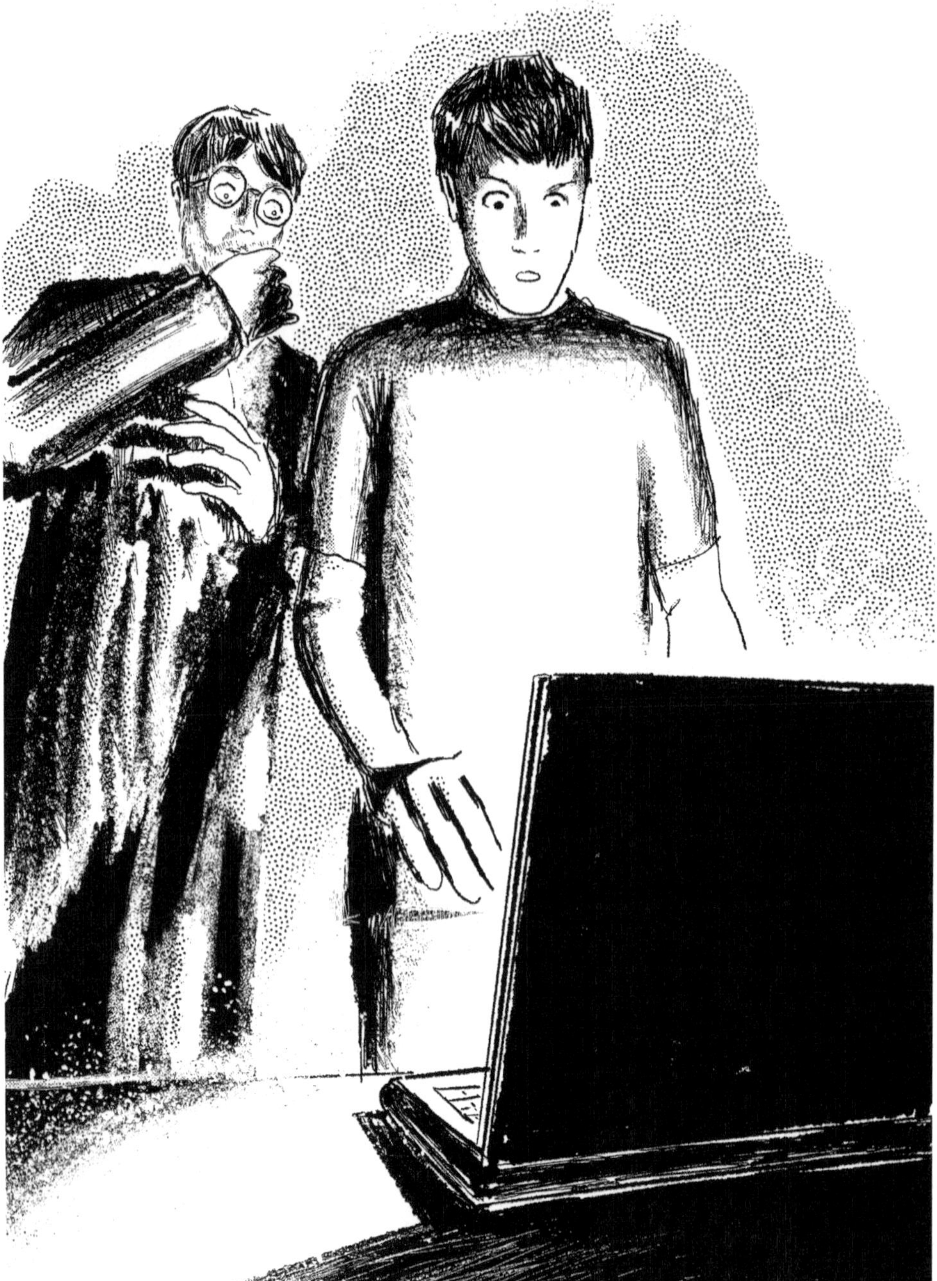

Ghost in a machine appear on my computer and translate my BM ghost story to English.

It's not a scary horror story. In fact, it is a very bad one. But I like it because this is my story. It's honest, pure and based on a true experience. The story is told exactly as it is. It was written with the help of a computer technology.

I'm a writer. Not a famous one. Nobody remember my name and books I wrote. But I write because it's fun and I enjoy writing. Mostly I write in Malay language. However, something strange happened as soon as I finished writing this, my writing changed to English. This is not the first time this has happened. I noticed since I used this computer, all my writing accidentally changed to other language.

The computer im using to write this story, I bought in a second hand computer shop. It's not really fancy look but just enough for me to scratching a Words into it. It's an old computer with big monitor, like televisyen set in the 60s and windows 2005. I bought it just for RM200 and for a broke writer like me, that's a bargain.

Well I always believe in a spirit that hold onto a 'old 'stuff'. Like a helmet I once bought was actually a helmet from a man who once died in an accident using it.

At night, the helmet scream. And sometimes blood drips from the head of the helmet. But it's a helmet, a thing that people put in their heads – a computer is another thing. Never in my wildest imagination, imagination, evil spirits can infiltrate a computer. Not to mention changing words into another language.

What happens next is easy to predict. Every night, I would write from 8 to 12. I wrote silly horror story about this modern bomoh with Matthew McConaughey hairdo who let go of the evil spirit that disturbs the UKM girl's computer. Mostly, a day I manage to write 1000 pages, which is less than Stephen King usual words perday but still, I think that enough for me. And after done, I would save the writing and save it to folder with title "Horror." I only open up the file next night when

I'm starting to continue my writing right after I finish my night prayer. What shock me is that everything I wrote, turn into English. It happens almost everyday. Now maybe I'm sleepy when I press the wrong button or whatever but as far as my logical thought refresh, it's almost impossible for me to wrongfully tick the wrong button for almost everyday. Only then did I believe that my computer had been possessed by an evil spirit.

On the advice of my brother-in-law, I met with a supernatural investigator. Of course, in the beginning, the idea for me to see any shaman to cure my computer was nonsense. But since I felt the meeting with such a shaman was something interesting, I also agreed with his suggestion. Perhaps, meeting this strange shaman is able to give an idea to my latest horror book essay.

For a horror writer who doesn't believe in shamans, I have to admit that it's an embarrassing statement. But since I wrote about them, and made a living by writing the story of this shaman, I feel to some extent I am indebted to people like them and their professional careers. So I agree.

He lives in a remote house at the mouth of the Gombak River. He was a popular shaman and his time, from morning till night he was busy healing machine that were beamed by evil spirits. I was lucky because one night he answered my phone call. Through a phone conversation the day before meeting him, I explained my real purpose in seeking his advice.

"I believe my computer is possessed by an evil spirit, tok," answer me when asked why I called him that night.

"Tell me more." He had a calm voice as expected. As if that was a common complaint to him. There was no sign of shock in his soft voice. From his voice I imagined he was a man with a Long beard that covered his entire mouth.

And I kept telling stories. After the end he was silent for a while. As a shaman who usually solves the problem of machines that are interrupted by spirits, it is something he usually hears. Either he thinks im bullshitting him or just playing prank.

"You don't believe me tok?"

"I must admit this is first time I heard such stories but for a shaman who believes in advance spirit that can live thorough electricity and new technology, I have no reason to call you a liar. Bring me that computer, let me take a look at it," he said ending our conversation.

So the next night, after 10 pm, my brother in law and I got into the car and moved to the shaman's house. When he arrived, and when he opened the door of his house, I was surprised to find how young the shaman was. He is around early 20s, with a babyface and glasses he looks more like Harry Potter instead of Nasir Bilal Khan. But behind the baby's face, his eyes showed a ray of fear, a sign that he had succeeded in fighting and driving away the evil ghosts.

He greeted us and I ushered the computer into the house under the full floating moon.

The house is moderately large, with worn out beds in the living room. On the edge of a wall full of broken computers heaped up in every corner of the house. In addition, there are also machines and other electrical tools such vacuum cleaner, espresso machine, blender dan grass cutter machine. Like me, waiting for the time to be fixed by the young shaman.

"I've seen a lot of computer possessed, but never saw a computer that converts Bahasa Melayu to Bahasa Inggeris," he said. "Put the computer down and show me."

When the time came for me to face him, I showed him the nature of the computer that made me believe that the computer had been beamed. I wrote something in Words and then saved it. And when I open it again, my writing changes language. His face was shocked.

"Have you seen anything like this, tok?"

"I've seen virus that destroy computer before, a skull appear on screen before everything when blackout. But nothing like this before. As if this was done by Sundar Pichai himself. This was done by Google Translate's wild spirit."

I gasped. That's the wildest explanation I could imagine. I turned to see my brother in laws sitting next to me, he was also gaping. Never in my imagination search engine that kills Ask Jeeves and Yahoo could become demon.

"What is google translate wild spirit tok?"

"That's the name I give it to the spirit." He gave me a sharp look. "You use Google Translate before?"

"Yes. Of course". Who doesn't, I said to myself.

"To cheat on your writing?"

"If the technology is legal and there is no issue whether the technique is legal or not tok. But of course it's legal!" I almost got mad at him. He paused.

No any connection. Hopefully he never ask further but I admit I was using a lot Google Translate. Especially when I translate my BM to English. Now let me explain something about Google Translate. I think it's a cool invention-the best since tagging in FB. I admit I use Google Translate when I was a degree students.

Of course, some people look down on software like Google Translate, as they look down on Wikipedia. But to me, those are friendly user technology, I use it very wisely. I know it can translate the language into 'funny words' but I don't care. Google Translate is art.

But what tok bomoh mention just now give me trigger. So I check all the BM that translate to English. I copy paste them and put it to Google Translate. Surprisingly, it turns exactly as the exact words I've been transfer. Maybe the wild spirit that this computer beam is indeed using GT to change my writing.

"So what should I do now tok?"

"You have several options. First, find out who the first owner of this computer is. Second, throw this computer far away into the deep sea. Or third, stop using Google," selamba tok answered.

"Stop using Google? I can't do that tok. It's impossible."

"Then go find the first owner. Get their stories why and how it turned to be what it is," said the shaman to end our conversation.

As my brother-in-law and I came out of the house, the atmosphere was dark but the moonlight accompanied us. Tok Bomoh saw me leave by standing by the door of the house waving.

I came home feeling disappointed that he failed to save my computer. But I agree with his opinion: The first owner of this computer is worth looking for. Only from him will I get the answer I am looking for how the computer is possessed by evil spirits.

That night I couldn't sleep. The computer is on next to the bed. His words gaped as if asking me to write and save something.

"Who are you? And why you haunt my computer and change my language?" ask me to the computer before I close it down.

I did not take long to find the original owner of this computer. A few days after I met with the shaman, I go to the computer shop where I bought the used computer. Although at first, the owner of the shop was a man of Pakistani descent reluctant to reveal to me the original owner, but after I told my problem to him, he agreed to share the address of the original owner of the haunted computer.

The computer was owned by a single mother living with her only son. She lives alone in a large mansion on the Selangor-Kuala Lumpur border. The road to her house is full of big creepy trees along the way. Its shadow fell on my car all the way across the road.

When I got to his yard, his son, who I assumed was 10 years old, was playing football alone on the short grass lawn. When he saw me getting off the train while lifting the computer on his chest, he stopped playing, as if he was looking at something that appealed to an old memory.

I was then picked up to enter the house by his mother. She is a beautiful woman with long, wavy hair that reminds me of Lana Del Rey when she was younger. We sat in front of the living room. The woman treats me to dry biscuits and hot tea chicks. I took a sip of the hot water after putting the computer down on the floor.

"You took him home," said the woman. His son who was sitting next to him looked at the computer with a fixed look.

Then he tells a horror story that makes skeptics hard to believe.

"Puan know this computer is haunted. Tell me how it happened."

He signaled for his son to leave. The boy got up and went upstairs.

"It happened in one night. All of a sudden, my husband, who was writing in the upstairs room, disappeared," she said, pointing to a room upstairs.

"My husband at that time was writing the last chapter for his Master's dissertation. You know, he's not a true academic. He actually almost gave up on preparing his thesis. I personally suggested that he just stop. But at the urging of his family for him to succeed and get a doctorate, he went ahead as well. He came from a family that was looked up to by everyone. His older brother is a well-known academic of the country, his failure to complete this thesis is unacceptable.

"At first he wrote in Bahasa Melayu. Because he thought that language was easy for him. But Bahasa Melayunya also ke laut. Then, at the suggestion of his supervisor, he switched to English writing. Actually his English is also bad. The truth is he can't write in any language. But he worked tirelessly. Day and night he wrote until he forgot about his son. He skip his daily lunch and dinner. And because his English is bad, he try to use dictionary but that doesn't really helpful. The only way for him to escape is by using… something called Google Translate. God bless the internet he said. Still… it's not easy for him. He works harder. Until he became…a man I did not know. He became irritable. He began to confine himself.

"One night, I still remember that night. The sky thundered. When I knocked on the door, he did not answer. I knew he didn't write because there was no sound of keyboard knocks on his computer. That's when I knew something bad had happened to her. In my mind, he was probably fainting from writing fatigue. I slammed the door. And when I managed to get into the room, I found the room was empty. There's no sign of him in there. And you know? The computer was still open brightly. What is plastered is…"

"…Google translate," I continued, slowly. Me and the single mother bowed.

"I believe he was swallowed by the computer. But I can't explain it how. Ghost in a machine does exist. I see it. It happens to my husband. Up until now he's nowhere to be seen."

Then to support his story, I showed him this computer. I wrote something and then, google translate changed my writing to English. He shed tears when he saw that. What others did not believe in him, now I have proven his words are true.

"I'm glad you believe me sir. Cause the police don't. Up until now they keep coming here for a statement. They believe I kill my husband and hide his body somewhere here in the yard."

Before going home, I gave the computer back to her. But to die she did not accept. Satisfied I persuaded him. But he still doesn't want to accept it.

"That computer will always remind me of my husband, sir. You better take it back. It's yours."

He continued to refuse my offer and once again, I returned feeling disappointed.

While putting the computer in the car, his son came to me. He spoke behind an iron net.

"My mom was right. The computer should be in the hands of the man who deserves it the most."

"You are the most worthy. You are his son."

"No, you. You the writer. Use it. Keep writing. Only that way my father will continue to live," he said. Sounds too matured for a boy that age. But I must admit, I was stunned by the verse he used. In silence I acknowledged the truth of his words.

He was right. I must own this computer and use it.

✕

A few weeks later I bought a new computer, complete with Microsoft Word and so on. Anti-virus that is so expensive I don't think any Trojan virus or wild spirit will mess up the computer. I continue writing horror story.

Six month later, my book being published. It has nothing to do with ghost in the machine story I'm experiencing before. It's just an ordinary horror story involving a highway and a yellow Volkswagen car, but somehow, fans love at its writing. Finally my novel becomes bestseller in MPH chart list. Only later I realized the book becomes a bestseller and my name as a horror writer is back famous not because of my writing, but because without my knowing, my story and this haunted computer spread widely on social media. I don't mind, anything can make me famous and my books became bestseller again, I don't care. People, in social media, asking either the story is truth or not and I deny it immediately. Sometimes I just give hint to them that the story must be true.

One day I read about writing competition on horror story stories. One of the requirement is it should be in English. I really want to join the competition. I have only one problem though – my English not that good. But I don't think that could be a problem with me. So I wrote this story in BM that will turn into English using that old computer. If readers, or even the editor question why the language is so bad, I just want them to know it's not really my fault, that it's not my doing. It's the work of bad spirit of Google Translate that haunt my computer.

The Break-In

✕

Terence Toh

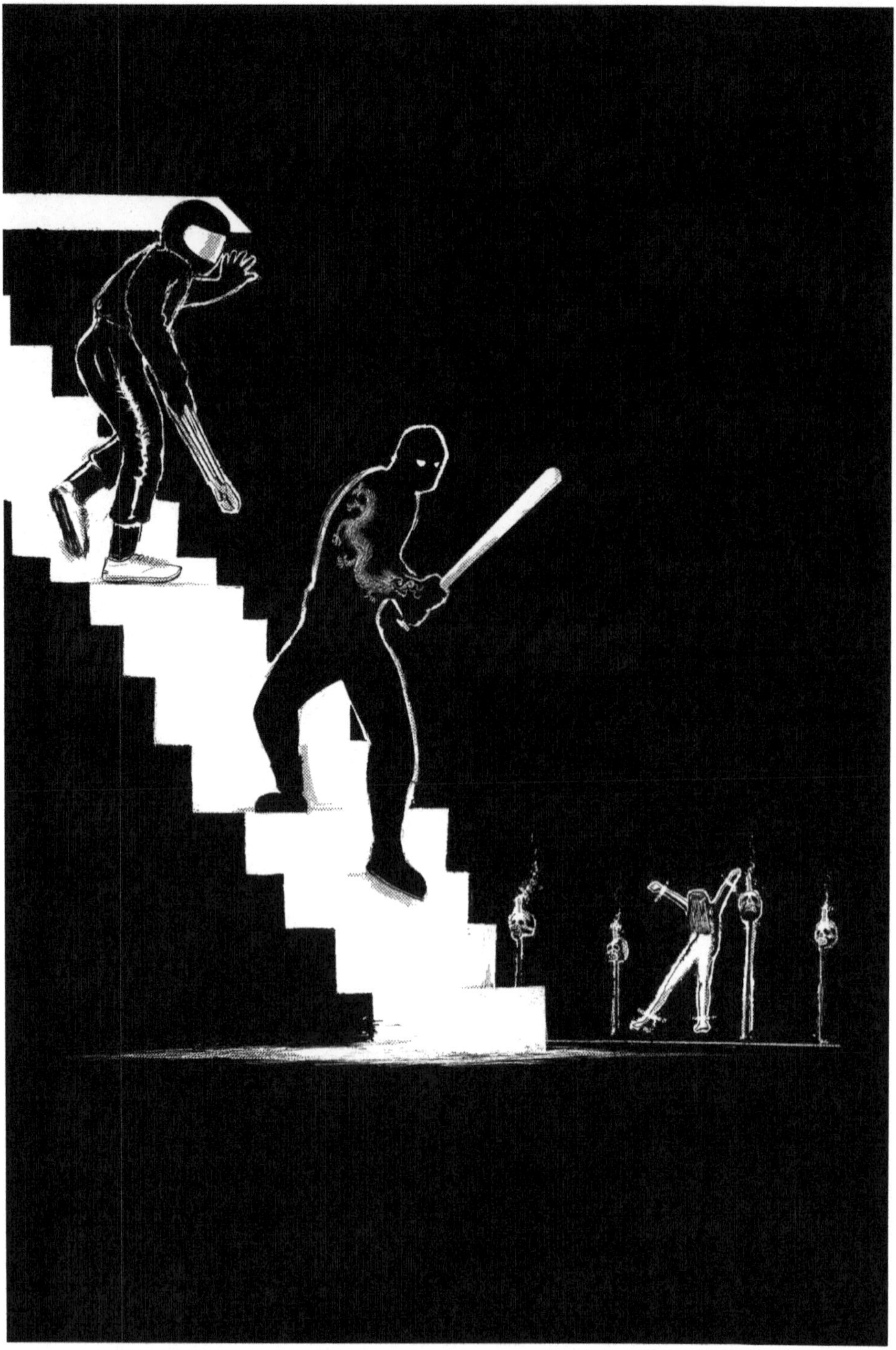

Cheng slammed the bolt cutter's handles together and the lock fell apart with a loud snap.

"Eh chill lah," Hafiz smiled, taking a puff of his cigarette. His hair was wavy, and his tanned face was marked by a knife scar, a souvenir from his last prison stint. "Treat the Crocodile with respect. Nanti dia makan kau!"

The sun was setting. The two were standing outside the bungalow at the top of the hill. A posh place. It had a lush garden with a water feature, a swing beneath a shady tree and a bird feeder with a Cupid.

The bungalow owner was bald and bearded, in his fifties or sixties. He did not know them, but Cheng and Hafiz knew him very well. They had been watching him for almost a month.

They knew he was retired or unemployed, and lived by himself. He was a bit of a homebody: he left his house only on Friday afternoons to go to the mosque, or to bungkus dinner from the mamak at the bottom of the hill. They knew he was fond of buying things online: delivery riders were a common sight at his gates.

Most importantly, they knew he always went for a walk on Sunday evenings. Like clockwork, he would drive out at 7 p.m. to Bukit Kiara Park, where he would walk for an hour. Then he would have dinner at a nearby coffee shop. By the time he came back, it was usually about 9pm.

Which gave Hafiz and Cheng about one and a half hours to do what they needed to do.

Cheng tucked the bolt cutters into his backpack. He was a tall, lanky youth with a shaven head and dragon tattoos covering his arms. Hafiz put on a motorcycle helmet, while he pulled on a balaclava. It was a present from an ex-girlfriend.

He pushed the bungalow doors; they swung open silently. Cheng braced himself for the sound of an alarm. Mercifully, nothing came.

He looked around one final time to ensure no one was watching.

"Relax lah," Hafiz laughed at his friend's tension. "No one is at home. Plenty of time."

✕

"Shit," Hafiz whistled. "Damn nice lah this place."

The bungalow's hall could only be described as magnificent. An ornate chandelier hung from the ceiling. Two sofas and a coffee table stood atop what Cheng guessed to be a Persian carpet. Opposite the entrance was a wide-screen plasma TV, complete with a DVD and Blu-ray player, and home audio system.

Cheng pointed to a garish painting of multi-colored squiggles on one of the walls. "How much do you think that's worth ah?"

"Should be at least a few hundred," Hafiz said. "Aku ada member kat art gallery. He can help us sell."

As Hafiz took down the painting, Cheng felt a vibration in his pocket; he took out his phone.

It was Imran, their lookout. Right now, he was sitting in the mamak at the bottom of the hill, pretending to read a novel while sipping a glass of teh tarik. In reality, his eyes were glued to the main road, looking out for the old man's familiar red Daihatsu.

←You guys in??→

←Yeah. Everything gud→ It was a little hard to type while wearing gloves, but somehow Cheng managed.

←Great. Anything I SOS, watch ur phone ya→ Imran replied.

←Roger→

Cheng was still a little uneasy about him. Hafiz had vouched for Imran, saying the two went way back. Used to be his number two in turf wars or some shit like that, Cheng couldn't remember. He hoped the guy was trustworthy. Or it would be back to jail for all of them.

The two quickly got to work. They had agreed on their roles: Hafiz for electronics, Cheng for valuables. And Hafiz was certainly having a field day. Within minutes, he hauled up the man's stereo set, DVD player, and laptop. All of which he placed in a neat stack by the door.

"Can Imran drive here?" Hafiz asked as he struggled to unravel the plasma TV's twisted wiring. "I tak larat lah, carry all this."

"Make two trips lah," Cheng said, rummaging through a row of shelves. "Don't waste petrol!"

He picked up a china vase and overturned it before tossing it to the floor, where it shattered loudly. Experience taught him that people hid stuff in the strangest places. Especially old people, with their irrational fear of banks. In one of his previous outings, Cheng found almost RM15,000 cash, wrapped up in newspaper and hidden at the bottom of a fridge.

There was little else to take in the hall, so Cheng moved into the rooms nearby. Not much luck there. The man didn't seem to have any jewelry, and didn't leave much money lying around.

His bedroom was sparse: a simple bed, dresser and wardrobe. A quick search revealed little of value. A few hundred ringgit notes in a drawer. An antique pocketwatch with a gold chain in the dresser, alongside a digital camera and a non-functioning tablet.

One of the other rooms was filled with books. Most of them Islamic texts, although there were a few in some strange writing he could not recognize. Hafiz confirmed it wasn't Jawi. These books were full of bizarre, often gruesome illustrations. Mostly nude humans being tortured by demons wielding various torture instruments.

What the hell? Just looking at them gave Cheng the creeps.

There was a tiny safe in the wardrobe. He cracked it open in excitement with the Crocodile, only to discover a copy of the Quran, a foreign book with yellowing pages, a staff with a crescent-shaped handle and what appeared to be a flask of water.

All the curse words in the world would not have been enough for Cheng. *Great. Just great.* All the houses in Mont Kiara, and they *had* to choose the strange kinky old man. What he did with these weird instruments he had no idea, but Cheng knew they would not sell for much.

He was about to try his luck in another room when he suddenly heard Hafiz's voice.

"Eh bro! Check this out!"

Cheng met up with Hafiz in the kitchen. His normally jovial face was now contorted in fear.

"See the fridge. It's damn freaky!" he muttered.

"Got cockroach, is it?" Cheng said. "Aiyo, bro, cannot so pussy lah."

But even he had to gasp when he looked inside. Dozens and dozens of glass bottles. All filled to the brim with a thick red liquid. And on one of the bottom shelves, smelling rancid, was what appeared to be the heart or kidney of an animal. It looked fresh: blood was still oozing from a cut in its side.

Cheng picked up one of the bottles and shook it. A long object swirled to the surface; perhaps it was his imagination, but it looked just like a human finger, complete with chipped fingernail.

He suddenly felt nauseous. Against his better judgment, he opened one of the bottles and touched its contents: it was thick and viscous.

"Is this what I think it is?" Cheng gasped.

"Fuck, man," Hafiz said. "What is this shit?"

It was just then that the two men heard a scream. It was high-pitched and faint, but unmistakably human.

"Did you hear that?" Cheng asked. He glanced around the kitchen nervously.

Hafiz nodded. His face was white. "Macam orang cedera."

"It came from over there." Cheng indicated a door to the right.

"Bro, let's get out of here," Hafiz said. "This is fucking creepy."

As he said that there was another scream, far louder this time.

Cheng paused. Shouldn't they get out of here? They already had quite a decent haul.

Yet he had always been the curious sort. If he left now, he would probably live his life in constant frustration, never knowing what had been behind that mysterious door. Could he live with himself after that?

And besides, what could possibly be down there that they could not handle? Hafiz had once taken on five men in a fight. And he had only been

16 at the time. It was one of the proudest moments of his friend's life. Heaven help whoever decided to mess with the two of them.

"Let's check it out," Cheng said.

The door was locked. Cheng took the bolt cutters out of his backpack and passed them to Hafiz, who nodded. Cheng then reached into his backpack again and pulled out a baseball bat. His palms were sweaty as he gripped its handle tightly. Cheng remembered the last time he had used it, and suddenly felt faint.

One last time, he thought. *Then, never again.* He was just a thief; he never liked hurting anyone.

Hafiz broke the lock and pushed the door open to reveal what appeared to be a tiny closet. There was a wooden trapdoor on the floor.

Cheng pulled it open, and his nostrils were immediately accosted by an overwhelming stench of decay. He covered his nose and mouth with his T-shirt, trying not to retch.

"Ya Allah!" Hafiz groaned. "Busuknya!"

The trapdoor opened to a flight of stairs. Grasping their bat and bolt cutters tightly, Cheng and Hafiz descended into the darkness.

✕

"This is a bad idea, bro."

The two made their way down the stairs slowly, groping against the wall for a light switch.

"We'll just check it out then we go, okay? Don't be so scared!" Cheng said. "Maybe we'll find something cool."

"Aku tak takut." Hafiz did his best to seem stoic, but was not doing a good job. "I just…okay, ya, aku memang takut, you got problem? Kau tak takut ke?"

"Just shut up and find the lights, can or not?"

A feminine voice suddenly rang out, making the two jump. "Help! Help me!"

"Shit bro," Hafiz muttered. "What the hell is going on?"

After five minutes of fumbling in the dark, Hafiz finally found the light switch. Cheng muttered a prayer of gratitude as the place was illuminated.

What they saw shocked them. A huge black cauldron stood in the middle of the basement. It smelt funky, putting Cheng in mind of vinegar. Surrounding it were four candles on tall stands; human skulls resting at their bases.

Not far from the cauldron was a girl. Her neck, arms and feet were bound by iron manacles, on rusty chains attached to the basement's back wall.

"Ya Allah!" Hafiz was stunned. "Apa ni?"

"Help me," the girl pleaded.

She was pale, with dark hair that flowed over her shoulders. Young, she couldn't have been more than 17. The girl wore a frayed white dress which looked as if it would come apart any moment. It was ripped along the right shoulder, exposing part of her breast. Cheng couldn't help but blush.

"What happened to you?" he asked. "Are you okay?"

The girl's eyes filled with tears as she looked at Cheng. "

My father put me here."

"Holy shit," Cheng said, stunned. "The old man?"

"This is like that story," Hafiz said. He had taken off his motorcycle helmet. "Ingat tak? In the news last time? There was this guy in the US, who trapped these women in a dungeon for ten years..." His hands were trembling visibly. "Fuck, man, fuck."

Who would have thought the old man capable of something like this? He had seemed so…normal. Like those old uncles you saw on the street selling newspapers. Cheng would have thought him the kind who'd find a 10 ringgit note on the pavement and turn it over to the police.

It was always the respectable-looking ones you had to be worried about. There were two kinds of men in the world: men who knew how to hide their darkness, and men who shamelessly displayed who they really were.

"I haven't eaten in three days," the girl's voice was a harsh sob. "Help me!"

"We'll get you out soon!" Hafiz said. He brandished his bolt cutters like a knight's sword. "This is a job for the Crocodile."

As Hafiz got to work, Cheng spoke to the girl.

"What's your name?"

"Dyana."

"How long have you been here?"

"I don't know. But…maybe three years?"

Cheng cursed. He took her hand, and held it tightly. "Don't worry, Dyana. We'll get you out of here."

There were ugly burns on the underside of her arm. "Did your father do this to you?" he asked, sick to his stomach.

"Yes." Her eyes filled with tears.

"This will all be over soon," Cheng reassured her. He turned to his friend. "Hafiz, why so long wan?"

"Ini besi kuat ni," Hafiz said. His shirt was soaked with sweat. He passed the bolt cutters to Cheng, and sighed. "Sorry, I tak larat."

Cheng tried the Crocodile for a while, but Hafiz was right. No matter how much he strained, he could not break the chains.

"We need the keys," Cheng said. "Do you know where they are?"

"I think they may be upstairs. Or with my father."

"What do we do now?" Hafiz asked.

"Call the police," Dyana suggested.

Cheng and Hafiz exchanged nervous glares. Both of them knew this was out of the question.

Summoning the police would mean explaining what they were doing in the house in the first place. And given how open-minded and sensitive the nation's boys in blue were, admitting they had intended to burgle the place would not play in their favor.

The two, after all, had six previous convictions between them. Cheng had been specifically warned not to steal anymore by the magistrate in his previous hearing. One more strike, and they would be put away for a long time. Especially as they could no longer be classified as juvenile offenders.

"We should go up," Hafiz said. "Maybe there's a saw there or something."

Just then, there was a whirring sound from his pocket; Cheng almost jumped in shock. He pulled out his phone and cursed. In the heat of excitement, he hadn't noticed it vibrating.

11 messages and 12 missed calls. All from Imran.

←SOS→

←SOS→

←SOS BRO, Get out of there!→

←He's back!→

←His car just pulled up→

←where the fuck u guys→

←Bro are you out bro→

←PLS get out→

←He's walking up now→

←Ssos→

←Get out of there BRO→

"Shit," Cheng said. "The old man. He's back."

"No." The girl's eyes widened in fear. "No, no, please, no, don't let him get me…" The chain around her neck clanged loudly as she struggled, and a panicked Hafiz begged her to stop.

Cheng sent a reply.

←Stay low bro. Its ok. Well get out→

"Now what the fuck do we do?" Hafiz asked.

"We turn off the lights," Cheng said. "Then we hide. Under the stairs. And on my signal, we attack."

"Kau pasti ke?" There were beads of sweat on Hafiz's brow.

"We have to," Cheng said firmly.

"Be careful," the girl said.

"Don't worry," Cheng said. There was an ugly clamminess in the pit of his stomach, but he forced himself to ignore it. "We'll protect you."

✕

After what seemed like an eternity and a half, there was the sound of movement.

A creak, a sliver of light that snuck into the basement like a bandit. And then there were footsteps: a slow and heavy tempo, the plodding gait of an old man. Cheng's stomach clenched.

"Dyana!" the old man cried. "Kenapa semua barang bersepah?"

In the silence of the basement, the girl's heavy breathing seemed like the echoes around mountains.

"Dyana!" The old man walked downstairs, his steps quickened by rage. "Apa berlaku? Jawab!"

There was a click, and the place was flooded with light: the old man had reached the switch.

"*Now!*" Cheng shouted. The owner stared as the two boys rushed out, screaming and waving their weapons. His shock turned to anger as he realized what they were up to.

"Jangan!" he screamed as Cheng and Hafiz attacked him. "Dia –"

He raised his arms to shield himself, but it was futile. There was a sickening crack as Hafiz smashed his bat against the man's head. He crumpled and fell, his blood forming a pool on the floor.

"Shit," Cheng said. Suddenly he was exhausted; his knees gave out and he collapsed, his back against the wall. His breath was heavy and came in spurts. "I think you killed him."

"Padan muka!" Hafiz said. He raised his bat and bashed the man's head one final time. "Bloody fucker."

The two rifled through the old man's pockets. Handkerchief. Phone. Wallet. Hafiz pocketed all of those. In his back pocket was what they were looking for: a ring of keys. There were about a dozen – one key, however, was stained with what appeared to be blood.

Cheng tried it, and his hunch was right. Within minutes, the two unlocked all the manacles around Dyana: her neck, her arms, her feet. They helped her up.

"It's okay," Hafiz said. "Everything is all right."

"You were so brave," Dyana said. She reached out for a hug, which Hafiz gladly accepted. There was a huge smile on his face.

As Hafiz and Dyana embraced, Cheng walked over to the cauldron, curious to see what exactly was in it. *Just what the hell has been going on here?*

Suddenly, he stopped – there was a piercing pain in his right foot.

What the hell? He had stepped on something. Cheng winced as he pulled the offending object out. Whatever it was, it had been sharp enough to pierce through the sole of his (admittedly low-quality) canvas shoe.

A thorn. About two inches long.

Cheng looked down; to his surprise, many of them were scattered all over the floor. With all the crazy shit going on, they had somehow escaped his attention.

His first impulse was to kick them away. Halfway through, however, a dark thought entered his mind.

Wait a minute. These are mengkuang thorns, aren't they?

He had read about something like this before. In old ghost-story books. Wasn't this how they protected against –

A cold shiver danced spider-like down Cheng's spine.

He turned back to Hafiz, who was still in Dyana's embrace. It was at that precise moment he noticed the tiny fangs peering shyly out of the corners of the girl's mouth.

Dyana grinned at him. It was as if she could read his mind.

And then she struck.

Hafiz could barely react as Dyana, moving with unnatural speed, sunk her teeth into his neck. He let out a tortured scream as the girl shoved him to the floor. Her mouth was stained with his blood.

"Dyana?" Hafiz was confused. "Apa ni?"

To their horror, Dyana's head slowly rose into the air. There was a sickening crack as it wrenched itself free from her shoulders. Blood gushed from her neck as her intestines and other organs slowly emerged, all attached to her head through thick, cord-like entrails. The rest of her body fell to the floor, like the last pieces of a cocoon left behind after a caterpillar's metamorphosis.

"Pe…penanggal!" Hafiz stammered.

Dyana's head let out a hideous, piercing shriek. It struck at Hafiz, taking a deep bite of his flesh. Hafiz tried to get up, but the creature was too strong for him. His last words were a gasped, "*Run bro!*"

Terrified, Cheng fled as what-was-once-Dyana feasted. Her abnormally long, fat tongue darted in and out of her mouth as she lapped up his poor friend's blood.

He did not get far. Cheng was barely at the stairwell when he heard another hideous shriek. Suddenly, he lost his balance and fell on his back.

Cheng screamed. One of Dyana's hideous entrails had wrapped itself, tentacle-like, around his ankle. He struggled to escape, but its grip was like steel: he could do nothing as he was pulled towards her.

Dyana's head hovered above him. It resembled a grotesque jellyfish, its blood-drenched entrails reaching all the way to the floor. Its eyes were a sickly yellow. It drew close to him, and Cheng felt its hot breath on his face. The stench of vinegar strongly assaulted his nostrils.

"You set me free," she crooned. "Thank you."

She sank her fangs into Cheng's neck. He screamed and made one final attempt to escape, but it was no use. He could not move: all his limbs had been pinned down by her ghastly entrails. All Cheng could do was close his eyes, and pray the sweet release of death came quickly.

Soon, Dyana was done drinking, and it was time to feast on his flesh. She was so caught up in her meal, she did not notice the vibrations coming from her prey's pocket.

←Bro, everything ok ke? So long no sound?→

←Bro, u ok?→

←Bro?→

←Satu jam bro where r u→

←U in trouble?→

←I masuk. Don't wori I tolong→

←Where r u bro→

Dyana would eat well tonight.

The Red Kebaya

✕

Venoo Kuppusamy

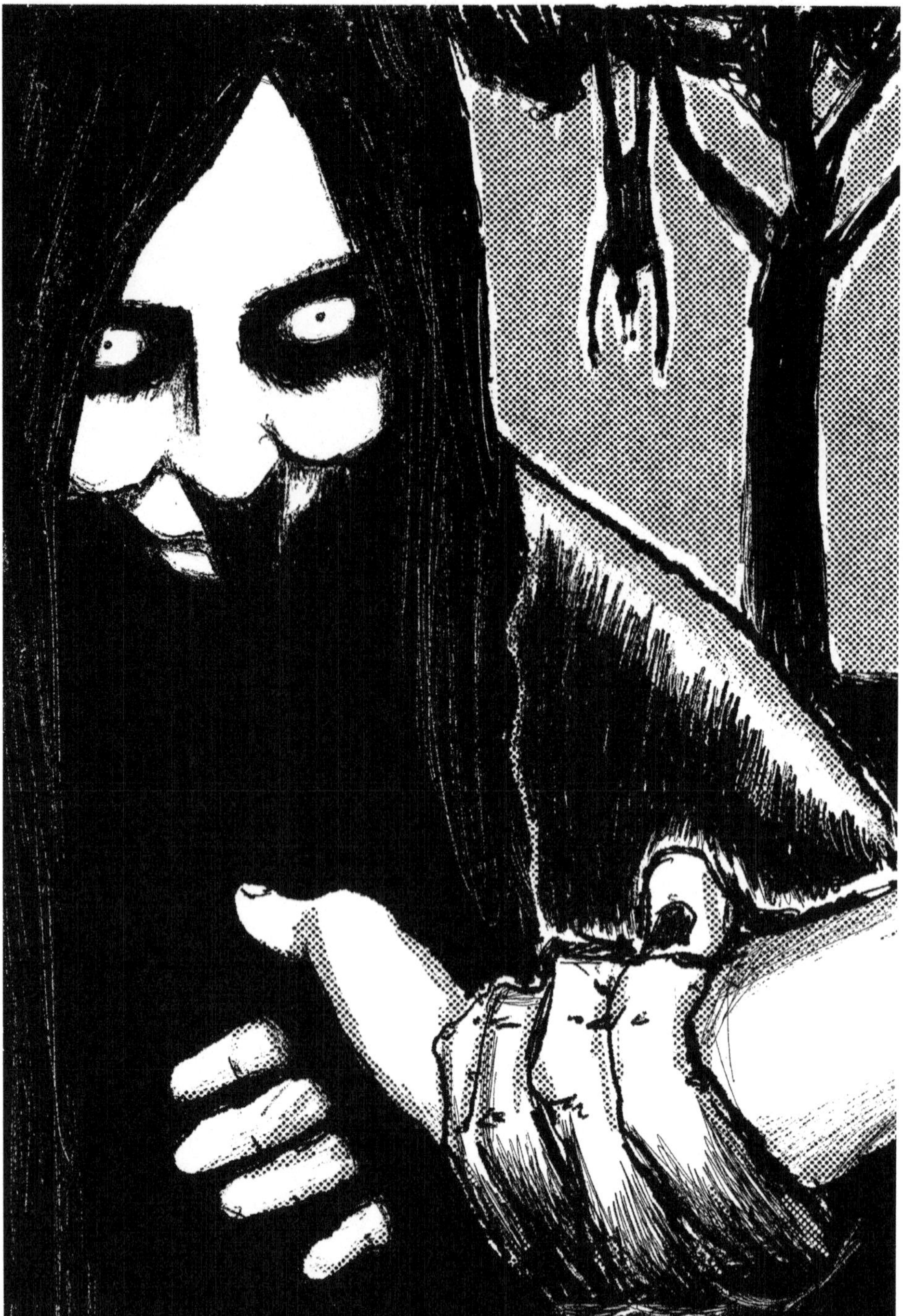

The night was silent and colder than usual. Samad walked slowly, taking in every detail. An eerie feeling had fallen upon the village for the past few months, but Samad braved the night. He was determined to find out what happened to his son.

Samad's son was the latest victim in a chain of events that started four months ago. Samad's life was shattered when he saw the body of his 16-year-old son, eyes gouged out, hanging naked from the angsana tree at the end of the village. The image haunted Samad's dreams every night.

One month later, Samad's despair turned into anger. The next month transformed his anger into vengeance. Every night he roamed the village, looking for the monster that killed his only son. Samad searched the night – oblivious that there was a pair of eyes lurking in the dark, looking right at him.

✕

Inspector Rama arrived at Kampung Seangsana from the nearest police station in Pekan. Pak Mat's coffee shop was his first stop. Accompanying him was Constable Dahlan.

"Tuan." Pak Mat served them coffee with a nod of respect.

"Pak Mat, join us," Inspector Rama requested.

Pak Mat glanced around his shop. Only Uncle Chong who came every day to read the newspaper was there. Pak Mat sat down.

"Are you here about the murders?"

Inspector Rama smiled; he was supposed to do the questioning. "Yes, I am."

"Don't talk about it. It will happen again. Better not talk about it."

Rama knew it was futile to question Pak Mat. He could see the fear in Pak Mat's eyes; not ordinary fear, either. Rama paid for the coffee and waited for Dahlan to get the Honda C70 they rode to the village.

"Tuan, where to now?"

"The house of the first victim," Rama answered, tired from the noonday heat.

They arrived at Satnam Singh's house as the family was having lunch. It was not a joyous lunch: no cheerful talk, no signs of enjoyment from the food. They had come at the worst possible time, but there was no turning back.

As soon as Satnam knew the purpose of Inspector Rama's visit, he brought them to the backyard. There were wooden benches in the open, surrounded by chicken coops. After being seated, silence followed with only the clucking of the chickens filling the air.

"What can I do for you?" Satnam asked, knowing well the questions that would follow. The investigation had been going on for months, and once again they had sent someone new – back to square one.

Satnam explained what happened four months ago. His son Sarjeet was 15 and studious. Rarely was he seen playing around, as he would spend his time studying. But on the unfortunate day, he requested permission to play football with the boys. Since it was a rare request, Satnam obliged.

The football match ended late in the evening and the boys dived into the river for a swim. It wasn't until the azan for Maghrib was heard that the boys rushed out, cycling back to their houses. Sarjeet sat at the back while Rashid pedaled hard. Suddenly –

"Rashid, stop. Someone is waving at us." Sarjeet tugged on Rashid's wet T-shirt.

Rashid stopped and from afar they could see a silhouette of a woman near the angsana tree.

"Who is that?" Rashid asked.

"I don't know but she was waving at us. Maybe she needs help."

They quickly turned around and headed to the tree. When they got there, the woman was missing – and the darkness hampered their search. Sarjeet saw her first, behind the angsana tree. They approached her. She was in her early twenties. She looked beautiful but a bit pale, with glistening lipstick matching her red kebaya. Her hair was in a bun and she had a sweet smile.

"Can you help me?" She held out her hand.

Sarjeet went closer with Rashid behind him. "What can we do?"

Suddenly she grabbed Sarjeet's hand, still smiling. Her grip was firm. "Let go. What do you want?" Sarjeet tried to pull away anxiously.

With an angry high-pitched shriek the woman said, "*I want your soul!*"

Her face changed, decaying in front of Sarjeet as her eyes bulged. The stench of rotting flesh filled his nostrils as he screamed his lungs out. But the woman's shriek drowned his scream.

"*I want your soul!*"

Rashid bolted, not looking back, the shriek fading away as he ran for his life. By the time the villagers were informed, there was no one at the angsana tree. A night-long search by the village men was fruitless. A few of the villagers went to Pekan to inform the police. Their story fell on deaf ears; the police were skeptical. Sarjeet's dead body was found the next night, hanging from the same angsana tree. The body was naked with eyes gouged out.

Sitting at the back of the motorcycle, Inspector Rama smoked away while they headed to the next victim's house.

"You believe that story?" Rama asked.

"Yes, Tuan. What other explanation can there be? Rashid was the only witness, why would he lie?" Dahlan replied confidently.

Rama was lost in thought. "Yes. Why would he lie?"

The next stop was Zulkifli's house. He lost his father two weeks after Sarjeet's incident. The hesitancy to tell his story was apparent. The villagers no longer trusted the police, who were seen as merely taking statements for their reports. Zulkifli didn't want to elaborate, his story was simple.

His father Shamsudin had gone to his sister's house. According to Shamsudin's sister, he had left the house around 10 pm, but never got home. The rest was obvious; His body was found hanging from the angsana tree, naked, eyes gouged out. There were no witnesses.

Rama stood beside their motorcycle, again smoking away, not uttering a word.

"Tuan, you want to go to the next house?"

"Maybe if anyone goes missing, they should just go wait at the angsana tree, the killer is bound to go there," Rama grunted.

"But…"

"But what, Dahlan?" Rama was agitated.

"But the killer is a ghost. Didn't you hear the stories?"

Rama burst out laughing, "So what do you want me to do? Write in the report the murders were by a female ghost in her 20s, in a red kebaya, and close the case?"

Dahlan was silent.

"Dahlan, there is a serial killer on the loose, and the whole village is sitting here telling me ghost stories," Rama said sternly. "We're getting to the bottom of this before anyone else gets hurt. Come."

Fauziah's house was their last stop. The fourth and fifth victims were Samad's son and Samad himself. They did not have any other family or relatives, and no one saw what happened to them. Fauziah was emotional; it took time for her to calm down and start narrating her story.

Amin was Fauziah's younger brother, a university student coming home for semester break. From the main bus stop it was a long walk into the village. Fauziah was adamant about waiting for him at the bus stop so they could ride her bicycle back to the village. She didn't want Amin walking back alone, especially with two deaths in the village already. No one went out after Maghrib anymore, but they had no choice. The only bus from Kuala Lumpur arrived in Pekan at 10.15 pm and Amin had to take the last bus to his village.

The road was dark, no streetlights. Fauziah looked left and right, muttering under her breath. She had only been at the bus stop 10 minutes, but it felt like hours. She was scared, even the slightest rustle of nearby bushes startled her. She felt like she was being watched. She squinted and looked down the road; it seemed like a silhouette, *Is that a woman?* Before she could take a second look, the glaring light of the bus blurred her vision. Amin was the only one getting down at the stop.

The bus rolled away, and Fauziah hurried. "Come, quick. Sit and pedal fast. Give me your bag. Don't stop. Just keep pedaling."

"Yes, Kak. Okay." Amin waited for Fauziah to sit and started pedaling.

As they got on the laterite road into the village, Fauziah turned to look –with the light from the bus fading away in the distance, and darkness consuming the road again, it was there: the silhouette of a woman.

Fauziah looked away, her voice trembling. "Amin, go faster."

Amin nodded and pedaled faster. Fauziah kept on turning back, her eyes wildly searching if the woman was following them. Suddenly, Amin stopped and jumped off the bicycle.

She looked around, anxious. "Why did you stop?!"

"Kak, calm down. The tire is punctured. We have to walk," Amin explained.

"Punctured? It's okay, leave the bicycle. Come, start walking." Fauziah took a few steps and she stopped cold. "No, why did you stop *here*?"

Fauziah's voice was almost muffled. To her right stood the angsana tree. A chill went down her spine. Before Fauziah could grab his hand and start running, Amin uttered the next words.

"Eh, who are you?" Amin said, looking behind Fauziah.

When Fauziah turned, standing inches away from her was a beautiful young woman in a red kebaya with red glistening lips curled in a smile. She grabbed Fauziah's hand.

"Let me go! Amin, run!" Fauziah struggled to free her hand.

Amin didn't run. He grabbed Fauziah's other hand and tugged hard. The woman let go of Fauziah, but grabbed Amin's hand instead. Her grasp was strong, her lips fixed in the same smile. Fauziah started hitting the woman, screaming to let go of her brother. The woman just kept smiling.

Her high-pitched shriek froze Amin and Fauziah: "*I want your soul!*"

The beautiful young woman began decaying, the stench of rotten flesh filling the air. Her eyes bulging out, she looked into Amin's eyes.

"*I want your soul!!*"

Fauziah passed out – the villagers found her the next morning. Amin was nowhere to be seen. The villagers knew where to find him and started their search around the angsana tree. The search went on and some of them braved the night in a small group to the angsana tree, with lit torches. They didn't see anyone. Suddenly there was a rustling above the tree and Amin's body dropped down hanging, naked, eyes gouged out.

"Cik Fauziah, are you sure what you saw? A young lady in red kebaya that started rotting and wanted your soul?" Rama asked.

"No, not my soul. It wanted Amin's soul," Fauziah sobbed.

Inspector Rama got up and left with Constable Dahlan tailing him. He was angry. Outside Fauziah's house, he took out a cigarette but it fell to the ground. He stepped on it furiously, took out another and puffed away.

"Are these people for real? They expect me to believe a ghost story?!"

"Tuan, they believe the story because that is what they saw. This story has been told for decades." Dahlan was a bit agitated with his superior's disbelief.

"Decades? The killings started four months ago." Rama was taken aback.

"Yes Tuan, but the previous killings happened decades ago." Dahlan was calmer now. "It's a very old story, the village's haunted past. The story of the woman in red kebaya. The best person to tell you would be Tok Wan."

"Who is Tok Wan?"

"The oldest man in the village."

It was nearing Maghrib by the time Rama, Dahlan, the village head Pak Ramlee and a few other villagers were seated on the mengkuang mat at Tok Wan's house. Tok Wan was 93, but he looked in his early 70s. He kept coughing and clearing his throat.

"I'm sorry, I've not been well for the past few months," he coughed again. "Let us get on with things. The woman in red kebaya."

The first incident was over 70 years ago. Tok Wan, or back then known as Wan Aziz, was the sole maker of Wau Pungguk in the village; a skill he learned from his mother before being orphaned at age 12. Wau Pungguk is unique to Pahang, and Pekan specifically. Made from bamboo, pinang, nibong and rattan, Wau Pungguk has a long tail different from the usual Wau Bulan. It also makes a violin-like buzzing sound when it takes flight.

The first victim was Jack Grant, a British officer stationed at the village. His maid saw him with a woman in a red kebaya outside the house at night, and he went missing after that. The next day his body was hanging from the angsana tree, naked, eyes gouged out. No one had seen this woman in the red kebaya anywhere else before.

"Did you see her the first time? How about the body?" Rama asked.

"No, I didn't. No one saw her, except for the maid. I didn't get a glimpse of the body. I was down with an unknown disease, fighting between life and death," Tok Wan explained.

In 1948, the communists occupied the nearby forest and looted the village for food and supplies. The British often had shootouts with the communists. Deaths occurred daily, including villagers caught by stray bullets. One such bullet hit Tok Wan, but luckily, he survived. During this period, one of the communist soldiers was found hanging from the angsana tree, naked, eyes gouged out. Rumors from the communist camp spoke of a woman in a red kebaya lurking in the forest a day before the body was found.

The last incident was in 1965. There was a dengue outbreak. This time, the village healer Esah saw the woman in the red kebaya. On the way back home after attending to numerous dengue-afflicted villagers including Tok Wan, Esah saw a villager, Lokman, holding hands with a woman in a red kebaya. The woman was young and beautiful until she transformed right in front of Esah's eyes, shrieking that she wanted Lokman's soul. Esah didn't remember what happened after that. The body was found as usual at the same place in the same condition.

Rama could not wrap his head around this. Three incidents decades ago, and now five incidents in the span of four months. Who is this woman? Is she real? Has she been killing for over 70 years?

Rama and Dahlan decided to stay the night. Pak Ramlee kindly offered his house. It was almost midnight, but the discussion went on between the three of them, still to no avail. Suddenly a thought struck Rama.

"What is the one thing that is still here since the killings started over 70 years ago?" Rama asked.

"The angsana tree?" Dahlan didn't understand the relevance.

"Not the tree. Let me rephrase. Who is the one person still here since the first incident?"

Pak Ramlee shook his head. "Don't tell me you suspect Tok Wan. He is 93. The victims were healthy young people. Impossible. You have to accept the fact, there are supernatural things beyond our understanding."

"Maybe he did it alone previously, but now that he is old, he has an accomplice," Rama was laying out all the facts he could think of. "Tok Wan had alibis for all the incidents. He was sick with an unknown disease during the first incident, injured by a bullet during the second incident and had dengue the third time. Isn't that weird? Where was he during the incidents in the past four months?"

Pak Ramlee pondered. "Most of the time he was in the hospital in Pekan. He has been very sick lately. You saw his condition today."

Rama got up. "It's him. I'm sure. Did anyone go see him in the hospital? He has been using his sickness as an alibi to murder people!"

"Why?" Pak Ramlee and Dahlan asked at the same time.

"Come, only he can answer that."

The three of them arrived at Tok Wan's house. It seemed empty. Tok Wan did not have any family. Hearing Pak Ramlee calling Tok Wan's name, the old lady Kamisah from the opposite house came over.

"Tok Wan went out with my son, Bakri. They left on bicycle a while ago." Kamisah's explanation brought fear to them.

Rama told Pak Ramlee to gather some villagers and go to the angsana tree. He sped away with Dahlan on their C70. They had to stop Tok Wan before he did anything to Bakri. After a few minutes they could see Tok Wan seated behind the bicycle that Bakri was pedaling. Dahlan called to Bakri to stop. As they neared Bakri and Tok Wan, Bakri stopped the bicycle, hearing their voices.

Rama quickly held on to Bakri and looked around. "Where are you going at this hour? Where is Tok Wan taking you?"

Bakri seemed confused. "Tok Wan is sick. I'm taking him to the hospital."

Tok Wan was crouched at the bicycle, coughing. He had fresh bloodstains on his shirt.

"Dahlan, take Tok Wan to the hospital on the motorcycle. Quick," Rama instructed, realizing he might have been wrong about Tok Wan.

Before Tok Wan got on the motorcycle, there was a scream a few meters ahead. Rama and Dahlan ran towards it. As soon as they reached, they saw a woman in a red kebaya holding on to a villager – the one screaming for help.

"Let him go!" Rama yelled. "I'm a police officer!"

Bakri and Tok Wan arrived and they saw the woman in the red kebaya. She kept smiling, still not letting him go. They knew what would happen next:

"*I want your soul!*"

The woman started rotting in front of them. Suddenly there was a scream from behind Rama.

"Maaakkkk, stop Mak. Don't do it!"

It was Tok Wan, who was in tears and screaming. Before the woman transformed, Tok Wan had recognized his mother.

"Mak, let him go. Don't hurt him Mak," Tok Wan cried.

The woman stood still, her bulging eyes looking straight at Tok Wan. Her face was emotionless, but a tear started to fall. She let go of the villager, who ran straight to Rama. Tok Wan moved towards the woman slowly, coughing.

Dahlan tried to stop Tok Wan, but Rama stopped Dahlan.

Tok Wan stood in front of the woman. "Mak, why are you doing this? Stop it, Mak, please. Don't kill anyone, Mak."

The woman held out her hand and Tok Wan reached out for it. As soon as he took her hand, flashes of images filled his head. He knew what was happening. He dropped to his knees and started crying his heart out.

Wan Aziz's mother, Mastura, passed away when he was 12. He grew up alone, making and selling Wau Pungguk. All the while, his mother was watching over him in the form of a spirit. When he was infected by a disease at the age of 23, Mastura didn't know what to do – but she needed to save her son's life. That's when she decided to commit a terrible sin.

Jack Grant was her first victim. She sucked out his soul through his eyes. The life force from Jack Grant was passed on to her son, and he survived the disease. It was a sin she didn't want to commit ever again, until her son was shot by a stray bullet during a shootout with the communists. Her desperation to save her son had her sucking the soul out of the communist soldier. The third time, she killed to save her son from the clutches of dengue.

The three souls were more than enough to give Tok Wan a long healthy life, until he was diagnosed with lung cancer. That was when she killed Sarjeet. Tok Wan deteriorated again after two weeks. The life force was not enough. Each time his condition worsened, she would kill and suck out another soul. In four months, she murdered five people to keep her son alive – and he was still getting sicker.

"Mak, don't do this. Mak, please let me go. Please," Tok begged Mastura. "I've had a long life. It's enough. My time is near, let me go in peace, Mak."

With tears in her eyes, Mastura disappeared from everyone's sight. That night, Tok Wan was admitted to the hospital. Within a week, Rama completed his report, citing there was no evidence for further investigation and closed the case. There was no mention of the woman in the red kebaya in his report.

Two days after he was admitted to hospital, Tok Wan's condition became critical. He was alone in the wardroom accompanied by the beeping sound of the cardiac monitor. But he could feel his mother's presence. She was there, beside him, in his final seconds, finally able to let him go.

I am a Triathlete

✕

Lai May Senn

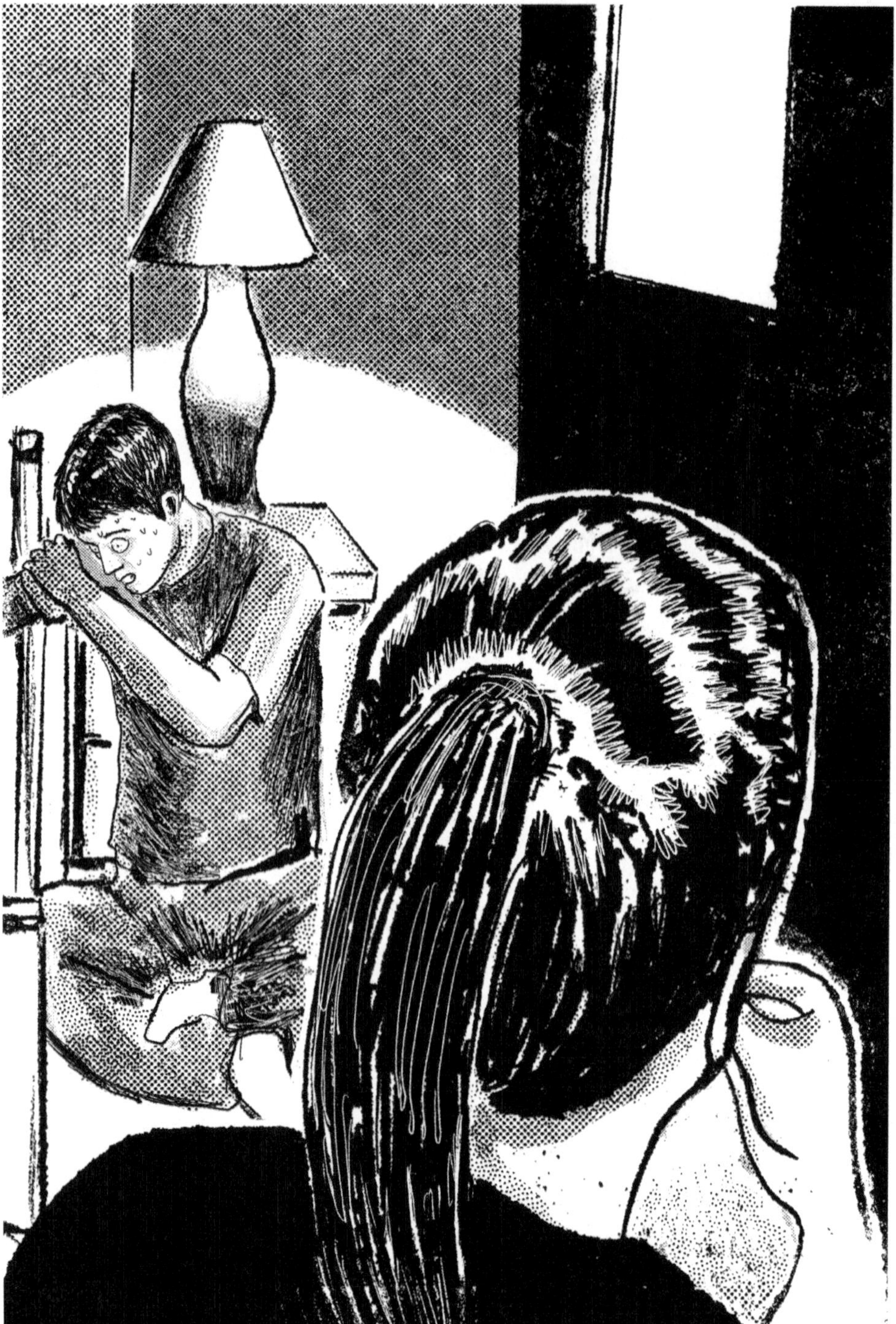

I am a triathlete.

There's a running joke in the circle that goes, *"How do you know if there's a triathlete at your party? They'll tell you."*

Guess there's some truth in that.

Every year around the month of February, my fellow triathletes and I would make our way up to Langkawi for the annual Langkawi Ironman. We would take a week off from work just to arrive on a Monday or Tuesday, prep for the week to race on Saturday and leave immediately on Sunday to make it back to work the next day. Why? Because the Monday after race day is the day we wear our tan lines proudly and tell our colleagues what we did over the weekend.

And that year was no different.

✕

It was 2009, and we had just driven our transit van onto the connecting ferry. There were five of us – always just five. Marcus owned a bicycle shop in Petaling Jaya; he's the hero that brought us together. Then Tarmizi and Rajan, besties since school, and finally my husband, Johan, and I – all loyal customers of Marcus' bicycle shop.

We made quite an entrance as Marcus had just purchased a second-hand transit van. He made the effort to wrap the van with his company designs, and with our bikes strapped to its roof, we looked smashingly professional.

Our go-to hotel was a three-star establishment just one turn from the finisher's platform. A strategic location for our tired bodies to return to after the race. When we arrived at our regular hotel, we checked in with our usual arrangement. Tarmizi, Rajan, Johan and I took the three-room family suite whilst Marcus checked in with another fellow triathlete. Everything was as it should be, every year the same arrangement.

Except this year, things were different.

On our first night, I heard what sounded like a bicycle going up and down the corridor outside our room. It was about 2 a.m. I was groggy, and half-annoyed that either Tarmizi or Rajan had decided to check their bicycle at that hour. *Triathletes,* I thought and tried to go back to sleep.

Just as I was about to fall back asleep, Johan patted my chest. I pushed his hand away and groaned. *No, wait – Johan is sleeping on my right; why was his hand coming from my left?* The hand patted again. Gently at first but harder as it continued, determined to wake me up. I pretended to stay asleep; a million things ran through my now fully-awake mind. The hand felt small, slightly clumsy, and even though the pats had turned into slaps, it didn't hurt.

I heard breathing. *Oh my god, it breathes!* I refused to open my eyes. I refused because I knew I see *stuff* and I didn't want to *see* stuff. I knew that if it looked anything like that first one when I was nine, I'd pee my pants and die of a heart attack. *Yup, not worth it.*

Remember that neighbor? Shu Mei's friend that passed away. What's his name? a voice in my head said.

Don't know don't care, I replied.

Yeah, you shared her bed the night he came back, remember?

Whatever, I replied, frustrated that I couldn't control the conversation nor the incessant patting on my chest.

You saw that bluish thing rising at the edge of the bed – inches from your face, the voice said.

I was now haunted by the patting on my chest and the memory of watching this bluish glow rising at the edge of the bed, wondering what it could be. I was nine at that time, and my cousin Shu Mei was friends with a boy that lived behind her house. He had died in an accident the week before, seven days prior, to be exact. I was visiting her and stayed the night his spirit was said to return.

There I was in bed, my cousin next to me, watching patiently as the bluish glow slowly rose. I freaked out when I realized I was looking at a set of eyebrows emerging. I knew what came after eyebrows, so I turned away just before my eyes met another set of eyes. I had not seen anything since, and I was not about to break that streak now.

The patting stopped.

Don't open your eyes; it's still there – breathing, I told myself.

I heard a sigh, and suddenly the hand grabbed the front of my T-shirt. In shock, I opened my eyes and saw a little girl trying her best to get onto the bed using my T-shirt as leverage. I looked, paralyzed beyond words, as a little girl no more than five-years-old heaved and struggled to climb on. Part of me wanted to help her, but instincts told me there shouldn't be a little glowing girl with a thick fringe covering her eyes in the room. So I did what I did when I was nine: I forcefully rolled to my right and jolted awake.

Confused, I wondered if I had dreamt the entire ordeal.

The next morning, I mentioned our secret code to Johan. A secret code we used only when travelling. From the many years of touring across Malaysia to race, we had become accustomed to the possibility of being checked into a haunted hotel room. It never happened to us, but we'd heard enough stories to make the code. The code that said *Mayday, spooky place.* Of course, it would have been easier to just say it out, but we grew up with the superstition of not announcing their presence as *they* would know, and then they would follow.

"You sure?" he said after I told him *the bed was lumpy* as we lined up at the race registration counter, a distance away from our hotel.

"Well, I woke up like it was a dream. But no, pretty sure the bed is *lumpy.*"

"Hmm, been here three times. Nothing like it before."

"Well, maybe we got a bad bed."

When our turn came, the race organizers took our attendance and clasped a plastic band around our wrists to mark our registration. Like branded warriors, we proceeded to collect our race kits. We waited for the rest to complete their registration before telling them about my *lumpy bed* and that it would be better to seek out a new place. They took heed, and we started searching for a new hotel, but it being one of the most anticipated events in Langkawi, all the hotels were booked except for the ones that *definitely* had those lumpy beds and the ones on the higher end of the price spectrum. At this point, it would be good to note that while we would willingly spend thousands to shave off a milligram from our race equipment, we couldn't justify paying more to switch hotels – even if it meant roughing out on a lumpy bed. Priorities, I guess.

By the evening, we all decided that we would give the lumpy bed another try, and if it happened again, we would check into the nearest luxury resort. *Maybe*.

The night came and went without any disturbance, so we stayed on.

The remaining days leading up to Saturday were fantastic. We had a great time exploring the race route and visited our favorite snack hubs along the way. The island was abuzz with more triathletes arriving from all over, some as far as the United States. That's the thing about the Ironman race: It is the only sport I know where weekend warriors like us can compete against international champions. Well, it was more like getting flat out dropped at the race circuit by the professional racers, them passing us as if we were standing still – but I digress.

Anyway, on the eve of the race, I walked into the bedroom to find Johan sitting cross-legged on the floor. He sat next to the bed, facing the door. I had just returned from a girly day out with the female triathletes in our group and had bought his favorite goreng pisang from a roadside stall. He looked down the moment he saw me, and I could see he was starting to look worried.

"What's wrong?" I asked.

He said nothing.

I approached him, and he avoided my eyes. He looked like he was about to cry. "Are you okay?" I asked. Still nothing, so I sighed. "Look, I bought goreng pisang. Have some."

I handed the plastic bag to him, but he would not take it. Thinking he must be terribly upset, I tried again, this time by opening the plastic bag and holding out a goreng pisang to feed him. He squirmed a little and pushed it away.

"Hey, if you're not going to eat it, don't waste it," I said firmly as I picked up the crispy golden treasure from the floor. I dusted it and ate it. *Five-second rule.*

He watched with a slightly disgusted expression on his face.

"What? It's good! I waited while she made it extra-crispy today." I rummaged in the plastic bag for another piece. "You sure you not going to have one?" I was losing my patience with the man-boy I married.

"We have to leave –" he finally said softly.

"*Whoy?*" I asked with my mouth full and slightly ajar to let the steam from the goreng pisang escape my mouth.

"Please, let's go home."

"The race is tomorrow," I said bluntly, chewing the remains of sweet fried banana in my mouth.

"Let's forget everything; this place is lumpy. Let's just go home."

"No!" I suddenly shouted as I stood up. I'd had enough of his nonsense, probably just pre-race jitters.

We trained all year, I said.

It's just one more lumpy night, I said.

We are going to race tomorrow, I said.

"*I* am going to race tomorrow – with or without you," I insisted.

Just then, my girlfriends walked into the room. "Is everything all right?" one of them asked.

"Johan thinks I should go home," I replied sarcastically. "I think I should stay with one of you gals tonight instead," I added, and started packing my belongings for the night.

None of them stood in my way; I guess they knew me well enough not to provoke me further.

When I was done packing up, I walked straight out.

"See you at the race start tomorrow – or not." I shrugged as I left the room.

×

Race morning was how I always experienced it: dark, a little eerie with the vast black waters at the pier, and filled with anxiety. I felt bad about the way I walked out on Johan and kept an eye out for him, but he was nowhere to be found. I asked Marcus and a few others; no one had seen him either. I laughed nervously at pre-race jokes and exchanged well wishes for a safe race ahead. I put on a brave face, but I was beginning to get very worried about Johan.

At the hint of dawn, we moved towards the waterfront. 800-odd triathletes bopping around, their color-coded swim caps like bright markers in the water. I looked around for Johan, wading among my chatty friends as we waited for the flag off.

With the sound of the air horn, I said a silent prayer for Johan's safety and started swimming. The waters were calm, and my mind soon entered the zone. My swim strokes were strong, my navigation on point. I smiled as I exited the water, running towards the transition tent to prepare for the cycling leg.

It was a beautiful day to ride. Sunny, with just enough cloud to make the hottest race of the year manageable. I was pushing hard on my bike and knew I would suffer during the run, but I didn't care. The wind seemed to always be on my tail, pushing my bike to a comfortable cruising speed. I passed many friends along the route, and they cheered me on. I felt on top of the world, though at the back of my head, I wished Johan was around to experience this incredible race day.

I ended the cycling leg 30 minutes faster than my usual time. I did a flying dismount off my bike and rolled it effortlessly to the volunteers waiting to catch it while I ran into the transition tent to change into my run gear.

As expected, I suffered on the run segment. My legs screamed for mercy, and they wobbled whenever I hit a downhill. Gradually, the afternoon sun turned to dusk and into the darkness of night. By the time I was on my last ten kilometers, I had been reduced to walking. No longer able to achieve a new personal best timing, I settled for just finishing the race.

By the time I arrived at the finishing line, it was past midnight, and it was empty. I had missed the official race cut-off time. My heart was heavy as I approached the short ramp to the finisher's platform. It was quiet; they had even switched off the lights. I fell to my knees and cried when I crossed the finishing line.

I felt a gentle hand on my back.

I looked up and saw a little girl.

It was the same little girl from my dream. The one whose eyes were hidden behind a thick fringe. At that moment, I thought I would scream, but I was probably too tired to feel afraid.

"It's okay, you can try again tomorrow," she said, and I was strangely comforted.

I heard my name being called.

I looked behind me, but the area was empty.

I looked back at the little girl, and an old woman stood next to her.

I fell backwards, stunned, and scrambled to get back on my feet, falling back each time I tried.

I heard my name again.

I looked around with panic-stricken eyes; a group of people dressed in gray robes were walking slowly towards the finisher's platform. I finally found my footing and started running. My legs wobbled, my chest burned, but I tried my best to run away. The hotel that Johan and I checked into was just around the corner. I headed towards it without looking back. The people in gray robes followed me. I didn't know how close they were, but they were close enough for me to hear them call my name.

I turned the corner and my hotel came into view. My heart became hopeful when I saw that many lights in the hotel were on. I bit down on my lip and mustered every last bit of strength in me to reach the hotel.

When I entered the brightly lit lobby, it was empty. I looked back towards the glass-paneled front and saw more people in gray robes walking to the hotel from various directions. I made a dash for the elevators.

"C'MON!" I screamed as I frantically pressed the elevator button. The people in gray robes were now spilling into the lobby like the gentle overflow of a stream.

I abandoned the idea of the elevator and ran towards the emergency exit. *Third floor – I just need the third floor,* I kept encouraging myself.

I was so relieved to reach the third floor. I was even more relieved to see that my family suite door was open and all the lights were on. I heard my name again, but this time I recognized the voice that called me.

"Johan!" I called out as I ran into the family suite. He called me from our room, and I headed straight for it, saying his name with tears of relief.

The smell of kemenyan smoke hit me before the fog in our room. Johan called for me again, and I called back, but I was unable to find him.

"Sara! Can you hear me?!" he shouted.

"Yes! But I can't see you!" I yelled back, my hands stretched out to feel through the fog.

"Sara! Can you hear me?" he shouted again.

Then I heard a second voice.

"En. Johan, saya sudah jumpa Sara. Dia dah ada kat sini," said the voice of an old man.

What is he talking about? Of course I'm here. I've been shouting!

"Panggil dia pulang," the old man's voice said again.

"Sara – come home. Come home!" Johan started repeating.

"I *want* to come home!" I screamed, but it seemed he could not hear me.

I heard more voices urging me to *come home*, the voices of my other friends. I heard Marcus, Tarmizi, Rajan, the gals – everybody, but saw none of them.

I was now livid and screaming in tears, "I WANT TO COME HOME!"

A tiny hand held my fingers. I pulled away and looked down, at the little girl with her hidden eyes.

Even more voices were shouting.

Sara, come home! they shouted.

Sara, pulang! they shouted, some beginning to be cries of despair.

Amidst the chaotic voices of Johan and my friends calling for me to come home in different languages, I heard the voice of the old man reciting unfamiliar Quranic verses. I looked down at the little girl, my chest heaving from confusion and the fear that I was beginning to realize what may be happening.

A slight smile crawled across the little girl's face.

"Saya tak nak pulang," she said.

My eyes grew wide when she said that, and my jaw dropped as I heard my voice come out from her smiling mouth.

The fog immediately disappeared, and the room was filled with the people in gray robes. Tears welled in my eyes as I looked around at all their unworldly ghost-like features.

"Maaf, Encik Johan," the voice of the old man said.

I heard it clearly, but I could not see the old man.

My heart sank when he said, "Kami dah jumpa Sara. Tapi masalahnya – Sara tak nak pulang."

✕

It has been five years since my world disappeared.

I no longer see anyone except the people in the gray robes and the little girl with the hidden eyes. Her name is Khalifah.

I hear voices of the living, though, and I'm always hopeful I will one day hear Johan again. The unfamiliar voices of the living always talk about me, especially if they check into my family suite. A few exaggerate the actual account, but the base story is always the same: She disappeared the night she checked in, and they suspected she was *taken*; her husband managed to see her once, but she offered him maggots in dirt and claimed they were his favorite goreng pisang; she ate the maggots and dirt; they tried for months to make her come back and one day she just said she didn't want to. Occasionally, someone would say they eventually found my decaying body by the pier.

I honestly doubt I ate maggots in dirt, and life on this side of the spectrum isn't all that bad. Khalifah is mischievous, but I guess she just needed a friend to play with. I can understand why. I mean, it's an island; the folks on this side of the spectrum are more mainstream and boring, especially with their generic ghostly features and plain gray outfits. The food Khalifah brings me is always great, and the weather is always cheerful. On days I feel like racing, I miraculously wake up to race day morning. Sure, race day always starts awesome, but I will never give up until I cross that finishing line victorious.

So, yeah. Five years since my world disappeared.

The plastic band from the organizers is still neatly fastened to my wrist, unblemished by time.

The last Ironman race was organized back in 2010, but I heard that the organizers are planning to bring it back. I look forward to that happening. It would be nice to hear familiar voices again. Maybe I'll even get to race alongside them!

I am, after all, a triathlete.

Bipedal

✕

Paul Gnanaselvam

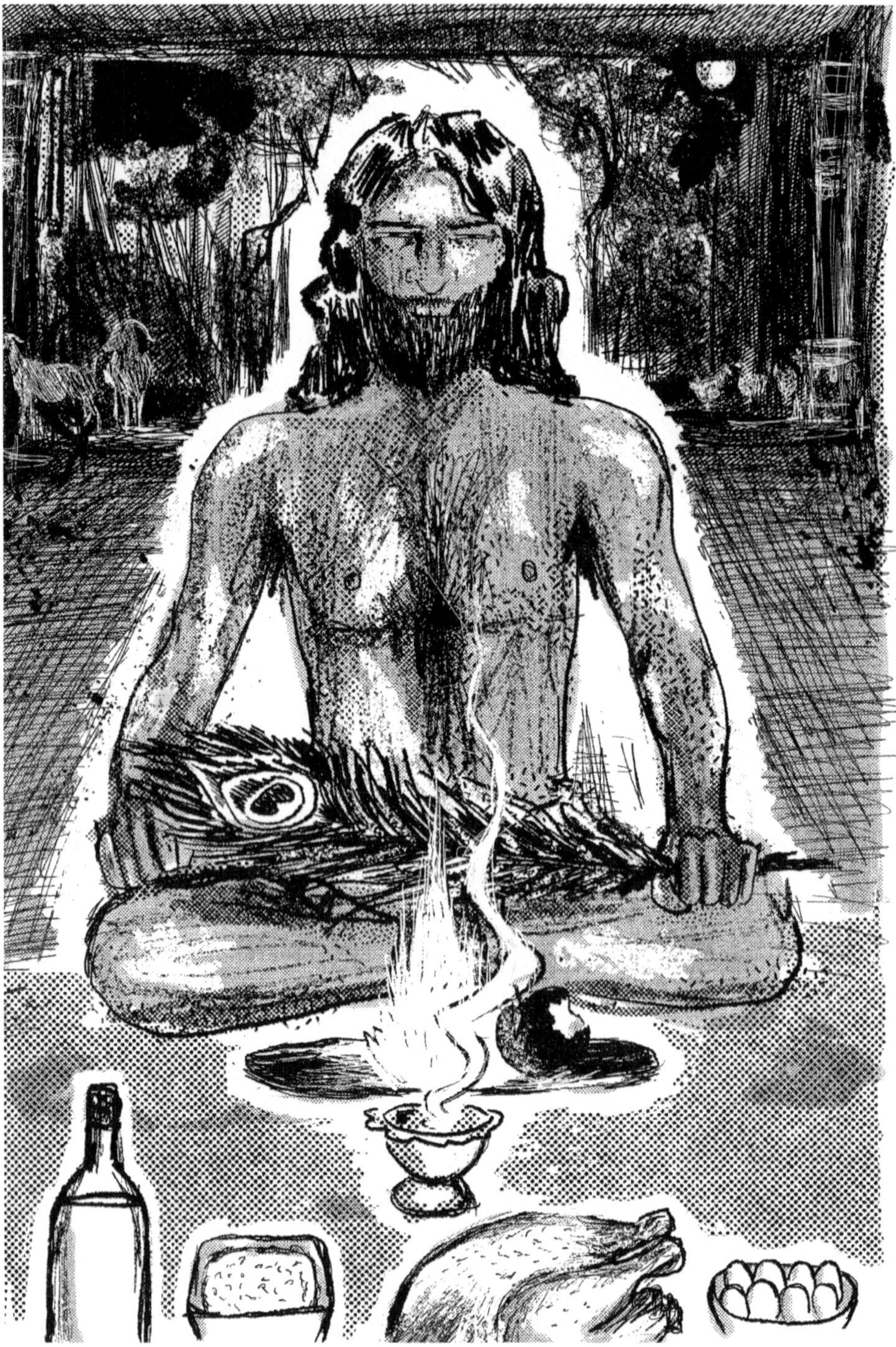

The muezzin's call for prayer filled the evening air as Arjunan drove cautiously into the narrow parking lots of the Rawang KTM station. The setting sun had cast a golden hue on the edges of the dark clouds sprouting like cauliflowers on the horizon. He couldn't help but notice an unusually quiet Dato' Jefri, his employer for 15 years, fiddling with his cigarette box and lighter. Dato' Jefri let out a short sigh as Arjunan pulled the hand brakes and turned off the engine. For a moment both men sat in silence, watching an overloaded train snaking its way into the station.

"Dato', we must leave now," Arjunan announced while unbuckling his seatbelt. "She will be waiting," he said and proceeded to the car boot. It took a while before he heard the slamming of the car door. Peering from the side of the boot, he saw Dato' Jefri leaning against the car and lighting a cigarette. It annoyed Arjunan, who wanted the day's affairs to run as planned. It was not advisable to be in an isolated pocket of urban forest, their affairs under the disposition of the madman Kirukkan. Above all, he had a fearful anticipation that their arrival would not be welcomed by her– since their, or rather Dato Jefri's, promise of a return was two years overdue! *There could be repercussions*, Arjunan thought, and the very sense of it made him anxious.

"Dato', I'll carry the fruits and toddy. The offering tray and kemenyan are also with me," he informed Dato' Jefri, whose sight seemed to be fixed on the vacant car park. "You may carry the rooster, I've got its legs tied up. Won't be a struggle as it's rolled up in the newspaper," he instructed. Leaving the rooster on the ground, Arjunan slammed the boot shut and waited for Dato' Jefri. Minutes passed until the deepening dusk brought out the mosquitoes which took an interest in their elbows and earlobes. Dato' Jefri scratched himself and took a few deep breaths.

Much to Arjunan's surprise, he did not walk to the back of the car but stood away from it instead. "You know, Arjunan," he began, "I wish not to partake in these rituals. I can follow you to see her, but you know, I find these activities nonsensical. Time has gone by so quickly, I have put this behind me now. The accident in the forest was a coincidence,

I think. Quicksand is rare, but accidents happen all the time. Lives and machinery are lost during such clearing of land, especially in unexplored areas because we have little understanding of the soil. Just like landslides and flash floods, they are all natural, aren't they?"

"But Dato', the accidents were rare at first. Now they are occurring more often. *'Excavators and four Bangladeshi workers swallowed by earth'* hitting the newspaper headlines is not good, especially when your investors are threatening to pull out," retorted Arjunan, his hands weighed down by the goods he was carrying.

Dato' Jefri sighed. "Can you kindly carry the rooster?" he asked. "Since you did all the talking the first time. Me, I have no inclinations for all this, especially with the one you refer to as 'her'. Doesn't have to involve me, Arjunan, hope you understand. I'm a land developer. Furthermore, this is forbidden. I should not be seen in such a compromising position, especially by my party members. Nowadays everyone walks around with cameras in their phones."

Arjunan was at a loss for words. He managed a faint smile. It was half past seven and there were things he needed to do. Bats were already swooshing across the wide intersection of the railway tracks and the sky was free of birds. It was going to be dark soon. And there was the hurdle of crossing the railway tracks and looking for that one small clearing in the fence to enter the dense jungle opposite the station. *Idiot,* thought Arjunan angrily. *I am only a go-between, an interpreter and car driver. Two years ago, when you lost favor with your party members and business partners, you turned to her. You bore gifts, pulut kuning and roast chicken on the wretched pournami night. And now you are hesitating?*

"Dato'," Arjunan cleared his throat. "You learnt about her from your Chinese partners and decided to come to her, you wanted permission for your development project. You initiated that meeting. You felt there were signs, right, especially when your wife's illness could not be diagnosed by the doctors, even the bomohs? Furthermore, she's looking for you. Not me. By right, you should carry this offering to her. Besides, it was not me who pocketed the 30 million wang saku from the contract you won, come on, Dato'. She helped you, didn't she?"

"Haram jadah! Don't talk so much!" shouted Dato' Jefri, raising his index finger toward Arjunan. "Biadab!"

"Like it or not, you have one leg in this. Just fulfil your promise," Arjunan retorted boldly. He waited.

Dato' Jefri shook his head and nonchalantly tossed his cigarette butt into the nearby bushes. "You're right," he said, walking up to Arjunan and patting his back. "Workers killed, tractor overturned, ground swallowing entire excavator, rains washing out the concrete – yes, yes, I get it. You have been with me for so long, Arjunan. Have you paid the station master?"

"Done, Dato'. We can cross from the end of the platform. There is less vegetation now, so we have to be swift."

"Good. Pass me the rooster now," Dato' Jefri said. Arjunan deftly picked up the large black rooster, wrapped neatly in large newspaper sheets.

"Hold it like this," said Arjunan as he rested the rooster in the crook of Dato' Jefri's arm and secured it to his side. "He won't struggle, Dato', his legs are bound tightly by raffia strings, he won't get your blazer dirty."

"Only if he knows what lies ahead of him," murmured Dato' Jefri.

The station master nodded suspiciously at the familiar MP clutching a rooster while walking up the platform in smart and expensive apparel, followed by a plump man in a pink batik shirt carrying large grocery bags. They exchanged salams before hurrying down the long platform, looking to their left and right before toting their goods across the eight-lane track.

"Ah, there it is." Arjunan pointed to a small hole cut into the fence.

"Are you sure that's the one? There are so many others in the fence now," he chuckled as they entered.

A small kongsi appeared, with a row of huts carelessly perched on bricks with plywood walls and zinc roofing. A colony of Bangladeshi workers was lounging outside, wearing colorful lungis amidst men bathing in their underwear at one corner and others preparing the evening meals in large cauldrons. They gazed at the two men, talking in low voices as Dato'

Jefri and Arjunan turned into a small path toward the jungle and vanished from their sight.

Arjunan sighed in relief when he looked up to the sky. His calculations were correct; there was a full moon. Except for the breeze that shook the trees and bushes, it was quiet as they went further into the jungle. Arjunan was glad the narrow dirt road was still visible. He walked ahead, mindful of Dato' Jefri's heavy breathing. He was aware that the hard-drinking, cigar-smoking businessman who'd turned to politics two years ago was tired. His business had collapsed when he lost his investment in gold schemes, and he was bracing for bankruptcy when he was led to her to save whatever was left of him. And as if that was not enough, he was at loggerheads with the insurance company that was reluctant to pay out for the mysterious disease consuming his wife. Now, the accidents at the construction site had sounded off the alarms and only Arjunan knew precisely why they were happening. It took a while for Dato' Jefri to be convinced to make this overdue trip.

A small clearing revealed an open platform with shoddy tiles and a dilapidated roof. A fluorescent light hung loosely on one of its four poles. A black trident rested in the middle and the cement around it was littered with dried leaves and soot from partially burnt things. They were greeted by a few large Boer goats – probably offerings that were let loose by those who came to consult her. And the place was literally overrun by roosters and chickens of all colors and sizes. Arjunan put down the grocery bags and surveyed the clearing. He nodded to Dato' Jefri when he caught sight of Kirukkan, the medium resident of the old abandoned temple. Arjunan walked up to him and found him prying open a half-rotten jackfruit. Kirukkan looked up and grinned when Arjunan stepped on one of the discarded seeds.

"She has brought you here, I see," he said, biting into the large fruit. The sweet fragrance of the fruit wafted into the air. Suddenly, the rooster Dato' Jefri was holding crowed loudly. "There, she will be coming soon," he declared, his eyes fixed on Dato' Jefri. He gorged on another piece of the fruit, licked his fingers and wiped them on his matted hair. "Sit here," he said, pointing to the trident after placing a huge banana leaf by its side. Dato Jefri looked away from the unkempt Kirukkan who was clad only in dirty boxers, his skin muddled with ash and sores.

Once they were seated, Arjunan took out a silver tray and quickly unloaded the fruit, bottle of toddy and frankincense.

"Why toddy?" asked Dato' Jefri.

"The drink is natural, sweet and pure when unfermented. Pleasing, I suppose," Arjunan explained.

"More for your friend looks like it," said Dato' Jefri, slapping on his neck and elbows. "Look at the size of these insects," he grumbled.

"Don't question anything, Dato'. Just focus on the intention," Arjunan said curtly, wiping away beads of sweat from his forehead. From another bag, he fished out plastic containers with pulut kuning, roast chicken and boiled quail eggs, and laid them in a row.

Kirukkan lifted his hands in a short prayer and sat down. He lighted a camphor. "She is a goddess to those she's pleased with, a demon to those she detests." He squinted after sprinkling water over his head. In a small pit before him, he dropped a spoonful of ghee and threw in the lighted camphor. Arjunan shifted his buttocks away from it. Kirukkan signaled for Dato' Jefri to move forward, and picked up the bottle of kemenyan from the tray.

"Slowly, bit by bit," Arjunan whispered. The pungent smoke filled the air. Kirukkan took an apple from the tray and bit into it. Then he rolled it into the fire, causing more smoke to rise from the pit. Arjunan and Dato' Jefri covered their noses and mouths with their handkerchiefs. They bumped into each other while pushing themselves sideways and backwards to avoid the flames that shot up when Kirukkan poured toddy over it. Kirukkan sniggered at them and laughed. Then, they waited. Dato' Jefri held the rooster close to his side, making sure it remained in its place. As the smoke thinned, Dato' Jefri squeaked in wonder. Before them, Kirukkan's face had changed. His matted hair rested neatly on his head. He now sat in a lotus position, his face defined with robust clarity, beaming with a thin smile, his eyes half-closed. He held the iridescent feather of a peacock.

"What's this?" asked Dato' Jefri, bemused.

Kirukkan opened his eyes and looked at Dato' Jefri. "You have come," he said, his voice now in a sharp, intensely feminine tone. "Late is the hour that you have chosen to come."

"I apologize, Amma," Arjunan butted in quickly. "I hope you will accept these offerings," he said meekly.

"And what about you?" asked Kirukkan, looking Dato' Jefri up and down.

"This," said Dato Jefri, lifting up the rooster still in its newspaper wrap.

"Is this what I asked for?" Kirukkan almost shouted. Clearly his serene face was transitioning into one that was unpleasant.

To Arjunan's dismay, Dato' Jefri let out a short snort and laughed. "Also some fruits and food. You like samsu, I'm sure," he said and pushed the bottle to Kirukkan.

Arjunan took a deep breath. *There is something wrong with the offerings.* His mind raced to the first meeting when he was here. Dato' Jefri was sitting before her, his head lowered when she spoke, and nodding to her demands. Bestowing permission to start land-clearing, reviving his business and promising prosperity, she had asked for a two-legged creature as an offering, a year after on the Friday of a full moon. She uttered a riddle he remembered:

A bipedal life,
that stirs at daybreak, but,
rests by dusk.

Dato' Jefri shook his head and lit a cigarette. "Here, take your rooster. Be done with this."

"You are now in my abode. Nobody messes with me!" Kirukkan said furiously. "It is not your privilege to do as you like. Your arrogance is a plague. I can and will take away what I gave you!"

Arjunan was lost for words. He brought his palms up to his forehead and clasped them reverently, hoping it would pacify the situation. But Kirukkan was now trembling, his long fingers trotting about like frenzied spiders on the mat he was sitting on. They were moving synchronously with speed, as if searching for something around him. A loud gurgling noise seemed to erupt from his belly. And it grew louder.

Dato' Jefri turned to Arjunan and whispered, "I am done here. He should be happy with the black rooster."

Arjunan tried to protest, but no words sputtered from his lips. He knew this spelt trouble. *A bipedal. Isn't a rooster a bipedal that walked on twos? Isn't this the norm, to offer birds? There are so many roaming around the small shrine. They were probably offered by the many Chinese contractors who came here asking for her permission to break ground for housing projects, or the punters seeking lucky numbers. Appeasing her with animal sacrifice ensured protection from wild animals and menacing spirits. Sometimes black pigs or black dogs were offered to her apart from goats, but they all walked on four legs. What is she angry with? What could she have meant? Had she changed her mind?*

"Look," Dato' Jefri spoke up. "I have to go. I hope you are happy with what I offered you. A rooster walks on two legs, crows at daybreak, sleeps at sunset. Thank you. Furthermore, if you want money, I can give."

Arjunan began to shiver.

Kirukkan laughed. "Of what use is your money to me?" he asked angrily. "You have forgotten I gave what your heart desired. And now, despite going against your promise, you encroached on my forest. All day you come cutting, hacking, banging and chopping. The noise from your machines disrupts my sleep. The absent trees pain my eyes against the glare of the sun. You have no respect for all that is living and all that has lived here."

Dato' Jefri threw his hands up in the air and shook his head. "You are a madman!" he shouted at Kirukkan before getting up.

Arjunan, panicking, also stood up, wiped his face and remained hunched before Kirukkan, breaking into a cold sweat. He understood that Dato' Jefri had done the unforgivable: angered her. His legs wobbled unsurely, between staying and fleeing.

Kirukkan gave out a yelp and laughed heartily. "I did not ask for a bird, you foolish man. I asked for a human life!" From underneath the mat he produced a large sickle, glinting in the ambers from the pit.

Dato' Jefri wiped his forehead. "I'm not buying any of this crap. Let's go!" he called out to Arjunan.

"You don't know what I am!" shouted Kirukkan, now shaking violently. In the glow of the moonlight, blood could be seen trailing down the middle of his forehead. "Run, run away!" he screeched. "I will come after you. I will open your eyes as I crawl up your chest, break your neck, sink my teeth into your throat and draw out your warm blood."

Arjunan shrieked in horror and turned to leave, only to find himself alone, surrounded by the gray shades of the wood. "Dato'…" he called out. But there was no response. He looked behind him; Kirukkan too was missing. The trident stood in its place, the fire in the pit dying slowly. He clenched his teeth, *Myrandi, abandoned me, didn't you?* Arjunan rubbed his eyelids. The small dirt road that led them to Kirukkan's shrine appeared. Braving himself, he walked up the path, straining his eyes for Dato' Jefri among the shadows. After a few yards, he picked up the unmistakable scent of tobacco and as expected he found Dato' Jefri strolling down the road, cigarette in hand.

"I hope it's over, sheesh. I'm not coming here again," he said when Arjunan caught up with him. Arjunan nodded – but suddenly he shrieked, seeing the black rooster in Dato' Jefri's hands.

"What the hell, Dato'! Why… where did you pick it up?" he asked, bewildered. "Drop it," he pleaded. "Drop it, don't bring it with you." However, their focus on the rooster was replaced by relief when they heard an ETS swooshing down the tracks. "We must be near the station, Dato'," said Arjunan. Dato' Jefri smiled.

Soon, they reached a junction where the path forked in opposite directions. "Where is the damn kongsi?" Dato' Jefri asked after a while. "It must be here somewhere, we walked past the kongsi after we entered the hole in the fence, right?"

"Yes, Dato'," agreed Arjunan. "I should have brought the torchlight. Left it in the grocery bag at the shrine."

"*Now* you remember it. Which way should we go? I think it's the right."

"No, Dato', it's the left, I remember we turned right before reaching the shrine," Arjunan tried to justify.

"It's 9:30 p.m., Arjunan. It's getting cold and I am hungry. We go to the Sungai Ujong clubhouse for dinner. Put all this behind us."

"Let's get out of this place first," said Arjunan, tapping on his mobile phone. "There's no signal here at all."

"Wait," cautioned Dato' Jefri, "I hear something moving. Behind us, Arjunan, use the flashlight in your phone."

They turned around. Both men screamed at the top of their lungs, for what stood before them was a stark naked Kirukkan, his muscular body smeared in turmeric, his bulbous eyes staring out like a feral boar's with tongue hanging out beyond his chin, which was reddened with blood. Kirukkan gave a piercing cry, raised his sickle and charged toward them. Without wasting a second, both men scampered off as fast as their aging legs would allow.

Arjunan reached the kongsi and found the hole in the fence. He climbed up the gravel-covered embankment to the railway tracks and rested. Dato' Jefri was nowhere to be seen. Arjunan looked up. On one end he could not see the platform except for a burst of brightness that shot up into the night sky. *That must be the KTM station*, he thought, somewhat relieved. On the other end, the full moon dazzled in all its glory. Exhausted, he stayed where he was, convinced that Dato' Jefri would appear soon from one of the many entrances he had reported seeing earlier along the fence.

"Arjunan," he heard a voice calling out from the thicket. He saw a large figure clambering out from the fence and falling onto the ground.

"Dato'!" Arjunan called out, relieved at last. "This way, Dato', the station is behind me!" he shouted, waving his hands. He began to walk toward Dato' Jefri, hoping he was not injured. Suddenly, he saw the man getting up and twirling his blazer over his head. He was saying something Arjunan could not decipher. He continued to walk toward him, hoping to help him up the steep embankment – when Dato' Jefri stopped waving.

Arjunan groaned in disappointment when he sighted the wrapped rooster still tucked under Dato' Jefri's arms. "Throw it away," he signaled to him, moving his hands sideways. The moon seemed to have been freed by the clouds and it was now bright enough to see Dato' Jefri staring in his direction. Arjunan gathered his strength to fetch his boss when he heard Dato' Jefri frantically yelling to him, "Run, run, Arjunan! Get off the tracks!"

Is there a train coming? But there's no vibration, what's wrong with this man, he wondered. As he looked down, he saw two large shadows on the ground. He realized there was something behind him but he dared not turn around. The shadows grew longer and bigger, and there were whispers like deep groaning. A terrible stench hit his nostrils and he wanted to vomit. His stomach churned and he fell to his knees. Two large heads could be seen in the tall silhouettes. They had long chins and hooked noses. Their wide-open mouths revealed sharp fangs and serrated teeth and their long limbs had claws. *Kaateri? That's it, this is my end*, he told himself. But the creatures walked on, now revealing their backs. The 12-foot creatures had bony spikes protruding from their backbones. Their thick black manes bounced with each step. Arjunan grew weak from fear as he saw them walking heavily in the direction of the full moon on their large hairy feet.

Arjunan was unable to get up and run. "Drop the rooster!" he called out to Dato' Jefri. His boss dropped his blazer, turned and ran back into the forest with the rooster still under his arm. The creatures turned at the very spot the blazer was lying and followed Dato' Jefri into the darkness. Arjunan then heard the unmistakable cries of Dato' Jefri. "Jembalang, tolong, tolong!" he cried for help. "Arjunan!" The pleading voice broke and faded into the stillness of the night. Then, nothing stirred.

Arjunan heard men speaking in strange voices. Darkness came over him and usurped all his remaining senses.

In The Vines of Paranoia

✕

Reuel Rawat

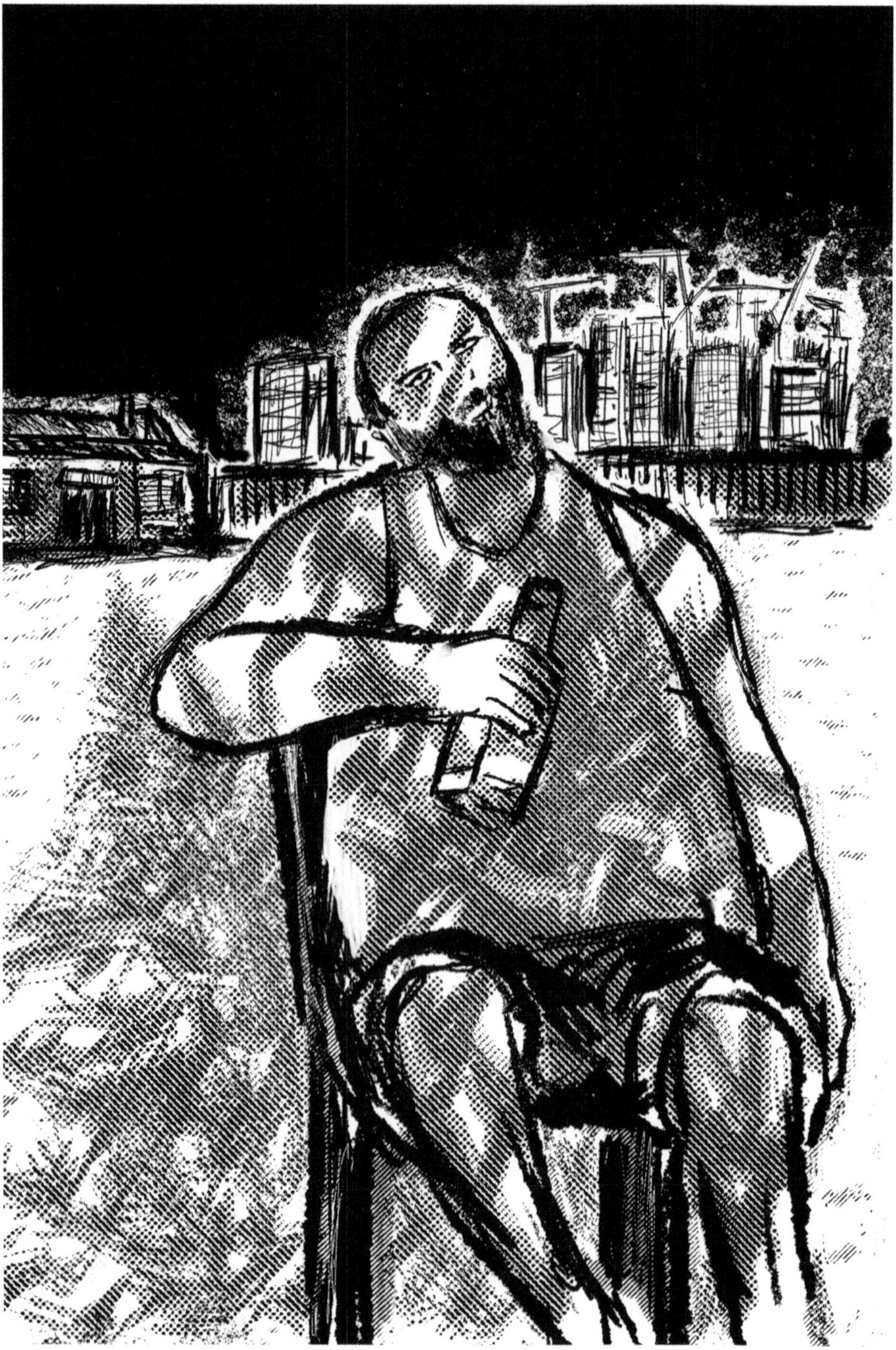

Anand Satyanarayan had no choice on how most of his days went. As a cocoa farmer in Kuala Lipis, Anand had spent most of his childhood in the fields with his father Rajan, who taught him the ropes and helped him develop his skills. Anand might have grown up to be like his father, had he been able to spend more time with him, but Rajan met with a fatal car accident when Anand was eight years old.

The year's harvest had been destroyed by a devastating flood. The rampaging body of water drowned many of their cocoa trees with its sheer volume, and its destructive charge uprooted the younger saplings and whisked them away in its murky depths, never to be found again. The local drinks corner had never been more full, though – with dozens of troubled men trying to lift their spirits with the aid of sweet and nutty toddy. Rajan rarely drank a lot, but he had a cup too many that time. As he was driving home in his Myvi, just at the turn to his house, his car skidded on the still-wet road and spun out of control.

Anand was the first to see the wreckage in the early hours of the morning.

The sturdy, blue frame of the car had been burnt to a corroded brown, and the surrounding grass seared to bulbous clumps of ash. The family's trusted vehicle had crashed directly into the wild birch tree that stood there with its bone-colored bark. Anand just looked at it, breathing in the smoke, unable to comprehend what had happened; he thought his dad would just come out of the destroyed wreckage and take him to the field to continue with the farming. Yet, a voice inside him told him that he wouldn't see Rajan again. The shade of the birch tree had covered the burnt remains of his childhood.

With a sickening thwack, the ax cut through the hard exterior of the tree, like a knife through butter.

Three years after the accident, Anand was the sole breadwinner of his family. His mother had to take care of his two siblings, so she couldn't do much apart from the occasional tailoring project. Anand started to work harder and harder in the cocoa farm. It was tough for an 11-year-old, but eventually he got a contract signed with a fair-trade company under his mother's name. Anand was glad things were finally looking up for his family; for the first time in years, he felt that they might get a chance at happiness. He poured his blood, sweat and tears into the trees. The way he measured the volume of fertilizer, water and pesticide – accurate to the nearest milliliter. There was no one more suited for the job.

The harvest did nothing but prove it: the cocoa he produced were of such amazing quality that the buyers wondered if it was imported. However, this still wasn't enough to fill the plates of his family. Since neither he nor his mother knew how to assert themselves while haggling with the buyers, he never managed to get a good price; that was why the new fair-trade contract had been a godsend to his family. He could finally get the money his produce was worth.

Looking out the window with a steaming Milo in his hands, he stopped to take in the sight of the rainy landscape. Mist arose from the ground like wisps rising from graves. The trees seemed to be merging into one: a colossal wall of brown bark standing tall as if protecting them from the hardships outside, all more or less the same color, with the exception of the ghastly alabaster presence of the tree that had caused his father's accident. It stood there among the other plants, tall and menacing. He had wanted to cut the tree down, to try and bury the memory of what had happened; to try and move on. He'd just never found the right time.

But now he was ready.

Anand took his tools from the shed and set everything up. He prepared to take the first swing of the ax, but he heard a voice call out, "Ey, boy, what are you doing? That's not safe, get out of there!"

Anand turned around and came face to face with a middle-aged man in a suit and tie. Anand immediately knew he was not from around here. His clothes made him stick out like a sore thumb: the sharp and straight edges of his well-ironed coat seemed to clash with the organic shapes of nature. Where people in Anand's neighborhood wore T-shirts and shorts, this man wore deep blue pants with a contrasting lighter shirt and a matching coat.

His shoes, polished enough to reflect sunlight, seemed to repel dirt- even when mud fell on them, a simple shake of the leg was enough to make it look brand new again, almost as if to show he didn't belong there on the damp ground with the likes of the boy in front of him. His face didn't show any form of compassion, rather a mix of irritation and contempt. Anand tried to open his mouth to explain but found he had forgotten how to speak, he was afraid that his crude words would offend this mysterious entity.

After a while he just decided the best thing to do would be to attempt to quell any worries the stranger might have.

"Don't worry, Sir, I am okay. I am very careful with the trees. I am used to working with them."

The man's expression changed a bit. He stopped glancing around to look at the farm, and focused on Anand instead.

"You're used to working with the trees? How old are you?"

"I am eleven years old, and after my father passed away, I've been taking care of the trees."

What happened after was a blur for Anand. He recalled taking the man to his mother, they spoke for a few minutes, and then the tears started. His crying mom seemed to be pleading with the man, who still wore a stoic expression. After a while, the man left and his mother sat in the living room, still weeping.

Later, Anand found that the man was the fair-trade inspector who had come to discuss the deal with his mother, but after he saw Anand cutting down the birch tree and spoke with him, he wanted to cancel the contract on account of child labor. What was more, he charged a hefty fine to Anand's mother. There was only one way to pay it off.

They would have to sell the farm.

It was inevitable. The accursed tree's bark had been pierced.

The construction site was probably as far from nature as you could get. The cold steel spires and large mechanical constructs were colored bright neon to stick out from the surrounding darkness. All the workers in the large crater wore the same expressions: tired and resigned without any glimmer of excitement or hope. Eventually, all their faces seemed to meld into one, and they stopped communicating with each other when not required, afraid to find a reflection of themselves in their peers.

Anand, now 24 years old, finished marking the last section of a colossal, concrete column that was to be connected to an equally gargantuan set of concrete rows to form a frame whose size was almost incomprehensible to him – a person who spent his life caring for trees. Life had been harsh for Anand after his father's death, but it got worse after his family had to sell their cocoa farm. The contractor who bought the farm was kind enough to let the family keep their house on the land, but had no intention of letting the farm continue. Despite many pleas from Anand, the contractor deemed it would be a financial loss for him. His beloved cacao trees were burned to the ground. The fire, smoke and ash had returned after years to make him suffer yet again.

If only he hadn't tried to cut the birch tree; he should have known better. Maybe the tree was no normal plant: first it took away his father, and now as revenge for trying to chop it down, it summoned the destruction of his beloved farm. Even still, it stood tall in the backyard of his house, mere meters away from what used to be the farm property, as if to mock Anand every day as he returned home.

Anand realized that if he wanted to be happy, he would have to keep the tree happy. From that time onwards, a chunk of whatever Anand earned went into supplies for the tree. Imported fertilizer, advanced pesticide, you name it. This, of course, meant Anand had less money for himself and his family.

Anand got married at age 21 as his mother had already arranged it a few months prior, hoping to give Anand a better chance at happiness with a family of his own. He did not mind getting married, but he worried about how he would find the money with his job at the toddy shop his father used to visit. In a stroke of good fortune, Anand's new father-in-law used some connections to find him work at the new Sime Darby office construction site. It was going to be hard work, but it would bring in the cash.

Before he knew it, Anand was the proud father of twins: Karan and Arjun, named after the favorite movie from his childhood.

However, it wasn't going to be a happy ever after for long.

His wife Lakshmi started to worry about him. He would sometimes go nights without sleeping and had spent so much money on products for the tree that he stopped buying toys for the children and almost never took them out anymore. Now, he'd even stopped talking to the boys and just had a monotonous routine of going to work, coming back, sleeping and then repeating from the start. It was time she confronted him.

The task was already halfway done. A few more strikes and the wretched birch would fall.

"Anand, what's going on?"

"What do you mean, dear?" asked a tired and confused Anand.

"You don't spend any time with us anymore. The kids miss their father, I miss you!"

Anand let out a deep sigh. "Lakshmi, please, can I go sleep? We can talk about this later."

"No! No more 'later's', Anand, you have to tell me what's going on. And don't get me started on the bottles of booze I found in the cupboard. It's like you only spend money on that and that tree…"

"Shut up, Lakshmi! You don't know about that tree. It took away my father first, then my family's livelihood, if I don't keep it happy, then… then…"

Lakshmi was now in tears; never before had her husband talked to her so roughly. She had had enough.

She first woke the young Karan, then Arjun, before calling for a taxi.

"Lakshmi, where are you going? I'm sorry! please we can talk about this, please…"

With a curt turn, she looked at Anand; cold eyes brimming with tears and slapped him as hard as she could. She then walked away into the rainy night, leaving Anand alone. Again.

Sitting there, he reflected on his life and remembered how his father had taught him to love and care for nature.

Anand unthinkingly walked to the shed. Not a sound as he picked up the rusted ax. He didn't bother wearing gloves or a raincoat. He didn't flinch as the cold drops of rain struck his face. He just kept moving forward. Anand quietly raised the ax in the air, and brought it down full force on the dirty white bark of the birch tree. He could vaguely hear thunder, but continued the assault. His hands could feel the vibrations from the wood splintering, *crik crak crik*.

With the final blow, the tree was severed from its base. What Anand should have done years ago was fulfilled now. All that was left was to wait for the tree to fall. Any minute now.

Anand closed his eyes; the lack of sleep had gotten to him. He yawned, imagining how he was going to make it all up to his wife. How she would forgive him. And he eventually drifted away into his dreams.

Midway through his slumber, he was surprised to find he couldn't stretch his arms and legs. There appeared to be no space to do so. As his eyes opened, he realized he couldn't see a thing. Where was he? Did he get a concussion? Did the tree fall on top of him? With every breath he took, the pungently sweet smell of sap invaded him. Anand yelled at the top of his lungs, but his words were lost in the labyrinth of echoes surrounding him. What was happening?

"Help! Someone help me!" Anand kept screaming for minutes until he couldn't bear the reverberations anymore. He felt his throat squeeze tight from thirst before he calmed down. His best option would be to wait until he could hear someone outside, and then try to get their attention.

After what felt like days, the only sounds he heard were the birds chirping and branches swaying. In horror, he wondered: Was he inside the tree?

And then he cried.

Line(age)

✕

Nat Kang

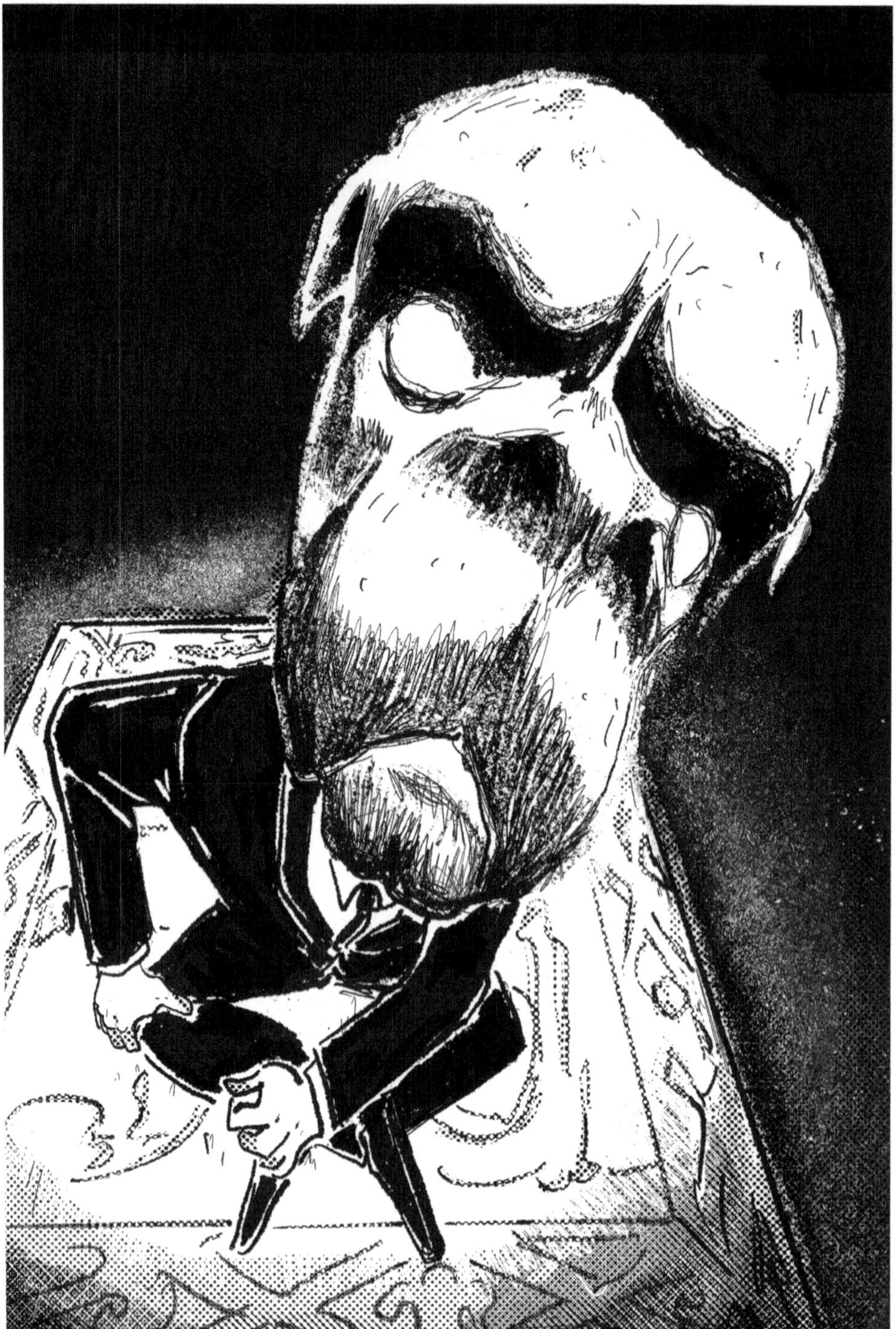

As expected, the brick wall materialized, blocking off the road ahead. As planned, I floored the accelerator. Split seconds before my car would crash into the mossy bricks, I felt that familiar popping in my ears, and my vision blacked out for a moment.

When my sight returned, I wasn't on that dark stretch of the Karak Highway anymore. Instead, I was seated at a bus stop surrounded by dense forest, under a flickering street lamp.

She always did love Totoro.

It wasn't long before I heard the sound of an approaching car somewhere to my left, and I turned to see a familiar set of headlights drawing closer. By the time I could make out the Volkswagen's glossy yellow paintwork, I could also see the silhouettes of its driver and a passenger in the back seat.

Just as it had many times in the past, the Volkswagen parked in front of the bus stop. The driver staggered out, every bit as physically uncoordinated as I remember him being, and opened the back door.

Poor bastard. Almost a century in her service, just because he had the misfortune of being gunned down by the communists in her domain.

"My dear, it's been too long!"

I stood, bowed, and gave her a smile knowing she'd see through it anyway. "As always, I am honored to be in your presence, Toh Puan."

"Pish posh, flattery gets you nowhere," she said, pushing her driver to one side. "Henry, be a dear and wait inside, would you? I won't be too long."

She walked over and sat down at the bus stop, even as Henry got back into the car. "Now, what brings you back here? You've stayed away for so long, I was wondering if you'd forgotten about me."

"Toh Puan, I believe you already know why I'm here," I replied, staying on my feet and keeping Henry in the periphery of my vision. "And also that I'll never forget you, or your kindness."

"Such sweet things he says, and yet he only comes here when he wants me to do something for him," she retorted, speaking more to her driver than me. "Granted, that's what you men do all the time anyway, one would think I'd have gotten used to it over the centuries. So, I presume this is about the final rites?"

I got down on one knee, and bowed my head. "Actually, it isn't. With all due respect, Toh Puan, it's about my daughter."

"And what makes you think I'd know where she is?"

Looking up, I met her gaze for the first time that night. "With all due respect, you always knew where all your children were. Even those you chose not to bless, in your wisdom."

Silence, save for the sounds of the forest and the purring of the Volkswagen's engine.

"That I do. Go look for your old friend, the Kepala Anjing, and he'll tell you everything you need to know. I believe these days he goes by 'Winston'."

Despite myself, I raised an eyebrow. "He's the one who put the bounty on my soul–"

"Times change, and yours is finally starting to run out." She shrugged, stood up and walked to the car. "Go to him."

I nodded. "You have my deepest gratitude, Toh Puan."

"Don't thank me yet," she said, already seated in the back of the Volkswagen with one hand on the door handle. "And one more thing?"

"Yes?"

"I'll be seeing you again soon, one way or the other. Know that the road leading here wasn't as straightforward as you might expect, and I had to make some tough decisions I'd have rather avoided. It was all for a reason."

Before I could reply, she slammed the door shut. I caught Henry's gaze briefly and to my surprise, he wasn't wearing his usual sour expression. Instead, he almost looked sympathetic. It didn't take long for them to leave, his face passing out of my sight but not out of my mind.

Once again, my vision blacked out and the next thing I knew I was back in my car, parked safely on the shoulder of the Karak Highway.

No brick wall, no yellow Volkswagen. Just me wondering what the tormented soul of Sir Henry Gurney knew that I didn't.

×

I kept an eye on her through the years.

"Always remember, we are children of Belum."

She did magnificently, far beyond what anyone could have expected of one who hadn't been blessed by the Elders.

"What does that mean, Papa?"

One day, a healing. Another, warding off a pelesit that had been unleashed by developers trying to evict some farmers.

"It means we are one with both Man and Nature. That we have a duty to preserve the spirit of the land and forests, in a world where spirits increasingly submit to the advances of Man."

I recall being so proud the day I heard of her performing an exorcism which ended in her facing none other than Kuan Kong, the Chinese God of War, and finally helping a possessed war veteran go to his final rest.

"I don't understand, Papa..."

Still, I honored her wish for me to stay out of her life.

"One day you will, and by the time you meet Toh Puan to receive the blessing of the Elders, you will be ready."

×

The flat was in a dodgy part of town, a bastion of human tenacity and suffering.

She would have known that the mortal auras would have been more than adequate to obscure hers from anyone who might have cared to search for her. And the residents of the flat itself knew to avoid those like us, so ordinary humans wouldn't have been a threat to her, either.

Smart girl. And yet, not smart enough.

Her flat looked like a hurricane had torn through it, and the front door all but fallen off what was left of its hinges when I gave it a gentle push. My flashlight gave me glimpses of the wrecked living room and the flayed carcass of a large animal, even as I played a hunch and slowly made my way to her bedroom.

The bedroom made the living room look positively unscathed. Deep gouges and streaks of what was probably blood were all over the walls, and two halves of a Ouija board lay in a corner. A dreamcatcher dangled from the curtain rail, still glowing with the telltale traces of whatever had tried to come in through the window, but which had ultimately decided to just enter through the front door. Faintly, I could hear the roaring of a tiger still echoing in the gutted room.

Even without Toh Puan's blessing she had been strong, and her tiger guardian was no slouch, either. But as I stood there surveying the ruins of her bedroom, I caught the faintest whiff of jasmine, and knew she'd bitten off more than she could chew. It didn't take me ten minutes to get back to my car and on the road.

Next stop, the Karak Highway.

✕

"Six months, maybe slightly more if you take it easy."

"I see."

"It's spread to the outer parts of your brain, which explains the symptoms. Unfortunately, the tumors are almost impossible to tell apart from your own brain tissue. So, targeted removal is too risky."

"I understand."

"Does your daughter know?"

"She will, once I find her."

✕

Taking a deep breath, I placed my faith in the Elders and put my left foot forward. The water held, and I walked out onto the surface of Sungai Gombak. Up ahead, the river flowed into a dark tunnel: a mere sewer for ordinary mortals, but so much more to those of us who live between worlds.

I walked on, the currents beneath my feet somehow not giving way beneath the weight of my thoughts.

As I crossed the threshold into the tunnel, the air around me seemed to shimmer, and the darkness broke into a mosaic of colors. Chanting prayers to the Elders, I kept moving, breaking through barriers that I'd not crossed in almost twenty years. Around me, the colors shifted, forming a tunnel that led to my destination, a cavern as bustling as its mortal counterpart, Pasar Seni.

Within minutes, I arrived in the cavern. Much of it was different than what I recalled, but then again, it had been a while.

I was back in Undertown.

✕

No one disturbed me as I navigated the cobblestone roads of Undertown, heading for the lair of he who had once put a bounty on my soul. Having said that, the sheer fact that I hadn't been attacked within minutes of my arrival suggested he had rescinded it.

"Oh my."

He'd come up in the underworld, that was for sure. What had once been a rundown, smoky shrine in a hut was now a neat little bungalow, with signage out front warning trespassers that they would be sacrificed to Bujang Senang.

"Come in," called out a voice from a little speaker next to the front door as I walked up to it. "Wipe your feet on the rug."

Yup, it was him, all right.

When I entered the bungalow, I realized that some things hadn't changed, after all. He was still seated cross-legged on a low dais as I remembered, and the room still smelled of sandalwood incense. But he didn't look the same: gone was the face of the pariah dog and the stained loincloth, replaced by the head of a bulldog and an immaculately tailored suit.

Clearly, brokering information called for a more professional setup than he used to have when he harvested human heads to be buried in the foundations of buildings.

"Winston?"

He nodded. "You know my name, and I know why you're here."

I shrugged. "Thanks for lifting the bounty."

"Oh well, the cancer will do it for free anyway," he said, with a wave of his hand. "So, your daughter. You probably already know that Madam came for her with Dumb and Dumber, and the fact that you're here tells me you want to know where she is now."

"She's strong, she's still alive, I'm sure of it."

Winston snorted, and offered me a look that almost seemed…sorry?

"Last I heard, they've already sent her to the Doctors. If she isn't there, try Temple Street."

My stomach tied itself into knots. "No."

"Yes."

I turned to leave, but stopped in my tracks when Winston spoke again.

"For what it's worth, she didn't deserve this. None of their victims do. And if it comes down to that…keep in mind that he's all but immune to mortal fire. He sent Madam to round up some coastal folks when land reclamation destroyed their homes, they keep him safe from fire."

I left.

✕

"Say when."

The tiger spirit growled as I poured him a bowl of tuak.

"Look, she doesn't want to see me ever again. Not since she found out she wasn't going to receive the blessing of the Elders."

He blinked slowly, ghostly reflections of the candlelight dancing in his bright green eyes.

"Toh Puan decided to end the line with me, you ask her!"

A low growl, followed by a soft sniffle.

I paused, trying to swallow nothing but air, yet somehow feeling as if I was choking. "Just…just watch over her for me, all right? I'm sure Toh Puan had a reason for all this."

He knocked back the tuak and shrugged his massive shoulders with a sigh.

"You know it, so do I," I said, throwing back a shot of my own. "I just thought she'd pass the blessing on to my little girl. Take care of her for me."

×

"Papa, what happened?"

I watched my daughter curiously approaching the stone remnants of Si Tanggang's ship.

"He and his Mama lived a simple life. Then he grew up, went on a long journey, and he had to leave his Mama behind."

Her brow furrowed in thought. "Why didn't he bring her with him?"

Picking her up, I laughed. "Those days, it was more dangerous to travel. So he had to leave her behind."

"And then what happened?"

I swept my gaze over the ancient, worn rock. "When he got back, he was a rich man. His mother came to greet him on his ship, but…something went wrong. He and his ship got turned to stone."

Eyes widening in shock, she hugged me tight. "Oh no!"

"It's all right, sayang," I chuckled, putting her down. "It's just a story, all right? How about we get some ice cream?"

"Strawberry?"

"Only if you share it with Papa."

"Okay!"

We turned and left the stone ruins, walking hand in hand.

Maybe someday I'd tell her the full story as it had been told to me, of a descendant of Medusa herself, senile beyond salvation, turning her own son into stone when she'd failed to recognize him during his homecoming.

✕

I found my daughter on Temple Street.

Falling to my knees before the statue of Kali, I saw the goddess all but *glowing*, her features rendered in volcanic rock and varnished with blood.

I cried, witnessed only by the goddess, who wore my daughter's skin over her shoulders like a cloak, and with a garland of entrails looping around her neck.

✕

"She's one of the most powerful majordomos around these parts."

The nenek grasi doorkeeper let me into Bar None after reading the letter, a penanggal bouncer hovering silently next to her.

"If you ask me, better reject this job. She won't hold that against you, but once you start, there's no end to it."

For such a notorious club, it was surprisingly homely inside. Two sides of the club lined with booths, with the remaining two occupied by a well-stocked bar and a low stage, respectively. In the middle of the club, small tables and a cozy dance floor.

"Everyone knows her as one hell of a sadist. Word has it, she forces girls into prostitution and sends them to the Doctors to sell off their organs when they outlived their usefulness. Just because she wants people to suffer like she did during the Japanese Occupation."

There at the bar, dressed in bright red and with a flower in her hair. As always, the Kepala Anjing's intel didn't let me down.

"Bro, as a friend, I'm telling you, don't do it. You know who she works for, right? He grows more powerful with each girl who gets defiled and dies under her watch, and believe me, you don't want him as an enemy."

Her back was to me as I approached. By the time I got close enough to make out the rips and tears in her cheongsam, I realized she was wearing jasmine scent.

"Madam?"

She turned around, and I stifled a gasp of shock.

✕

Once more, I walked the streets of Undertown. This time, I was prepared.

Having made a trip back to the mortal side of Kuala Lumpur, I'd made some discreet inquiries and done some quick shopping. Then back to Undertown it was.

I headed past the street market peddlers with their love potions and charms, into the dimmer roads that led to party central. Soon enough, I saw Kelab Kay-Hell looming ahead, its neon signage announcing that Sudirman was going to be performing there for one night only.

Despite the wistful urge to go and see the great singer one last time, knowing I could easily get past the massive queue, I kept walking. It didn't take long for the bright lights and loud music of Kelab Kay-Hell to fade behind me, as I continued down the road into even darker places.

And there it was, looking exactly as I remembered it from all those years ago.

Bar None.

While Kelab Kay-Hell was the hotspot for nightlife in Undertown, Bar None was where the most powerful individuals on both sides of Kuala Lumpur's mortal divide headed for their nightly entertainment. Name a vice or a VIP, odds are that you'd find them all at Bar None eventually.

I was walking up to Bar None when the front door burst open, almost slamming into the crocodile spirit bouncer who had been giving me the evil eye as I approached. Seconds later, a half-dressed man flew through the open door and landed on the grimy street outside.

"Bloody fool!" a familiar, raspy voice snapped. "Do this nonsense again, I'll have you chopped up and fed to the pigs!"

Sure enough, Madam stepped out onto the street, flanked by her two bodyguards. "Whatever happened to the days when being a Dato' Seri meant they had class? Get lost, scumbag!"

Sidestepping the fleeing man, I nodded to her. "Madam."

Her bodyguards moved to get between us, but she ordered them back. "You. What do you want?"

"Where is he?"

The charred ruins of her face gave nothing away, as she pulled out a cigarette and a lighter. "Down in the basement, of course. You seriously believe you stand a chance against the Master?"

I shrugged. "What have I got to lose?"

We stood there for a while, her blowing smoke rings and me bracing for a fight if it came to that. Madam herself wouldn't be too hard to deal with, but her bodyguards were an entirely different animal. The two of them may have looked like normal headless ghouls, but years ago I'd seen them drawing those knives they had sticking out of their stomachs for some close quarters carving with deadly efficiency. Clearly, she'd kept them around since they retained much of their Japanese military expertise.

"Go on, then."

I cocked my head to one side. "Just like that?"

She gestured to her goons, and they stepped aside. "Doesn't make a difference to me. By all means, go to your own death. Either way, I'll survive. Always a demand for whores, no matter who's in charge."

Not bothering with a reply, I walked backwards into Bar None, not breaking eye contact with Madam until the front door closed between us.

✕

The stairs into the basement went further down than I'd expected, although the bartender had mentioned they took you wherever you wanted to go. So maybe it was that.

After what felt like hours going down the concrete stairs I arrived at a landing illuminated by strips of fluorescent lighting, which was unexpected.

What *was* expected, though, were the three – no, four humanoids dressed in rotting clothes waiting for me down the corridor, covered in slime and reeking of mud flats during low tide. Their bodies were so bloated, I couldn't even tell if they had been male or female, though the fourth one was decked out in some shredded kebaya.

I unzipped my backpack, and drew out what resembled a bundle of firecrackers.

"Who's first?"

The three bulkier ones ran towards me, and I snapped the tops off several of the custom incendiaries. I threw the flares at them, stopping them in their tracks as the thermite mix literally burned through them, causing them to shriek in agony.

Just as I was about to ignite more of the flares, my chest felt as if it was freezing over from within, and I could no longer breathe. My vision began to sway even as the three of them burned out into puddles of pungent slime, and I fell to the ground as the fourth water spirit walked up to me.

Before my eyes, I saw the flares turn waterlogged on a perfectly dry floor, one by one. Forcing myself to move despite feeling like I was drowning on land, I snapped open the last of the flares, and threw them unsteadily towards the kebaya-clad spirit.

One must have hit, because I saw the flash of light as its clothes caught fire. The shrieking spirit collapsed, and for a brief second, our minds met. I saw its final thoughts, and couldn't help but let out a choked sob as it slowly burned up.

The air turned sweet with the smell of fresh rain, even as the last of Melaka's river nymphs died.

✕

Dazed, I walked towards my final destination, toying with the lighter in my right hand. Would have preferred a thermite flare for this, but beggars can't be choosers.

I knew I'd arrived when I saw the pulsing column of black liquid just several meters ahead of me. Smelling the odor of crude oil, I knew it was him, even as the column shaped itself into a massive human head.

Madam's master himself, the Orang Minyak.

Last I'd seen him, he had still been humanoid. Winston had clearly been right, in that he had transcended his original physical form thanks to his work with Madam.

Speaking without words to the deepest recesses of my mind, he mocked me for being too late, asking me if I thought that a mere lighter was enough to destroy him.

"He's all but immune to mortal fire."

Probably true, and those water nymphs sacrificing themselves in his name would have worked some powerful magic in his favor. But just as they had died for him…

I uncapped the lighter and sparked it to life. "I am the last human blessed by Belum."

He hesitated, uncertainty creeping into our mental bond.

If mortal fire wasn't enough, maybe the spiritual might of a forest fire's fury would do. And maybe that was why Toh Puan chose me.

"I call upon the spirits of flame and ash."

Fear radiated from him as he surged towards me, the smell of burning wood filling the space between us as the fire gods accepted my sacrifice.

The Orang Minyak reached me as my hands burst into flame.

BIOS

✕

Shepherd by day, aspiring writer and painter by night, **Rizal Ramli** used to work in KL. He retired early and is now back in his hometown in the East Coast. All thanks to Covid.

Raja Ummi Nadrah exiled herself from the royal family. She then dabbled in witchcraft and kept a few loyal "servants" who never left even after several exorcism attempts. She has traveled to 57 countries to try to run away from her demons. One of these sentences is a lie.

Joshua Lim has lived in Klang all his life. Born in 2002, he is the author of one short story published in the anthology *KL Noir: Magic*, and he hopes to publish more stories in the future. He is currently a medical student who spends too much time creating fantasy worlds that don't exist… yet.

Chua Kok Yee's debut novel *Not A Monster* won the 2nd Fixi Novo Malaysian Novel Contest. His short stories have been published in various anthologies and periodicals including *Ronggeng-Ronggeng* (Maya Press 2019), *Remang* (Terrerbooks 2017) *Little Basket: 2016* (Fixi 2016), *KL Noir: Blue* (Fixi 2014), *Black and White and Other New Short Stories from Malaysia* (CCCPress 2012), *Selangor Times*, and *Esquire Malaysia*. He co-authored *News From Home* with Shih-li Kow and Rumaizah Abu Bakar in 2007, and his own collection *Without Anchovies* was published in 2010. Three of the stories from *Without Anchovies* are required reading for the SPM English Literature paper.

Adrian Chase is *not* a Mat Salleh, nor is he a villain from Arrowverse. He is an immortal spacefaring Gallente in EVE Online, switches between a tank and a healer in Final Fantasy XIV, and a wizard in Ragnarok. In the spaces in between, he sometimes writes. Rarer still, he posts on his Instagram, @adrianchasewrites. His novel *Wayward Arrows* is out on Amazon.

Yanna Hashri is a Malaysian writer, poet and editor. Her works have been published in online publications including *ISUU Mag*, *Eksentrika* and *Metaphors*. In 2018 she self-published her first poetry chapbook, *At Night We Come Out*. She has translated fiction and non-fiction books by prominent Malaysian authors.

Collin Yeoh has been writing advertising copy for 17 years. He now prefers to write things that have plots, characters, themes, genres, and that won't be subject to notes like "needs more product benefits". He had a story published in *KL Noir: Magic*, as well as several horror and sci-fi drabbles in anthologies by indie presses that earned him no money but were loads of fun to write.

Nurul Hafizah is a wordsmith from Kuala Lumpur. She is currently living with ten cats who have appointed themselves the masters of the house. Nurul's interests include overusing pretentious words, singing along off-key to bad music, and pretending she is cooler than she actually is. Nurul is in no way affiliated with man-eating red bugs, nor is she secretly a million red bugs in a human shell. That would be ridiculous. Bugs cannot type.

Joni Chng is a writer and photographer. In her spare time, she reads and draws. But in between doing photo shoots of stage performances, urban sketching and interviewing professionals from some interesting academic field for magazine articles, she continues building and expanding her own imaginary universe – one story at a time. Follow her on Twitter and Instagram: @jonichng.

Civil litigation lawyer turned writer/actor/vocalist, **Tina Ishak** has published numerous short stories, including achieving Runner-Up for the DK Dutt Memorial Award for Literary Excellence 2015, and being featured in the Short Story Collection of the 2015 SciFi Film Festival in Parramatta, Australia. Recent publications include "Last Farewell" in Fixi Novo's *2020* anthology using experimental writing techniques, an erotic horror story "Pontianak" in the international anthology *Under Her Black Wings: Women Monsters* and a multi-POV story "Confluence" in *Anak Sastra* literary magazine.

Muthusamy Pon Ramiah has been writing articles for a trade union quarterly for more than fifteen years. Lately he has been writing short stories. Two of his stories were published in *Anak Sastra*. His stories have also been included in *UNMASKED: Reflections on Virus-Time*, *KL Noir: Magic* and *Tapestry Of Colours Book 1*.

Ethan Matisa has been writing since he was eight years old, and has always had a special fondness for the horror genre. As a young boy, he moved from town to town all over Malaysia with his family, and despite multiple attempts (and studying engineering in university), he is still unable to kick the writing habit.

Hadi M. Nor is a TV script writer. He's the author of *Pengembaraan Laki-Laki Scorpio*, *Family Values*, *Sepucuk Pistol Di Dalam Laci* and *Suci*.

Wong Jo-yen has been writing since childhood to limited success. She did her BA (Hons) in English Language and Literature at the University of Nottingham Malaysia (with an elective in Creative Writing) and then her MA in Linguistics at NUS. Previous publication experience includes work with *The Star*'s now-defunct *Stuff@School* pullout, second place in Inklewriter's Future Voices Competition, and a story in Daphne

Lee's horror anthology *Remang*. She also freelances as a fiction translator, ghostwriter, and proofreader. Like everyone else, she has a novel (or two) constantly in the works.

Creative Writing graduate **Nadiah Zakaria** writes bloodcurdling horror and thriller when she's not trauma-dumping in her poems. Her characters are cunning and fearless, but in real life Nadiah can't step into a room without turning on the light. Now she spends her weekdays creating content and writing captions for ads that you skip. She wouldn't last five minutes in her own stories.

Malachi Edwin Vethamani is a Malaysian Indian poet, writer, editor and bibliographer. He is Emeritus Professor with University of Nottingham. He has five collections of poems and a collection of short stories, *Coitus Interruptus and Other Stories* (2018), all published by Maya Press. His stories have also been adapted into short plays, and published in *Ronggeng-Ronggeng: Malaysian Short Stories* (2020), *Queer Southeast Asia Literary Journal* (2020), *Creative Flight Literary Journal* (2020), *Business Mirror* (2018), *Lakeview International Journal of Literature Arts* (2017) and the *New Straits Times* (1995, 1996).

Ismim Putera (he/him) is a poet and writer from Sarawak. His poems and fiction can be found in many online journals and his latest works can be found in *Men Matters Online Journal* Issue 1, '*to let the light in*' *Poetry Anthology* (SingLit Station) and *Tapestry of Colours 1: Stories from Asia*.

Former journalist **Bissme S** wrote his first collection of short stories, *Doubt* in 2013. Two years later, he produced his second collection *Bitter*. Sometimes. he believes he does not choose the story he writes. Instead, the story chooses him.

Atikah Wahid is a contemporary author, hailing from the Klang Valley. This is her fourth short story published in an anthology since 2015. To read more of her writing, check out her website atikahwahid.com or follow her on Instagram at @literally.atikah.

Eileyn Chua is a burn survivor, writer and motivational speaker. Having miraculously survived a gas explosion in 2016, her perception of life has changed. She plans to live this life to her fullest potential. Currently, she is writing her memoir about her life as a burn survivor in Malaysia.

Nathaniel Sario is very sure that he'll end up a reclusive hermit just like JD Salinger.

Izaddin Syah Yusof is a graduate of Lancaster University, UK and is currently residing in Shah Alam. When he is not prancing around his poor cats at cat shows, he can mostly be spotted as the creepy loner at the cinemas watching trashy low-grade horror movies, offering the excuse "so that you don't have to".

Saat Omar: This is the first time he writes short story in English. He may or may not using Google Translate while writing this.

Terence Toh writes articles by day and fiction by night. He has written arts and culture articles for various publications, including *The Star*, for many years. He was the editor of Fixi Novo's *PJ Confidential*, and his short stories have appeared in local and regional anthologies including *KL Noir: White, Lost in Putrajaya, Cyberpunk: Malaysia, Hungry In Ipoh* and *KL Noir: Magic*. His debut novel *Toyols 'R' Us* won the first Fixi Novo Malaysian Novel Contest.

Venoo Kuppusamy has a degree from the Moscow Medical Academy, Russia, and is now an assistant regional manager for Clinical Research Malaysia. His Malay novel *Akan Ku Jejaki* was published by MPH.

After experiencing an awakening, **Lai May Senn** was propelled onto a spiritual journey. Finding spiritual books too dry and hard to comprehend, she felt the dire need to help others facing the same challenges by adapting what she has learnt into relatable stories. Her first fiction entitled *O.R.B.: 300A.L. – The Last Known Prophecy* was published in 2020 and she recently published its sequel, *O.R.B.: 330A.L. – Rise of the Dark Lord*. Join her journey via Instagram: @laimaysenn

Paul GnanaSelvam is an Ipoh-born writer whose work often focuses on the experiences, issues and identity conflicts of those in the Indian diaspora. Since 2006, his short stories and poems have been published locally and internationally in e-magazines, anthologies and literary journals. His first collection of short stories, *Latha's Christmas and Other Stories*, was published in 2013 while *The Elephant Trophy and Other Stories* was published by Penguin Random House SEA in 2021. He currently lectures at UiTM Seri Iskandar (Perak Campus).

Reuel Rawat lived in Mumbai for 11 years before moving to Kuala Lumpur for five years and now lives in Ontario, Canada. He's always loved reading and writing stories. Enjoys completing tough video games (spent nine hours beating Malenia, Blade of Miquella) just as much as mastering the lore of different franchises. Sitting cozily with a good book or his laptop when it's rainy is his idea of a relaxing day. Rolled a nat 20 on writing this bio.

Nat Kang is an optometrist, and also a musical stand-up comedian in his spare time. With experience working as well as performing in Malaysia and Singapore, he now resides in his hometown Petaling Jaya. He retired from writing fanfiction in 2013 after almost a decade on Fanfiction.net.

NOVO

Printed in Great Britain
by Amazon